Praise for the novels of Maisey Yates

"[A] surefire winner not to be missed."
—*Publishers Weekly* on *Slow Burn Cowboy*
(starred review)

"This fast-paced, sensual novel will leave readers believing in the healing power of love."
—*Publishers Weekly* on *Down Home Cowboy*

"Yates' new Gold Valley series begins with a sassy, romantic and sexy story about two characters whose chemistry is off the charts."
—*RT Book Reviews* on *Smooth-Talking Cowboy*
(Top Pick)

"Multidimensional and genuine characters are the highlight of this alluring novel, and sensual love scenes complete it. Yates's fans...will savor this delectable story."
—*Publishers Weekly* on *Unbroken Cowboy*
(starred review)

"Fast-paced and intensely emotional.... This is one of the most heartfelt installments in this series, and Yates's fans will love it."
—*Publishers Weekly* on *Cowboy to the Core*
(starred review)

"Yates's outstanding eighth Gold Valley contemporary... will delight newcomers and fans alike.... This charming and very sensual contemporary is a must for fans of passion."
—*Publishers Weekly* on *Cowboy Christmas Redemption*
(starred review)

MAISEY YATES

The Heartbreaker of Echo Pass

HQN

ISBN-13: 978-1-335-44808-8

The Heartbreaker of Echo Pass
Copyright © 2021 by Maisey Yates

Solid Gold Cowboy
Copyright © 2021 by Maisey Yates

Recycling programs
for this product may
not exist in your area.

This edition published by arrangement with Harlequin Books S.A.

For questions and comments about the quality of this book, please contact us at CustomerService@Harlequin.com.

HQN
22 Adelaide St. West, 40th Floor
Toronto, Ontario M5H 4E3, Canada
www.Harlequin.com

Printed in Spain

CONTENTS

THE HEARTBREAKER OF ECHO PASS   7

SOLID GOLD COWBOY   339

To my readers: Iris's story is for you.

THE HEARTBREAKER
OF ECHO PASS

CHAPTER ONE

IRIS DANIELS WONDERED if there was a particular art to changing your life. If so, then she wanted to find it. If so, she needed to. Because she'd about had enough of her quiet, baking, knitting, *underestimated* existence.

Not that she'd had enough of baking and knitting. She loved both things.

Like she loved her family.

But over the last couple of months she had been turning over a plan to reorder her life.

It had all started when her younger sister, Rose, had tried to set her up with a man who was the human equivalent of a bowl of oatmeal.

Iris didn't *like* to be mean, but it was the truth.

Iris, who had never gone on a date in her life, had been swept along in her younger sister's matchmaking scheme. The only problem? Elliott hadn't liked her at all.

Elliott had liked Rose.

And Iris didn't know what bothered her more. That her sister had only been able to imagine her with a man when he was so singularly beige, or that Iris had allowed herself to get swept along with it in the first place.

Not only get along with it, but get to the point where she had convinced herself that it was a *good* thing. That she should perhaps make a real effort to get this guy to like her because no one else ever had.

That maybe Elliott, who liked to talk about water filtration like some people talked about sports, their children or once-in-a-lifetime vacations, was the grandest adventure she would ever go on.

That she had somehow imagined that for her, dating a man who didn't produce any sort of spark in her at all, simply because he was there, was adventure.

That she had been almost eager to take any attention she could, the idea of belonging to someone, feeling special, was so intoxicating she had ignored reality, ignored so many things, to try and spin a web of lies to make herself feel better.

That had been some kind of rock bottom. Truly terrifying.

It was one thing to let yourself get swept away in a tide of years that passed without you noticing, as things around you changed and you were there, inevitably the same.

It was quite another to be complicit in your own underwhelming life. To have willingly decided to be grateful for something she hadn't even wanted.

But as horrifying as that was, it was also what brought her down to the vacant shop where the Sugarplum Fairy bakery had once been.

She had been turning over the idea of leasing the building for months now.

And she had finally developed her plan enough that she was ready to dive right in. She had projections and products, had found out what permits she would need. She already had a food handler's card. She had a whole business plan. The only thing she didn't have was the building, and a business name.

One thing at a time.

There was a number posted on the sign on the window for a property management company. She took a deep breath, and dialed it.

"Hi," she said when the woman on the other end answered. "My name is Iris Daniels, and I'm interested in renting out the building at 322 Grape Street."

"Of course, Ms. Daniels. If you want, I can send over the information packet that I have here."

"I would like that."

A couple hours later, Iris was sitting at Sugar Cup Coffee House feeling morose. The email that the management company had sent to her was comprehensive, and included all of the information that Iris could've wanted. As well as the astronomical sum of money it would cost to rent the space.

She did know that it would be expensive. Any place in this part of town was bound to be. It was just that Gold Valley was a tourist attraction, and the historic buildings in town got heavy foot traffic. So many people came from California, dreaming of a simpler life, and they brought California money with them. The kind of money that was rare for people in Gold Valley to have.

In fact, she imagined the building itself was owned by a Californian and managed by a local company.

She felt a sense of impotent regional rage. Californians and their lack of turn signals and deep pockets...

She hadn't had a dream in so long. The idea of giving up on this one was... It was crushing. Crushing in ways that she didn't really want to think about.

She closed the laptop, and stared into her coffee.

Sugar Cup was the most adorable redbrick coffee place, with wide pastry cases overflowing with cookies, scones and cakes. The floor was all scarred barn wood, and from the ceiling hung a massive chandelier, all glittery and proud in the middle of the rustic flair.

Iris couldn't even enjoy it right now.

"Hi."

She turned and saw her sister Rose standing at the counter with her now fiancé, Logan.

Rose patted Logan on the shoulder, then scampered over to Iris's table.

"What are you doing here?"

"It's strange for *you* to be here," Iris said.

Logan and Rose worked full-time at Hope Springs Ranch, her family's ranch. Iris still lived in the house. She was basically a rancher wife, without the benefit of the husband.

She had spent years of her life taking care of her cousins and siblings. Cooking for them, cleaning. It was a full-time job even now.

But it was a full-time job that didn't have any pay, and didn't have a lot of personal satisfaction at this point.

Her brother was married now, and while Sammy had always been involved in the household to an extent, she now lived in the house. And was… Well, it was her house.

It made Iris feel like there wasn't as much to do. And like she didn't really have the authority to do it.

It was the same with her sister Pansy and her husband, West. They were firmly established at their own home, raising West's younger brother. A family unit apart from the one the Danielses had spent years building after their parents had died when they were kids.

And now that Rose and Logan were engaged, Rose had moved out of the main house too, and Iris just had…less and less to do.

She and Logan no longer came to the farmhouse for every meal. Instead, they usually ate at their place.

It seemed fitting that they were all settled first. Well, she couldn't have imagined another way for it to go. She was a practical girl, and she tried not to give in to self-pity. Self-pity didn't help anyone. But she'd always occupied a particular position in her family. She was steady and she was well-behaved, and she was…well, she was the one who had to shepherd them all into the safe, happy, finished places of their lives.

Ryder had taken care of them, it was true. But the emotional well-being of her siblings, that she be a good example…all of that was an essential part of who she was.

Of what her mother had needed her to be.

And sure, there were hard things about that, but she'd never seen the point of arguing with the way things were.

She'd tried. But she'd lost her parents at fourteen. She'd exhausted her lungs arguing with the universe back then. And it hadn't changed a thing.

And yes, it burned a little more at the realization she was the only one left alone. And maybe she was irritated by the fact that a few months ago her pride had suffered a mortal wounding at the hands of her sister.

Unintentional of course.

But when Rose had tried to set her up with Elliott, who had ultimately been after Rose and not Iris, it had driven a splinter deep beneath Iris's skin.

She should be grateful, she supposed.

With everyone so decidedly moved on, that left her in the house with Ryder, Sammy and baby Astrid, feeling like a third wheel.

Her poor eldest brother had his maiden spinster sister living in his house with him while he was trying to adjust to being a husband, and a new father.

Of course, being in the same house as her niece was

wonderful. And she knew that Sammy appreciated having help with the baby.

But it just served as yet another reminder of what Iris didn't have for herself.

She was always enjoying things through other people.

Their milestones. Their triumphs. All of them falling in love. Having children.

It made her ache, and it was inspiring her to act. And this bakery was supposed to be her way out of that.

And now it just felt like she had been shaken out of an impossible dream.

"We decided to have a date morning." Rose frowned. "You look upset."

Iris hesitated. She knew that if she told Rose about what was going on, Rose would immediately go into scheming mode. And when Rose schemed, things tended to go... Well, they *went*. Awry or well, that was never a guarantee, but something always happened.

She might as well see where Rose's momentum could take her. She was currently stagnant. And sure, sometimes Rose had terrible ideas. Like trying to set Iris up with Elliott.

But Rose also had a sort of mischievous magic that Iris herself didn't possess.

"I called about the bakery."

"Yay!"

"*Not* yay. It's being managed by a different company now, which means I think it got bought by someone else. And the rent is higher than it was when I looked into it a couple months ago. I just don't think there's any way I could ever afford it."

"You know Ryder would help you."

She nodded slowly. She did know that. But she didn't

want to put strain on her brother when he had just started a new family. Plus…

"But that's not what you want, is it?" Rose asked.

Iris nodded. "I want to be independent. And maybe I'm jumping into it a little bit too fast. Maybe I'm being too ambitious."

"I don't think so," Rose said. "I don't see why you can't have everything."

She had a feeling her sister was being overly supportive in part because of what had happened between them a few months back. But she appreciated the support either way.

"Well," Rose said brightly. "We just have to figure out another way to problem solve this. Is there a way to figure out who bought it?"

"It might be… Somewhere. I mean, I don't know what difference that would make."

"You don't want to deal with the management company. Whoever has this all set up probably has a management company because they don't have a business brain. They probably don't have the resolve to handle all this kind of stuff. Which means if you talk to them directly, maybe they won't hold firm on the rent. You can't go through the rental company, because they're set up to be a barrier. You need to remove the barrier."

"I don't… That's not how it's supposed to work, though."

And even as she heard the words come out of her own mouth, she realized what she was doing.

She was wimping out. She was taking this first hurdle, and allowing it to be insurmountable. Well, she couldn't do that. She was going to have to make it… Surmountable.

"Okay. Where do you suppose I might find the information?"

Rose sat down, and Logan pulled a chair up to the table, while Rose helped Iris scour the document.

If Logan was irritated by Iris co-opting his date, he didn't show it.

Logan had grown up with them on their ranch. His mother had died along with Iris's parents and aunt and uncle in a plane crash on their way to a joint family vacation.

The kids had all been staying together while their parents had gone on the trip, and they had remained together thereafter.

They had created a tight family unit, which had been a blessing growing up, but was now part of what Iris suspected was holding her back.

"What is it you're looking for?" Logan asked.

"We're trying to figure out who owns this place," Rose said.

"Which place?"

"The one that used to be Sugarplum Fairy. Iris wants to rent it to make her own business."

"Oh," Logan said. "Well, I know who owns that."

"You do?" they both asked in unison.

"Yes. West was looking into it because the guy who used to own Redemption Ranch also owned those buildings, and he decided to sell. But then, some out-of-state guy made an offer that the guy couldn't refuse. So, West decided to back out. He didn't want rental properties that bad."

"And you remember the buyer's name?" Iris pressed.

"Yeah. I think so. Griffin… Griffin Chance. Very California. You don't forget a name like that."

"I don't suppose you do," Iris said.

"Well, do you know where to find him?"

"I bet it would be easy enough to find out." Rose had a wicked gleam in her eye.

"You can't ask Pansy," Iris said. "I'm sure that she's not allowed to get that kind of information."

"Maybe she just knows it. Because he's a new person in town, and he bought a sizable amount of property, so honestly, she might…"

"I'm not one hundred percent sure he's in town," Logan said.

"Oh, right," Iris said, feeling deflated.

"Well, all we can do is ask," Rose said.

She was in full Rose mode, and this was when Iris had to be thankful for her sister.

Because Iris was very good at putting her head down and enduring whatever hardships came her way.

She was good at creating calm. At creating quiet.

When she was in her element, she was strong. She'd wrangled Rose and Pansy even before their parents had died. They'd been two of the most high-spirited kids Iris had ever seen. And it had been up to her to keep them corralled from an early age because she was naturally more…well, more of a rule follower.

She was used to taking that role at Hope Springs, but outside of it she tended to shrink back a little. Some people even read her as being shy or timid—Iris didn't feel she was either—but she definitely didn't have a lot of practice with taking charge away from the ranch.

She was in a space now where she needed to push, and Rose was an excellent pusher.

Rose scurried off, and made one phone call, and Iris could see from where she was sitting that Rose was wheedling. She exchanged a glance with Logan.

"Try living with it," he said.

"I did," Iris said, deadpan. "I raised it."

"Yeah, well," he muttered. "You're not as much of a sucker for her as I am."

"That is true," Iris responded.

When Rose returned a moment later, she had a triumphant grin on her face. "I have an address for you. 9020 Carson Creek. That's all the way up Echo Pass."

"There's not... There's not even electricity out there," Iris said. "He can't live out there."

"Well, that's the address that Pansy had for him. Honestly, he's probably got some huge fancy house up there with satellite internet and a generator and stuff. Anybody that owns that much property in town has to have some fancy spread way out there. He's probably some rich old guy. You should bring cookies."

Iris didn't know how she had gone from standing in front of a shop window only a few moments ago to being sent on an errand up into the north forty to meet a man she'd never even heard of.

"Rose, I don't know..."

"It might be worth it," Rose said. "And you won't know unless you try."

Her sister had a point. And as this sort of thing went, it was better than being with a guy who didn't excite her. She had been offended before when she'd thought Rose had imagined that she couldn't handle a fantasy more compelling than Elliott.

At least this felt like the start of something exciting.

GRIFFIN CHANCE WAS impossible to get a hold of, it turned out. Or maybe it was just that he declined to be gotten a hold of. Iris couldn't be sure. But in the days since she had discovered he was the owner of the property that she was interested in renting, she had left messages on two different phone lines, both with robot voices that had given her no indication of what the man himself actually sounded like, and had written two emails.

So it couldn't be said she hadn't tried to warn him.

But Iris had spent the last several years of her life in a place of absolute stagnation, and she was over it. Absolutely and completely. That meant that she wasn't accepting no response for an answer. You would think that the man would get back to her. After all, she had matters to discuss with him. Well, she was trying to finagle a way to get lower rent. And maybe he sensed that. Maybe that was why he wasn't getting in touch with her personally. But she had a plan, a plan that involved about two dozen cookies.

Shortly, Mr. Chance would see that what she was proposing was going to be so profitable that in the end he would benefit.

If there was one thing Iris knew about herself, it was that she was a fantastic baker. She didn't have a whole lot in the way of self-esteem. But what she had was pretty solid. And that was how she found herself driving her sister's truck up the back roads toward Griffin Chance's house.

She hoped that he was home. But if not, she would leave everything behind with a detailed note and go from there. The important thing was that he try her food. It was very, very important. Much to her chagrin, the road narrowed, and turned to gravel long before her phone said she was set to arrive at his house. And then there was… There was a damn log in the middle of the road, not five hundred feet from where she was supposed to turn to get up the drive to his house.

She parked her truck and sat there, looking around. She didn't know what the hell she was supposed to do. *This is it. This is the first challenge. You can either fall down, or you can keep going.*

Keep going.

She was not going to be thwarted now over something this stupid.

She got out of the truck, her plate of cookies and her just-in-case note in hand. She pocketed the truck keys, locked everything behind her and marched right over the tree, carrying on up the road.

"If there are any cougars out there," she said. "Do not eat me."

She was not about to die a thirty-one-year-old virgin with no career.

Whose one and only attempt at dating had resulted in facing the truth that things were as she'd often feared.

Given the option, a man would choose her younger sister over her.

As much as that bothered her, of the two, currently the business situation bothered her the most. Because it was the one she felt motivated to fix.

The other… Well, she'd lived this long with it. It wasn't going to hurt her if it stayed. Anyway. She had a feeling that her biggest problem was the fact that she didn't do much of anything. This business was the start of that. The start of the change. Shoving all thoughts of her virginity to the side, she continued on up the narrow road. She tightened her hands on the plate. It was beautiful out here, but a touch eerie.

The trees were tall and green, and it was impossible to see too deeply into the woods, because the plants were so dense. It was wild out here. And for being so near to town, it felt wholly removed.

She took a left from the gravel road, onto an even narrower, more harrowing road. It was a hike up toward his house. Whatever vehicle the man drove, it had to have tires that were bigger than the truck she'd come in. She muttered as she hiked up the trail. And then she saw it. It was not a grand custom home. It was a little cabin, dilapidated and run-down.

"This is ridiculous," she said. "There's no way he even actually lives here."

And if he did, there was something wrong with him. He was like a full-on ax murderer or something.

She shoved that thought to the side. At least she had told Rose where she was going today. And her other sister was the police chief. So, Rose would tell Pansy, and Pansy would come up guns blazing if Iris were gone for too long. So, there was that.

"That would figure," she thought. "I try to do something out of my comfort zone, and I walked myself into a horror movie."

Yeah. It was just a little bit too on the nose.

But she was determined, and she wasn't going to back down now. Steeling herself, she picked her way over the uneven ground and walked up the porch, nearly losing her balance on a loose board. The place was an absolute dive.

The wood was old, and part of it was covered in moss. The siding was split, and the porch… Well, she was afraid she was going to fall right through it.

She took a breath, and knocked on the door. And waited.

"This was stupid," she muttered under her breath. There was no way anyone was actually here. There was no way anyone could actually… Live here.

But then, she heard footsteps. And she waited.

The door jerked open, and her heart tried to take a hard fast beat through the front of her chest. Because standing in the doorway was the biggest man she'd ever seen. Tall and broad, a black cowboy hat resting low on his head.

His eyes were wild, intense. If she'd hoped to find a welcome there, she could see she wouldn't. He had a full, dark beard, and tattoos running up his massive forearms.

He said nothing. He only stared her down, the glint in his blue eyes so hard it made her feel like she was pinned to the spot.

But she had left her truck halfway down the mountain, trapped behind a fallen tree. She had hiked up this narrow road... And no amount of glaring was going to deter her from her mission.

"Griffin Chance? I brought you some cookies."

CHAPTER TWO

GRIFFIN CHANCE LOOKED down at the plate of cookies, and then at the extremely plain, mousy woman who was holding them.

He wasn't sure which was the bigger surprise. The woman, or the baked goods. Really, anyone coming out of nowhere and materializing at his chosen retreat was a surprise. One of the things he liked about living so far up Echo Pass was the fact that he was isolated. Alone.

That was how he liked it.

"Do I know you?"

His voice was rusty. He didn't think he had spoken in a couple of days. Not unusual. In fact, he was pretty sure the last thing he'd said was a vile expletive when he'd hammered his thumb working on the house a while back.

And before that… He couldn't even remember.

"No," she said. "No, you don't. Though, I did leave a couple of messages for you?"

"My business manager handles that." His words sounded disconnected. They felt disconnected.

He didn't think about that side of his life often these days. It was why he paid someone to manage it. A payment that left his account automatically and required no effort or thought on his part.

The woman looked at him like he had grown a second

head. He had to acknowledge that it was probably weird to hear a man who looked only *just* this side of Sasquatch say that he had a business manager.

But what this creature found weird or not weird wasn't really his problem.

"Well. I haven't heard from your business manager. But I got your address and I thought that I would come up here and talk to you. With… A peace offering."

"The cookies."

"Yes. The cookies."

She looked around, the disdain in her muddy green brown eyes obvious.

"Are you going to invite me in?"

"Wasn't going to." He crossed his arms and leaned against the door frame.

"Well, if you don't let me in, I'm not going to be able to give you a cookie."

"I could take it off the platter if I felt like it."

"Well, you won't be able to have milk."

"I don't have any milk."

She didn't seem to be deterred by that. "Well, what do you have? Coffee?"

"Whiskey."

She straightened her shoulders, looking comically proper. Like a 1950s housewife in the thick of problem solving a dinner party dilemma. "Well, perhaps we can have cookies and whiskey."

He stared at her for a long moment, and she didn't shrink back.

When he'd first set eyes on her, he'd thought *mousy*. But *mousy* wasn't the right word at all. "Why are you here?"

"To talk to you about the building that you own on Grape

Street. Which I said in my message. Which I left for your business manager. Who quite frankly isn't doing his job."

"Her job."

She blinked. "Fine. Her job."

She just looked at him, expectant. "I can let you in, but there's nothing nicer in there than there is out here."

"Okay," she said, taking a seat in one of the rickety wooden chairs that sat on the leaning porch.

He stayed where he stood. "So you want to talk to me about the building."

"Yes. I do. I want to start a bakery."

He looked at her, then at the cookies. "That's why you brought these cookies."

"Yes," she said, brightening visibly. "To show you that my offer is a good one. It is. Very good."

"And that offer is?"

"I want to rent out the building on Grape Street and make it a bakery. But the rent that you're charging is astronomical."

"What am I charging?" He didn't have a clue. He wasn't entirely sure what building she was even talking about.

She named a figure that didn't sound especially astronomical to him. But that was the problem with him these days. He didn't know if it didn't sound like much because living in the Bay Area had made him numb to real estate prices. If it didn't seem like much because he'd made and spent more money in thirty-eight years than most people would ever see in a lifetime.

Or if it just didn't seem like much because he didn't care anymore. About much of anything. About money or expenses or...

Much of anything.

"I can't pay it. I was going to rent the building, but then you bought it."

"My business manager probably did that too."

"Well, whatever. The bottom line is that you own it. And, now it's kind of hindering my dream."

"What's your name?"

She blinked. "Iris."

"Maybe you need some more realistic dreams, Iris."

He'd expected a reaction out of that, but she remained nearly sanguine in appearance. "I am actively trying to make my dream more realistic by changing the circumstances around it."

"Coming up here and negotiating with me is not exactly dancing with realism. Here's a tip. Life is tough. It's not fair. I don't exist to make it fair for you." He started to step back into the house, but Iris advanced.

This time, he'd succeeded in making her mad.

If she'd been a bird, her feathers would have been ruffled. As it was, her cheeks turned pink, her lips pulling down at the corners.

"I've never labored under the illusion that life was fair. You're making assumptions about me because you think you can just look at me and see exactly what I am, but you can't. I'm strong and I'm determined. I'm a hard worker and I've dealt with enough *life* to be certain I won't buckle underneath stress. We can both make money on this business. I will promise you a percentage of my profits."

Something about her persistent optimism made him feel mean. "And you're so confident that your little bakery is going to make a profit on the main street of a nothing town where any number of businesses on that main street struggle to break even in their first five years of business?"

It was weird to hear that come out of his mouth. Weird to remember that at one time he'd been something else. Something different.

Different than a loner up at the top of the mountain?

It was difficult to remember life before that. Before days spent in this cabin, getting up when it suited him, putting in a hard day of labor before collapsing back in bed. Some days he allowed himself the time to ride his horse. Another echo from another time. This, though, this was part of a life long gone. But somewhere, inside of him, apparently dwelled a developer. He hadn't really missed him.

"I'm telling you, I have an idea. It will be primarily sweets, but I would also like to make fresh meals to go."

"Seems like splitting your focus."

"Maybe. But the more something can be convenient, particularly right in Gold Valley, the better. Oftentimes to get a variety of food people need to go into Tolowa, and that's forty-five minutes away. The more they can shop local, the better. If they can make a stop for a treat, and also pick up a convenient, healthy meal, I think they will. And there's plenty of single men in town who would like a home-cooked meal."

"Okay. So you're proposing what? There's a bakery counter and then..."

"The fridge. With to go meals."

"What else?" He didn't know why he was indulging this, and he was out of practice at reading his own motivations. Because one thing about being by yourself, having your life taken down to the studs, was that you didn't have to.

He ate when he needed to, drank when he felt like it. Moved with the sun if he needed to, or didn't if he was tired early, or not tired at all.

It didn't matter. And because it didn't matter, he didn't have to engage in any internal dialogues about his intent.

He was curious about it now, though, and lacked the inner vocabulary to sort through it.

"I make bread. There will be a bread rack."

"All right. Well, I guess that's not the worst thing I've ever heard."

He was struck by the absurdity of it all. That he would be standing there on his front porch, talking to this little creature still plaintively holding a tray of cookies.

"But really," she said. "You should try my cookies. And then, you might agree with me."

"I've had any number of cookies in my lifetime, Iris. What makes you think yours are so special?"

Color mounted in her cheeks, and he searched the recesses of himself and it dawned on him that there were definitely two meanings to something like that.

"Just try them," she said, quiet, but insistent. She was a strange thing. But by no means as timid or plain as he'd first imagined.

"Did you walk?" he asked, suddenly realizing there was no vehicle in sight.

"From a ways back," she said. "There's a tree in the road."

There hadn't been a tree the last time he'd been down. But that had been a couple of weeks.

"And if I try one of your cookies, will you leave?"

"Depends."

"You're trespassing," he said. "I could call the police."

"Sure. But my sister is the police. So, I'm not sure how far that would get you."

"They say you can't negotiate with terrorists, but apparently here you can't negotiate with terrorists or little brunettes bringing cookies? Because you have the police in your pocket."

"In this instance, yes. I do."

He reached out, and picked up one of the cookies. It looked like it was chocolate chip. Standard cookie fare. Big mistake. If you were going to come all the way up the mountain and try to impress a man with your baking, you had to get beyond the basics.

Unless she put cyanide in it.

Entirely possible.

The thought of that didn't really…faze him.

He popped the cookie into his mouth whole, and chewed.

And had to revise every thought he had previously.

Because it was the *best* damn chocolate chip cookie he'd ever had in his life.

And that was saying something. Especially nowadays. He didn't really eat for pleasure. Didn't do much of anything for pleasure. He ate to not die, he drank to not feel.

Dessert? Unless it was a convenience, he couldn't remember the last time he'd had something sweet.

And maybe that was coloring his perception on these cookies. But there was something about them that was almost painful. A window into something domestic that he didn't have anymore.

A look at another life.

Who knew that butter and chocolate could accomplish such a thing?

"It's good, right?" she asked.

And the strangest thing was he knew that she was just confirming. Because she knew it was good. And there wasn't a hell of a lot else that made her interesting. But her confidence did. That flat-out assurance that she had something here that was better than average. That she was better than good. And she had come all the way up the mountain to make sure he knew it.

Spare few things intrigued him, but that did.

He picked up another cookie off the plate, and her grin became that of a satisfied cat.

"I told you," she said.

"I'm a soft target," he said, "I can't tell you how long it's been since I've had a cookie."

"I don't have a lot of money," she said. "A little bit that I have saved up from…things. And, what I'm anticipating I'll make on the bakery. But by and large, the start-up is going to be pretty cost prohibitive." She took a deep breath. "If I could do some things for you around the house, or bring you things…"

"Are you suggesting we should barter?"

"Yes. That is exactly what I'm suggesting. I'll bring you food. I'm going to be making dinners anyway, and I'm going to be making baked goods. I'll cook for you."

"How do you know I need someone to cook for me?"

She looked past him, at the decrepit cabin. "Just a hunch," she said.

"What makes you think I want that?"

"I don't know. But I'll trade you. Domestic services. And the percentage of my profits. And if after twelve months it's not worth it to you, then it's done. But it's just empty right now, and I guarantee you that very few people in town are going to be able to make that rent. Even if they do, it's going to be some fool who came up from California—no offense—and thinks that they know how to run a business here. They're going to think they know better what people here want. They're going to aim to please tourists, ignoring the fact that you have to give something to the locals as well. I know this town. I know these people. Like I said, my sister is the police. My brother is one of the most well-respected men in town. My cooking is something people know about." She straightened, lifting her chin. "I'm something of a legend."

"Are you?"

"Yes."

"You're very small for a legend."

"And you're awfully talkative for a mountain. But here we are."

And he didn't know what to say to her. Mostly because he had no reason to argue with her. Not really. He could give her what she was asking for. The only thing he needed money for these days was the equine facility down in Santa Barbara. And most of his previous investments handled that.

And yeah, there was the house. And it had to be finished. A promise was a promise. It had just taken him a while to get here. And then, taken a while to get to where he could think about starting. But in the meantime, he didn't need exorbitant rent money. And if he had someone bringing him food, he could leave the house less often. He could actually get a decent start on building.

And yeah, doing it by himself was something a little bit past foolish, but he'd gotten to where it was possible. And anyway, it was about the only thing he could do to occupy himself.

"Come on in," he said, jerking his head toward the door.

Likely, when she saw the place, she would run.

He kept a close eye on her as they entered, trying to gauge her response.

And at this point, he wasn't sure whether he hoped she would go, or hoped that she would stay.

He looked around the dilapidated cabin, trying to see what she was seeing. It was... Well, it was a mess.

The furniture was in disrepair, and everything was shoved into one room, and the floors were buckled. It was dim and dark, and it didn't bother him any. But she looked bothered.

"Do you have electricity?"

"I have a generator. Sometimes I bother to run it. Mostly I don't."

"So, you live here...alone."

"What gave that away?"

"All right," she said, as if steeling herself for a battle. "All right. I will clean this place twice a week, plus provide dinner for every day. And dessert that goes with whatever I'm making at the bakery. And twenty percent of the profits."

"Twenty-five."

That lit her face up like a beacon. "Twenty is more than generous."

"And no rent is something a bit past generous. And I'm not known for that. So, if I were you, I'd take a deal when one is offered."

She looked mulish. "Fine." Still holding the plate of cookies in one hand, she extended her other for a handshake. "Griffin Chance," she said, "you've got yourself a deal."

"Sounds good, Iris." He grasped her hand in his, and for a moment it was like the world tilted.

She was soft. And warm.

And right then, he was trying to remember how long it had been since he'd touched another person. He'd never even had another person in this cabin.

"What's your family name?" he asked, dropping his hold on her hand.

"Daniels."

"Sounds to me like we're business partners, Iris Daniels."

"Sounds like it."

"You start Monday."

"That's tomorrow," she said. "That's not very much time."

"Then I suggest you get busy."

CHAPTER THREE

IRIS WAS VIBRATING with energy by the time she got back to Hope Springs Ranch. She had done it. She had… Gone up the mountain a hausfrau and come down a bakery owner.

Sort of.

There was still so much to consider. So many things to put into place. Thankfully, she knew that the building had the facilities she needed to do what she wanted, more or less, since it had been a bakery prior to her taking over. But she was still going to have to… Well, bake more than she ever had in her life, figure out a name, figure out so many things.

And somehow, add cleaning a cabin that seemed entirely made of dirt and cooking dinner for a hermit.

He was not at all what she expected.

The *cabin* wasn't at all what she expected.

Griffin Chance was a man who *seemed* to own real estate, and have the ability to negotiate business deals. The way that he talked about things made her certain that he was familiar with the practice.

And he lived in a hovel.

It didn't make a lot of sense.

But she had accomplished her goal, thanks to her cookies, so she was going to go ahead and call it a win and not worry about the rest.

She scrambled around the kitchen, finishing off the meat loaf that she was preparing for dinner.

Everyone was coming over tonight. Which made her very happy indeed.

It was a strange thing, wanting to distance herself slightly from the family, while also missing them desperately.

The way they were.

Because they'd been a soft cushion for her for so many years, and deciding that she needed to move on, deciding that she wanted more, didn't mean...

She missed it. Feeling satisfied with this.

It wasn't comfortable to want so much.

To be dissatisfied.

"Iris." Her sister-in-law Sammy came into the room with baby Astrid strapped to her chest. "I didn't want you to cook dinner by yourself."

"Oh it's fine," Iris said.

"We always used to cook together," Sammy said, looking down at her baby's beautiful, fuzzy head.

"And now you have Astrid to take care of," she said. "It's *fine*."

"I do have Astrid take care of," Sammy said, "but that doesn't mean I can't cook dinner."

"Well, I just want to... I want to help when I can."

Because she was going to have to tell them all tonight that help was going to be a lot less common.

The front door opened, and Iris heard the sound of the dogs rushing in. Their nails clicking on the hardwood. And then she heard three pairs of boots walking along with them.

"Can we not have the dogs in?" Iris asked, mostly just because it was what she always asked.

It was futile, at this point, to complain about the small pack having free run of the house.

She just didn't want them under the dining room table, or in the kitchen. But at this point, the dogs had won, and there was no sacred space for humans. And there was simply no enforcing it with Sammy as mistress of the house anyway.

Iris rolled her eyes, and took the pans of meat loaf into the dining room, setting them with the rolls and salad that were already on the table.

She also had an icebox cake ready to go for dessert. Lemon with vanilla cake and candied citrus peel, which was a family favorite.

She was gratified by the sounds of anticipation that her sister Rose, her fiancé, Logan, Ryder and Sammy made as they surveyed the table. West, Pansy and West's half brother, Emmett, joined them a few moments later, and made more proclamations of joy around the food.

It was almost enough.

Almost.

But she couldn't help but be conscious of the fact that everyone was paired off except for her and the teenage boy.

And it was things like that that just left her a little bit depressed.

She waited until they were halfway through the meal to make her pronouncements. Her reality might not be cheering. Her pronouncement was.

She might feel stagnant here in this familiar environment, but she wasn't. She'd gotten her deal.

"I did it," she said. "I made an agreement with the owner of the building on Grape Street today, and I'm going to be opening a bakery."

Everyone stared at her like she had grown a second head.

"Well," she said. "Say something."

"That's fantastic!" Rose said. "I knew that you could do it. How did you manage?"

"I…baked a plate of cookies and hiked up to the top of the mountain."

"I have *no* idea how that got you a bakery," Rose said.

"They are very good chocolate chip cookies, Rose," Iris said, sniffing.

"Good for you," Pansy added. "You've been wanting to do that for so long."

"Yes," she said. "And in exchange, I'm going to be giving my landlord twenty-five percent of the profits, and cleaning his house. And making him dinner. And dessert."

"What?" Ryder asked, his eyes narrowing.

"Well, he was charging a lot for rent, so I went to negotiate."

"Iris," Ryder said. "You don't even know who this guy is. Do you?"

"No. His name is Griffin Chance. He's from California, I think. But he lives here in town now. Well, not in town, he lives up Echo Pass. And well, let me tell you, he is in need of someone taking care of some things for him."

Everyone was staring at her like she'd grown cloven hooves, and was currently grasping her fork between the splits.

"I don't feel comfortable with it," Ryder said.

West was eyeing her closely, but as her brother-in-law, probably didn't feel like he could offer his opinion freely. Logan, however, as a surrogate brother who had known her all of her life, was clearly not so encumbered.

"I don't like it at all," Logan said. "The whole thing is weird. He might be some…some pervert, who likes to watch people clean his floors, you don't know."

Horror stole over Iris, as she tried to imagine what that

could even mean. Especially applied to the large, muscular bearded man she had met earlier today.

What sort of...perversion was related to floor cleaning? She didn't know.

She wasn't afraid of him, though.

He was a very large man. If he decided to harm her in some way, she wouldn't have any recourse, and even though for some reason she felt she could trust him, she wasn't entirely sure that could be enough. Maybe she could carry bear spray...

"Well, it's too late," she said, emphatically. "I made a deal, and I start tomorrow. And... I'm excited. Because it's the first thing I've ever done for myself, and I went and made the deal, and I'm not boring."

"Nobody said you were boring," Pansy said.

"You think I am. Because I needlepoint and knit, and Rose thinks that I should date a man in khakis."

"Are you still mad about Elliott?" Rose asked.

Irritation and something that felt deeper stabbed at her chest.

"I'm not *mad*," Iris said. "I was never mad. It's just... Look, I'm doing something for myself. And I'm excited about it, and I don't need commentary from a man who got his best friend pregnant, another man who slept with my sister even though she's a decade younger than him and he's known her since she was a child, and finally, from my sister's landlord, who is also an ex-convict who seduced her and stole her innocence."

The three large cowboys at the table had the decency to look chagrined, so there was that. And she could tell that none of them had expected quite such a definitive display from her. Well, they didn't know everything about her.

"That was different," Ryder said.

"Completely different," Logan agreed.

"How so?" she pressed.

"We are not potentially secret serial killers," Logan said.

"West might have been."

Pansy gave her husband a sidelong glance. "She has a point."

"How did I get dragged into this?" West asked. "I didn't say anything."

"You thought it," Iris said.

"You definitely thought it," Emmett agreed, in the fashion only a younger brother could.

Great. Not only was the teenager the only other single one, he also seemed to be the only one on her side.

That made Iris feel a little bit less confident in her plans.

"I appreciate the concern," she said. "But I'm a grown woman. I'm older than you," she said to her sisters. "And about the same age as you." She directed that to Ryder and Sammy. "I don't need to be taken care of or coddled."

"It's just… Where does he live again?" Ryder asked.

"Off-grid. Up Echo Pass. Yes. I know. But… I don't know what his deal is. But clearly he needs someone to do things for him."

"That seems stupid," Ryder said.

That earned him a baleful look from his wife. "Because you're notorious for making your own dinner after a long day out on the range?" Sammy asked, sweetly.

Iris looked across the table. At all the food that she had made. "I've been taking care of all of you, for a long time. And now I'm taking care of myself. So, some support and a little bit less questioning would go a long way."

"I support you," Rose said.

It did not surprise her that it was her youngest sister that immediately jumped on board. In part because as seemingly sketchy life choices went, Rose was leading the charge in their family. Her secret relationship with Logan had been a shock to everyone else, and it was easy for all of them to underestimate Rose, given her age. But she had proven that she was tough, and that she and Logan were definitely something other than logical. They were meant to be. And everyone would have told them not to do it. And they would've been wrong. Just like they were wrong about this situation. About her.

"I'll bring bear spray," she said.

That earned her an incredulous laugh from West.

"Right, now you're talking, Caldwell," she said. "Which means it's officially open season on you."

"I'm sorry," he said. "The image of you taking down a man with bear spray is funny."

Because they didn't think she was tough. That was why. She hadn't anticipated this whole thing being quite so annoying. She knew that her family had good intentions, but she didn't need to be saved from herself.

"I have cake," she said, getting up from the table and stalking into the kitchen.

She heard a chair scrape across the floor, and she expected to see Sammy following after her. But it was Ryder.

"I'm sorry," he said. "Let me help you with the cake."

"I don't need help with the cake that I already made."

"I just worry about you," he said.

"Stop," she said. "Stop worrying about me."

"It's not that simple, Iris, you know that. You're my partner in crime. If it wasn't for you, I don't know what would've happened to this family. There were things I had to do to take care of all the kids. But I was mostly the legal fulfillment. You were the heart of us. You made sure that Pansy and Rose looked nice when they went to school. You learned how to mend things, and make clothes and make sure that we ate well."

"Your wife deserves credit for that too. When she came to live with us…"

"Yes, Sammy helped. But you had already set the tone. You made sure that our house was still a home. Even after we lost our parents. I want you to be happy. I really do. And I'm supportive of you, I promise. But sometimes I worry that you missed out on a lot of the real world because you were here."

"I did," she said. "And that's what I'm trying to fix."

"I'm just worried that it's made you a little bit naive."

"*Naive?* And then you think I don't know that a random man living on the top of the mountain could be a pervert or a serial killer? I do. I have, like, three streaming services and I watch a lot of crime dramas. I have *seen* things."

"You know what, it's not even that," he said. "What if he's after something else?"

Iris blinked, then stared at her brother in disbelief. "Are you… Are you warning me that the man might be after my… My *virtue*?"

"Oh hell," Ryder said. "I didn't say that."

"You did, though. That is basically what you're saying."

She wanted to laugh except she was so angry. After everything…she couldn't even fantasize that a man like… well, that one would be *at all* interested in her in that way.

"I'm not. I'm really not. I just… He might expect something."

"Ryder," she said. "I know that you're my brother, but come on. The man is no more likely to want to take advantage of me than he would a small brown vole that came to his door. And you know it."

"You're not a vole," Ryder said. "You're a woman and…"

"And I'll bring bear spray," she said, feeling angry now. Honestly, it was like he was making fun of her. How could he possibly think that… He couldn't. He was basically just giving her a talk to give it. Being outrageous and over the top because he could be. "But I guarantee you that the prospect of a home-cooked meal is about the only thing that makes me appealing to him."

"Just be safe," Ryder said.

"Do not lecture me about safe sex," she said. "First of all, I'm way too old. Second of all, you don't practice it yourself."

"Iris," Ryder said, sounding like he wished he were dead.

"Don't lecture me," she said. "Don't scold me. Just support me."

"Make sure you have cell signal up there," he said.

"I don't think I do."

"Fine, then put a CB radio in your vehicle and figure out a way to call Pansy if you need it."

"Ryder, I promise you that I will be safe. But you have to let me go. You're right, I was the one who came alongside you and did this. Who helped you with the other kids. I was never one of them. Not in the same way. But we were a team. And we aren't now. We can't be. Not in the same way. I'm so… I'm so happy for you. For you and Sammy, and I love Astrid. Dearly. But I still don't have a life, Ryder. And that's not fair."

He looked at her, hard. "I'm sorry," he said. "I mean, really sorry. I didn't think of it. Not that way. I'm proud of you," he said. "For making it happen."

"Thank you," she said.

"You're stronger than I give you credit for," he added.

"I am," she said. "Stronger than I give me credit for too."

She brought the cake to the table, and the subject of her working for Griffin was dropped.

And she repeated what she just said to Ryder, over and over internally. She was strong. She was. She had lost her parents, she had helped raise her siblings. Cleaning up after one backwoodsman was going to seem easy in comparison.

She was certain of it.

CHAPTER FOUR

WHEN GRIFFIN WOKE UP Monday morning, he had the realization that today would be different than the one before it.

And that was strange.

He didn't really look forward to things. And he wasn't sure that he could say he was looking forward to this. Mostly, it was a strange mixture of alarm and anticipation. It was just knowing that the day wouldn't stretch on until it ended with nothing interrupting it. Knowing that another person would be sharing his space. Space that had been sacred ground since he'd moved in.

But he went out, and he worked on the house until the sun started to make his shoulders feel blistered, and he stripped his white undershirt off and wiped his face with it before shoving it in the back pocket of his jeans and heading toward the house, his stomach growling.

Her car was there. Gleaming in the late afternoon light. He had moved the log yesterday so she wouldn't have to hike up to the cabin the next time she arrived. It seemed the least he could do.

He walked up the steps and pushed the door open, and stopped when he saw her, down on her hands and knees on the floor, scrubbing vigorously. Her dark hair was hanging limp in her face, her brow gleaming with sweat. She was wearing a plain gray T-shirt that showed nothing of her body, and a skirt that fell down past her knees, and he didn't know why he was frozen there watching her work.

Maybe it was just the strangeness of having her there. It sure as hell couldn't be anything else.

She straightened, clambering to her feet, her eyes wide. Her mouth went slack, then dropped open.

"Hi," he said.

"Oh" was her response. She was staring at him. Or more accurately, at his chest.

Right. He'd taken his shirt off.

Which, he could see was maybe not the best move in context with the situation. But he had kind of forgotten how to do the whole people thing.

He stomped over to his dresser, which was pushed up against the wall, opened the top drawer and grabbed a black T-shirt out of it. He shrugged it on over his head. "Thanks for coming," he said.

She was still staring at him.

"Well," she said, clearing her throat. "It is what we agreed on."

"We didn't agree on a time."

"No," she said tentatively. "We didn't. That is true. But I thought… Well, since I don't have a key to the bakery, or anything like that."

"Give me your address," he said.

"Oh?"

"Yes," he said. "Give me your address and I will have it mailed to you."

"Thanks," she said. "Anyway. I figured since I didn't have anything to do at the bakery today I would come and get a head start on getting whatever needed to be done here…done."

"Enterprising. I admire it."

Of course, doing anything around this place was essentially a lost cause. It was dirt on dirt. Not that he cared. It was rustic. It was basically camping, and that was just fine with him. He'd tried.

He had tried to stay in the Bay Area. Had tried to continue to run his business in San Francisco, living in an apartment there. But there was no normal. And nothing had gotten better. So a couple of years ago he had come to Gold Valley. It had always been the plan, after all, so it made sense that he would follow that plan. And about six months into ruminating at the top of the mountain he had come to the conclusion that the house still needed to be built.

Even if it wouldn't be for its original intent.

Anyway. It gave him something to do.

And as far as the cabin went, he didn't mind it. Not in the least.

"I did bring food," she said, indicating a picnic basket sitting on the kitchen counter.

"You said you didn't have electricity?" she asked.

"No," he said.

"How do you…refrigeration?"

"Icebox," he said. "In the most literal sense of that word."

"Oh. Good to know. That seems…rustic."

He looked around the room. "Did you have the idea that I wasn't rustic?"

"No. I guess not."

Two days in a row he had talked to another person. It was strange.

He grunted. "Don't stop cleaning on my account."

"No," she said, scrambling back down to the floor. He nearly smiled. *Nearly.* Instead, he walked over to where that picnic basket sat and opened the top. There was a platter of fruit and cheese inside, artfully arranged. There was also a sandwich, made on what looked to be a homemade baguette, with little jars containing mayonnaise and mustard on the side.

There was also a small bottle of wine, and a bottle of beer. And he was starving.

He opened them up, pulling the plastic wrap off the top of the platter and digging straight into the cheese. Flavor. So different from what he'd been making on the stove top in this place. What he learned was that you could take TV dinners, dump them into a pot frozen and make something edible. He had gotten well acquainted with cut up hot dogs and baked beans. Had eaten a fair amount of canned chili.

It had been a long time since he'd had something like this. Something that had intense texture and flavor. Different kinds of cheese were a strange human luxury. The time and effort that must have gone into figuring out you could get a different result from letting milk age in a slightly different fashion from another batch of milk was one of those things he'd never wondered about before. Who had discovered that? Who had perfected it?

And to what end?

The nutritional value had to be the same.

It was just for taste. Just for pleasure.

Eating this cheese was just for pleasure.

Having been deprived of pleasure of any kind for the last five years, it was a revelation he hadn't expected. And it made him all the more eager to dig in to the sandwich. He took one of the small knives that she had included in the basket and slathered mustard on the inside of the baguette. There was also ham, and yet more cheese inside. He put a generous helping of mayonnaise in there as well. And he groaned, audibly, when he took his first bite. And didn't bother to hide it.

"I brought extra," she said. "It's just still in the car in a few different cases because I wasn't sure how you were going to store it. But I'm glad that I did."

"Thanks," he replied.

"You are out... Working?"

He nodded in the affirmative, but didn't offer any details.

"It must be lonely up here," she said.

"I live here by choice," he said. "It's quiet up here. Not lonely. That's the difference between enforced solitude and chosen solitude, I would imagine."

"Oh. I guess so." She shifted uncomfortably, then rose up off the ground. "I'm finished with the floor. I... Do you have extra blankets?"

"Yeah," he said. "One set."

"Could you direct me to them? I will... I'll bring these home, and wash them at my place. Then I can bring them back to you."

He lifted a shoulder. "No need. The creek works just fine when I get around to washing."

"No," she said. "I will take them, and I will give them a legitimate wash. That's what we are trading for. And I'm showing you what kind of worker I am. And what kind of quality customers can expect from me. If I cut corners with you, then what would I be showing you?"

"I don't know," he said. "But I have a feeling it matters more to you than it does to me."

"Well, I'm used to that," she said, the comment cryptic enough. And maybe some people would have been curious about what she meant by it. About the underlying truth in it. But he wasn't. He didn't much care.

With industrious movements she crossed the room and went toward his bed, yanking the sheets off, and the blanket.

"The extras are under the bed," he said. She paused, the

handful of bedding in her arms, then looked down skeptically.

"I'm half afraid I might find a live weasel under there."

"I call him Frank," he said. "But he only eats every other day. And even then, he doesn't eat brunettes."

He thought he might have even seen amusement glittering in those green brown eyes, and it surprised him. Mostly because he hadn't remembered that he could be amusing. Hadn't felt the desire to be in so long it was like a lost art.

But at one time, Griffin Chance had been known for being entertaining. Had commanded whole rooms at parties, and had conducted business meetings with authority. Had spoken at any number of charity events. People were easy. They always had been.

Until they weren't.

"Seriously," she said, walking to the door and dumping the blankets by it. "No weasels?"

"Not a one."

She got down onto the floor again, and reached beneath the bed, looking at him the entire time, as if he was going to pay if she encountered a small mammal or creepy crawly of some kind.

"I've learned to live with the nature," he said.

"How so?"

"There are spiders in here," he said. "Nothing you can do about it. Ants. Lizards. The occasional scorpion." She leaped back from the bed. "Why don't I get that?"

He crossed the space and reached down for the blankets, grabbed them and shook them out, finding nary a scorpion, before setting them onto the mattress.

"And you just…live with all of it."

"Hey, I chose to move to the woods. They didn't choose to have me here. So yes, I live with it. I live with it because it's the most tolerable place I've found to live. So, a few spiders don't really bother me."

"I live on a ranch," she said.

That simple statement made something in his chest turn. "Is that so?"

"Yes. I'm not really… It's not really my thing. But you know, I grew up in ranching. I live with my brother and his wife." She frowned. "Sorry. You didn't ask."

But he found he was suddenly curious. And she was in his domain, so if he wanted to know, why couldn't he just know? "Go on. I like to know a little something about the people who are in my house. Which in this case is just you. And has only ever been you. So you might as well go ahead."

"I want to open the bakery because I spent all of my life taking care of my siblings. Being part of a big family is like that." She bit her lip like she was holding something back. "Anyway. They're all married now. My brother is running the ranch, and he's married and they have a baby. My sister—the one who isn't a police officer—loves ranching. It's in her blood. And she and her fiancé also live on the property and do the rest of the work. I used to cook and clean, but now my sister-in-law does that. And now it feels so much like her house. It's just all different than it was. And I don't really have a place. But anyway. There are a lot of spiders on a ranch, believe me. And I never got used to them."

"There's an apartment above the bakery," he said. He had just been going over the specs of that particular building, because he actually did have a file on it, chucked under the couch, which would make Lucinda crazy. But his business manager had accepted the fact that if she wanted him to keep information, it was going to have to be analog, because up here he didn't have internet of any kind.

Another thing the Griffin Chance he'd once been would never have believed he might not care about.

But he didn't. Didn't miss it. Didn't want it.

But that meant he had files. Actual physical files about his various interests.

"Really?"

"I imagine I could rent it out separate to the bakery, to someone else. You're basically robbing me blind, Iris. But, that sounds like a lot of extra work. If you need a place to stay…"

"I… I hadn't even considered that."

She looked completely bowled over by the thought. By the offer. And it gratified him. He really didn't know why. He didn't know why he should want to offer it to her. Why he should care. It was just that she had spoken of the way that she no longer fit with her family, and there was something familiar about that to him.

He knew what it was like to simply not fit anymore. To walk the same streets he had always walked, going to the same halls that he'd gone into for years, and they were the same, but he was different. And it was just too painful.

Too much of a reminder.

Sometimes new scenery was the best and most important thing you could have.

"That seems awfully nice of you. You're not a serial killer, are you?"

He nearly spit out the bite of sandwich that was in his mouth. "Am I a serial killer? How did I get from being nice to being a serial killer?"

"My brother was concerned that you might be a serial killer."

He chuckled. "Yeah. I guess that's a good question for a brother to ask."

Guilt stabbed him. Because he was a brother. He was a brother, and he hadn't reached out to his sister in a long time. Hadn't reached out to anyone in his family.

"Well, are you? Because I would love to be able to answer him in the affirmative that you're not."

"No," he said, his voice suddenly rough. "I'm not."

"Well then, that's very nice of you, and I will think about it. It just... I wasn't really considering getting quite that much independence all at once. But... If I lived above the bakery, it would be so much easier to get all my work done."

"I'm sure it would be. Plus, solitude," he said.

"You're a big fan of solitude, aren't you?"

He considered that. "Not specifically. But I find it... about the easiest thing."

"You don't seem to have too much trouble talking to me."

"I've been saving up for this conversation for a number of years. Probably by tomorrow I won't have anything left to say."

"Well, I live in a house full of people. So there's no saving up conversations. But I don't mind. My family really is wonderful. We all had to... Really take care of each other."

Now this was territory he didn't want to get into. He didn't want to talk about family. He didn't want to think about it. No way in the world.

He finished eating while she finished tidying, and then he carried his blankets out to her car. In trade, she handed him one of the two giant insulated bags she was holding. "Your stove works, right? Your oven?"

"Wood fire. So it works as long as there's a flame."

"Some of these need the oven. There's soup, which you can do on the stove top. And bread. There's also meat loaf and mashed potatoes. Some roast chicken, green beans, rolls and salad. And this one has cake."

She handed him the second insulated bag. "And cookies. And I also put slices of millionaire bar in there. I made them for my brother-in-law. I figured he didn't need all of them."

"That seems excessive," he said.

"When do you think you'll need more?" she asked.

"I'm not really sure," he said.

He shouldn't be hungry. He had just stuffed himself with more food than he'd had in recent memory. But the prospect of eating everything she just said made his stomach growl.

It was weird.

How suddenly his hunger had been awoken. How something he hadn't felt in a long time had reared its head when he was reminded how good things could taste. He had forced himself to eat all this time. It had been all he could do to choke food down. And now there was this. Now there was her.

And that first taste of chocolate chip cookie had reminded him of how different it could be.

"How about I check back in with you tomorrow? You know, since I won't quite have everything with the bakery up and running yet."

"Sounds good. And that key will be on its way to you."

"Right. My address."

She reached into the car, and the loose skirt she was wearing blew up against her legs, outlining them. They were longer than they looked, considering she was so small. The thin fabric was tight against her bottom, and he couldn't help but notice the round, pert shape.

He blinked, feeling like he was in a haze. Feeling like he just had an out-of-body experience.

She grabbed a small pad with sticky notes on it, scribbled the address and held it out to him, stuck to her finger. He took it, without touching her skin. "Thanks," he said.

"You're welcome."

She regarded him for a moment, and looked like she might say something else. But then didn't. "See you tomorrow," she said.

Then she got back into the car, put it in Reverse and drove away. He stared down at the address stuck to his finger.

And he watched as her car faded into the distance. He went back into the cabin, and grabbed his cell phone. Then he went to the trail just behind the house, past the stables that were just behind the cabin, and in much better shape than his own dwelling. Where he found the rock. That stuck up just a little bit higher than everything else and put him at just the right angle to make a call.

As soon as he got there, his phone vibrated, four voice mails showing up.

He bit back a curse.

He didn't listen to any of them, instead he just called Lucinda. "I need you to mail keys to my new tenant," he said. He didn't bother to ask how she was, say how he was or give any kind of introduction. Then he explained the situation, and how he was bartering with Iris for rent.

"Are you insane?" Lucinda asked.

He looked around, at the stern silence of the towering pine trees all around him, the narrow wedge of blue sky and the needle covered dirt down below. His dirty, weathered boots on the boulder he was standing on. Doing a balancing act while he made a phone call to his business manager.

"Hell yes," he said. "But that's not a recent development."

"That is prime real estate. It's why you gave me permission to invest your money in it. And I don't want it turning into an albatross. For you or for me."

"I don't care. She made a case for it. I think the business will do well. Plus, she cooks for me."

There was a long silence. "She cooks for you?"

"As part of the trade," he said.

"Right," she said.

"Anyway. It's my building. You might manage things, but you're not the boss."

"I've basically been the boss for five years, Griffin."

"But you still aren't," he said.

"Fair enough. Do what you want. Give me the address and I'll mail the keys."

He rattled it off, and then quickly ended the phone call. Then he stared down at the voice mails. He hesitated for a moment, then started to play the first one. It was Iris. Asking about the property.

The next was just Lucinda, calling to tell him that there'd been an inquiry about the property, and asking what he wanted to do about it. It was over a week old now. Well, those problems had been self solving.

Then there was another one, two weeks old. He grimaced. And played it.

Griffin, it's Mallory. I'm just calling to make sure you're still alive. I really wish that you would keep in touch better. Mom and Dad want to make sure you're doing okay. But they don't want to pressure you. I think you could do with a little pressuring. He clicked the voice mail that had come a week before it.

Griffin, it's Mallory. I was just calling to wish you happy birthday. And tell you that I love you. I guess you don't have to call me back. It had been his birthday.

He hadn't really remembered. But then, it didn't really matter what time of year it was. He didn't mark it by number dates on the calendar. He marked it by the way the air felt. By how long the sun stayed in the sky, how early it rose. By whether or not the underlying feeling in the air was crisp with a sharp bite, or if the coolness had an overlay of warmth that seemed to coat your skin. That was how he could tell the changing of the seasons. He didn't need anything half so literal as a calendar.

Poor Mallory.

He did feel guilty. But he also wasn't in the mood to deal with his sister when she was mad at him, and given how mad she was in the last message, she was going to be even madder when he actually did call.

He would wait for another time. Maybe until he went down into town, which he did have to do sometimes. He couldn't get everything delivered.

Though, with Iris, he was a lot closer to being able to get everything delivered.

He shrugged off the guilt, and it rolled off his shoulders easily as he stepped off the rock and headed back toward the cabin.

Guilt was easy to shift from where it sat on the mountain of grief that rested on him. A mountain he didn't have the strength to move.

A mountain he wasn't sure he wanted to move.

Guilt. Hunger. Everything had to contend with that. And none of it could ever be quite so crushing as that real burden that he carried.

He might feel bad for his sister. But not enough to change anything.

And if that made him an ass, so be it.

He was a whole lot of things he didn't want to be.

Not being nice was the least of them.

CHAPTER FIVE

SHE WONDERED IF Griffin would like pancakes. And also wasn't sure if she should come up to the mountain that early. Or what she might find there.

They hadn't discussed the time frame. Which made things difficult.

But he had really appreciated the food that she had brought yesterday. Far and away above anyone else she had ever fed.

They hadn't discussed it, and he hadn't really particularly thanked her. But she had heard it. That deep, guttural sound he made when he bit into the sandwich had been evidence enough.

She had to wonder what the man was subsisting on up there. She had had a look around the cabin, and as far as she could see, the only foods he had were of the canned variety. And beyond that, there wasn't much of anything else.

He was...he was a strange man.

And when he'd made that noise, that strange, grunting growl when he bit into her sandwich, her stomach had turned over. And she had realized something else. She had been hung up on the fact that he was *big*. And, as a woman, that was something of a concern when dealing with an unknown man.

But she was starting to realize he was something more.

He was big. Muscular.

And behind that beard, he was beautiful.

His eyes were a deep blue, like denim. She hadn't ever seen eyes like his before. His nose was straight and sharp, his lips beautifully formed. The beard kept him from being pretty. But she could imagine that as a younger man he'd been stunningly beautiful.

She had spent way too long thinking about that on her drive down the mountain.

He was also weird. Which she had reminded herself multiple times whenever her mind had strayed that direction.

She had been thinking, as she had trudged up the mountain, that she wasn't going to allow herself to be a virgin who lived at home, and she wondered if her brain was inescapably trying to solve both problems at the same time.

Even thinking that as a joke made her face get hot.

She had never thought seriously about a man in that way.

Well, she had *tried* to think about Elliott that way. She had tried to imagine kissing him. But it had not made her warm. It didn't make her cheeks light up like a beacon. Didn't make her heart beat faster or her stomach stretch and twist like a ball of bread dough being kneaded.

Just thinking *virginity* and *Griffin* in the same sentence made all those things happen to her. Plus, she was sweaty.

And no closer to coming to a consensus on what she was going to do about her pancake idea.

She was standing in the kitchen considering it when Rose bounced into the room.

"What are you doing here?" Iris asked.

"I've been up working for hours," Rose said. "I came to see if there was food."

"And you couldn't see if there was food at your and Logan's house?"

"I was closer to here. Plus, Logan was out working too, so he wasn't cooking me breakfast."

Iris scowled. "Well, neither was I. In fact, I have to head to work."

She grabbed the bag of pancake mix, a mixing bowl and her griddle, completely laden down with things.

"Wait," Rose said, "you're going to make pancakes for somebody else?"

"Yes," she said. "Because I am *trading* for those pancakes. The pancakes are a form of payment. *You* don't pay me. You just expect there to be pancakes."

"I didn't mean it that way," Rose said.

But Rose never meant anything any way. Iris loved her sister so much. She had basically raised her. But only basically. Rose wasn't her daughter. And Iris hadn't been an adult. She had been a sad fourteen-year-old girl who had lost her mother, and had found some solace in playing mother to her desolate little sisters.

Because there was no one there to comfort her. So somehow, becoming strong and being the one to offer the comfort had Well, it had felt like getting it herself.

But that kind of emotional surrogacy just didn't last. Because now everybody was moving on and leaving her, and she was just this object. Someone who seemed comforting and warm and easy to everyone around her.

When she felt nothing like that inside.

She had pushed her own grief down. Kept it away. Had done her best not to deal with that at all, while she had poured herself into fixing things for other people.

And the added bonus had been hiding away.

Because the world was nothing more than terrifying to a child who lost their parents suddenly. A child who'd had to learn at an early age that you could wake up one morning expecting everything to be the same, and find that it was irrevocably changed.

Broken beyond repair.

She'd heard it said that it was always darkest before the dawn. That the night would end, and the sun would rise, but Iris had learned that when the sun rose, your grief would still be there. And the loss would remain.

That saying didn't mean that everything would be fine. That everything would go back to the way it was.

All it meant to her was that time would march on, whether you were ready for it to or not.

And here time was, marching on. And she surely wasn't ready for it. Not remotely. She was being left behind by it.

And Rose was here wanting pancakes. While she had a fiancé she would go home with tonight. A man who would hold her in his arms. A future that wasn't just assisting in the lives of other people.

Iris tramped out of the kitchen, through the living room and out toward her car, where she put all the pancake objects onto the passenger seat. Then she went back into the house, and opened up the freezer. She selected a couple of different meal options from there, held them to her chest as she stalked back outside.

"Don't be mad at me," Rose said from the porch, leaning against one of the support beams.

She turned and looked at her sister, who looked comically young and plaintive. And Iris didn't feel young at all.

She felt every inch the old maid spinster that she was. Having a fit with a bag of pancake mix, though. So, there was that. It was different, at least.

"I'm not," Iris said, even though her heart felt bruised, and she did feel a little bit mad, thank you very much.

"I don't take you for granted," Rose said. "I know that

this made it seem like I do. But I don't. You are the best, Iris. And if it weren't for you, I wouldn't have… I wouldn't have Logan, that's for sure. I wouldn't be any kind of well-adjusted. You took care of me. You put your life on hold for me. Don't think that I don't realize that."

"I know you realize it. And you tried to fix it by setting me up with the worst man in the entire world."

"Hey," Rose said, "he wasn't the worst."

Iris suddenly felt fatigued. "No. He *was*. Because you could have set me up with a guy with a neck tattoo, at least. And he might've been a terrible choice, but he wouldn't have been… Boring. Or easy. And I am so tired of boring and easy. I am so tired of the biggest thing in my life—the biggest feeling I've ever had—being grief. That is the most defining thing in my life, Rose. And I am really tired of it."

"It defined all of us," Rose said, softly.

"Yes. But now you're marrying Logan. You're going to be his wife. You're a rancher. You're strong. Ryder is a father, and he's a husband. He's a cowboy. Pansy is the chief of police, and West's wife and Emmett's… I don't know, surrogate mother. And what am I? I'm nothing different than I was back then. I'm just… Poor Iris. I am so sick of being poor Iris. I want to be more. I want to be everything. I want to have big crazy feelings, so that something over-shadows my grief. Maybe I can be a business owner. I can open the bakery. That's what I want."

And she thought of Griffin, and his compelling blue eyes. His hands, which she had noticed were quite large.

But she said nothing about that. Left it at *the bakery*, and nothing more.

She didn't understand the fixation she had with him, and had no real idea if it was real or something borne out of forced proximity and her deep need to rattle the foundation of her life.

Better kept to herself either way.

"I understand how you feel," Rose said. "But I promise you nobody just thinks of you as poor Iris."

But Iris had always been able to tell when Rose was lying. And this was no exception. She didn't say anything. Instead, she rounded the car, going to the driver's side, and got inside. Then she started the engine.

It wasn't up to Rose to see her different. Not when Iris wasn't *doing* different.

Iris had to see herself different. She had to change herself. No one was going to treat her the way she wanted if she didn't first figure out how to become what she wanted to be.

So she was taking the pancakes, and she was leaving. And she was well within her rights to do that.

Maybe it would surprise them. And as rebellions went, she had to admit that it was a pretty small and strange one. But she would take it. Because she didn't have much else.

She drove down the winding road that led to Echo Pass, humming a tune along the way. And when she realized it was a hymn, she abruptly stopped, because that certainly wasn't doing anything to shake up her image.

It was strange that this road felt familiar already. That the cabin seemed like a place she knew well even though this was only her third time here.

It was a haven, if nothing else. A symbol of the new steps that she was taking in her life.

Same as yesterday, when she approached the cabin, she didn't see him anywhere. And when she knocked, he didn't answer.

She pushed the door open cautiously, and found that— again—same as yesterday, he wasn't there.

She didn't know where he went during the day, and it wasn't really her business. Still, she found herself curious about the man she had struck up a strange business relationship with. More than she would like to admit. More than she would like to be.

But he was... She had never met a man like him before. She went into the kitchen area of the small cabin and began to open up the cabinets. She had already looked through them, so she didn't know why she felt compelled to do it again. But she found things much the same as they had been.

He had a bottle of Tabasco sauce. Salt and pepper. Canned chili. Canned vegetables. The kind of thing she would only eat in an absolute emergency. The kind of food they had eaten after their parents had died, actually.

When the casseroles had quit coming from the neighbors, when people had forgotten about their tragedy, and had gone back to their own lives, while the Danielses had settled in to a life that would never be the same again, there had been canned chili.

It was, to her, the kind of food that you got once your tragedy had been forgotten by those around you, but your grief remained.

The food of a person steeped in a half-life.

She touched the bottle of Tabasco. It wasn't open. So he might have the ability to add flavor to his food, but she wasn't certain he did. This was the kind of food a person had when they were in a life they didn't particularly like.

That was when Iris had learned to cook. When she was tired of being in a transition. When she was tired of feeling the loss of her mother so keenly.

There were recipes. And she had watched her mother make bread countless times. So, she had purposed to make some herself. She had decided that she would take their situation and make it into something more. And she had found that food had taken a life that had felt shattered beyond repairing, and had introduced joy back into it. It was one reason she loved to cook. One reason she loved to bake. Because those early birthday parties, when their parents weren't around, had been painful. But a beautiful cake had brought warmth back into it. Had made them feel like their mother was there in some regard.

And it didn't matter to Iris if she was the one baking them. Or even baking her own. It had connected her to the woman that she missed more than anything.

She still felt connected to her through her cooking. It was magical to her.

The way that food brought you back to places you could never go again. Brought back people long gone.

Canned chili brought back the acrid taste of grief, loss and loneliness.

Freshly baked bread brought joy.

She moved away from the kitchen, and took a turn around the room. There was a couch, one that dipped in the middle and looked well-worn. And she had to assume it had probably been here when he'd moved in. There was that upright icebox in the refrigerator area. And his bed shoved in the corner. This was the place that a person lived when all they were interested in doing was surviving.

It was basic. But maybe that wasn't fair. Maybe he really loved living here. Maybe he really loved the wilderness.

Somehow, she doubted it.

Well, he obviously loved the wilderness well enough, or he wouldn't be here. It wouldn't be a place to find solace in here if he couldn't stand the spiders.

She shuddered, and looked up at the beams. She was

going to clear out those creepy crawlies as best she could. They didn't need to have homes inside the house, that was for certain. He might be somewhat sanguine about them being there, but she didn't have to be.

No, she did not.

It became clear he wasn't going to be back for pancakes, and she set that idea aside—and her disappointment at not getting breakfast herself—and set about to work.

The house was small, and after getting into more dusting than she had managed to yesterday, she headed outside. There were flower beds. Or rather, there had been at one time. Perhaps a young couple had lived here before him and they'd planted edible flowers and other hipster things. Or an older couple. And they had made sure that there was cheer planted out in the yard. Such as it was.

Mostly, everything surrounding the cabin was untamed wilderness. There were a few walking trails, clearly forged by hiking boots and deer hooves. And there were those flower beds. Otherwise, the place might have been dropped into the middle of nowhere with no sign of human life at all. But the weeds had taken over.

Maybe she would plant some flowers.

He had hired her, after all, to make good use of her time up here, and the house was so small that, while it would definitely need upkeep, and would get dusty quickly because it was out here surrounded by all this nature, she would need to do other things to occupy her time.

Obviously, once she was running the bakery she wouldn't be up here every day, but still. She could plant him a flower garden.

She was good at this. At finding small moments in life to create beauty, or something sweet. Sometimes when the big things were sharp and shattered, when hope was gone completely, finding a way to breathe was all you could do.

Sometimes breath came from the beauty of the mountains around you. A piece of pie. A cup of tea.

From a flower garden.

She knelt down onto the earth and began to tug the weeds out, shaking the dirt from the roots and chucking them into a pile. She got lost in the repetitive motion of the task. She enjoyed this. Being outside in the sunshine, sitting in the dirt.

She had always liked this aspect of nature. Ranching had just never gotten in her blood. Not the way it had for Rose, Ryder and Logan.

Pansy had been so determined in her own path from an early age. She had been a hellion as a child, Iris could just vaguely remember. But after they'd lost their father, she'd gotten very serious. Determined to honor his memory by becoming the chief of police, just as he'd been.

And she had done it. Gold Valley's first female chief of police.

Iris couldn't be prouder.

But while Iris had never found her passion in ranching, unlike Pansy she hadn't really found it anywhere else either.

Not true.

She supposed it was in cooking. It had healed some of the loneliness in her. Had given her purpose when she'd been lost. It had connected her to people she loved.

It had always been a way for her to earn her mother's favor. If Iris cooked a meal, she was lauded for being a helper, and she carried that good feeling around with her for days after.

It made her want to use it to give that sort of feeling to others, even in a small way.

She might be arriving at it late. But she was finding her passion. A way to apply it.

She stood and surveyed her handiwork. The now cleared planting spaces. It was looking good. It was perfect. Everything she needed it to be.

With a song in her heart she picked up the scraggly weeds and went over to her car, where she found a bag and dumped them inside.

She would take them back to the ranch and give them to Ryder to go on the burn pile. That way they wouldn't leave any spores behind and replant themselves here.

She had a feeling that up this far the battle against weeds was a losing one, but she figured she would do the best she could.

She could leave. She was sure that she could. Because he wasn't here to give direction, and there was nothing else immediate to do.

But from where she stood by the car she could see a small path that led up into the trees. And she was curious.

Right. Because he seems like the kind of man who would hear your curiosity well.

There was a strange shimmer beneath her skin.

That she had opinions on what kind of man he was. It felt strange and intimate. And she didn't quite know why.

She shrugged it off, ignoring the feeling, and began to walk toward that path.

The deepest groove in the path was at the center, speaking to the narrow footprint spread of deer that must travel here frequently, and she wondered if there was water somewhere that way. But it faded out to shallower, bare dirt along the edges, which seemed to indicate that a person walked it often enough as well.

Griffin. It had to be.

Since as far as she could see there was no other life up here at all.

She began to make her way up the trail tentatively, conscious of the fact that while she had made bold claims about carrying bear spray to potentially fend off Griffin, she hadn't actually taken the steps to do so. She knew that her brother, Ryder, never ventured into the woods without a sidearm at the very least.

You never knew *what* you might encounter out in the middle of nowhere. From wildlife that was intent on making you a meal, to people who might be out trying to hide their more unsavory activities in the middle of nowhere.

Protection was a consideration.

But as Iris didn't frequently venture out into the wilderness, it wasn't one that she often thought of.

But she knew animal tracks. Her father had taught her. And she knew basic safety. So, she pressed on. She didn't see any tracks that she should be concerned about, anyway.

She passed a small clearing, with a boulder at the center, and looked around. There was nothing particularly special here that she could see. A thick grove of trees surrounded it. Maybe it was a place for pagan rituals.

Which wasn't something she would ever normally think. That kind of drama was more Rose's type of thing. She must be overly hot or hungry. Or maybe it was just… Maybe it was just getting out of her rut. And it was allowing her to think some strange things too.

She kind of liked that idea.

The trail went past the clearing, and she continued to follow it. But it wasn't a cougar that she found that surprised her. Rather a nice looking building, out there in the middle of nowhere. A small fenced in corral, and what looked to be a covered paddock.

And then she saw a horse exit the covered area, tossing its head, its black mane gleaming in the light.

Another horse followed, this one with a blond mane and tail. She wasn't an authority on horses, not in the least, but these two were glossy and well cared for, clearly round and well muscled, and enjoying their existence out here in the wilderness.

And they had to belong to Griffin.

The horses seemed to live in a better kept, newer home than their owner. And they were definitely more well-kept than he was.

It was the oddest thing. Of all the secrets she had managed to find out about the man, she hadn't expected this to be one of them. That he secretly had a pair of beautiful horses.

She heard footsteps, coming from the other direction, and she turned, to see Griffin barreling down toward her. "What are you doing?"

"I… I… I finished. And I didn't want to leave without finding you. And there was a path. And I followed it."

He stopped, crossing his arms over his broad chest. "Little Red Riding Hood, didn't anyone ever teach you not to go wandering into the woods?"

His voice was rough, the way he said those words making them change shape inside her. They seemed to fill her, scrape through her like velvet. Like a touch.

That thought made her insides shiver. But she couldn't quite pin down why. She was having difficulty pinning down exactly what this man made her feel in general.

Out here in the sunlight, with the golden rays pounding down on him, he was like an avenging angel. His dark hair was shot through with spun gold. As if the sun had reached down and touched him. She'd thought him a mountain, a rock, and he was. But there was something else too. Like magic. It was like discovering a different dimension of him, and that seemed silly. Fanciful. And Iris Daniels had never been accused of being fanciful.

It was the absolute strangest thing.

He moved, and that same sun caught the light in his eyes, and they were an even more startling, piercing blue than she'd realized.

His shoulders were thick, heavily muscled from hard labor, his forearms well-defined, the muscles visible even beneath that colored ink that was etched into his skin. His waist and hips were slim, while his chest was broad and thick.

He was holding a hammer in his hands, she realized, and that just made her think about their size and strength in a more visceral, specific way than she had done when she pondered their size yesterday.

He was not wearing khakis. He didn't look like a man who would own khakis. He didn't look like a man who would even know what khakis were. If she said something about dress pants to him he would probably curl his lip in disdain.

He looked like a relic of the land itself. A collection of the elements that had been breathed into life.

And somewhere deep inside of her, a voice that she hadn't known existed in there, whispered to her.

Adventure.

He looked like adventure.

He looked like a change.

Like something that nobody would ever believe she could handle.

The simple truth was Griffin Chance looked like something Rose would never believe that Iris might do.

And she would have said she wouldn't either.

But he made her feel like she was trembling somewhere inside, and it was an entirely foreign, and not unpleasant, sensation.

"What?" he asked, sounding angry. Dousing cold water all over that strange, half formed fantasy that had been blooming inside of her. Because he clearly wasn't thinking anything of the kind.

"I… You startled me, that's all. I'm sorry."

"No harm," he said.

"You ride horses?"

"Iris, I'm a damn cowboy."

That was… Slightly disappointing. Because cowboys were essentially all she knew. Other than water filtration guys. And she had never imagined that she might find herself interested in a cowboy, considering she was not a ranch type person.

Interested? A strange word, Iris. Wrong word. Intrigued by? In fascination with?

"Right. Sorry. I didn't know. I mean, I didn't realize you had a… Ranchette."

"A ranchette," he said, dismissive. "I have three hundred acres up here."

That did surprise her. That basically meant the whole mountain was his.

"It's just that my brother has a giant spread. Beef. So, by comparison…"

He snorted. "Not interested in comparing ranch sizes with your brother. Don't care. I like to ride horses. That's it."

"That's it?"

"Anymore," he said. "Yes."

"Oh. Well, they're lovely horses."

He huffed a laugh. "I'm glad they meet with your approval. I was obviously very concerned about that."

She wrinkled her nose and fought to keep staring at him with the full blaze of the sun in her face. "You don't have to be mean."

The ground was rocky, the light extra bright over the light gray surface of the rocks. There were scrubby yellow weeds popping up out of the dirt at odd heights, fat bees drunkenly twirling around the blooms. She could smell dirt and pine, hay and horse.

The scene was idyllic, really.

And she felt turned inside out.

He frowned. "I'd like to think that I don't take the kind of effort required to be mean."

She looked away then, a breeze stirring up, moving the air a bit. But her face still felt prickly. "You're a bit mean."

She didn't know why she'd said that. She didn't know why she was pushing the issue. She didn't know why she cared at all.

"Did you want to go for a ride?"

She whipped her head back to look at him. "A ride?" She couldn't have been more surprised if he'd stripped his shirt off and done a seductive dance.

But that made her think of yesterday when he'd walked in with his shirt off. And the fact that she'd seen every one of his muscles on display when he'd done it.

What she knew about his chest was that it wasn't just broad, it was clearly defined. And what she knew about his stomach was that it was flat and ridged in the most interesting way. But he had dark, compelling body hair covering his skin, and she had never been fascinated by body hair in her life.

But found herself more than a little fascinated by his.

Her face felt warm, and she still couldn't blame the sun. She kept hoping if she stood there long enough she might be able to. But the breeze was nice. It wasn't the air.

It was him.

"Would you?" he pressed.

"Yes," she said, finding herself agreeing before she had even thought it through. "Sure. But I'm not that good at it."

"You grew up on a ranch and you're not that good at it?"

She frowned. "I haven't ridden in years."

"That doesn't seem right."

"I'm just not a horse girl. I mean, I like them, but it's nothing like my sister. Rose was basically born riding horses and she hasn't gotten off of them since. Working the ranch is what she does. She's a real, proper cowgirl. And that's just never been me."

"Well, there's a lot of ground between doing a trail ride and becoming a bona fide cowgirl."

"I suppose."

Without a word he went past her, and opened the gate to the corral. The scent of him joined with the sunbaked earth and pine. Something spicy and compelling that made her stomach drop and her heart cramp painfully.

He paused for a moment and her breath froze.

She hadn't realized that could happen. That your breath could turn to a solid and just sit there, painful, in your lungs.

Then he moved, blessedly, and so could her lungs. He disappeared into the paddock, and she stood there for a while, not moving. He returned with tack, and made quick work of getting bridles and saddles ready to go. He did all of it without asking for help. He did all of it without looking at her, actually.

It was the strangest thing.

She couldn't help but be utterly and completely compelled by his movements as he strapped the saddle into place. The way each muscle worked, the way his fingers moved. Expert.

She had seen this done thousands of times. Had watched men with equal expertise handling horses. Her brother, Ryder, was so quick with this kind of thing you could barely see his movements. But she'd never found it *fascinating*.

She found this fascinating. She found him fascinating.

Like some of that wildness in him had possessed her somehow. And she didn't think that was something he meant to do, or wanted to do. He couldn't seem less interested in her.

Undoubtedly, he was not standing there pondering her scent and the way it mixed with the breeze.

She'd liked guys before, of course. She'd gone to high school. She'd had crushes. She'd found different men who worked in different places around town attractive. But she was invisible, and always overlooked. She'd always made sure that she didn't have the time to date, so that it never bothered her when she didn't get asked on one.

It wasn't like she didn't know what it felt like to have a crush. Like she didn't understand sweaty palms, a racing heart and a tightening stomach.

Except, this was different and deeper, and it felt altogether more dangerous. And she didn't want to believe that it had anything to do with a crush, because it felt utterly and completely… Well, stupid. She had made a business arrangement with this man. She couldn't go having it turn into anything else.

As if.

Yeah. This man. Tattooed and bearded and hard, was going to be interested in soft, dull Iris. Who would have done better to be named after a small dowdy bird than a bright, beautiful flower.

It had long been said in their family that Pansy had been given the meanest name. Because she was tiny and tough, and wanted to be a cop, and being named Pansy was an impediment to those things. Rose... Well, her name suited her. Her youngest sister was beautiful, vibrant and full of thorns.

Iris had always quietly felt that *her* name was a slap in the face. To be named after such a brilliant, glorious flower that couldn't be overlooked, deep yellows and purples, and all the incredible hues that it came in, being applied to her.

She was plain. And she knew it.

And adding insult to injury she was quite *dull*.

A little old lady before her time, and she liked it. So what was there to be done about it? She liked quiet. And she *liked* being at home. And yes, she had felt that she should be wanting more, the desire to make her own space in her own way. But she still didn't see herself going out on a Saturday night when she had the possibility of binge-watching an entire British detective series while knitting a new sweater.

She just was who she was.

More western meadowlark than an Iris. But nobody was going to name their baby western meadowlark.

And western meadowlarks didn't attract the attention of big, burly men who seemed to hold the secrets of the universe behind their compelling blue eyes.

End of story.

So she quit staring at him, and chose a leaf that was waving in the breeze to be the recipient of her attention. Then he opened up the gate, and the clanging sound brought her focus back to him. And he led both horses on through, and that was a picture. This man effortlessly guiding the two massive beasts, not with force, but with a gentle hold. His connection to the animals was clear, and even though she wasn't a horse girl, she found she couldn't deny the appeal of that.

"All right. Saddle up."

CHAPTER SIX

HE HAD NO idea in hell why he had invited her to go riding. He really didn't. But as he watched his plain little housekeeper mount the horse, as he watched a strange satisfaction flood her face and a smile spread slowly over her lips, he found he couldn't really care less.

Whatever she said, she *did* want to do this. And she was enjoying it.

Out here in the sun, her brown hair seemed glossier, her eyes more green than brown. He noticed that she had a faint dusting of freckles over her pale skin, and that her lips, while such a pale pink it was hard to notice them against the contrast of her pale skin indoors, were quite full. Soft.

Everything about her was soft.

And he'd lived through a lot of hard, so he found it more compelling than he ought to.

Soft was an indulgence to someone like him. An indulgence he couldn't afford. Because the soft and pretty didn't change the shape of the hard and sharp. It only went the other way. He might be a bastard but not enough of one to inflict himself on her.

Her food, though, was enough to make a grown man weep. That was just the truth. That food was filled with flavor and spoke of hidden depths. But then, so had her walking up the mountain and shoving a plate of cookies in his face.

She was a strange little anomaly. And now, perched on the back of a horse, she looked like a pretty damn pleased anomaly.

It was normal, actually. For him to want to give her something when she'd made him nice food. It was like a social contract. She'd done nice things for him, he was happy doing something nice for her.

At least, that was sort of how he remembered social things working.

"This way," he said, maneuvering Babe onto the trail that he knew would take them to the creek.

"What is this one's... What is my horse's name?" He could have laughed at the way she asked that.

"That's Carl," he said.

"Carl?"

"Are you maligning his name?"

"I'm not maligning his name. But I do question it."

"He came to me with that name. I went ahead and kept it as it was to minimize confusion."

"Well, that makes enough sense, I guess."

"I don't care if it makes sense to you or not, Iris. Anyway, why can't a horse be named Carl?"

"I don't know, it seems silly."

"Maybe the horse thinks it's weird you're named after a flower."

"See? Mean."

He felt a smile curve his lips. "Not mean. Honest. I don't have the energy to lie to people."

Another funny thing. Because Griffin Chance, back in his heyday, would have smiled and lied to smooth over just about anything. He hadn't been too shady, not as much as many people in his profession were, but if there was a situation that was difficult, he was more than willing to spread a little frosting over the details to make sure that he obscured the reality of the situation. Development was a hard game. And things were bound to go wrong, and landowners were volatile. Investors were always breathing down his neck. The one thing he was very good at was putting a smile on his face and BSing his way through a potential catastrophe.

And typically, he could make sure that it didn't turn into one.

But making sure that nobody ever saw him sweat was one reason he'd gotten so good at what he did.

Was one reason he had so much success.

He'd blown off steam at his ranch, at home, where he'd been himself, and he'd put his suit on, and put his businessman face on, whenever he needed to.

Now, the very idea of engaging in that kind of nonsense made him want to lie down, go to sleep and never get back up.

It was stupid. He couldn't see the merit in it, not anymore. It just... It didn't feel like him. Those memories didn't feel like him.

Not just another life. Another person.

"I guess that's a good thing," she said. "I don't think that I would lie to people."

"What do you mean you don't think?" The trail dipped down, and he leaned back on the horse, as the animal navigated the incline, stepping carefully around the rocks that came up out of the hard ground. He turned back to look at Iris, to make sure that she was all right. She seemed to be handling it gamely, and he felt like her claims of not being a horse girl had been greatly exaggerated.

She was doing just fine.

"I've never had a real job." He could almost feel her regretting that statement, the force of her embarrassment hitting him like a wave. "I guess I shouldn't say that to the man who is banking on collecting the profits from my business."

"Maybe not," he said, laughing. "But you know, I admire your honesty."

"Okay. So I've never had a job outside of my house. You know, like I said, I'm kind of the… The cook. For the ranch. Not a housewife." She made a small gagging sound. "Obviously. Because I'm not anyone's wife. But you know. It's actually like a job. Or, it was. Because we kind of ate communally as a family still, and now we do that less. And now it's Sammy's kitchen. My sister-in-law."

"Right. So you kind of got edged out."

"Yes. But I guess… I haven't had much of a social life. I haven't had a lot of situations where it had to be tested. I had friends, don't get me wrong. But it's gotten really difficult. I had friends in high school, and a lot of them went away to college, and I couldn't." She didn't elaborate on that, but he imagined it had something to do with money. In the world he'd grown up in, college was a given. An expected thing. But he'd learned that wasn't the case everywhere.

"Some of my friends came back, some never did. Some got married right away and started having children. You know, I have friends with kids in middle school. And that boggles my mind."

"Right," he said. His chest felt tight just then.

"But you know, that makes it harder to maintain friendships. Because they are busy. And they've made new friends from parent groups, and things like that. And I don't work outside of my house, and I don't have a built-in group of people that I have something like that in common with. So… I just… I found that my social life just kind of crumbled and fell away, particularly in the last four years. And I just kind of feel lonely. Aimless. Isolated."

"Yeah," he said, feeling almost guilty that he couldn't contribute more to the conversation. But he was isolated on purpose. And it was difficult for him to see it as a bad thing.

"Anyway. I guess that's going to change with the bakery. I should hopefully meet some people?"

"I would think."

"I'll actually be out there, in the world, in the community. I'll have something in common with people. I'll own a business."

It sounded to him like Iris had a secure world with a lot of people that cared about her. And while he could definitely understand why she felt like she had a failure to launch, or whatever, he also didn't feel that sorry for her.

It sounded like she had a lot.

"You're close to your family, though."

"Yes," she said. "I love them. But they've managed to be close to me, while having distinct lives of their own."

"Fair enough. No boyfriend, then?"

She laughed. The woman honest to God *laughed* like he'd told the funniest joke in all of creation.

How long had it been since he'd heard another person laugh? A real laugh.

He hadn't laughed like that in years.

And he hadn't shared laughter in just as long.

He'd heard it, he was sure. At parties he hadn't wanted to be at. Before he'd come to the conclusion that home wasn't home anymore. It had grated on him. It hadn't…made it feel like his lungs were full.

"No," she said. "Not even close."

It struck him as strange, right then. Because she was a pretty little thing, actually. He'd come to that conclusion out here in the sun. But maybe that was the problem. Maybe nobody looked at her for long enough to notice.

Because he could see how in a bar somewhere your eye might skim over someone so deliberately plain. Her long hair captured in a tight ponytail, or a braid. Her face completely free of makeup. Her clothes were serviceable, and that was about it. Long skirts and simple T-shirts. Or jeans, and the same simple T-shirts. He'd seen her a few different times, always in a variation of those things.

But there was a strength to her that was uncommon. A sort of deep stubbornness that was more than a little bit fascinating.

She was kind of incredible.

"Why do you say it like that?"

"Just… I'm not the kind of person that gets noticed."

"Maybe you should start bringing plates of cookies with you when you go out."

She laughed again. "You know, I probably should. That might bait them a little bit."

"You don't need to do that," he said. "I'm sorry. That was a bad joke."

He really did feel guilty now. It wasn't that he didn't feel guilt. It was just that he lived with it all the time. Though, actually noticing it was a strange thing. It was there like air in his lungs, so he took it for granted. Actually, having it change enough, shift enough for a moment for it to be apparent… That was weird.

"No, it wasn't. I'm realistic, Griffin. My sister Pansy, the one who is with the police department, she is adorable. Like a pocket-sized stick of dynamite. She scares men a little bit, don't get me wrong. I mean, she can arrest them. Or tase them. And would. But she's not somebody that you can ignore. My sister Rose is incredibly beautiful. Stunning, actually, and she has the kind of personality that men notice. She tried to set me up with someone a few months ago. But it turned out that he was hung up on her. And you know, I wasn't even surprised. Because anyone who gets in her orbit tends to be taken in by her spell. Some of us just don't cast spells."

He didn't know what to say to that. This wasn't the kind of conversation he'd ever had with a woman. He tried to rack his brain to remember if he'd ever had a casual conversation with somebody like this. Regardless of gender.

He'd had friends. But then, there had been a time when things had turned into business partnerships, and everything had centered around work, and the kind of small talk that laid the sort of inroads that you needed for business relationships. Everything had been centered around that.

This was just conversation. For the sake of it. Getting to know somebody. It had been a long time since he'd gotten to know anyone.

Yeah, he could remember the last time.

He didn't want to.

"Spells can be broken," he said. "That's all I know."

After that, they didn't talk much. They came to the edge of the creek, and he dismounted, leading his horse to the water. Iris did the same, copying his movement and bringing Carl to the edge of the water too.

"This feels a bit like a cliché."

"Well, you won't even have to try to make them drink, because it's hot."

She laughed, and a lock of hair fell into her face. He saw that it shimmered, gold hidden in the brown.

He just stood there for a moment, struck by the fact that he was noticing something like that. It was strange. And so unlike his experience over the last few years. Where people had been kind of transparent. He just looked through them.

He was looking at Iris.

"If men don't notice you in this town, then they're fools," he said.

Her head snapped up, her eyes wide, and he could see how they were more golden brown than mud, shot through with green. It was just that inside, it all sort of landed together, and out here he could see them clearly. "I... I..."

He had successfully stunned her into silence. "I haven't seen your sisters. But I don't need to. And you don't need to compare yourself to them."

"I don't think that I do. It's just that I try to be practical about these things."

"You're not being practical, you're wrong. In fact, I bet plenty of men notice you, and they don't think they can approach you."

"Why?"

"Because a lot of men would find you intimidating."

She laughed again, and this time she doubled over, putting her hands on her knees. "Me? Intimidating? I'm basically the least intimidating person on the planet. What am I going to do? Stab someone with a knitting needle? Hit them over the head with a pan?"

"No. You're trying to compare yourself to the kind of strong your sister is. The police officer. That's not the only kind of strong there is. You're the kind of strong that actually scares people, I think. Let me guess, men always want to challenge your cop sister to arm wrestling, or something?"

"Well, yes, I guess that is true."

"Because they want to test themselves against her physical strength. Deep down, they think that they're superior, and they want to prove it. But they can't read you. And I bet you sit in the corner of the bar and don't talk to anybody. You just have your drink, and you watch everybody.

And I bet you nobody can figure out why you're so happy to sit there by yourself."

"Because I feel awkward," she said. "And how do you know what I do in bars?"

"I don't think you feel awkward. I think you don't see anything compelling enough to move you from your seat. You're close to your family because you like them. But when you wanted to change, you marched yourself up the mountain and you found me. Not very many people would do that. And, I didn't scare you away. That would be true of even less people, let me tell you."

"I don't find you scary," she said.

"You don't?"

She looked away then, and he could see a flash of fear. She did find him scary, but maybe not in the way they were talking about. And that made his stomach feel tight. That felt a little bit like hunger. Hunger, which was such a foreign concept to him. He had lost it so long ago. Survival, that's what everything had been about. And appetites had gone away, completely.

But she had reminded him of what it was to be hungry for food that tasted good. To be hungry for the way it could comfort you.

And this felt like the slow-growing echo of a different hunger altogether. One he would rather not remember at all.

"No," she said, meeting his gaze again, having collected herself. "I don't."

"Maybe you should."

She shrugged. "Maybe. You know, I'm not very good at being told what to do."

"This is what I'm talking about," he said. "You're not weak. You're strong, and I bet it's the kind of strong that people can't quite figure out, and it scares them."

"Well, bully for me."

"How come you're not used to being told what to do?" He didn't know why he was compelled to find out more about her. Only that he was.

"Because I'm the one that told everyone else what to do. I'm the oldest girl. And... I spent a significant amount of time raising my sisters. That's the thing. I took care of them. And I've been independent for a long time. I use my independence to accomplish things on my own, though. I know a lot of people who would have gone a little wild. Actually, my cousins were kind of like that."

He sensed that he was missing a big chunk of her story. But he didn't really want to push for more. Because it would end in conversations he didn't want to have, and that he was certain of. That it would be far too easy to end up stuck there with Iris. And there was just no point.

"But not me. I used it to make sure that I can take care of myself. That I didn't need anyone."

That he understood.

How badly you could need to prove that you didn't need a person or thing to get by.

To shake your fist at the sky, and declare that you wouldn't be struck down.

That you could live, however grim it was. That you could go on.

"Anyway. I've never had any practice with being... With being a child, I guess. So, you can tell me what I'm supposed to do all you want, but that doesn't mean I'm going to do it. I'm going to do whatever I please." She frowned. "I never really realized that before. Sometimes I feel so domestic and boring that I think maybe I must be a pushover. But I'm not. I kind of just do whatever I feel like, and now

I feel like making a change, so I am." The entire set of her shoulders changed then. "Thank you."

"For what?"

"For telling me that I was strong. So that I could see it."

He didn't want her to thank him. And he didn't know what to think about the warm sensation that spread through his chest. He hadn't interacted with another person in so long that it was strange to have this now. Strange to have her react to him. To have her act like it meant something to her.

Stranger still, that it managed to touch something inside of him.

Mel would be happy about it.

He didn't know where that thought had come from. And he didn't like it, anymore than he liked the warmth in his chest.

"Well. Don't worry about it." He headed back over to his horse. "Are you ready to go back?"

"Well. If you are," she said.

"Yeah. More than ready. I got more work to do."

"What are you doing?"

"Nothing."

He wasn't going to talk about the house. He wasn't going to talk about anything. Already, things had gotten strange. Already, he had gotten in deeper with her than he had intended to.

There was no point.

Not for her. And certainly not for him.

He couldn't think of anything to say on the ride back, and Iris seemed determined to fill the silence. A sweet, melodic voice filled the air, as she began to hum.

And it took him only a minute to recognize the tune.

"Could you not do that?"

"Sorry," she said. "That song has been in my head lately.

I don't know why. We used to go to mass when I was a child, but Ryder was never all that intense about taking us, so I can't say why I've had a steady stream of hymns going through my head the last week."

"I don't like them," he said, his chest going tight.

"Oh. I'm sorry."

"It's okay," he bit out.

Because he could hear another voice singing that song. "How Great Thou Art."

For all the good it did you, Mel. For all the good.

But now, he couldn't shake it out of his own head. And if he needed another reason to hurry Iris along, he'd found it.

"Thanks," he said, when they got back to the paddock. "I'll put the horses away and you can head on out."

"Oh. Okay."

"You should get the keys today or tomorrow. Feel free to head over. You don't have to come over here."

"When do you want me back?"

"How much food did you bring?"

"Enough for the next couple of days."

"Then come back Saturday."

"Have you liked anything particularly well?" Her brow creased, as she looked up at him from where she stood on the dusty ground. She looked young, and he didn't think she was all that much younger than he was, but there was something about her that was fresh, new in a way that he simply would never be able to be again.

"Meat loaf," he said. "And mashed potatoes." And in spite of himself, he wanted to smile. "I hadn't had that since... My mom used to make it."

She smiled, and there was something sad in it. "So did mine."

"My mom probably still does," he clarified. "It's just I don't go around for dinner."

"Mine doesn't." That smile again. She didn't offer any more information, and he didn't ask.

"I'll see you Saturday, Griffin," she said.

"See you."

And more concerning than any of the other feelings he'd had in the last several minutes was the fact that he felt regret watching her walk away from him.

Regret that meant nothing, and could turn into nothing.

Best remember that.

CHAPTER SEVEN

THE KEY WAS there early Thursday morning, along with the mail, and Iris nearly shot through the ceiling. The excitement of the key did something to erase the strangeness of the interaction that she'd had with Griffin on their trail ride. The trail ride she wasn't certain why they'd gone on in the first place. She could feel a deep loneliness coming from him. And he could say that he liked to be alone all he wanted, but she could sense something underneath that. Something moving beneath the surface.

What was it they said? Still waters ran deep.

That was what he was like. Like a placid pool, but she could sense there was something beneath the surface, deep down under there, and it was going to take tenacity to get to it.

She wasn't sure she wanted to.

Or more accurately, she wasn't sure *why* she wanted to.

She'd had a life filled with people who needed care. And she had done her share of caregiving as a result.

She was escaping that. She was living for herself. That she should become almost immediately consumed with the problems of a man she didn't even know...

That made her wonder about her own sanity.

But he was compelling.

It's because he's handsome.

Her inner voice was pragmatic. And she felt like it probably had a decent read on the situation.

He was more than handsome. After the trail ride she had come to the conclusion that he was the most beautiful man she'd ever seen. The kind of man she hadn't known that she would find appealing, but she most definitely did.

And that was probably why she found herself so compelled by him. That was kind of normal. As those things went.

"I got my keys," she announced as she went into the dining room.

Rose was in there eating a bowl of cereal.

"Hey," Iris said. "Remember when you baked cookies to win Logan's affection? You can learn to make pancakes too."

"I like cereal just fine," Rose said, crunching noisily on the cereal, her nose wrinkled in such a way that it was clear she didn't actually like cereal all that much. "Of course, it would help if Ryder didn't buy old man colon-health cereal."

"What do you want? Something with marshmallows?"

Rose rolled her eyes. "Obviously. What's the point of being an adult otherwise?"

"You were raised by children," Iris pointed out. "Nobody ever barred you from having sugary cereal."

"True."

"I got my keys," she repeated. "I can go to the bakery today."

Rose brightened. "Oh! Your keys! We have to go over there as soon as possible."

"Don't you have ranch work to do?"

"Nothing hugely pressing. I mean, nothing Logan and Ryder can't handle. Make sure that Pansy knows she can meet us there."

Their sister was likely working in town, so it would be easy for her to slip away for a break and wander around the bakery. And the idea of that made Iris feel... Good.

She had supported her sisters through their various life changes, and that Rose wanted to return the favor...

It was nice to be cared for. Nice to be cared for in the way that she had cared for other people for a long time.

Iris poured herself a bowl of cereal, and sat across from Rose, agreeing silently that Ryder's choice of cereal was disappointing. But she wasn't buying groceries for this house anymore. That was something that just occurred to her. She chewed her lip.

"What?" Rose asked.

"Nothing. Just thinking."

"Well, let's quit thinking and go to a bakery."

They piled into Iris's car, and drove the short distance down to Gold Valley. They stopped at the four-way stop, and Iris peered anxiously around the corner of the redbrick building that was going to be hers. It was right there at the intersection of Main and Grape, a fantastic location, across the street from Sugar Cup. Visible, and adorable.

The redbrick facades of the buildings had old ads painted onto them, weathered with time. They were a popular backdrop for engagement photos and senior pictures, and it was easy to see why.

The whole town was imbued with historic charm. At Christmas there were white lights strung everywhere and deep green boughs, horse-drawn carriages and a parade. At Halloween the trolley led a haunted tour of the town and for Independence Day there was a big community picnic.

And this store would be right in the middle of all of it.

They parked their car right in front of the building, and she clutched the key tightly in her palm.

This was the moment of truth.

She'd been in the building before. But never when it was hers. Never when she felt like she could freely imagine all the things she wanted to do with it.

She took the key and pressed it into the lock on the blue door. It was lovely, with big windows that gave a view into the dining room. Right now, that room was empty. She would need tables and chairs. But fortunately, there was a beautiful counter with large display cases already installed.

The kitchen would be the real surprise. Good or bad.

Either it would provide everything she needed, or it was going to be a massive, disastrous money pit. And she wouldn't know until she went in.

She turned the key, and pressed the door open, and she and Rose stepped cautiously inside. The floor was black-and-white checked linoleum, the walls exposed brick, with gorgeous wood beams running across a crisp white ceiling. Modern light fixtures made of bronze hung down low in the dining area, evenly spaced.

"Well," she said. "Thank God the previous owners did a decent job with decor." She winced. "Of course, they might have taken everything from the kitchen. It all depends on what all Griffin bought. And I'm not even sure he knows."

"How has working with him been?" Rose asked, looking at her a little bit too innocently.

"He's… Weird. I mean, exactly as you'd expect any guy who lives up there to be." She shook her head. "I mean, he's not living in a nice house up there. He's in a cabin. He doesn't always run his generator. So mostly there's no electricity. I don't know what he does all day, but he's not there ninety percent of the time I'm cleaning. He seems to own a lot of properties. While cleaning, I stumbled across some paperwork underneath his couch. In folders. This isn't his only piece of real estate. But he has a manager and basically acts like he doesn't know any details. Or doesn't want to know."

"Young? Old?"

"Older than Ryder," Iris said, though as she said that, she wasn't entirely certain. No, he had to be. Late thirties, she would expect. His face was weathered and lined, and that only added to the appeal of it. He was a man who worked outdoors, and those hours spent in the sun were imprinted on him.

He smelled like the sun, like the mountain air.

She would not be sharing *that* with Rose.

"How much older?"

"I don't know."

"Is he good-looking?" Rose asked.

"He is…" She didn't know how to explain Griffin. Mostly, she didn't want to talk about him. Because whatever happened up there felt totally separate from her life down here. Because the feelings that she had for him didn't feel quite so simple as him being good-looking, though she had decided he was.

That made it feel cheap or easy. Like something silly. She couldn't explain the sensation that worked its way through her when she looked at him. Couldn't explain the way her eyes saw his brand of handsome and telegraphed it to her body.

Because it was more than a look. It was a feeling. One that ran deep and wide through her soul. And that didn't make any sense. She wasn't really that close to anyone that wasn't part of the inner Daniels circle.

Her sister-in-law, Sammy, had come to live with them when she was sixteen. Logan had been a family friend, and then when his mother had died in the accident that had also killed Iris's parents, he'd moved in with them too. Along with her cousins Colt and Jake. They'd grown up together. And they were the relationships in her life that endured.

She had friends, but it had never been anything like that. Never been anything like being close to people who knew your story. Who understood why birthdays were happy and sad. Who understood why Christmas and Valentine's Day, Easter and every other holiday were celebrated with an edge of happiness that bordered on silly, because they were doing their very best to honor what their parents had given them.

To make the best life they could, because they had all known that their parents wouldn't want them sitting around and crying on Christmas.

But that even when they laughed on that day, sometimes they wanted to cry.

They all just knew that about each other. Understood the loss.

She felt a little bit like an alien in school. An orphan. It was still such a strange word to her, one that she didn't really identify with. Because in her mind, orphans were usually singing while doing a coordinated dance and mopping. Or little street urchins that were smudged with dirt and asking for more food in a British accent.

Orphans, in her mind, were alone.

And she never had been.

She had lost, but she had never been by herself.

But the reality was, it was them. Technically. Orphans.

It had made her an oddity, a little bit of an outcast. And she knew that it had impacted their social lives. Not very many people wanted to let their kids come over and play at the ranch run by children. The place where the "responsible adult" was eighteen years old.

But the Danielses had closed ranks around those who lived on the ranch with them. They had made their own family.

Still, it meant that the relationships she'd forged outside of that were nearly nonexistent.

And for some reason, Griffin felt linked to her. In a way no one outside of that core group ever had.

But she sensed something in him. Some deep sadness beneath the surface, and she couldn't quite say why.

Because maybe a man who lived up there and punished himself by living such a Spartan existence had to have been wounded irrevocably?

Sure. It stood to reason.

"It's taking you a long time to answer me," Rose said, her eyes narrowed. "Handsome, or not?"

"He is," Iris said. "If you like big, muscular brutes with beards."

"And do you?"

Apparently she did. A lot.

"Rose," Iris scolded. "I'm not open for meddling. You did it once already, and you can't meddle here. He's my landlord, and he's my boss. He's…not nice, really. He's kind of grumpy. And I also feel safe with him. Like I know he's not going to hurt me, or anything like that. But he's not particularly pleasant." She was making him sound like an ogre. But all of it was true. All of it was true, and she still craved more time in his company. "And there's definitely no possibility of it becoming anything other than a working relationship."

She thought back to the trail ride. That was not explicitly part of a working relationship. There was something about it that had actually been quite personal.

He'd said she was strong.

And for some reason, now she seemed to feel a core of solid strength running through her body.

It had always been there, somehow she knew it. But it had taken his perspective for her to see it.

And she wondered…

She had to wonder if at least part of the problem of why she didn't have a lot of friends, why she had difficulty dating, was that she was just very set in her ways.

She liked things the way she liked them, and she had been running a household since she was fourteen years old.

She didn't have to do a lot of compromising.

She cooked what she wanted for dinner, she wore whatever she wanted to. She even helped her sisters pick their clothes out, so effectively, they wore what she wanted them to as well.

Yeah, she could see why it was difficult for her to arrive at compromises. To want to try and perform to be more interesting to somebody in a bar.

He'd said something to that effect. That he just didn't have the energy to lie to people.

Maybe that was it.

Maybe the real issue was that she lost her parents and it had devastated her. But with it had come a knowledge that life could be cruelly short. That it wasn't protecting you from anything.

And why bother with nonsense when that reality was so clear?

Why bother to twist and contort herself to be with another person?

She wasn't special. She never had been. Why bother to want something out of life you couldn't get?

"Well, at least he gives you something to look at, I guess."

Iris felt her face heat up. "I guess."

"You know, if he's handsome, and in proximity... It's not like you have to marry him."

Iris stood there and looked at her younger sister. Her younger sister, who was nearly nine years younger than she was. Who was *not* a virgin. At least, Iris assumed, all things considered. Her living with Logan made that unlikely.

There were these great mysteries in her world, and her sisters knew them. Her sisters that she had raised. Her sisters that had needed her to guide them and help them and take care of them all through their childhood.

Something about that seemed remarkably unfair.

Her sister was now suggesting to her that she engage in a fling. Because she knew that Iris was a virgin, and that made her feel horrendously exposed, inadequate and embarrassed. And she knew she shouldn't feel any of those things. There was no shame in the fact that she hadn't found anyone that was worth taking her clothes off for.

She wasn't going to do it just because.

That was another thing about that strength that Griffin had pointed out.

She didn't believe in doing anything just because. She was far too stubborn for that.

"I'm not having this conversation," Iris said.

And she was rescued, because a moment later her sister Pansy walked in, dressed fully in her police uniform, the bulky belt around her hips, with her pepper spray and service weapon comically large on her petite frame.

"This is great," Pansy said as she entered, looking around like she was scrutinizing a crime scene.

"We were just about to go into the kitchen," Iris said.

She looked between her two sisters, and remembered what Griffin had said. About not comparing. She was struck by the fact that she did, possibly more than she realized. That something inside of her had decided that they were particularly special and deserved a certain amount of effort dumped into them.

A certain amount of effort that part of her didn't seem to think that she deserved.

She blinked, and they headed back into the kitchen. She breathed out a sigh of relief, and gave a small prayer of thanks.

"Ovens," she said. "And big giant mixing bowls. And everything that I could ever need."

She wanted to run back up the mountain and give Griffin a big hug, because clearly he had purchased all the kitchen equipment.

His business manager did.

You should send her a thank-you note. You shouldn't think about hugging him.

No, and the thought of hugging him made her feel flushed, and she didn't want to be flushed in front of Rose and Pansy.

But she bet his body was hot. And very, very hard and… and…

She turned her focus away from that and fast.

At the back of the kitchen was a small door. And she wondered if that led to the apartment.

"I want to… I want to go upstairs."

"What's upstairs?" Pansy asked.

"It's an apartment," Iris replied, brushing past her sisters and heading toward the door, which unlocked with the same key. There was a small, narrow staircase, the stairs painted black. She walked boldly up, having the vague fear that there would be spiders. Spiders seemed to be a primary concern.

But when they got up there, they were welcomed instead by a beautiful open space with soaring ceilings. The natural lighting coming in from outside kept it from seeming gloomy or dark in any way. It had the same floor as downstairs, the same exposed brick and beams. The kitchen and living room were the same large space, and there was a large couch and coffee table at the center of the room.

She wandered to one of the doors, and pushed it open. A bedroom. Complete with a bed.

"This is a fully….furnished apartment," Rose said.

"I know," Iris said.

And right then, she knew the decision was made. Right then, she knew exactly what she was going to do.

"I… I think I'm going to move here."

"What?" Rose asked. "You can't leave Hope Springs."

Pansy, for her part, was silent.

"I think I need to leave Hope Springs," Iris said.

"Why?" Rose asked. "I've never wanted to leave. I'm perfectly happy there."

"I left," Pansy said. "I needed to. You love it, Rose, it's not the same. And it isn't that we don't love it. I mean, it isn't that I don't love it. But I had to move away to find my life. It's different for you."

Iris nodded slowly. "I don't know how to explain it. I don't think I can. All I can tell you is there's too much of my sadness wrapped up in that house. And there's so much happiness there too. But I'm one thing there. I'm a caregiver. And it has to stop. I have to take care of myself. I have to find… What I want."

Right now, what she wanted was a stern jaw and blazing blue eyes.

Yes, he was…something. A project, maybe.

But there was something that appealed about him in a

different way. He wasn't a safe space, at all. He didn't treat her like she was boring or sweet or soft.

He wasn't just a project. Wasn't just something for her to pour herself into.

He was something she could…test herself on.

He was a mountain, and she wanted to climb him.

"Nobody wants to stop you from finding what you want," Rose said.

"I know you don't. And you know what, it's not you. It's not any of you. It's me. I'm in a habit. I'm in a rut. And I'm comfortable. That's the thing. I take care of everyone else, but it doesn't mean I don't take care of me. I take care of me in a very particular way. That never tests me or pushes me or makes me contend with the big wide world outside, because it scares me. It's easy for me to just stay home. It's easy for me to tell myself that you and Pansy need something that I don't. But you need me to push you and take care of you, and treat you like little birds, while I recede into the background." Iris shook her head. "It's not martyrdom. It's self-protection."

It all became very clear. Because she might be strong. Stubborn. But she was also afraid. Very afraid.

And that stubborn streak was well in place to protect her.

"Iris," Rose said. "If this is still about Elliott…"

"It is," Iris said. "But in a good way. That forced me to realize that nothing about the way I'm living matches up with what I secretly dream my life is going to be like. And of course I have dreams. But they don't include being the spinster aunt in the attic at Ryder and Sammy's house. And if they have more kids, you know I'm going to end up in the attic once all the bedrooms are filled. I want to have my own house. And maybe my own kids someday. I want to have my own business. My own dreams. I want to fall in love. I am ridiculously offended that I have never seen a naked man and you both have."

Rose grinned, sly like a fox. Pansy looked like she might choke.

"So I need to reevaluate some things and change things. And I'm prioritizing the bakery. But this apartment is here. And I have the chance to live in it, and I think I'm going to use it to further my goals."

"Your goals of seeing a penis?"

Iris shot Rose a deadly glare. "Well, not living in my older brother's house would help with that."

She felt humiliated and hot and embarrassed. And she hated that most of all.

It was one thing to be untouched, it was quite another to be as… Repressed as she had let herself be. She had just kind of ignored that part of herself for a long time. More self-protection. Because mostly, if she put herself out there, she knew she was going to end up hurt. Even though everything had worked out for Pansy and Rose, she had watched them be devastated by various hiccups in their relationships.

She had watched Sammy tear through men for all of her teenage and adult life. And while she had seemed mostly untouched by it, it was just something that Iris didn't ever think she could do. Sammy and Ryder, on the other hand, had had an extremely intense time navigating turning their friendship into something more. And along the way there had been a lot of fights, a pregnancy and her brother getting his heart shattered for a period of time.

Iris had watched it all like a terrified spectator who was a little bit happy to be in the safe seats.

Basically, she hadn't seen a lot in the way of casual relationships. She questioned, deeply, if the Danielses were capable of having them.

Maybe that was another issue with them.

They had lost so much early on that when they found love, they wanted to cling to it hard. So casual seemed to be next to impossible.

But she was going to have to try at some point.

Immediately, Griffin came to mind, and she shoved his image aside.

That man had *heartbreak* written all over him.

That man didn't even have running water. He bathed in a creek and had an outhouse. He was not a good choice for a physical only affair.

Of course, now you'll have an apartment...

And he wouldn't come down from the mountain. So it was moot.

"I'm sorry you feel that way," Rose said. "And you know that you have our support whatever you do."

"I'm fine with you moving," Pansy said. "In fact, I say, it's about time. You don't owe anybody your eternal indentured servitude."

"She is not in service to us," Rose protested. "I thought she made pancakes because she liked them."

Being with Logan had changed Rose quite a bit. Their relationship had brought a certain amount of maturity and understanding to her younger sister. She had become a woman, not because she'd had sex, that was a severely antiquated idea. And anyway, that would mean Iris was a... a maiden. Not a woman herself, and that was not true at all.

Rose had become a woman because she had to learn how to love somebody who had wounds as deep as her own. Because she had to learn to care about someone else's feelings even more than her own, and she had to consider what life was like for someone else. What someone else was feeling.

All of that had worked to make her a much easier person to deal with. Because for all that Rose had always been a delight, she had also always been a handful.

But sometimes, she was every inch the girl that she always had been. And as far as Iris could tell, it was usually with her.

"I do like making you pancakes," Iris said, knowing she was placating her a little bit. "Don't get me wrong. But…"

"She needs to make pancakes for a naked man," Pansy said, and Iris could tell her sister was slightly triumphant that she'd been the one to say it.

Pansy and Iris would just never be as comfortable making intentionally suggestive comments as Rose was.

"Why not," Iris said, looking around the space. "Really. Why not."

"Well, when you tell Ryder you're moving out, maybe don't mention the pancakes for the naked man," Rose said.

"I should," Iris said. "Lord knows we actually made things a little bit too easy on him."

"That was a kindness on our parts," Pansy said. "Because Colt and Jake didn't make anything easy."

Her cousins had been hellions when they were younger. Of course, now they were the ones that were home the least, spending most of their time on the road with the rodeo.

But that was coming to an end, at least, as far as she understood it. Jake had talked about buying a ranch in town, and everyone was hoping that meant he would be around more.

"Nothing was easy for any of us," Iris said. "But I think we've all grown up pretty well. Or at least… I'm on the way to growing up."

"Iris, you were born grown-up," Rose said.

And there was something about that statement that settled wrong inside of her. She knew that it was a compliment. About her maturity, or whatever. But it made her question some things.

She was born grown-up, and she had never rebelled. Not ever.

And she had to wonder if she was overdue.

Well, not right now, she needed to start a business.

She did.

And she had all the means to do it.

She looked around the space again. "Okay," she said. "I'm going to need to make some lists. List of things I'm going to need for this apartment. And a list of what I'm going to put on the menu. Do you want menu items named after you?"

Pansy and Rose brightened. "Yes," they both said in unison.

"Then you're going to help me. And your favorites are going to be your namesakes." She grinned. "And, if you want me to make you food, all you have to do is come here."

She was suddenly feeling more confident than she had in a long time.

The proper lady in her wanted to write a thank-you note. To Griffin Chance.

Well, she could do better than a thank-you note. When she was finished making her menu, she could bring him a selection from it. And maybe, she would even name a specialty item after him.

She would just have to figure out what that would be.

CHAPTER EIGHT

HE HADN'T SLEPT at all the night before. Everything on his body hurt. Sometimes, he just had those nights. Not as often as he used to. But there were times when he just couldn't get certain images out of his head. There were times when he was forced to relive that night. Over and over again on an endless loop. And if he tried to dream, it only became clearer. Only became worse.

On those nights, he either got drunk enough to black out so there was nothing in his mind, or he got up. Last night, he got up. Ran some floodlights out to the homesite and had worked. For no real reason. But now, it was 9:00 a.m., and he was numb all over and regretting the decision.

He could go to sleep whenever he wanted, and he was about to do just that when the door to the cabin pushed open, and in walked Iris, laden down with platters.

"What the hell?"

"I'm here. To perform my... My duties."

He could only stare at her. She looked bright and chipper and altogether offensive. Her dark hair was captured in a low ponytail, one that spoke of deep practicality, and no concern for fashion. He was fascinated by that. That everything she did seemed to be about service. Seemed to be about what was easiest.

She was no-frills.

Except... Her love of sweets was definitely a frill.

And he shouldn't be wondering about the strange layers that she contained.

"I didn't know you were coming this morning."

"I didn't know that I needed to… But of course it makes sense. I guess I should make sure to prearrange things with you. But I went to the bakery yesterday and everything is great. I started baking last night. In the kitchen. The kitchen is amazing."

She said *kitchen* like some people might say *sex*.

And that realization sent a kick straight down to his gut. Desire? Lust?

He hadn't felt a particular inclination toward either of those things in so long he could barely recognize them.

Why? Why was it attaching itself to this woman? He had to be very honest and admit that he hadn't exactly thought about *when* he might have sex again. *If* he would. He just hadn't thought about any of it. It wasn't like he had decided one day that he wasn't going to have dessert. Wasn't going to enjoy the taste of food, was simply going to consume what he needed to survive. He had just done that, because it was all his body had demanded. But Iris had brought cookies, and had reminded him about taste.

Apparently, she was now reminding him of other things.

And that was forcing him to think. Forcing him to maybe make decisions.

Being up here is a decision.

That was true enough.

He had separated himself from the outside world and he had done a damn good job of it. He had isolated himself by design, and that, he was certain, had made it even easier for him to go on living as he had.

He had decided on a monastic life here. Joined the priesthood of grief and hadn't looked back.

When he'd been in the Bay Area still, his friends had always been checking in on him. Family. Always asking him if he would rebuild. If he wanted to go out. To a bar. To dinner. When he was coming in to the office again. And the answer had always been blank. It had been a feeling. A violent sense of simply not wanting to. And he had waited for it to change. But it hadn't.

Nothing had changed, not really, until he had left entirely. Driving up I-5, crossing the border into Oregon, had been a strange kind of torture.

Because there hadn't been any chatter in his car. No effervescent laughter or stream of consciousness ideas about what it would be like when they finally left. When they realized their dream of being out in nature.

I don't know. It will just be nice not to be tied to those people anymore.

Our friends?

People who care about image. I just want to live.

He gritted his teeth against the memory. Feet on his dashboard and long blond hair. Happiness. Most of all, he didn't want to remember the happiness.

"I'm tired," he admitted.

"Oh. Sorry. I would've brought coffee."

"I don't drink coffee."

"You don't drink coffee? What do you have with your sweets?"

"Milk? I mean, or whiskey, as discussed." His answer came from another time. Since before she'd come up the mountain, he hadn't eaten sweets.

"How do you not drink coffee?" she asked.

"Can't stand the stuff. Anyway, my mom always used to say it stunted your growth." He spread his arms wide. "Seems to me that you can't prove she wasn't right."

"I'm not that small," Iris said.

"You're half grown, little girl," he said.

She blinked, and shot him an evil look. "I am not a girl."

She made him feel about a thousand years old, that was sure. It was that brightness. That cheer. That brisk, stalwart sort of sense she had about her. Like a particularly bright-eyed rodent moving about industriously. She had that sense of someone who was uncrushable. At least, thought she was. Because she hadn't been exposed to anything intense enough to crush her.

That thought brought him up short. Because she had said something about her mother the other day…

He shoved his sympathy to the side.

Losing your parents was normal enough.

Callous, maybe. But he'd given a lot of thought to the natural order of things. And there were losses a man expected to endure.

And the losses he didn't.

It wasn't that it wasn't *loss*.

But there was a certain sense of unfairness when somebody young died. A certain amount of anger. Because it just wasn't the way that life was supposed to work.

Of course, he lost any idea that the world was supposed to work any kind of certain way.

It had screwed him from every direction.

That's nice. Little bit of self-pity. Wallow in it.

He gritted his teeth.

"What did you bring?"

"I brought breakfast. And baked goods. Because I started working on my menu. And I want to name a menu item after you. I'm doing it for my sisters and my brother. I wanted to give you something too because you're giving me this chance."

"I don't want to be a menu item."

"Why not?"

"Do I look like a cookie to you?"

She wrinkled her nose. "No. You have to be something sour."

"Like a lemon?" He felt like a lemon half the time.

She tapped her chin. "No. Passion fruit," she said.

That word sent a jolt down to his gut. *Passion.*

He couldn't remember passion. And hearing it on her lips, spoken so innocently… It was a strange and terrible thing. That's what it was.

He was angry at her then. In a futile way. That she could say that word without it carrying weight. That was soft and young and looking ahead in a way he never could. Not again.

"What?" she asked.

"Nothing," he said, ignoring the tight band that stretched between them.

"Oh. Well. It's just…" She opened up a Tupperware in her arms, then walked over to the counter and unloaded everything onto it. "I did make a few different things."

He looked down into the Tupperware. There was an array of bright confections. Cookies, and other things. "This is like a pavlova cookie," she said. "I love pavlova, and we don't have it in the States that much. But I saw it on a British cooking show and I got obsessed with it. I did a lot of research and saw that in New Zealand they have it with passion fruit a lot. And I really love passion fruit. I did think… This could be yours." She lifted the treat aloft. White and airy, with a bright yellow center.

"This is weird," he said.

"Try it," she said.

She shoved it toward him, and he took it, staring at her

while he took a bite. It was amazing. Sweet and extremely sour when you got to the center, and just the strangest thing, just like her.

Because what the hell was she even doing. At his cabin, handing him baked goods.

His life had been turned upside down in the weirdest way in the past few days. Iris Daniels was a low-key force to be reckoned with, and she didn't even seem to know it.

There were many a natural disaster that you could predict to an extent. You could try and figure out which way the wind would blow. You could predict where a hurricane might travel. Iris was more like an earthquake. You can know that a fault line was there, but you never know what might wake it up. It just hit one day.

With a plate of cookies.

And whatever the hell a pavlova was.

"It's good," he said.

She looked so hopeful that he didn't want to crush that hope.

It was weird. Caring a little bit about how someone else felt.

But she was kind of undamaged and miraculous, and he didn't want to be the one to harm her. No, he hadn't asked for her to be in his path. Hadn't asked for her to come here. None of it had been his idea at all. But he still didn't...

He didn't want to be the reason that she cried. That was for sure.

"Can I name it after you?" She deflated slightly then. "It won't be an honor for you. So what's the point?"

And just like that he was as angry at himself as he'd been with her a few moments before. He wanted to push her away. He wanted to keep her here.

He didn't like the pull she created inside him.

He was used to certainty.

That was one thing about being up here that was good. His life was easy, and it was stripped back to basics. This wasn't basic. It was something more. He couldn't make sense of it any more than he could deny it.

He didn't want her sad. That was all he knew right then.

"Why don't you name it the Mountain Climber? Because you climbed up the mountain to meet me. And… I don't feel like I deserve any credit for this. I'm not doing you a favor. Not really."

A small smile tugged at the corner of her lips. "Really?"

"Really. I mean, it's a business deal, right? So you don't need to go doing me any favors. We are trading." He looked down into the Tupperware. "What's that one?"

"Well, the trouble with my sister Rose is that if you name a cookie after her, I suppose it has to have some Rose in it. So this is rose and lemon. And then I've got Pansy's special, which is a sugar cookie with blackberry buttercream, which is of course kind of blue, for her uniform. Ryder's is chocolate chunk. Because he's kind of classic, but also… just him. Sammy's is my take on a hummingbird cake, but in a cookie. Coconut crushed pineapple. Because my sister-in-law is a whole thing, but very sweet with it."

"And this one?" he asked.

"Logan's. He's my…" She hesitated, and something in his chest hitched slightly. "Well, he's my future brother-in-law. But he's like a brother already. It's complicated. It's very complicated."

"Your family is obviously important to you."

"You have no idea. We just… We raised each other. Me and my siblings. And Logan. Sammy." She pointed to two other cookies in the box. "Colt and Jake. My cousins. Pecan sandy and white chocolate raspberry."

"I see." He didn't quite have it in him to ask. The silence stretched between them, and he wondered if she would offer. Clearly, she was deciding. Finally she said, "Our parents died in an accident. All of them."

"Shit," Griffin said.

It took a lot to shock him. Frankly, his tolerance for tragedy was blown way the hell out of proportion. But that did it. "How old were you?"

"Fourteen. Rose was six. Pansy was eight. Ryder was eighteen. He was the only one. The other boys were fifteen through seventeen. Sammy's parents didn't die, but they were abusive, and she was our neighbor. Eventually, she moved in with us. Well, she parked her camper on the property. It took her and Ryder a long time, but eventually they admitted that their feelings for each other were more than just friendship. But it was tough for them. Because... Nobody else really has what we do. We were so dependent on each other for everything. It was all hands on deck. The boys helping on the ranch, and me doing my best to take care of the household stuff. We just all did the best we could. And I guess that kind of explains me. I guess you can kind of see how I forgot to move on. How I forgot to get out of the role that I was in. I'm kind of an empty nester, I guess." She scrunched her face up. "It's the strangest thing."

He felt like an ass then, for thinking what he had about her, and that was a feat. But she'd been through a hell of a lot more than he'd given her credit for.

When she'd implied she'd lost her mother he hadn't realized this was the whole story.

"Sorry," he said. "About some of the things that I've said to you."

"You didn't know."

"Because I didn't ask."

"I realized that."

He let out a long, slow breath. "It's been a while since I've done… People."

"I assume you don't want me to ask," she said looking down.

He shook his head once. "That's true. I don't."

"And if I did?"

"I wouldn't answer you."

It was all dangerously too close to things he didn't want to think about. Things he didn't want to deal with. Not with her. There were just some things that were sacred ground, and there was no stepping on them. Not ever.

There was no use going over what couldn't be changed. There was just no use at all.

"Well, good to have boundaries, I guess."

"And dessert," he said.

"Indeed." She looked around the room. And he looked at her. At the fine line of her neck, that pointed, determined chin and surprisingly soft looking mouth.

He couldn't remember how he'd seen her that first time. Only that he thought she was plain.

She wasn't plain at all.

It would be better if she were.

"I better head out," he said.

"Oh?"

"Yeah," he said. "I have some work to do."

He might be tired, he might be damned sick of being outside, but he wasn't going to stay in here with her. Not any longer.

"I guess so… I guess I'll clean."

"You don't have to. Hell, don't you have a bakery to try and open?"

"Well, yes. But… I guess until I actually open there's

not a whole lot for me to do. I have to get a permit and things like that."

"Right."

"So, I'll just stay."

"If you insist," he said.

"I do," she said.

"All right. See you later. If you're not here when I get back."

"Right."

And for some reason, turning and walking away felt difficult. And he couldn't just blame it on lack of sleep, or his bad temper.

Couldn't blame it on anything other than the woman standing in his cabin.

And her damn cookies and sad life story.

A little bit of manual labor would do him good.

The only thing that sleep had for him was more nightmares anyway.

And he was all out of patience with that.

CHAPTER NINE

SHE HAD DECIDED on a few things before she had come up today. Not just his cookie, not just that she might share a little bit about herself and her life, but that she was going to make sure he had a fresh meal.

And so, she had outfitted herself with everything she needed to make a good camp dinner. She was going to make burgers. And she might even stay for dinner.

What exactly are you doing?

She pushed that thought to the side. She was being nice. She had briquettes and a lighter, and she was determined that she would get a perfect sphere on the hamburgers. She had cut up lettuce and tomatoes, and had pickles and mustard and mayonnaise. Barbecue sauce. Lots of cheese. Basically everything required to make a good burger. She was grilling onions and put the buns on the grill as well to add a little something.

Usually, it was her brother who did the grilling, but there wasn't a whole lot of cooking that she wasn't more than competent at.

And while she worked on dinner, she thought about the exchange they'd had earlier. About the way he seemed to fight allowing himself to enjoy anything.

About the way he had looked at her.

Like he was trying to see something beneath her skin.

It had made her feel hot all over, and like her clothes were particularly itchy.

She liked him.

Which made her feel stupid and juvenile. But it was more than just a crush like she'd had in high school. It was deeper, and came with some feelings that were decidedly adult. Ones that she couldn't quite untangle, because she...

She *knew* how sex worked. She wasn't young. She knew basically all there was to know. But that was just theoretical.

And in terms of what she actually wanted... Well, she didn't *quite* know all that.

She felt perplexed. By the deep attraction that was building on her end. And a bit embarrassed. She had never felt anything like this in her life. And she wondered if he could see it. Wondered if it was somehow written across her forehead. And how humiliating, because it wasn't just like having fluttery feelings for someone. Like thinking she might want to hold a guy's hand. This was fraught and deep.

She wanted to touch her mouth to his.

And how the hell did you have that conversation with a man anyway? Not that she wanted to kiss him, but that she wanted to kiss him, *and* had in fact never been kissed before.

Maybe that was the real reason she'd been drawn to Elliott. Because if there was one nice thing she could say about a guy that bland, it was that at least gaining some experience with him might have felt a little bit low stakes. Regardless of the fact that even he probably had more sexual experience than she did—because the rock next to the charcoal grill had more sexual experience than she did—she would have felt like they were somehow still on more equal footing.

She knew that she wasn't on equal footing with Griffin. Whatever his experience was. That was beside the point.

He was hard and intense, like a man carved from stone. He would be…

He was brisk and demanding. And she somehow had the strong sense that he would be that way in all areas of life.

And she didn't even know how she had that sense. Was it wisdom? Female wisdom that she just sort of had because on an instinctual level she knew how things could be between a man and a woman?

Or was she just making things up? Because it was too unsettling to have such a big void of knowledge and she wanted to pretend that there was something she could know?

She couldn't say.

So she angrily worked at grilling burgers.

She tried not to think about him telling her explicitly that she wasn't to ask about him.

His past.

It made her chest hurt. Because there was something. She knew it.

Maybe that was what drew her to him.

That certainty that on some level she could understand him. She was certain of that. She didn't quite know how. But maybe deep sadness and loss called out to like wounds. She didn't know.

She didn't know a whole lot.

But wasn't that the point? She hadn't pushed herself in that kind of situation before. She had been quite easy on herself these last few years. And this was where she… Well, it was where she pushed herself, she supposed.

Grilling burgers and pondering sexual attraction. She sighed heavily.

She had just wanted to open a bakery.

In the beginning.

Now things were complicated.

She finished, and waited. She had been at the house all day. Had run back into town to get some supplies, to get the grill and come back, and she hadn't seen him at all.

She wondered where he went. Because his truck was here, so he couldn't have left, and he had indicated that he didn't often leave the mountain anyway. So what was he working on?

He had the horses, maybe he had even more of a ranch than he let on. It was possible, she supposed. But he hadn't been over there where she had found the horses, so he was somewhere else, that was for sure. There was another path. One that led in the opposite direction to the one that she had taken the other day. Somebody had to go and get him for dinner.

She ignored the disquiet that flared through her when she took the burgers off the grill, and decided to go and look for him rather than continue to wait.

Because something in her knew that he probably didn't want to be found. But he hadn't wanted to be found in the first place, and he was happy enough about it now. And he did like food.

She had noticed that.

She wouldn't go so far as to say that it soothed the savage beast. He never seemed all that soothed. But he was slightly more…manageable when there was food on offer.

So she took a deep breath and headed down that path, looking around as she did. It really was beautiful up here. She could see why he liked it. Or… Did he like it? He had never really said. He had made it clear that he preferred isolation to the company of strangers. Or anyone. That didn't mean that he liked it.

She continued walking until she heard the sound of a hammer hitting metal. And then, she came around the curve of the path, and saw the beginnings of the house. At least, that's what she assumed it was. A foundation and some skeletal wood. And Griffin, shirtless, hammering away. She couldn't take her eyes off of him. Everything about him was beautiful. His entire body finally honed. As he hammered, the muscles in his shoulders shifted and bunched, his abs, his chest...

And she was mesmerized. By absolutely everything about him.

And as if he could feel her eyes on him, he suddenly looked up, and his expression shifted. And when it did, it was to one of absolute, unquestionable fury.

He pulled the hammer back one more time, then tossed it onto the ground. "What are you doing here?"

"I... I came to get you for dinner."

"I didn't give you permission to go exploring, did I?"

"I didn't know I needed permission. I'm kind of in all your stuff cleaning, anyway."

"Well, I didn't tell you that you could come here. And I don't want you here."

It was like her fantasy had been a delicate paper lantern, and he'd grabbed it in his fists and buckled it. Extinguished the light.

His anger was painful, and she hadn't expected that. That it would hurt to be on the receiving end of his displeasure, but it did.

"I'm sorry," she said.

He was *so* angry. She could feel it coming off of him in waves. And she could see that he wasn't entirely reasonable. This was about something else. And she couldn't quite figure out what. Because she didn't know anything about him, and he refused to tell her. Because whatever she thought was happening with him, it wasn't. That much was clear. Because he had forbidden her from asking anything about his past, and she had been sitting there... She was such an idiot.

She was an idiot, and she felt unnerved, with this large, angry man barreling toward her. He stopped, still with a healthy amount of space between them, but she could feel deep, unchecked emotion coming from him.

"Just stick to the cabin, Iris. Stick to what you do. This is my stuff. My business."

"It's a building," she said. "I don't magically have insight into you that you don't want me to have because I saw it. You can calm down."

"Just… I didn't ask for you to come up here in the first place," he said. "I didn't ask for you to bring cookies. I didn't ask for you to cook me dinner."

"Well, I did," she said, taking a step toward him. Anger spiked through her veins.

She didn't often let herself get angry. She didn't let herself get angry because it was often pointless. Because what was there to say half the time when life wasn't fair? When the people around her weren't fair. Nothing. There was nothing but coping, and she was damn good at that. She was good at putting her head down, good at telling herself that she liked quiet life. That she was fine with the way things were. But she wasn't fine with this. For the first time in her life she had met a man who interested her in a deep and terrifying way, and he was…infuriating and unknowable.

He was creating desires inside of her that she wasn't even sure she'd known were there. At least not this strong. And he was… He was pushing her away. And it enraged her that she even had that thought. That she wanted to be something other than *away* from him. That she felt entitled to anything from him at all. Because he hadn't opened her chest up and put those feelings inside of her. Because he hadn't asked for her to feel this connection to him that she did. But she still blamed him.

And this pain that was rioting through her chest felt like his fault too.

Was this what being a teenager was like for most people?

It wasn't like she didn't know what it was like to have crushes. It was just…she'd never been able to afford to have her emotions be unchecked. She'd always had to be levelheaded.

Always.

And he made her feel… *Not* that.

"I cook for you because I'm being nice," she said, taking a step toward him. "I'm not sure if you know what that looks like. Or what that means."

"Iris…"

"No. I made you hamburgers. And you…" She moved even closer still, and she could smell him. Musk and man and spicy skin.

His sweat.

It should disgust her. But it didn't. Instead, it made her want to draw closer. Made her want to… She didn't even know. She didn't even have the words for the things that he made her want, and it wasn't fair.

She suddenly felt desperately, horribly lost.

She'd never had anyone to ask about all this.

About sex and wanting and what you did when a man's sweat was more attractive than it was repelling.

She'd been the mother figure.

She'd been the one that was supposed to know everything, but she didn't know anything.

Not about this.

And suddenly, he shifted, and it brought him just that much closer. So close that a whisper separated them. So close that a breath might have closed the distance between their mouths. Heat prickled over her skin, made her skin feel too tight for her body. Her heart thundered, out of control, and she could barely breathe.

Would he kiss her? Was that what was happening?

Would he actually…

She felt weak with it. Terrified. Brave. She wanted to take that additional step. Wanted to close the distance between them. And she also wanted to weep because she didn't know how.

"I need you to do your job. And that's it."

She could feel his heat. His mouth was so close she would only have to incline her head to touch her lips to his. She felt dizzy. Giddy.

"Griffin," she said softly.

Then he took a step back from her, leaving her feeling cold. Bereft.

"Just go, Iris."

"I made you hamburgers."

"Take them home. Take yourself on home."

She didn't have the words to argue. Didn't know how she even would.

So she did what he asked. She stepped back, and then she turned around on the trail and headed to the cabin. She looked around at the food she prepared. She had half a mind to push it onto the ground. Because what was the point of trying to do anything nice for him? What was the point of any of this? Of feeling like she should do anything for him? Of feeling anything at all?

Was she just pathetic? Pathetic and so desperate for a man that she'd attached herself to the first one she had any proximity to who wasn't related to her?

You know that isn't true.

She wanted to howl in frustration.

Instead, she slowly collected the food, and then took

it into his house. Putting the carefully sliced vegetables and the hamburger patties inside the icebox. She sealed the desserts and made sure that they were properly stored. She didn't know why. She knew less than nothing at the moment, it seemed.

But... No one was up here to take care of him. And he clearly didn't want her to. He would probably rather she had a huge tantrum and kicked the grill over. Would probably rather she took the food home for herself.

She wouldn't let him do that. She would leave it for him, regardless of his behavior. She would take care of him, regardless of his behavior.

Because that's just what you do? Take care of everyone else?

She didn't really think she could win. With herself or with him. So she left, driving back down to town full of frustration, but most of all, sadness.

Because this was supposed to be some kind of big emancipation. And somehow, she felt younger and more confused than she ever had in her life.

GRIFFIN KNEW HE'D crossed the line. She hadn't asked to be treated like that. And she didn't deserve it. She'd cooked for him. Made him dinner. And he knew what the hell his problem was, but that didn't give him any excuse.

It was just that... He'd seen her standing there, and he'd wanted to go to her. He'd seen the way that she was looking at him. Really looking at him. And what he'd wanted to do was go to her and wrap his arms around her. Had wanted to pull her up against his chest. Had wanted to taste her mouth, rather than lecturing her.

Hell.

He felt like an ass, and somewhere beyond redemption.

Redemption was a strange word. One that didn't quite fit with his life. With where he was. With what he needed.

And that was how he found himself sitting on his cell phone rock knowing that he needed to call his sister. He'd avoided her for too long.

It was perverse, and he knew it. He wasn't calling her because he missed her. He was calling her because he wanted a reminder. Of who he was and why he was here.

It wasn't that he didn't miss his sister. It was just that he… He didn't really have a sense of what missing a person was anymore. It was just with him, all the time. Part of who he was. So, he couldn't separate out missing her more than he could missing anyone else.

"What the hell, Griffin?"

"Nice to hear your voice too, Mallory."

"Well, you know, I spent a good amount of the last few weeks thinking you might actually have killed yourself up there on that mountain."

He didn't say anything.

"I didn't mean…" She stumbled over her words. "I meant, you know you could have an accident. How would I know? How would you get help?"

"I'm fine," he said.

She breathed heavily into the phone. "Yeah. *So* fine. What is your plan?"

"I'm building the house."

"Griffin…"

"What?"

"I don't think she would want you up there building the house by yourself. I get what you think you're doing, but…"

"You don't know what she would've wanted. And you know what, it's not about what she would have wanted. I don't know what else to do. I don't know what else to do, and I'm here. You don't have to worry about anything happening to me. I'm alive."

He bit back everything he wanted to say in addition to that. It wasn't... Worth much of anything. Because he'd said it all. He'd thought it all.

He could have all the questions in the world about why he couldn't swap places. About why it hadn't been him. About why it had happened at all. It didn't change anything. It never did.

"I wouldn't do anything to... It would be disrespectful."

"Come home."

"It's not home for me," he said.

"Enjoying small town life so much?"

He looked around at the wilderness. She wouldn't be able to believe what he'd traded in. What he had here, and how different it was to what he'd left behind.

She wouldn't believe what it was really like up here.

"Yeah," he said, finally. "It's quaint."

"What should I tell Mom and Dad?"

"Tell them I'm...fishing."

There was a brief pause. "Are you?"

"I could."

"What do you do? Just tell me that you're not drinking too much and..."

"I'm definitely drinking too much. But I've got horses up here with me. I ride."

This pause felt painful, he wasn't sure why. "You talk to other people?"

He cleared his throat. "It just so happens I've got a woman cooking for me."

"A woman."

"She works for me," he said. "That's all."

"All right," she said. "Just… Don't go that long without calling me again."

"All right," he echoed. "I promise."

"You're just going to go now, aren't you?"

"I think that would be best."

"Goodbye, Griffin."

And as he walked back down to the cabin, he realized the phone call with his sister hadn't really helped anything. The only thing it had served to do was highlight the fact that he was caught between two things. A life that didn't exist anymore, and one he didn't want.

And then there were Iris Daniels's greenish eyes, and the way she had looked at his body.

And for the first time, what he really wanted was to pretend that there was no old Griffin Chance. That his life had begun here on this mountaintop. Because if it had, he would be free to grab her, kiss her, answer all the questions he'd seen on her face.

He growled, throwing open the door of the cabin, and then going to the refrigerator. Whatever he'd said to her, he was hungry.

And when he looked in the icebox, he saw all of the burger fixings carefully wrapped up and placed there.

There was a lot of food in that fridge. Thanks to Iris.

Food that reminded him he could be hungry.

Damn Iris Daniels for reminding him about hunger.

For reminding him he was human.

For reminding him he was a man.

CHAPTER TEN

IRIS WOKE UP crabby and avoided her family as she got up and slipped out of the house, making the drive down to the new bakery. It was still early, the sky just barely blushing pink as the sun peeked over the mountains.

It was a beautiful morning.

Too bad she was far too vile to appreciate it.

Griffin.

She shoved his name far to the side. She didn't need to be thinking his name.

She needed a name for the bakery. She hadn't thought of one yet. There were puns, of course. And anything involving her name. But so far, her baked goods themselves had gone toward being named after the people in her life, rather than being anything terribly cutesy.

Except for the Mountain Climber.

Well, she might not name one even vaguely in his honor, after all. He was being difficult. Completely unreasonable.

She parked her car and got out, squeezing her eyes shut for a moment, then crossed the street and headed toward the front door of the bakery.

She pushed the door in, and the warmth greeted her. And the strangest sense of belonging. She had never felt that outside of her house. Had never felt that outside of Hope Springs. It was amazing.

The sense of belonging. Of purpose.

But her unhappiness with Griffin was like a grain of sand, agitating against the warmth in her chest. It felt rough and uncomfortable. And she hadn't asked for it.

She tortured herself with it as she sat down behind the counter in the space. She was intent on making lists of names for the place, and finalizing an opening date. She had filed everything for permits with the county, and it was looking very straightforward. Especially since it had passed inspection only recently.

Really, she needed to get going on everything.

Instead, she sat there, thumping her pen against a piece of paper.

She saw a flash of movement out of the corner of her eye, and realized it was her sister Pansy standing there in front of the door.

Iris frowned and slid off the stool, heading toward the entry. She pushed the door open and let her sister come in. "What're you doing here?"

"I thought you were here, and I came by to check in. I took an early shift this morning."

"Oh. Well, so did I."

She smiled, but knew it was a rueful smile. Considering she had come in early to avoid her family. And yet, there her sister was. She couldn't quite seem to escape them.

"What's wrong?"

Iris narrowed her eyes. "I didn't say anything was wrong."

"You look like something is wrong."

"It's not," she said. "I promise." Except she was lying, and she was a very bad liar. She didn't have any practice with it.

"Are you nervous about the bakery?"

"No. Not at all. I'm excited about this. I… I want this.

But it's a change, and I want to focus on that. On the change. And so is moving away from Hope Springs, and I am going to do it."

"I know you are," Pansy said. "I really do understand, Iris."

"I know you do. Rose doesn't like change, and everything she needs is right there at the ranch. She... She fell in love there."

"There's life off of it, though. Ryder and Rose might've found love there, but I didn't. I found it in an unlikely place."

"Yeah. I know."

"I really don't want to pry."

"Well, then you could not pry."

"No," she said, looking incredibly, falsely sad. "With great regret I'm going to. This guy that you're working with... The landlord..."

"I think my problem is that I haven't been in the vicinity of an attractive male that I'm not related to in...ever."

"You're not related to Logan," she pointed out.

"But he's like a brother to me."

"Didn't stop Rose."

"Well, clearly he's not like a brother to Rose." She sighed. "He is to me."

"So you think that you are just having some kind of testosterone overload?"

"It occurred to me. I mean, what's wrong with me, that I go out to make a life for myself and immediately get... fixated on a very unfriendly man that I'm working with. It's not like he's nice," she muttered.

"Did something happen?"

"He got mad at me yesterday."

"He's not dangerous, is he?" Pansy asked, and she could

sense a shift in her younger sister. Her protective instincts going into overdrive. Pansy might be Iris's younger sister, but she was also a police officer. And Iris knew that she wouldn't hesitate to go handle a man who had gotten violent with her.

"No. Not like that at all. Just… Angry. He's angry. And I've had my fill of caregiving and taking on projects." Unease spiked in her chest, because that was close to the truth, but it wasn't quite it. And she didn't want to get any closer to *it*. "I have this bakery," she continued. "And I think he's *beautiful*. And yesterday even when he was mad I wanted to… I don't even have the words for what I want. And I feel so horrifically frustrated by it." Tears pricked her eyes, and she didn't know why. It wasn't sadness. It was a deep frustration.

"I took care of you. You and Rose and everyone else. I did the best I could. But I… I didn't really have anyone to take care of me. And it isn't that Ryder didn't do his best, he did. But I think he considered me in his boat. It's okay. I'm not… Upset about it. But there was no one there to talk to me about dating, or sex, or anything like that. And the idea of caring for someone that way just scared me anyway so I kind of shut it off. I didn't want to go to bars and hook up. Because I couldn't imagine giving that much of myself to someone I would never see again. I still can't imagine it, but I don't want… I don't want to care about someone that much. But I want him. And I don't know what it means. I don't know what to do with it."

"Well," Pansy said after a long moment. "I know that I didn't do the caretaking. But I understand… I understand feeling like you missed something. Something big. West infuriated and frustrated me, but not half as much as what he made me feel. I don't have the same reasons as you, Iris, but I wanted to be the chief of police. And being a police officer at all in a small town, knowing you might have to pull over some guy that you hooked up with… I was never into that. It just sounded like too much work. Like too big of a risk. So I kept it all locked down until I met West. And I didn't intend to fall in love with him, I just did. Just because that happened to me doesn't mean it will happen to you."

"What are you suggesting?"

"I'm suggesting that you're in a season where you're trying to change. And you're doing things for yourself. And you're going to have your very own apartment. And if you want a man, maybe you should see where it goes?"

"But I…"

"Why haven't you been with anyone?" Pansy looked at her intently, her sister's bright eyes glittering. "Is it because you don't want to? Is it because it doesn't feel right to you to be with someone you're not going to marry? If that's the case, then don't do it. But if it's just because you're afraid, if you're holding yourself back…"

"I am," Iris said. "I am."

And she wouldn't have been able to admit that only a few days ago. But what Griffin had said to her about her strength was resonating inside of her. She was strong, and she had built strong walls to protect herself.

She had done what she felt was necessary to survive. Had chosen to put other people ahead of herself because she didn't want to contend with what it might mean to put her own self out there. To let herself want something. But she was doing it now. With the bakery. Why not with him too?

"What do I do if he doesn't want me?"

"I… I mean, do you think he wants you?"

"I don't know," Iris said, spreading her hands. "I really

don't. I don't have any idea about the finer points of this kind of thing. Or the…blunter points even."

"I guess it's like opening a bakery. Or becoming chief of police. There are no guarantees. But you kinda have to try, or you aren't going to know. Nobody can tell you it's going to work. Nobody can tell you that you won't be disappointed."

Iris nodded slowly. "It was so easy to complain my life was boring while I wasn't doing anything about it. Boring is safe." Stupidly, tears welled up in her eyes again. "I got mad at Rose for pushing me toward a man that I thought was boring. I was upset that all of you had moved on. And I kind of saw myself as poor and left behind. But I'm afraid. I'm afraid of wanting more. I'm afraid of getting more. And the easiest thing to do is to put everyone and everything in front of yourself."

"I'm not unfamiliar. It's pretty easy to put a cause like chief of police in front of grief. A tribute to Dad instead of actually dealing with how I feel about losing him. I feel you."

"I guess I should be grateful that I'm not alone?"

"I guess. I understand feeling like you want to protect yourself from going through any more than you already have. Believe me. I don't think anyone understands more than… Well, the rest of us."

"But you have to spend a lot of time hiding in order to do that, don't you?"

"Definitely," she said.

"So what do you suggest?"

"You're going for what you want. So, go for what you want."

"But what if I don't know exactly what I want?"

"Then you make a mistake."

"But you didn't actually make a mistake. And I feel like you're awfully comfortable talking about me making one."

"I might have," Pansy said. "And whatever else happened with me and West, I did make some mistakes. And so did he."

Iris stared down at her blank pad. The one that still didn't have a single name for the bakery written on it. It's true. She was trying to not make mistakes. She was trying to be certain before she even tested anything out.

And so she started writing. Lots of names. Stupid ones. Flowers and puns and personal things.

While she wrote, Pansy gave her a hug, and said goodbye. And Iris kept on thinking. She stood up from her stool and walked into the kitchen. And without thinking, started to make sugar cookies. Because sugar cookies were the perfect blank canvas sort of treat.

And it would help her think. Mostly because she could do this entire recipe without paying attention at all.

"The Hungry Raccoon," she said to herself as she got the dough into the mixing bowl. "The Place That Has All of the Baked Goods." She had a distinct memory then. Of Pansy being small and stealing cookies out of the cookie jar. And she paused. "The Cookie Jar. *The Cookie Jar.*" The name filled her with warmth. It felt good. It reminded her of better days. Of when they'd been children and things had felt simple. Of her mother making cookies and putting them in that little jar at the back of the counter. It was long gone, that jar.

Even as far back as she could remember, the mouse on it had a broken ear. But she had still been cute, with a pink dress and white apron. And of course, she always held cookies so that made her all the more compelling.

The Cookie Jar.

There. She could make choices. She could decide things. Things like the name of her business.

Things like whether or not she wanted a man.

Griffin Chance.

The idea of trying to...*seduce* him seemed ridiculous. Mostly because she didn't think of herself as seductive in any way.

But she also hadn't imagined a few months ago that she would do something like this. That she would jump into starting her own business, into moving in to the apartment above the bakery. The way that she'd fought for this was unlike anything she'd ever fought for in her life. For herself, anyway.

She was proud of it. So why not go a step further? And if he rejected her... It didn't matter.

She ignored the slight pain in her chest at the thought. She finished the sugar cookie dough, and put it in one of the large fridges, to be rolled out later.

She felt somewhat resolved. It seemed a bit ridiculous to think that she might seduce a man she hadn't even kissed. But that was the thing. She wasn't a child. And she had left things far too long. So as it stood, it was all a little absurd. She couldn't imagine that a man like Griffin would merely want to be the subject of her first kiss. He would of course assume that there would be more. And she did want more. She imagined the problem with waiting until her age to have sex for the first time was that kind of put you on an accelerated track once you did start.

When you were sixteen, there was a whole lot of fumbling and uncertainty—as she was led to believe, anyway—and fear that parents might catch you, concerns over teenage pregnancy...

Iris winced.

Well, pregnancy wasn't really a concern. She'd been on the pill for a while just for cramps, so that was covered.

But there was a matter of condoms, which she knew was responsible, pregnancy not being a fear aside.

Though, that would require a trip into Tolowa. She was not buying prophylactics *here*. No. There was no way.

The very idea made her wish she was dead.

That was it. She was just at the age where she could be pragmatic about these kinds of things. She should celebrate that. It was a gift, really.

That she didn't have to romanticize. That she didn't have to turn it into something bigger than it was.

She wasn't going to fall in love. She couldn't. Wanting more would mean needing more, trying to earn more, and she couldn't face that. But that was another gift of age. She knew enough to know that sex didn't mean love.

But…she didn't think she'd have been silly enough to think it did even when she was younger.

She couldn't seduce him in his cabin. And it was entirely possible she wouldn't be able to seduce him while he was mad at her. So that was another issue altogether.

She walked slowly up the stairs to the apartment, and looked around the vacant space. It was really almost move-in ready. She would need to bring bedding, and things like that, but otherwise…

She walked over to the kitchen sink, and turned on the water, and a spray shot up from behind the faucet. Like a sign from heaven.

Well, that was maybe not a very good way to think about it. Perhaps she couldn't attribute that sort of thing to heaven. But either way, someone had helped her out. Because there she had it. The perfect excuse to ask him to come down here.

You don't think he'll just hire someone else?

She thought back to the work he was doing on that house he clearly didn't want her to see.

No. She didn't think that he would just hire someone else to do it. He would want to do it himself, because he was that kind of man. The kind of very stubborn man who liked to do physical things on his own, and would never see any point in paying someone to do it. He might have a business manager, but Iris had a sense that that was different.

At least, she hoped it was.

For all the little she knew about men, she did have her brother, her cousins and Logan. And they were that kind of hardheaded man.

First things first, she had to get the place a bit more habitable. But since he clearly didn't want her coming up to the cabin in the meantime, that seemed fair enough. And maybe in the end, she could outlast him. He'd come down here to get food, because she would be too busy to go up for the next couple of days.

As seduction plans went, it wasn't a bad one.

If you couldn't lead with experience and skills, you might as well lead with excellent cooking.

She may not know all the places to touch a man, but she knew how to make mashed potatoes.

And in the grand scheme of things, that was pretty good.

She was committed to working with what she had.

CHAPTER ELEVEN

HE HADN'T SEEN hide nor hair of Iris for a couple of days. He'd overstepped. Yelling at her like he had that day she'd come to the housing site. He didn't know what the hell he'd been thinking. Well, that was the thing. He hadn't thought at all. It had been nothing more than feeling.

He'd felt cornered. Invaded in some way. He'd felt like she was getting close to treading on sacred ground and he didn't like it.

Then she left dinner in the fridge for him, had left all that food for him...

Of course, now it was nearly gone.

It was what enticed him back to the cell phone rock. To see if she'd gotten in touch. He was gratified when a voice mail came in, and he could see that it had come from Iris.

"Hi, Griffin. I didn't want to surprise you again up at the cabin. Not until we talked. But I'm moving in to the apartment and there's an issue with the sink. I don't how to fix it. I need you to either hire a plumber for me or maybe you can come take a look?"

There was a strange note in her voice, and he had a very odd feeling in the pit of his stomach.

"I'd like to see you."

That pit grew.

It wasn't just an odd note. It was breathy. Strange. And

he recalled the tension that had arced between them when he'd been angry with her.

He'd wanted to…

That was the problem. He hadn't wanted to *hurt* her. He hadn't even wanted to shout at her. What he'd wanted to do was grab her, claim her mouth with his. Punish her with every bit of pent-up rage and desire inside of him in the form of pleasure.

He growled, gritting his teeth.

This was not helping.

He didn't want to acknowledge it. He didn't want…

He didn't want it.

Still, he found himself hitting the return call button and waiting.

She answered. "Griffin?"

"Are you around? Because I could come over and fix that leak."

What the hell.

"Yes," she said, her words altogether too bright. "I am."

"Great. I'll be down in a couple of hours."

"I have… Some food for you."

"Thanks." He hung up.

He hadn't misread the look on her face when he'd moved toward her the other day. He hadn't. She might've been upset at him. She might have been a little bit frightened, but she had also been intrigued.

Maybe even aroused.

There had been a time in his life when he would have taken her up on that offer without even thinking about it. Hell, that was just a Friday night. He didn't *need* to know a woman to have sex.

At least he hadn't.

But that was before Mel.

When he'd met her it had changed everything. It had made him want different things. It had made him something else. And then he'd lost everything. Everything that had made him who he was. And he didn't know who he was on the other side of it.

If he was anything.

Why does it matter? If she wants to have sex...

He took a sharp breath. It mattered. It just did. Right now, it did.

Anyway, her asking him to come fix a leaky pipe could be nothing. Nothing more than his body overreacting to having a woman in close proximity.

Because one thing was for certain, this was most definitely the longest span of celibacy he'd ever had in his life. And it hadn't mattered. Not one bit. Until Iris Daniels had given him a bite of a chocolate chip cookie, and looked at him with those eyes that seemed to be the last thing he saw in his mind before he went to sleep.

It wasn't that. If there was one thing he was certain of, it was that Iris wasn't... He couldn't imagine her being into that kind of casual thing. She seemed far too sincere. And anyway, she hardly had the wardrobe of a siren.

Seems to be working well enough on you...

Yeah. Well, he was hard up. Whether he wanted to admit it or not.

Honestly. Grief was a bastard that kept on giving. If it could just be there and insulate him from wanting anything, then it would be all right. He could just come up here and hang himself on his cross, work himself to death, suffer but live as a tribute, everything would be fine.

Not fine. But alive, at least. There was a comfort in wanting nothing.

In having no appetite.

There was control to it.

But now all of a sudden his *body* wanted things. And *he* decidedly did not.

The grief hadn't faded. It was still there. It was still telling him the same things.

Not that he was a married man. He wasn't. That wasn't the issue.

But he was alive. Mel was gone.

And he didn't know how the hell he was supposed to keep living, enjoying that life, when she couldn't.

When her smile and her laugh were gone from the world, and he remained.

He knew how to survive.

It was the rest he wasn't sure about.

"Well," he said. "You're just going to fix a pipe." He sighed heavily. "And you're talking to yourself. So you really have reached a good space."

And he couldn't deny that the realization he would be talking to Iris in person soon made his blood run hotter.

Couldn't deny it, no matter how much he wanted to.

IRIS HAD PUT on the sexiest thing she owned. Which she felt wasn't that impressive, in the end. A pair of faded blue jeans and a scoop neck T-shirt that revealed just a hint of cleavage wasn't exactly going to set the world on fire. Or Griffin, for that matter.

She *had* put on lip gloss, though.

It was the only makeup she had.

She felt a little bit frustrated by that tonight. It would have been nice to be able to fix herself up a little bit more, but Pansy wasn't really a makeup girl either, and she wasn't sure Rose even owned a comb.

She could have talked to Sammy, that was true. Her

sister-in-law was a feminine goddess, who wore makeup, or didn't, who wore dresses, or denim with the same amount of ease. Who let her blond hair dry naturally and fly wild around her, or occasionally straightened it if the mood took her. Sammy wielded her femininity with ease. Let it take whatever shape she felt like in the moment.

Iris admired that.

It scared her a little bit, though. And, she hadn't wanted to talk to Sammy, because Sammy was no longer a safe space. Because if she told Sammy, Sammy was going to tell Ryder.

That had always been a little bit of a tricky situation. But Iris had never had any secrets to keep from her brother.

She did not especially want him to know that she was intent on trying to seduce a man in the apartment she was going to move in to.

She hadn't even told him that she was moving.

After the reaction she had from Rose, she hadn't really wanted to get into it.

A text popped up on her phone and she looked down at it.

I'm at the front door. You have to let me in. I don't have a key.

Her heart scrambled up into the base of her throat, and before she could chicken out, before she could talk herself out of it, she flung the door to the apartment wide and scrambled down the stairs inelegantly. Then she righted herself, fussing with her hair before heading toward the door.

There he was.

She just stood there for a moment, inside the empty shop, staring at the broad, tall figure on the other side of the glass. He was wearing a black T-shirt, and a black cowboy hat. The sight of him made her shiver, even though she wasn't cold.

Not at all.

If anything, she was a little bit warm.

She realized, suddenly, that she had never seen Griffin outside his natural habitat.

The cabin, the wilderness. She did think of it as his natural habitat. It was hard to imagine him in any other space. And here he was. In town, like a normal human being and not something mythical that was larger-than-life.

He cocked his head to the side. "You going to let me in?" His words were muffled against the glass.

"Oh," she said, fumbling with the knob and pushing it open. "I'm sorry. Come in."

"This is a nice place," he said, looking around. "Good thing I bought it."

"You haven't been here before?"

He shook his head. "No."

She frowned. "What kind of business do you have?"

"Mostly real estate investments."

"And you buy things you don't even look at?"

"All the time. I own property around the world. I don't go visit every single thing that I buy. It wouldn't make any sense. Wouldn't be practical either, come to that."

"But this isn't across the world. It's in Gold Valley, and so are you."

"Yeah. Well. My business manager thought it was a good idea. There's a reason I hired her."

"How did you… Get into owning property? I mean if you're not interested?" She couldn't quite wrap her head around it. "Financial success doesn't seem like something you just fall into."

Then again, he didn't seem particularly successful. She

only knew he was because he had…a business manager and a portfolio.

He was a study in contradictions. On the one hand, he seemed like he would have to be dirt poor, but he owned this building that she could certainly scarcely hope to afford in one lifetime. He seemed to be able to barter the rent money away just fine.

He was building a house. But by himself. At least, that was what it looked like.

He probably came from California. Where there was certainly more money in real estate than there was here.

"I used to be more interested than I am. But there came a point in time when things changed. And I outgrew where I was."

"Why?"

"It doesn't matter." He walked past her, heading toward the back of the building. "I assume the stairs are this way?"

"Yes," she said, scampering after him.

He had a toolbox clutched in his hand, the muscles in his forearm shifting as he walked. "Very early on," he said, "I just had to fix a lot of my own things. I got my first investment property really young, and I became a landlord. Then it turned out I was really good at all this. Got into bigger stuff."

"I see."

He paused, turning toward her and arching a dark brow. It was the closest thing to playful she'd ever seen on his face. "Did you want to ask if I'm rich?"

"The thought did cross my mind," she said, embarrassment heating her cheeks.

"Yes," he said. "Yeah." He looked around. "I guess I am."

For some reason, there was a heaviness in his voice that settled hard and strange in her chest. Like she could feel the weight of it. The cost of whatever it was beneath the surface.

"The sink is this way," she said.

Her hands felt sweaty again.

Great.

How was she supposed to seduce a man if she had sweaty hands? It seemed like a losing proposition to her. And very much like a humiliation just waiting to happen.

She stood there, her heart hammering in her ears, and she just had so many questions. *How did you... How did you do this?* This was the first time in her adult life she had been all alone with a man who wasn't family or surrogate family. She looked at his broad back, his muscular shoulders, lean waist and hips. And she felt. Not just desire, but what was filling up her chest was something else altogether. Something deep and overwhelming. Something that almost hurt. She couldn't explain it. Not if she wanted to. Fortunately, she didn't want an explanation. Not for any of this. She felt gloriously not herself, in this apartment that would be hers, about the business she was going to open. With a handsome man right there.

Not Iris, who took care of everyone else and pretended she didn't even know what she wanted. Iris, who didn't think about whether or not she was beautiful, or if a man might look her way or not. Iris, who had basically become a housewife at fourteen.

No. She didn't think she was that person. Not now. She was some new adventurous woman who might do any number of things.

Who could be anything she wanted to be. Who wasn't afraid to take chances.

Who wasn't hiding.

Behind responsibilities.

Behind fear.

She let out a long, slow breath. And she could see herself, crossing the distance between them. Putting her hand on one of those strong shoulders.

She didn't need experience. She only needed to follow instinct.

She steeled herself, and took that first step. He pressed his strong hands to the edge of the countertop and leaned forward. And she put her hand at the center of his back. Sliding it up to his shoulder.

Oh. There was no pretending that wasn't making a pass at him. It felt so much more sensual than she'd intended it to.

It was amazing, how loaded a touch could feel. How very not innocent that simple contact could be when there was intent behind it.

When there was nothing but the two of them in this room. No rules. No limitations.

She felt him go stiff beneath her touch.

"Iris…"

His voice was hard, and she wouldn't let him put her off. She moved her hand down farther, to his chest.

An arrow of desire shot through her. She wasn't confused. Not now. Because the places that were lit up from touching him were not confusing at all.

She wanted him.

She really did.

He turned around suddenly, his blue eyes wild. He was so close to her, like he had been that day at the house. He pushed his hand over the top of hers, pressing it flat to his chest, and she could feel his heartbeat raging there. Her own was most certainly keeping time with it. She felt overwhelmed. Overwrought.

Deliciously so.

She had spare few opportunities in her life to feel this way. To feel this much.

Not when it wasn't bad.

She knew the crushing, absolute devastation of grief. Of shock. The kind of loss that left you feeling hollow. Yes, she knew that.

But this. This exhilaration. She didn't know what would happen. Perhaps she had put herself out there for nothing. Maybe his heart wasn't beating for the same reason hers was. Maybe he didn't want her.

But this felt... Dangerous.

As if she had stepped up to the edge of a precipice and was gazing down at the bottom, impossibly far away.

As if she was staring into that abyss and nearly laughing at it.

She was lost in all that blue. The blue in his eyes, a flame flickering low and hot.

"What are you doing?"

"Isn't it... It's pretty obvious, isn't it?"

"I want to be very sure."

Her tongue suddenly felt thick, her throat tight. She didn't know how she was supposed to speak, not now.

She was shaking. Down to her soul, she was shaking.

But again, it was different than fear. Different than sorrow. She was familiar with both, and this was something else altogether. This shivering that was happening beneath her skin. As if the blood in her veins was turned to effervescent lava.

"I..."

"Tell me," he bit out.

"I..."

He reached up, gripping her chin firm between his thumb and forefinger. "Tell me," he said again.

"I thought maybe I might...seduce you. You know. Since there's no one else here. And there is electricity. It seemed like maybe something I could... That perhaps it was a good..."

"Is your sink really broken?" The question came out hard, filled with grit.

"It is," she said, brightening. "It really is. I didn't lie. But I did think that maybe you could... Fix the sink and also... Help me out."

"Help you out." That was horribly flat and it made her stomach slip down an inch or so in her midsection.

"Yes."

"*Help you out* as in you want to have sex?"

"I do," she said, heat flaring in her body, a blush blooming hard and heavy in her cheeks. She could feel it. She didn't have to see it to know what was there.

"Why?"

She blinked. "I... I didn't know that would matter."

She didn't want to get into her virginity. Didn't want to get into the fact that she'd never felt this way before.

"I want to know why. Because you marched up to my cabin just a few days ago holding cookies, and you wanted to open a bakery. I'm fine with that. I'm fine with helping you with that. But I don't understand what would make you want me. We had a couple of conversations, most of them have ended very well. I was an absolute ass to you the other day, and now you're standing there telling me that you want me?"

"I don't know what to say," she said. "I'm attracted to you. I..." Tears started to fill her eyes. She felt stupid. She felt small. "I didn't mean to do something wrong. I... I guess you don't want me. And that's... That's fine..."

"Iris, stop talking. I want to make sure you're not doing

this because you think you owe me. That's it. I don't need to know about your feelings. Except I need to make sure that this isn't payment."

A rush of relief filled her.

"It's not," she said. "It's not. I find it very inconvenient that it's you. That I want you. Because I guess it's really messy, and it might cause problems. And I didn't really want to be in that position, and I didn't want you to be in that position either. I guess there's not really anything either of us can do about it. I mean, attraction is what it is, and I… I'm not paying for the bakery with this. I would rather that I felt this way about some guy in a bar. Or maybe a family friend, like it was for Rose. Not that I mean… I'm going to stop talking now."

So she did. So she went up on her toes and pressed her mouth to his. For the first time in her life.

Sensation exploded inside of her. Need. Longing.

His lips were hot and firm beneath hers, and she was nearly panicked with just how much it made her feel. How did anyone survive this?

He was motionless, but only for a moment. Then he growled, tightening his arms around her and nearly lifting her up off the ground as he angled his head and consumed her.

Her heart was thundering wildly, desperation clawing at her.

This was why people went crazy over a person. She had never understood it.

She had watched Pansy turn her well-ordered life over for West. Had seen Rose and Logan risk breaking the family apart in order to be together. Had watched Ryder and Sammy nearly consume each other with the desperation of their passion and the fierceness of their need to deny it. But she hadn't understood.

Hadn't understood how it could make you so crazy. So gosh darn crazy.

But she did now. She understood it. She did.

Because his tongue was tracing black magic spells over hers, and his mouth was firm and perfect. Because she hadn't even understood why she would want to kiss a man like this, all deep and slick, and in an instant he had brought her into a state of full awareness and understanding.

Because his hands were large and warm as they pressed hard against her back, and made her feel fragile, but shielded, strong and desired all at once.

Iris had never experienced any sort of particular magic in her life.

Her world had been all about practical things. About survival and coping, about giving and learning how to press on when it was necessary.

But this made the case for fairy dust. For the mystical. For the unexplained.

This made a case for miracles. This man's kiss.

And the fact that he was holding her in his arms.

She didn't know what she thought seduction might entail. Perhaps more talking. Perhaps her removing some clothing. What she hadn't counted on was that he would seduce her. Completely. Fully.

Her breasts felt heavy, her nipples pointed into painful buds. And between her legs, there was a raw, hollow ache that seemed to echo inside of her, going on endlessly.

She wanted him. She wanted him more than she could explain. More than she had anticipated.

She didn't know what she had thought it might be. It had been gauzy and unclear in her head. A tangle of feelings inside of her. An increased heart rate, the barest hint of sensation shivering over her skin when he looked at her. When he got near.

Her stomach getting tight, her heart turning over.

But this was something else entirely. An explosion.

Blooming heat in her stomach, slick need between her legs. Decorum was completely demolished. In her mind, she could already see them, naked and tangled together. And the idea of it didn't frighten her. Didn't embarrass her at all.

She suddenly wanted things that she had never even imagined before. Desired him in a way she had thought… Well, that she hadn't even thought of before.

She could see how you might do anything for another person. How you would crave any touch, any tastes. Whatever their hands, their mouth would offer.

And how you would want to give it in return.

It was all blindingly clear. Just from a kiss.

But suddenly, he was pulling away from her, dragging in deep gulps of air, his muscular chest pitching violently with each indrawn breath.

"What?"

"No," he said. "This isn't happening."

"Why?"

She sounded petulant and small, and she felt utterly defeated. Because everything had been there. Like a thunderclap, and a flash of lightning that had given her everything.

And then he had taken it away. And it was like the clouds had covered the sun again.

"Why?" she asked again, knowing that she sounded small, that she sounded sad, that her pride had been utterly demolished by that one question. And not knowing what she could do about it. Not even knowing she cared.

"I don't know what you want," he said. "But I'm not up to giving it to you. I'm not. I can't."

"I just want… I just want…"

"I don't care what you had to say. Whatever you have to tell me. You don't want some guy to fuck you and then walk out, do you? And that's all I've got in me."

That word felt like a slap. Hard and vulgar and unlike anything they'd been doing. He'd said it for that reason. To be hard. To be mean.

To prove his point.

"I wanted to be with you," she said. "That's as far ahead as I was thinking."

"That's the problem. It's way too easy to only think that far ahead. But there's life beyond the orgasm, Iris. It would be easy to lay you down here on the floor and have my way with you. You know how long it's been?" His voice went rough, hard and intense. And his grip was iron on her. "You know how long it's been since I've touched a woman? It would be the easiest damn thing in the world to take what you're offering me. To take it and not feel an ounce of guilt. I could leave you satisfied. You'd call out my name more times than you've ever said it. And I want it." He wrapped his arm around her then, one hand hard on her behind as he pressed her against his body. As he let her feel the evidence of his arousal. Shock mixed with desire, mingling with rage that stole over her.

"Please…"

"No. You feel that. I want you. You made me want you." He sounded mystified. Angry.

And she had no idea what she'd done to incur his wrath. But then she hadn't understood it the other day either. And that was the problem, wasn't it?

She didn't know him.

She thought maybe she could have sex with a relative stranger, because Pansy had done it. For all that it had ended up working out well for her, that was how it had started. And she made it sound like it was good and easy. But the problem was, he had trigger points, and she didn't know what they were. She was watching them explode right now, and she didn't understand what it meant.

She was wretched.

Wretched and filled with need, and he was only stoking the fire by holding her against his hard body.

Stoking it for both of them, while denying them.

"Let me go," she said. "If you're going to say no, then just…don't touch me."

He released his hold on her. And she stumbled back. "Look at this," he said, his voice rough. "This is your first apartment. Your first job out of your house, owning your own business. You're starting out. And I'm done. I'm just done," he said roughly. "Don't waste any time worrying about me."

He turned and started to walk out of the room.

"What about my sink?"

He stopped, his shoulders going rigid. "Get a plumber."

"But I…"

"Bill me," he said.

"What are we going to do? About the rest of this?"

He turned to face her, and his expression was… It was terrifyingly bleak.

"We're going to pretend this didn't happen, because we're still at the point where we can. I don't think you understand, Iris. But this could turn into something that we can't come back from. That we can't fix. And then what's going to happen to your business? What's going to happen to our arrangement?"

She wanted to say that she didn't care. But she realized that wasn't true.

But this was like the first adult hurdle that she had to cross over. And she was on the verge of failing. Because she was pretty sure she would happily burn her dreams down to kiss him again. And what did that say about her? That she was on the verge of begging to be kissed?

When Elliott hadn't wanted her, when he had wanted Rose instead, it had stung. But it had also been absurd. Because she hadn't wanted him. And it had wounded her in strange and complicated ways, but she would never have begged him to pay attention to her. Not ever. She was on the verge of cutting her own pride to pieces over all this. Over the need to be with him. The desire to have him as her own.

Maybe she wasn't strong, after all.

Maybe she was just a foolish girl.

This had all felt magical only a few moments ago, and now she just felt bedraggled.

"No," she said. "Right. Just... Okay go then."

"Iris..."

"No," she said. "Don't you dare apologize to me. It's humiliating enough, throwing yourself at a man and being rejected. I... Thought men basically threw caution to the wind when it came to sex. Whether it's a bad idea or not."

"If it was just a bad idea for me, I might have. But it's a worse idea for you, and that... That's the problem."

He started to walk out again.

"I thought you said I was strong?" Pathetic. On the verge

of begging. Even that sounded plaintive and tragic to her own ears.

"You are," he returned.

"Then why are you pretending that it's me you're protecting?" She didn't know what had made her say that. But she knew it was true. She did. As sure as anything.

"I'm not pretending."

She felt stronger then, buoyed by her realization. "You are. You're protecting *you*. But that's fine. Get out of my apartment."

He didn't have to be asked again. He nodded once, then went down the stairs, and when she heard the door close, she stumbled over to the couch and lay across it, her heart beating a steady rhythm of pain.

You've been through worse.

She had. She had been through much worse. But it didn't help. Not now. Because this was bad enough.

So this was living.

Being an adult making mistakes. Living on your own.

She wasn't sure she liked it.

She hadn't told Ryder yet. Hadn't told him she might move up here so she could always go back…always go home.

What she really wanted to do was go back to her brother's house, curl up in a ball and sink into familiarity. She wanted the kitchen that she knew and her familiar bed. Wanted to be surrounded by her family. Wanted to hit rewind on the last hour.

But that would be losing for real. That was basically the only way she could lose. Quitting.

And she wasn't going to quit.

That, in the midst of the pain, gave her a sense of determination. A sense that maybe it wasn't quite so bad.

Because she wasn't going home. She wasn't letting his rejection decide what she was going to be.

She had changed. Her life had changed.

And as she lay there, coated in misery, she tried to let that matter.

At least she wasn't stupid enough to fall for him.

CHAPTER TWELVE

HE WAS A damn fool. And he cussed himself the entire way back up toward Echo Pass. A damn fool. He should never have touched her. He should never have let her kiss him.

But he had. And he'd been... Consumed by it. Like it was a flame. Like it was everything.

Chocolate chip cookies had nothing on Iris Daniels's mouth. If he could savor one thing for the rest of his life, it might be that.

It was the sweetest damn kiss he could remember.

And that made his head feel messed up. Made everything feel sideways.

He wasn't married. He knew he wasn't.

He pulled over, his heart pounding so hard that he felt sick.

There had been a time when he would have thought the kinds of emotions that he grappled with made him soft.

His dad had raised him to be a man's man, after all. Stoic in all things. Strong. Not emotional. Not led around by anything half so fickle as feelings.

But that was before grief had become his second skin. That was before he'd cried rivers over things he couldn't change. Tears hadn't felt weak, not then. They'd left him hollowed out. Left his throat raw and his body in deep, unending pain.

Tears like that weren't for the weak.

That was before he'd found out sorrow could make you sick and there was a kind of feeling that existed beyond that. A gray haze. Where you felt nothing. Couldn't see the end of it. Couldn't see your hand in front of your face.

You couldn't work your way out of it, drink your way out of it. Couldn't punch your way through it.

There was no being man enough.

No being enough at all.

And that was worse than the pain.

It was better to be retching your guts out on your front lawn, overcome by the dark, awful truth of your life, than it was to feel like a ghost, hovering over the world, unable to be in it or out of it.

He didn't worry about whether or not he was strong or weak. Not anymore.

He was alive. That counted for something.

He rested his head back on the truck seat. "Okay," he said in the nothing. "You know, the least you could do is haunt me a little bit. So that I know you're okay."

There was no answer. Nothing but the ticking sound of the remaining heat, popping and settling in his truck engine.

"I don't know how to live. I don't know how to do it. And why should I? Why should I when you don't get to? Why should I be happy or satisfied? Why should I enjoy anything?" He gritted his teeth, memories of his past life scrolling through his head.

"We weren't finished. You weren't. It's not fair."

He took a breath, hollow and shot through with knives. His life stretched on ahead of him and...

And this heat that burned inside of him reminded him too much of fire.

And fire killed. It destroyed.

It had burned down his whole life.

"I'm sorry," he said.

And as always, there was no answer.

No advice. No epiphanies.

No meaning.

He had no idea what to do with that. No idea what to do with the desire that still roared inside of him like the beast.

He steered back on the road and drove on.

Yeah, it had been easier to want nothing. To survive without feeling any sort of craving.

This… This was some kind of hell.

And all right, maybe a lot of it had to do with him. But he wasn't lying about protecting her.

She had no idea what she'd be getting if she took him on. And he was supposed to end the five-year bout of celibacy with her? She was inexperienced, that much was clear. She'd been shaking like a leaf when they kissed. Her touches had been tentative, even though she'd been enthusiastic. And he wouldn't have been able to be as soft as she was.

Iris was all softness and baked goods, and caring. And she'd been through enough. She'd been through enough without him dumping his shit onto her. And he had shit. She had no idea.

It was best if she didn't know him. It was best if she didn't get involved at all.

Keep telling yourself that.

It was true, though. Even if he couldn't shake that accusation she'd made. That he was only protecting himself.

When he pulled the truck up to the cabin, killed the engine and went inside, he stood in the middle of the living room for a long time.

No. He wasn't protecting himself. There was nothing

left to protect. That was the problem. He was nothing but a shell. Burned completely from the inside out.

Just like his house in the hills.

Just like everything he had ever loved.

And the kind of ash it had left behind was the kind nothing could grow out of. Desolate. Devastated.

There would never be anything there again.

And if there was one thing he could do, it would be to spare Iris from trying to grow something there, when he knew it was impossible.

He opened up his fridge, and the only thing in it was food she'd made.

He couldn't escape the woman.

He slammed the fridge shut, and went and sat on the edge of his bed. He was headed for another sleepless night. But it was no less than he deserved.

He didn't really care.

He didn't really care.

He repeated that, a few times over.

Until he could feel it.

Until he could believe it.

Surviving had been enough for the last five years. It would have to keep on being enough.

IRIS DIDN'T KNOW what to do the next day. So she set about finalizing her bakery plans.

She contacted the local print shop and had some basic flyers made. Because there might be endless reach for things on the internet, but if you wanted to let someone around Gold Valley know what was going on, then you had better put physical advertisement in brick-and-mortar spaces.

She decided on an open date, and commissioned a local artist to make her a sign.

So there, she had at least been productive in her day, after all.

The clouds hung low in the sky, and she felt that they might open up at any moment, drowning the land in rain, which seemed fitting in many ways, because she was feeling awful, and a sunny day would have been an assault.

She spent the night at the bakery.

In the apartment.

It still wasn't fully habitable. In that it didn't have internet, and she wasn't able to watch any movies or shows. She also didn't have any of her knitting with her, which was inconvenient.

But she hadn't wanted to go home. She hadn't wanted to face Rose, who probably would have been able to tell that something was wrong, and then would have questioned her on it.

She didn't want to have that discussion. She wanted to pretend that nothing at all had happened. Wanted to pretend that things were exactly as they had been.

That she was working with a man who was a little bit grumpy, and that was the end of the story. That she certainly hadn't put her hand on his shoulder, then pressed her mouth to his. That she hadn't taken a risk only to be rejected.

But thankfully, she had an endeavor to keep her busy anyway, so she had a reasonable excuse if anybody noticed that she was scarce. She wondered how they were feeding themselves. But it wasn't her problem. She had a life all her own, and so did they.

Her life might suck, currently, but she did have it.

"This is the problem. You weren't supposed to be doing

this, but then you did, and now you've gone and made it difficult. When it shouldn't have been."

She growled internally at herself. There was something else going on with him, and she knew it. She just didn't know what. But when he pulled away from her, it hadn't just been disinterest.

She'd been over it a hundred times. And he'd said as much. He'd said that he wanted her. He'd said he hadn't been with anyone in a long time.

Was that why he was isolating himself on the mountain? Had something happened? Had his heart been broken?

She wasn't going to find the answers inside of herself.

She could only ever get the answers from him. It was just sadly obvious that he didn't want to give them.

The next day, she was still upset about it, and the sky had broken open, what might have been a brief summer thunderstorm turning into a muggy, overcast day with a constant drizzle that occasionally changed to a downpour.

And, it was her day to bring food up to the cabin. He hadn't told her not to.

And if she didn't come, then he would know it was because she had been defeated by that kiss. That she had let it affect their arrangement. Which was what he said he was trying to prevent.

And she had way too much stubbornness to let that happen. She had her pride, kind of. Maybe not as much left as she would like, but she had done something to preserve what remained. She couldn't not come. He would think she was a coward. She would be a coward.

Devastating her dreams over a kiss.

She wouldn't be able to respect herself. So she gathered up food items—extra food items—because she was not going to allow this to impact her job with him at all. If anything, she was going to do it better. She was going to be even more competent. More amazing.

She drove up, determinedly not thinking about what it would be like to see him.

The rain was coming down in big, fat drops that hit her windshield, then radiated outward, creating intense pools over the glass, making it difficult to see. Her wipers could barely keep up.

But her anger fueled her on, and when she was at the top of the mountain, she realized she was barely conscious of having gotten herself there.

The weather was vile, so she was almost certain he would be inside the cabin. Not working on his mystery house that he would give no details on. Because why would he be out in this weather?

She walked up to the front porch, her arms full, and knocked with her elbow. But he didn't answer. She knocked again, and again, no answer. So she pulled the door open and went inside and found the cabin empty.

She tried not to feel concerned.

She shouldn't. If he wanted to be out in a thunderstorm that was his too bad. If he wanted to be out there getting soaking wet, there was nothing she could do.

And she shouldn't care.

She huffed around, straightening, and cleaning.

"How does one manage to make a mess in such a small space in such a short amount of time?" She kicked a pair of muddy boots to the side. "Why do you even have more than one pair of boots?" she yelled down at his shoes.

It didn't make sense for the man to have more than one pair of shoes. He only did one thing. He never went anywhere.

He was ridiculous.

Everything was tidied, and Griffin still hadn't appeared. She didn't want him to anyway.

She didn't.

Except, she found herself stepping out of the cabin, standing on the porch. She crossed her arms, and looked out at the weather. She hugged herself, rubbing her hands up and down, trying to ease her goose bumps. But she found it didn't work.

The drops were coming so thick and fast she couldn't see farther than a couple of feet. And then, through the sheet of water, she saw movement. A stark silhouette in the gloom. No jacket, a black hat, water pouring down over the brim. His head was lowered, at least as far as she could tell as he got closer, and when he looked up, he stopped.

"Hi," she said.

"Didn't figure you would still be here."

"But you knew I would be here."

"It's your day," he said.

"Yes, it is. I'll get out of your hair."

She started down the steps, and he reached out, his hand going to her arm. "Iris. There are things I don't like talking about. Things about my past. It just seems... It seems stupid to bring it up. Because I came here to get away from it. It's not the kind of thing you can get away from. But it's the kind of thing you can... Everyone knew. Everyone in my life knew. And every time they looked at me. It was all they thought of."

"What?"

He opened his mouth, then closed it. "I... I lost my wife. A few years back."

It took her a moment to process that, but when she did...

Grief pierced Iris's heart like an arrow. His wife.

His *wife*.

"Oh. Oh. I…"

"That's the problem. I've been there, and I've done all that. I've got nothing left. I've got nothing left in me at all. I haven't been with a woman since… And yeah, I want you. But I can't care about anyone. There's a reason I'm here. There's a reason that I'm not part of the rest of the world."

"I don't… I don't know what to say." She took a step closer to him, and the rain was pouring down on her now too.

"No one ever does."

She nodded slowly. "I know that. I know how foolish people can be when it comes to grief. How they can hurt you without trying. Without realizing. They turn away from you because it's too hard." She put her hand on his face, his skin cool on the surface from the rainwater, but warm underneath. "I'm sorry."

His pain was naked. Raw. She understood why people had looked away from her all those times, all those years ago. But she had lived in a house of grief, of pain. She knew what it meant. She knew what it was. And she knew how isolating it could be. He didn't share this with anyone else. Thus he was in a house by himself. Cut off completely from any potential support.

She wanted to give him a lifeline. The kind that no one else had, at least, so it seemed. She wanted to… She wanted to do something. She wanted to fix it, but she knew that was impossible.

Because these were the kinds of things you didn't fix.

They were wounds. And they stayed there. You could walk around with them, just fine. But nobody could ever take the loss away.

He'd been in *love*. And he had lost that.

He was just so powerful, so stoic and imposing. So hard,

that the idea the world would have dealt him such a cruel blow seemed especially wrong. She didn't know why. Why it seemed worse because he was larger-than-life. Why it seemed particularly cruel.

"I'm just sorry," she said.

Because there was nothing more to say. She was sorry. Or rather, she was filled with sorrow. For him. For the pain he'd been through, the pain he was still going through.

She'd known. Looking around this cabin she'd seen a life scarred by pain.

"I don't need pity."

"Sure you do. Everybody could use a little bit of pity." The rain nearly drowned out her voice.

But she spoke anyway. "Do you know what the hardest thing was? When we lost our parents." She swallowed hard. "It was when everybody else forgot. But *we* hadn't. Other people felt bad for us. And their lives changed for a while. But ours changed forever. There was no fixing it. There was no...reclaiming it. We had to take the pieces of what we had left and move forward. For a while, the whole community felt affected by the tragedy. But in the end, people have to go on with their lives. But when you're the one that lost, you can't. Not in the same way. Because you never forget. The only time they remember is when they see you. Somehow, impossibly, you need to make a life that's about more than that. And it's this terrible two-edged sword. People don't just think of you. And when they do, they only think of loss. And you think of it every day. And then feel sorry when some days you don't."

He said nothing for a moment, the rain pounding on the ground, filling the silence. "I think about it every day."

She looked around. At this place, removed from the rest of the world. Of course he thought about it every day. This was his monastery of pain. Designed, in many ways, to be a constant reminder of what he'd lost, free of any distractions or comforts.

Free of food that he enjoyed. Free of pleasure. Of any kind.

She could understand that. She had felt like perhaps they were entirely different people. That he was a man who'd lived an experience entirely different from hers. That seducing him was insane because he was clearly beautiful and experienced in ways that she wasn't.

And that may be true.

He'd been *married*, after all.

Had loved someone enough to vow to be with them for the rest of his life.

For the rest of hers.

But at the base of it, down deep at their hearts, they weren't different.

They were both scarred. Devastated by the loss that they'd endured. Parents... It was a terrible thing to lose your parents. Always. More terrible still when you were children and there were so many years, so much more time that you should have had. And particularly cutting because childhood was supposed to be magical. A time that was sacred, in some regards.

And theirs hadn't been. It had been dark. And the kind of monsters that haunted other people's closets haunted their regular, daily lives, great and toothy and visible. Those things that other kids saw in their deepest, darkest fears, they had lived.

But falling in love, and losing that person, that must be such a deep cut. People expected to have to lose parents eventually. And how to find a way to live without them. With a husband or wife it was different. One of you would lose the other eventually, but if everything went well... You shouldn't have years and years of figuring out how to live without the other. And he did.

But he was too beautiful. Too compelling to be up here forever. To cut himself off from every good thing. She just wished that there was some way she could... She just wished...

She angled her head, lifted up on her toes and kissed him.

It was absolutely the most inappropriate thing to do to a man who had just said he thought about his wife every day. That he lived with the pain of her loss constantly.

It was wrong, but he seemed to accept it. Sipped the water from her lips and pulled her in close. He held her, like they might both break if he released her. Held her like she mattered. And she... She poured everything into the kiss. All of her sympathy, all of her sorrow. Sorrow that she had for him, but for herself as well. She felt absolutely helpless to do anything to fix this. To fix him.

And she wanted to.

Oh, what she wouldn't give to be able to take them both back to a place where they were new.

Maybe if her parents hadn't died she would be a normal thirty-one-year-old woman. She would have had lovers, maybe a few of them. She would be confident in herself and in her body. She would be equal to the task of having him.

And maybe he would be charming. Easy.

Maybe they could flirt. Maybe they could go on a date.

Instead, they were sharing a fractured kiss in the rain. And she felt like they were drowning.

Sinking into an endless well of need that she wasn't sure they would ever escape.

Her clothes were sticking to her body, and so were his.

She pushed at the hem of his shirt, and he gripped the end of it, pulling it up over his head and taking his cowboy hat with it. His skin was slick and hard, and he held her flush against his chest. Her hands were pinned there, and she could feel his heartbeat raging against her palms.

This was insanity.

Or maybe it was the first real thing either of them had done for a long time.

Because there was no forethought here. No decision to seduce. No decision to turn away. It was out of their hands. Swept along by the raindrops that fell from the sky. At the mercy of this torrent of desire rushing through them.

But wasn't it better than being at the mercy of fear? The mercy of grief?

They both knew how that went. They both knew pain. Why couldn't they know *this*?

His hands slid down her back, and he let them wander down, all the way to her bottom. He cupped her, then lifted her up off the ground, urging her legs around his waist as he held her there in the rain, one hand cradling the back of her head as he took the kiss deeper. Harder.

She moaned into his mouth, letting everything they talked about wash away. Letting this cleanse them. For in this moment, maybe they were new. Maybe they were fresh creatures that had never known anything but this. This overwhelming sense that they needed each other more than they needed their next breath.

This was better.

Better than deciding to be with him, with all her nerves and insecurities jangling through her.

This was more than just wanting an experience. This was real.

They were real.

They were alive.

A hysterical bubble of laughter welled up in her chest, but he swallowed it with a voracious kiss.

She had *lived*.

To have this moment. With this man.

And all those years it had been so easy to hide away. To protect herself from loss, to protect herself from pain. But this was what life was for. To kiss a man in the rain, and to revel in it. And everything they could be. Whatever happened after this, it didn't matter. Because now was perfect.

She was sorry, so sorry about the journey he'd had to go on to get here.

But he was her reward.

This felt inevitable, and right, and like it was what she'd waited for.

He carried her up the steps, her legs still wrapped around his waist, and pushed open the door. They all but stumbled inside. He stripped her wet T-shirt up over her head so that she was only wearing her bra. She was frantic to see more of him. To touch him everywhere. And so she did. Moved her hands over that broad, well-muscled chest, down his stomach.

Watched as drops of water rolled between his perfectly outlined ab muscles.

Desire swept through her like a wind. Stole the air right out of her lungs. Carried it off somewhere. And she didn't even care.

Kissing her still, he backed her toward the bed, and lowered her down, his body slick over the top of hers. When he undid the snap on her jeans, her breath caught. But he lowered the zipper slowly, and then worked the denim down her damp legs as best he could. He was kissing her still, like a man possessed. Desperate. She was sure she must look like a drowned rat, but she never felt more beautiful. Because he was beautiful. And he wanted her. In this moment, he wanted her.

With trembling fingers, she undid the button on his jeans, dragged the zipper down, but she was too clumsy to divest him of the damp denim. She cursed, which was something she almost never did.

"I got it," he said, his words slurred. He pushed his jeans and his underwear down, kicked his boots off along with them, and his socks. He was naked.

But he pulled her back up against his body so quickly she barely had the chance to see. But she could feel him. Hard and bare and hot pressed against her hip.

He reached around her back and unclipped her bra, tugging it off and exposing her. His hands were rough as he palmed her sensitive flesh. Her breasts were impossibly needy for his attention. And in another set of circumstances she might have been embarrassed. But not with him. Not now. There was no embarrassment at all. Nothing but a deep, intense desire. To give pleasure. To receive it.

For they were held in thrall by this equally, and she couldn't be embarrassed about that.

He kissed her neck, her collarbone, drew one nipple deep into his mouth, and she gasped.

Her mind was blank of everything. Potential expectation, everything she'd ever known about herself.

She wasn't her past. And there wasn't a future.

There was just this.

Just this brilliant, white-hot need.

And it was perfect. He pushed his hands down beneath the waistband of her panties, sliding fingers through her slick flesh. She was shocked by the white-hot feel of pleasure there. How it burned.

Gloriously.

She found herself arching her hips in time with the rhythm of his hands, her need escalating inside of her with each glorious stroke. He pushed one finger inside of her and she gasped at the unfamiliar sensation. At the invasion. She knew there would be more. Bigger.

She could feel that part of him still against her. And she shivered. Now wasn't the time for nerves. She didn't want fear to have any part of this.

She arched her hips against him, and he moved his thumb over that sensitive bundle of nerves at the apex of her thighs. And pleasure broke over her like a wave. Sending her soaring. She was sobbing with desire. She had never felt anything like this. It was beyond. She could scarcely breathe. Then he wrenched her panties down her legs, a wild look in his eye.

She realized what they were missing.

"I'm on the pill," she said.

"I…"

"I haven't…"

He nodded, as if he understood what she was trying to say. But she was pretty sure he didn't.

Instead, he positioned himself between her legs, nudging the untried entrance of her body, before thrusting into her completely. She gasped, the pain a lot more intense than she had imagined.

And then he started to move. And this was just different than she thought it would be. Raw. Physical. Not soft and romantic with a gauzy veil drawn over it. Something that connected her. To him, his breathing and her own. The beating of their hearts. The bed. The room.

It was everything. Everything real and terrifying that she had never known and always avoided.

And then as she began to ascend the peak she had the thought that this was what she'd been looking for. Something sharp and hard that might match that intense violent grief she had experienced all those years ago. That might transcend it.

But she should have known that it wouldn't be a sensation of undiluted joy. Of something purely good.

It wasn't a piece of cotton candy. Sweet and one-dimensional. Fluffy and easily dissolved.

It was sweet and bitter.

There was a darkness here that called to the darkness in her. To the pain that she had experienced. And it was richer for it. She knew that it was. For all the hurtful things they'd endured.

But there, in the midst of the storm, a shaft of light broke through. And she knew that it was brighter for all the darkness around it. That the peak of pleasure would be more exhilarating because of where they had been.

She didn't *need* cotton candy.

That was easy. For people who knew easy and needed easy.

She was stronger than that.

This was for her.

She needed it strong. Strong enough to block out the pain.

And this was.

More than. It made her feel like her chest was going to break apart. Like the light in need in her soul was expanding beyond that which she could accommodate. But she welcomed it. Because this was how you found a new way forward. It was a fight. She knew that.

It was why she had stayed where she was for so long.

Because she had sensed that. That there was no way she could be new without first going through a hurricane.

And he was a hurricane. A storm that moved through her like a devastating monsoon.

And she clung to him. Like he was the anchor.

The anchor and the stormy sea, all at once. The reason she was being tossed. The reason she was held secure.

The source of her danger and her delight.

His movements became hard, fractured, along with his breathing. And pleasure overtook her thoughts. Pleasure overtook everything. She clung to him as her climax grabbed her and pulled her under, a current she couldn't fight, even if she wanted to.

And then he broke too, shivered and shook as he took his own pleasure on the heels of hers, and when he collapsed against her, sweat slicked and breathing hard, she realized that he had been in the middle of the same storm.

Not a force larger than nature, but a man held captive by it the same as she had been.

They were slick with rain and sweat and breathing hard. And she clung to him. Because she was afraid he would let go if she didn't. Because she was afraid that he would throw her out. Because she wanted to lie there for a while, rocked by the experience between them. By the change that had just occurred. And it was a change.

She was changed.

Made new from the inside out somehow, and she didn't know how she was supposed to move forward. She just wanted to stay.

He didn't seem in a rush either. Instead, he turned over, his arm heavy over the top of her.

And it took her a moment to realize he had fallen asleep.

She looked at him, at the lines on his face.

He didn't look restful, even asleep. The lines on his forehead were still creased, his brows still drawn together.

A man whose heaviest weights didn't lift from him even when he had passed out of consciousness.

It made her heart hurt. To know that his was a burden that didn't lift even then.

She could remember that. Being in the thick of grief and having nightmares chase after you as you tried to find some peace. She lay there on her back, staring up at the ceiling. The light was gray. It wasn't night yet.

But she didn't want to get up. She'd had sex for the first time.

And she had to face the possibility that it was with a man who had been thinking about someone else.

That made her ache. He had told her about his wife, and then they had kissed. She knew that he hadn't been with anyone since. That he had turned her away the first time, likely because…

Of course he was still in love with his wife.

He should be. It was… Understandable and reasonable. It was okay.

She tried to breathe, and found that it was far too shallow. Found that it was making her dizzy.

She slowed down, deliberately.

Of course it hurt her to imagine that he had thought of someone else.

But wasn't she using him to work out her own issues? To help move her on in her quest for finding that new stage of her life?

She hadn't thought of any of that when they'd come together, of course. And she didn't think he'd been thinking anything either.

No. Whatever had happened, it wasn't manipulative.

Or deliberate. They'd both been lost in feeling. She was confident in that.

But if for him it had been a moment to recapture something he'd lost, and if for her it was to find that new piece of herself, that wasn't wrong and wasn't less.

And it didn't mean she didn't matter at all. At least, that's what she would cling to now.

Finally, she dozed, and when she woke up it was dark. And she needed a bathroom.

She had deliberately not stayed up here long enough to need to deal with that.

She turned over onto her stomach, wiggling against his hard body. He was hot like a furnace, and still naked. A thrill of erotic desire shot through her, and she frowned deeply at herself.

She rolled over onto her back, feeling aggrieved.

"What is it?" His voice surprised her in the darkness.

"I… Bathroom."

"I'll get a flashlight."

"Oh no," she said, her cheeks heating up.

"I'm not having you walk out there in the dark by yourself. You don't even know where it is."

"But I might die," she said.

"Of?"

"Embarrassment."

"I'm not really sure how you could die of embarrassment over me walking you to an outhouse after what we just did."

"Then you haven't known very many women."

He chuckled. "I have, actually."

"I don't want to hear about it," she said, feeling grumpy.

"Get your shoes and a blanket," he said.

She felt petulant and annoyed. "I don't want to."

"Iris," he said, turning over to face her, pressing his

thumb against her chin. She didn't know how he'd found it so unerringly in the darkness.

And it was dark in here. There was no light pollution at all. "Do as you're told."

She huffed. He got out of bed, and found a flashlight quickly in the darkness, shining the beam over to the door by her shoes. The rest of her clothes were littered about.

"Just my shoes?"

"Yes," he said.

She angrily got out of bed, and he shone the flashlight on her with no regard for her modesty at all. It was different to be naked in front of him now. When she had to pee, and not when they were in the middle of having sex.

But she got her shoes, and then grabbed the blanket from the bed and swaddled herself in it. For his part, he had pulled on his jeans and a pair of boots. But nothing more. He still had the beam of the flashlight pointed on her, but there was a bit of residual glow coming from the back of it, illuminating his stomach and chest, the hollows and planes of his face.

"Scamper along," he said.

"I don't scamper," she muttered, heading for the door. The light followed her.

"You do."

"I don't. I'm too dignified to scamper. Though, if we take any longer, I am going to have to ramp it up to a *scurry* to make it to the outhouse."

"God forbid," he said.

Following the path he let the light blaze, they ambled down the trail to a very simple wooden building. He handed the light to her.

"Don't drop it in."

"I'm not going to drop it." She gathered the folds of

the blanket, and the flashlight, and went into the rustic building. She heard his footsteps move away, and she was grateful.

Wrangling both blanket and light, she managed to take care of the necessities, and with great relief stumbled back outside.

And he was there.

They walked in silence, heading back to the cabin.

When they got back inside, she went to the bed, still wrapped in the blanket. He relieved her of the flashlight and went over to the fireplace. He started to light one, the glow of the flame casting orange ambient light all around them. Warmth quickly beginning to fill the space.

"You hungry?"

"A little," she admitted, curling herself deeper into a ball at the center of the bed.

"Well, thankfully I'm well stocked with food."

"Imagine that."

"I'll get us some."

"Thank you," she said, suddenly way too tired to continue to be obstinate. It had been a fine shield for a little while. And had made her feel not quite so vulnerable. But now the weight of holding it up was just making her cranky. He got a cheese tray out of the icebox, said nothing as he began to slice a loaf of bread with the flashlight nearby, then brought two beers and the bread and cheese back to the bed.

"I don't really drink beer," she said, wrinkling her nose. But she took the bottle anyway.

He cleared his throat. "We going to talk about this?"

"What?" But she felt prickly, and afraid that she knew what he was going to ask.

"You."

"Me?"

He sighed, heavily. "Have you never been with anyone before, Iris?" he asked, his voice grave.

She could feel her face heat. "Oh."

She took a piece of cheese off the plate, stacked it on some bread. Took a bite. Chewed very slowly.

"Iris..."

Really no point lying. "No. I haven't been."

"I was afraid of that."

"You don't have to be afraid of anything. I lost my parents. I raised my sisters. That's not normal. Sex is normal. I missed a whole lot of normal because I was busy trying to be an adult when I was still just a kid. I skipped a lot of steps. I'm trying to fix that. You don't need to worry about me. I'm really, genuinely fine."

"I feel like you're just starting out. And I'm not. You deserve better than that. Better than me."

"Why? I don't see myself that way. I haven't been innocent for a long time. Sex isn't about... Innocence. You know what takes your innocence? Finding out that nothing in the world is all that safe. That your parents, who take care of you, who are supposed to be the strongest people, were just human. And that you were never safe. Not ever. Not a single day of your life. And then you have to figure out how to walk through the world knowing that. Somehow. It's the worst thing. The worst. Suddenly, everything in the world looks dangerous. And it's taken me all this time to figure out how to be brave again."

"But there are things you don't have. Things you haven't had and haven't done. I do understand, Iris. I do. But there... The only thing I think that might be worse than what you went through, is being the one that failed to protect the people you were supposed to."

"I'm sure that must be..."

"You don't understand." Everything seemed to stop for a moment. Somehow, the air went completely still, and neither of them dared draw a breath in that space of time. There wasn't even the sound of a critter rustling anywhere. Not a cricket. As if time itself had stopped to listen to Griffin Chance. "I couldn't protect them. I didn't. I didn't protect my wife and my baby girl, Iris. You don't come back from that."

CHAPTER THIRTEEN

HE'D SAID IT.

And there was no going back.

He'd said it, and now his whole mind was full of flames.

Images of that night that he worked so hard to never, ever see.

But they came to him anyway. Awake or asleep. And pretty much the only time he could escape was when he was wielding a hammer, the motion and the sound of the metal hitting nails doing something to drive all thought out of his head.

And he often thought that if he could…if he could just *never* think. If he could be like an animal and move through life focusing on survival. Maybe, maybe it would be endurable.

But he couldn't.

Because no matter how deep he tried to go back into nature. Back to nothing, he was still a man.

A fact well proven tonight.

Dammit but he was weak.

He had wanted her. So much. And then she'd been standing there, all wet and glorious, looking at him like he might have answers.

She was about to be very disappointed. Because he didn't have an answer. Not a single one. To anything.

"I hate it," he said.

He didn't say what, because it was too many things. Maybe everything.

No, not everything. Not her.

She said nothing.

She didn't press him to continue. Didn't ask him to clarify. And for that he was grateful.

She just sat there. Still and steady and Iris.

This strange creature that had come into his life when he hadn't wanted her to, hadn't asked her to. And there she was. Holding a plate of cookies and demanding that he let parts of himself that had been asleep for a long time rejoin the world.

And so… Maybe she did deserve his story.

He'd never told anyone before.

Everyone he knew…they just *knew*.

It had been in the news.

And no one had ever made him talk about it. In fact, they had gone out of their way to never talk about it. There had been a whole lot of *sorry*. And then, other than his parents and Mallory, a push to try and bring him back into the real world.

As they called it.

But no. The real world for him was gray. That space where Mel and Emma didn't exist anymore.

"I worked in the city and sometimes I worked late," he said.

He was surprised how flat the words were. But there was something about that that made them easier to get out. Because there were whole boulders lodged in his chest, in his throat, and he didn't know how he was supposed to speak around them. Again, he was met with her silence, and he was grateful for it. He knew it didn't mean she wasn't listening. Didn't mean she didn't want him to speak. It just meant she was going to let him do it at his own pace.

He didn't know what that pace was.

The story of how his life had fallen apart could actually be distilled into two lines. Which seemed wrong. But taking a long time to tell it didn't feel right either.

It hit him then that it would just always feel wrong. Always.

He would never be able to reconcile that moment in time. Would never be able to make it fit. Would never be able to… Put it in a place. It just was.

And it was wrong.

"I came home and the house was on fire," he said, battling against the images in his mind. He was trying not to relive it. But it was damn near impossible.

To not see the flames glowing like hell as he had driven up his driveway. And he'd seen the lights, and he'd been sure… He'd been sure that they were out. That they had to be. Because it was this five million dollar *damn* house with every safety system known to man, and alarms that were supposed to go off and everything designed to have easy exits.

Everything had been thought of.

And he would never know for sure what had happened.

They'd told him it was smoke inhalation. Which was the kindest of scenarios, he knew.

And he was always afraid they were lying to him.

But that meant somehow there had been smoke and no alarms had gone off in time. But he couldn't figure that out either. Nothing made sense. That was the bottom line. And they could investigate it and comb over the debris that was left of his life and try to give him answers, but none of the answers would ever be good enough.

None of them would change the outcome.

"I tried to go into the house. It took three people to stop me. When I realized they weren't out there..." It was all around him, even now. Like he was there. "You know how ash flies through the air. It's like pieces of a broken world. And that's what it felt like to me."

He was lost right then. In that moment when he'd been on the ground, on his knees, watching that ash float through the night sky. "Like it was my life broken in pieces. My life...burned to nothing. It *was*. It wasn't just *like that*. It was."

He could see himself in the memory. Screaming like a wounded animal, cut from trying to get through the glass. He could even see...he'd hit one of the firefighters. Punched him. The man who'd been holding him back. He hadn't decided to do that, not in the moment. It was just... He'd been a man possessed of a supernatural level of rage and strength, wanting to fight the flames that had consumed his world.

And there just... Hadn't been anything he could do.

He had been a rich man. An important man. A man with all this supposed power and influence the world required. And he'd realized that night that it meant nothing. Nothing at all.

He was less than nothing.

Because he couldn't put out a blaze with his money and his influence. He couldn't turn back time. He hadn't even been able to throw himself into the fire, and God knew he'd tried.

He'd been stopped even then.

Five years, and it didn't make sense. It didn't make it easier to breathe around.

"Everything was gone," he said, rough. "Just like that. Everything."

She still didn't speak. Instead, she moved toward him, put her hand over his.

"I stayed," he said. "I lived at an apartment near my office building. I didn't sell the property the house was on. It just didn't seem... I didn't want anyone else to have it. Because it was a memorial. But I did never want to go there either. And people wanted me to get back to normal. Do who I was... I think even before I married Mel. You know, there were guys I've known since college, and they figured I was single again." He laughed, and it sounded so bitter even to his own ears. "Isn't that the stupidest damn thing? Like... Like I would just go back to who I was before. Like I just wasn't a husband or father anymore. Like I'd never been those things. I'm not, is the thing. I get that. I can't hold my daughter. I can't take care of her. I don't have school drop-off and pickup, or artwork on my fridge. I don't have a wedding ring, or an anniversary to remember. I'm not that. But I can never be the man I was."

She pressed herself against his back, her bare breasts flush against him. And she wrapped her arms around his waist. He felt her cheek pushed up against his shoulder blade. Felt wetness there.

She was crying. For him. He'd made her cry, and he truly felt bad about that. Or maybe just felt bad.

"Mel loved horses," he said. "That's something we both enjoyed. I run an equine facility in the Bay Area. For at risk kids. And there's another program for sick kids. It just... It seems like the thing to do? But basically it's the only thing I need money for. Except the house."

She didn't ask any questions. So he just kept talking. "We drove up here before Emma was born. Mel fell in love with it. She wanted to get out of San Francisco. She didn't like it anymore. And we had the money and we knew I could work remotely. I could fly to San Francisco if I needed to for meetings and things like that. But she wanted a different life. Slower. And we bought this place. We spent months working on the house. The design. But I had a few things to wrap up down there. So we weren't going to start building just yet. And then it was too late. It was just too late. But…"

He didn't finish, because he didn't need to, and he knew it. He knew that Iris understood. That he had to build Mel's house. Because it was the last thing she'd wanted. Because he couldn't go back and rescue her from that house that had burned down around her.

"I've been over and over that night," he said. "And I wish I had been there. So that I could've saved them. Or…"

"No," she said. It was the first time she'd spoken. "Not so that you could die."

"I wished it more times than I can tell you. That if I couldn't have saved them I could have just gone with them. But you don't get to make those choices. You don't get to re-arrange the world like that. I mean sure, I could kill myself."

That sounded awful, but there was no way around the truth of it. No pretending it hadn't crossed his mind.

He kept on talking. "I could have." She didn't argue this time. Not even an indrawn breath. "But that… I really couldn't do it. Because… I'm alive. Aren't I? They aren't. What a… What a shitty response it would've been to take my own life. No. I couldn't do that. Even when it was the worst. I had to keep breathing."

She still didn't say anything. And he thought back to their earlier exchange. Before they'd made love.

Before, when they'd been standing out in the rain. When

they had talked about her parents. About how there were no words. And how people tried anyway. And usually failed.

But what they did was pull away. And so her, pressed against him, just being with him in the grief, he realized was the kind of gift no one else had ever offered.

Everyone in his family wanted to fix him. His friends wanted him to be fixed so that they could be more comfortable.

But she was just sitting with him. And all this broken discomfort.

His story was an awful one. In part because it was senseless. You couldn't find the meaning in the death of a young woman. In the death of a child. You couldn't lay blame, not when the house had every safety system in place. You could do nothing but sit with the *senselessness* of it. And that, he had a feeling, bothered people most of all.

That this wasn't something he could make sense of, box up and stick on the shelf of past wounds.

It was a cloak laid over the top of him that he had to figure out how to wear. Like a new skin that he couldn't shed. And in many ways didn't want to. Because how did you let go of something you *needed* to remember?

"Would you like to talk about them?" The question was spoken softly.

"What?"

"Would you like to talk about them? That was the hardest thing. For me. Is that sometimes I wanted to just talk about the good things about my parents, and not the tragedy of losing them. I wanted to be able to have good memories, and I didn't know how. And people… They wouldn't let me. They were sad and my sadness made them sadder. I imagine that's been even worse for you. So do you want to tell me about them?"

He didn't talk about them. Ever. Because it… It hurt too much. Except… Suddenly he did. He wanted someone else to know. The good things.

And it didn't make any sense at all. That he should talk to this woman he just slept with about his wife. It was strange, though, because after five years he wasn't confused about whether or not he'd been released from his marriage vows.

He was all too aware of it, every day.

That he wasn't a husband. Not in a practical way.

That was where the grief came in. That he couldn't give love to Mel or Emma in the way that he once had. Couldn't be those things to them he'd once been. He was just a man who *remembered* those things.

"I met Mel ten years ago. At a work function. Her dad was CFO of a company I did business with. And… It was *not* love at first sight. Not for her. But we ended up talking and decided to see each other again. And then again. We dated for longer than she'd have liked before we moved in together. Then I waited too long to ask her to marry me."

The thought made him smile. Now. They'd fought about it a lot back then. "We got married seven years ago. And Emma… We had Emma about a year later." He stopped for a long moment, grief a boulder that he couldn't shift. This was too heavy. But he could see her. Chubby and blonde and dimpled, and he wanted Iris to know. "She was the cutest baby that you've ever seen. And I've never liked babies. But… I knew the minute that I saw her that I would die for her." He lowered his head. "I would have. I would have, Iris. And I didn't get to. That is failure that I cannot get out from underneath. To have loved someone so much… You know, people say that. That you'd run into a burning building for someone. I would have and I was too late. If I could've saved her… If I could've saved Mel…"

A sob shook Iris's frame. "I'm so sorry. I'm so sorry." She said it over and over again, and her jagged sobs covered up any emotion of his own. And he was damn grateful. To share his feelings and have some privacy in them as well.

Then he gathered Iris close, and laid them both down on the bed. And he closed his eyes, clinging to her. Committing to memory her softness. Her face. Making sure that as sleep began to drag him back down, it was Iris that he saw in his mind.

He wanted her, not nightmares. Her, and not memories that brought him straight down into hell.

He was only sorry that in sharing with her, he had certainly given her a few of his nightmares as her own.

CHAPTER FOURTEEN

WHEN IRIS WOKE the next morning, she was drained, both physically and emotionally. Griffin had turned to her two more times in the night. And she had opened herself to him willingly.

This morning, she felt tangled in him. Because of what they had done with their bodies. Because of the things he had told her.

She had known that he was a man in pain, but she had no idea. Not really. He'd lost everything.

Everything.

The two people he loved most in the world, his sense of himself as a man. Any sense of control that he had in the whole world. And she could relate to it. To pieces of it. But it hadn't been her job to protect her parents, and as much as she had grieved them, she hadn't suffered the kind of regret that she knew he did. The fear that he had failed them so profoundly. She knew that he carried that in a deep and real way.

But she didn't know where that left them. And she didn't know if it was even fair to try and figure out where she fit in the equation.

Of all the things to have entangled herself in.

Pansy had talked about having a fling.

It had been pretty obvious since she'd met him that he was a man grappling with something heavy, something intense. And she'd told herself before she ever set out to seduce him that there was no way she could get too emotionally involved.

But now she felt…even more convinced of that.

She could help him. She'd been through grief. It might not be the same as his, but she knew what it was like. To experience loss. To experience the way people treated you as a result of that loss.

But she wanted a new life. And this was too perilously close to what she was trying to escape.

It would be fine. She just had to…not fall for him. If she fell in love with him she would want him to love her. And he loved his wife.

Her stomach went tight.

A lifetime of trying to live up to someone else. Of being second. Trying to earn first place…

She just couldn't.

She extricated herself from his hold, slipped her clothes back on and walked herself over to the outhouse. And on the walk back, tried to make some decisions.

Mostly, she thought she might need a little bit of distance. Because she was overwhelmed. Not just with his revelations, but with the one she was having about herself.

And she didn't quite know how to fit all those pieces together.

Because she wanted to… She wanted to be there for him, but she needed to figure out how to be there for herself too. Because aside from all of the sharp and painful things she had learned about him last night, she'd had sex for the first time.

She stopped right there, in the middle of the woods, feeling awed by that realization.

She was finally not a thirty-one-year-old virgin.

That seemed revelatory. More than a little bit incredible. But somehow, she had managed to attach herself to the most complicated man in the general area. Maybe Rose was right. Maybe she would have been better off with khakis. Khakis and water filtration, and no deep, emotional scarring that tested her own.

Maybe that was why some people opted for easy partners.

He's not your partner. Settle down. He's a guy that you slept with. And he couldn't have made it more clear that he's not ready for more.

It was true. He'd tried to warn her off, in basically every way, and she hadn't listened. Because she had been so certain that she knew, absolutely, what she was doing and what she wanted.

And on the one hand, she had. On the one hand, it had been amazing. On the other hand... Complicated. Painful.

She paused in front of the cabin door. She just didn't quite know what she was going to get, not with Griffin. Not really ever. But there was no turning coward now. The thing was, she had done the brave thing, and so had he. Now there was just the fallout. And she wondered what the fallout would be. If he would regret telling her. If he would regret touching her. Well, she'd been ripping the Band-Aid off a lot the last couple of weeks. Might as well do it again.

She pushed the cabin door open, and saw that Griffin was already up. He was at the woodstove, wearing only jeans, cooking something in a skillet. Bacon.

"I... Didn't know you cooked."

"Of course I cook. I mean, minimally, but bacon is not beyond my reach."

She stood there, awkward. "Good morning," she said.

"Morning," he said.

"I don't really know what the protocol is for this. I mean, virgin. Until recently."

He shook his head. "I have no idea. But there's bacon. So I figure, we can have some of that."

"Yeah. That sounds like a plan." In the absence of clarity, she would take bacon. Well, truth be told, she rationalized to herself as she watched Griffin, muscular and compelling, standing at that woodstove and cooking. As she watched his skin, his muscles, his movements. She did have some clarity. She didn't regret last night. Not even a little bit. She had wanted it, and she had wanted him. And what had happened had been more than she'd bargained for, sure. But if she was truly honest with herself...

She had known. She had known that he was a man with unspeakable pain at his core. He hadn't been dishonest about that, not in any of their interactions. He practically bled grief. He had also been a brilliant, desperate lover, who had woven fantasies around her that felt like they'd always been there. He created desires and satisfied them just as quickly. And standing there even now, she was filled with the strangest sense of satisfaction combined with a hollow, aching need for more.

What was clear was that she cared about him. Was that she had enjoyed last night. Was that his body matched hers in a very specific way.

What was clear was that she wanted to be standing here, watching him cooking bacon. She wanted it more than anything in the world.

"It's so unusual that someone cooked breakfast for me."

And some of that was that she tended to jump in and help, even if breakfast was already going by the time she got into the kitchen. But she wasn't going to. Not now. Instead, she took herself to his bed and curled up at the center of the mattress, waiting for him to finish. And when he did, there was stove top coffee, eggs and bacon. And he brought them to her.

"There's no call for you to wear clothes while you're inside," he said.

"I'm not sure about eating naked."

A smile lit his face up, and she realized that she had never seen that. Not really. It seemed to surprise him as much as it surprised her. "Why does eating make it a problem?"

"It just is," she said. "I mean, the risk of bacon grease burns alone…"

"I would never let that happen."

"You can't protect me."

The words hovered between them, and suddenly felt leaden.

He cleared his throat. "I mean, suit yourself."

"You still have your jeans on."

"What's good for the goose," he said. "If you're wearing clothes, so am I."

She weighed that, but lay out on her stomach, still fully clothed, holding a piece of bacon. It was the strangest thing, but she felt younger. And it wasn't that she felt light or unburdened, because there had been some pretty hefty weight shared last night. It was just that her world felt freer. Her world felt like it was this room. This moment.

"What are your plans for the day?"

"Well," she said slowly. "There are things I could do back at the apartment. I need to talk to my brother about the fact that I'm moving out. I basically need to tie up some loose ends at the bakery. But I don't think I need to do any of that today."

"Really?"

"No. I think… I think that I would rather stay here. And I think that we should just forget everything."

"That's what I've been trying to do for the last few years."

"But you've been alone. Today you won't be."

CHAPTER FIFTEEN

THAT WAS HOW Griffin Chance found himself sitting by a campfire down at the river, Iris cooking trout in a pan, which she had helped catch quite handily. She was wearing a combination of the outfit that she had come in yesterday, and one of his shirts, which was overly large on her, the flannel rolled up at her wrists so that it didn't totally cover her hands. Her dark hair was a mess, loose and wild around her face, and her cheeks were red, maybe from the sun, or just from living. She was just so alive. And he sat there, and wondered, really deeply wondered, how he had ever thought her plain, because she wasn't. She was a deep, still sort of beauty like the mountains. Like the water. The trees and the sky. The kind that settled over your skin, and became what grounded you. That rooted you to the earth.

So intrinsic to the makeup of the world that some days it was easy to look at it and not fully realize. But when you did, when you stopped and took it all in, it could still your breath. The kind of beauty that a man couldn't possibly take in all at once.

She knew. She knew his story. The strangest damn thing. And she was there with him still. Smiling.

But he wasn't going to think about it. Because she'd said... To just pretend the rest of the world didn't exist. And to be with her. So he was.

It was a gift. This sliver of time.

And he didn't want to think of what lay beyond it. But for now he wasn't going to.

"Fish is almost done," she said. She shook the pan, and a lock of hair fell into her face, at the same time as the shoulder on his shirt fell. It didn't expose any bare skin or anything like that, but there was something about seeing Iris Daniels so undone that unmade something inside of him too.

"Do you go fishing a lot?" he asked, when she was settled next to him, picking pieces of fish out of the pan with her fingers.

"Not really. We used to. Me and my dad."

"Tell me about your dad."

"He was the chief of police in town. And he was… I thought he was the strongest and best man in the entire world. A close second was my uncle Todd. When it was just me and my older brother, Ryder, and my cousins Colt and Jake, we'd go fishing with them on the weekends. They were just very good men. And my mom… We would come home with fish, and she would cook it, and she always made it taste amazing. I remember telling her one time that I didn't like trout because of all the bones. She picked every single one out. Tried to make it into something that I would enjoy. She was just like that. She took care of us. And things got a lot busier when the younger kids came and it changed, like families do. But yeah… My dad. You know, my sister Pansy, she became the first female chief of police in town. That's all she ever wanted. Was to make our dad proud."

"What about you?"

"I wanted to take care of everybody. It's such a funny thing, but I figured if I couldn't be taken care of, then maybe… Making a space where all that care still was…

Building that same kind of feeling, that sense of home that my mom did, that maybe it would be enough. That maybe it could go some way in healing some of the hurt. And it did. I mean, it really did. Until I realized that… It was more of a barrier than it was a crutch. At least now. It wasn't always. But you know, life changes. Things change."

"Yeah. I know."

"I'm sorry. I shouldn't have said it like that."

"No," he said. "It's just, that you're right. Things change, you can't go back."

"Sometimes I think maybe I tried to go back a little bit too much. Sometimes I think that by trying to make the same kind of house, I didn't really ever figure out what kind of home I would make. What kind of life I wanted to have."

He nodded slowly. "You know, they say time goes on, but it's a funny thing about grief. And about people. You can sure as hell do your damnedest to stop time. To pull yourself right out of it. To make it so you've got nothing but you and your grief."

"Yeah," she said. "That's very true.

"So," she said, her tone changing to something comically conversational. "Are you from California?"

He didn't know why. But he laughed. It caught him off guard about as much as when she had made him smile earlier. But damn, she had made him smile. "Yes," he said. "I am. The Bay Area. Kind of outside of San Francisco. Born and raised."

"I see. Rich family?"

"Yes," he laughed. "So I never really appreciated it, I have to say. Things were just kind of there. And yeah, I did a pretty good job managing all my money and things like that, but to be honest so much of that came from having learned how to do it way back when. My dad was always managing lots of portfolios and things like that. But the best thing is we had a ranch. So I grew up with horses. And I just… Oh I love them. I always have. Horses are the best part of life."

"Then you really are a cowboy."

"I really am. On a good day."

"Are you going to make a ranch up here?"

"I don't know."

The subject of the house loomed large between them, but she didn't push. And he wasn't in the mood to talk about it. It didn't go along with this. This light, getting to know you stuff that was like something he'd forgotten existed.

"Favorite color," he asked.

She closed her eyes and smiled. "Raspberry buttercream."

"That's not a color."

She opened her eyes again. "Disagree. It is a food, a flavor and color. And it's a very particular color that you get when you put fresh raspberries in buttercream, and it is both beautiful and delicious."

"Okay," he said. "Favorite food."

"This could get repetitive really quickly." She tapped her chin and looked at him. "First kiss."

"Molly McDonald. Fourth grade."

"No way."

"There was no tongue."

"A relief."

"You?"

"Well," she said, her cheeks turning rosy. "That would be you."

"How the hell, Iris?"

"I don't know. I mean, I guess I do. I just kind of closed myself off. And then I decided to step out and go for it, and it turns out I can start a business, and find a man to kiss. I had no idea."

"There you go."

"First time?" she asked. "And I'm not asking so you can ask me too. The answer is going to be boring."

"Lacey Anderson. An older woman. I was sixteen, she was seventeen. She taught me a thing or two."

"So, not big on virgins, then?"

"Not historically."

"Do you have any brothers or sisters?"

He nodded slowly. "My sister, Mallory, is quite a bit younger than me. She worries. A lot. All the time. And is frequently unhappy with me for my lack of contact."

"What about your mom and dad?"

"They're giving me space. You know, like good new age California parents do. Which is nice since, if we were in the same vicinity, they'd give me no space at all. If my dad is talking, he's sharing his opinions. So. Space is being given."

"But your sister's not giving you space."

"No. And anyway, half the time I'm convinced she's acting as an agent for my parents while they pretend to be a lot more okay with me doing my own thing than they actually are."

"I know all about meddling siblings. I might not have my parents, but believe me when I tell you my older brother more than makes up for it. Plus, my sisters are always in my business. Then there's my cousins, and Sammy."

He probably wouldn't meet them. It would be for the best if he didn't. This thing that they were doing up here... It didn't have anywhere to go. That was the problem. It was stuck up here, because he was stuck up here. Because there was nothing else.

And as nice as it was to sit and talk, it wasn't really an

appetite for talking she had awakened in him last night. He brushed her hair back from her face and kissed her. The desire that flared inside him was instant, hard and deep.

"Ever had sex outdoors?" he asked.

"I think you know the answer to that."

"Well, we better fix it."

He pushed that flannel off her shoulders, tugged her T-shirt up over her head. She gasped as the air hit bare skin.

That braid of hers was plain and simple, and inflamed his desires in a way he couldn't quite articulate. And didn't even want to. He didn't want to articulate. Not anymore. He just wanted. For the first time in his life not every feeling was his enemy. And he was damn happy with that. Because this felt good. She felt good.

She had brought cookies, and her beautiful body, and moments in the sun, and it was a form of magic he hadn't thought he could have.

Her lips were sweet, the curve of her breasts over that bra plump and delicious. He lowered his head and licked her skin, and felt her shiver beneath his touch.

"You're beautiful," he rasped. "I want to make sure you know that. Beautiful like I've never seen."

And he didn't care about anything but the truth of those words. He didn't care about the past. He didn't care about the future. He didn't care about anything but holding her soft, sweet body in his arms. And it was sweet. So damn sweet. He moved his hands down her back, pushed them down beneath the waistband of her jeans so that he could cup her ass.

"Griffin," she whispered.

"What?"

"Just… You."

He stripped those jeans off of her, her underwear. And

all he could do was stare. At that enticing thatch of curls there between her thighs, at all that smooth, creamy skin. He had forgotten. All the things he liked about women. The things that made him so happy to be a man. She was all of them. Every last one. She was everything. She wiggled out of his hold, and stood, shaking out her long dark hair. And he could only stare. Then she turned away from him, her hair cascading down her back, ending just above where her waist nipped in. He looked at her hips, generous and lovely, at the dimples just above her behind. The round curve of that plump flesh. He was struck by a deep, completely aggressive urge to have her. And also rendered completely motionless by the sight of her.

It was a hell of a thing. And so was she.

She looked over her shoulder, her expression one of shy innocence, mingled with a slow roll of seductive thunder. Whether or not she knew that was there, he didn't know. But it was. At least, it was to him. It reached out and grabbed him. Compelled him to stand. Then she looked away from him again, her dark hair shimmering like a wave when she took a step forward into the water. She jumped back, a reaction to the cold. But then she stepped forward again, this time more determinedly, putting both feet into the slow moving stream. "I've never done this before," she said, and he could tell that as she lifted her arms to wrap them around her body.

"What?"

"Skinny-dipping."

Then, as if she was compelled by an invisible force, she took two large steps forward, then lay forward in the water, shrieking as it closed over her skin.

"Cold," she said.

"Yeah, I figured."

"Are you going to join me?"

"I could," he said. "But the view is awfully nice."

"Come on," she said.

And he felt like she was beckoning him to something else, though he didn't want to pin it down. He wanted it to keep on shimmering inside of him, moving around like an invisible force. Weightless. Wonderful.

Because so few things in his life were. Nothing, if he were honest. For the last five years, nothing. And then, there she was. A forest sprite or an angel, he didn't know. But she was something.

And he wanted her.

He stripped the rest of his clothes off, and his eyes caught hers. Her gaze was… Hungry, there was no other word for it. He thought a lot about his own hunger. About how long it had been since he felt these things, since he'd touched another person. Since he felt connected in any way.

Since he felt sexual desire. Stripping it back to its most basic, taking away even that human connection element, he had just been starving for pleasure.

But she was too, and that made him feel something.

Something deep and immeasurably satisfying.

"I've never seen a naked man before," she said. Her words were small, and he knew she didn't mean those to be seductive. But dammit they were.

"Really?"

"I mean, not… Like that."

He looked down. "Aroused?"

"Yeah," she said, her cheeks turning the most delicious shade of pink.

"Turned on."

"Yes," she said.

"For you."

"*Definitely* not."

He waded into the water, and wasn't concerned at all that the cold would have a dimming effect on him. There wasn't a possibility of that. Not when Iris was right there.

Want and need blurred together as he moved closer to her lithe form. He closed the distance between them and wrapped his arms around her wet, naked body, pulling her up against him. She gasped, turning fully into him, her breasts sliding against his chest, their legs tangling. Her eyes widened, he assumed when she felt his erection pressing against her stomach.

It was completely silent around them except for the sound of rushing water, and the breeze in the trees. The sun was shining down on the river's surface, tossing light onto the ridges of movement there, a glow surrounding them. A halo surrounding her.

There were very few perfect moments in life. And Griffin had been absolutely certain he would never live another one.

He'd been sure that he'd used them all up. And that when life had come to collect payment for all those moments, the cost had been dear enough that he would never be able to feel it again. He'd had his perfection. And there would be no more.

Except this moment was perfect. This woman was perfect, and if he could have stopped time then and there he would have done it.

But time rolled on and his hands roamed over her body, hers over his, tentative at first as they explored his chest, and then down farther. His breath caught in his throat, and she leaned forward, kissing him just beneath his jaw.

He groaned, tightening his hold on her, flexing his hips forward.

"I didn't think I was like this," she whispered.

"Like what?"

"Sexual. I mean, I knew that I… That I would like to. With… With a man. It's just… I didn't think I would…" She brushed her hand over his cheek. "Outside. In the water. I didn't think that I would feel like I might die if I didn't have someone. Not after I went so long not having someone."

"Because you didn't know."

"It's safer," she whispered. "To not depend on anyone."

"I know." He felt bereft, hollow then, not because of his loss, but because of the inevitability of these kinds of conversations. The inevitability of this truth. That any time you made a connection with someone you were at risk. No matter what you told yourself.

"I know it, but it doesn't… I'm so glad that I'm here."

"I'm glad you're here," he said, his voice rough.

And as he moved his hands over her curves, he realized that this was a lot like fire.

He had just cooked fish at a fire. Sat in front of it for warmth.

He had to make his peace with it. Because of the way he chose to live. Because he had gone off-grid. He had to surrender to the fact that it both gave life and took it.

And he supposed this kind of connection was a lot like that.

He knew that it could destroy.

But he also realized that he needed it a hell of a lot more than he'd allowed himself to believe.

It was all about control, really. Fire out of control killed. Fire in control gave life.

Control, that was the thing.

But not now. Not here. Here, control didn't matter. Here, he didn't have to think about those things.

Here, he could just be with her.

And let there be nothing else.

He tilted her back, kissing her neck, down to the edge of her collarbone before moving back to her lips, sliding his gently over hers, the water making them slick. Then he tasted her, deep and long, lapping at the inside of her mouth until she shivered, and this time not from the cold.

He kissed her chin, her throat, the valley between her breasts. Then he moved across to one tightened bud, sucked it deep in his mouth, desire bursting in him like a bomb. He moved to the other breast, another moment he could live in for the rest of his life. This deeply captivating moment where only her breasts, only her body mattered. There for him to worship, there for him to indulge himself in.

That was a miracle that he had forgotten about. This miracle of sex. Where you could give and take endlessly and in equal measures. In the same moment. He had never seen anything like the joy on Iris's face, tinged with wonder as he touched her. As he stoked the flames of her desire.

A fire that could destroy.

A fire that could heal.

He moved one hand between her legs, traced a pattern of pleasure over her slick folds. She gasped, and he moved his thumb in a circle over that sensitized bundle of nerves at the apex of her thighs, pushed a finger inside of her as he continued to tease and torment her. As he sucked her nipple deep into his mouth. He felt her explode around his fingers, pleasure rolling through her body like a wave. Then he kissed her. Deep, long and endless, and he could have just kissed her like that forever. With the water lapping gently against them, with her body shaking and shivering from the orgasm she just had. With the sun in the sky as a witness, and the blessed silence of the wilderness enveloping them in all its velvet glory.

But then he carried her up out of the water, all limp and boneless, and was thankful for the blanket they brought with them. He spread it out on the ground, and brought her up against him, kissing her, kissing her like the answers to everything might be found there.

Even though his mind was blank of questions. Void of absolutely everything, which made touch all the more heightened. The cool temperature of the surface of her skin giving way to heat beneath. The water droplets there. Smooth flesh, puckered nipples, that slick, sweet spot between her legs. Lips like a rose petal. Hair like silk.

She grabbed hold of his face, kissing him hard, deep, her intensity increasing as she rocked against his body. She met his gaze, and didn't turn away. And he maneuvered them so that he was between her thighs, testing the entrance to her body with the blunt head of his arousal. She gave, easily, much more so than last night, than that first time where breaching her had been a marked event. This time it was a slow glide into heaven as she opened to receive him. As she let her head fall back, her eyes fluttered closed, but only briefly as she let out a low moan of pleasure.

And then she opened those beautiful eyes again. Green and gold—more than brown, he'd decided—shot through with strands of the sun, and it was like he heard that color. Echoing in his heart. He began to move, the sounds of their pleasure the new soundtrack to the forest. And when he found his pleasure, she did too, her nails digging into his shoulders, the plaintive cry on her lips balm for his soul.

And they lay there together like that, on the blanket, beneath the sun. He moved his hand down her arm, laced his fingers together with hers.

That had been more than one perfect moment.

Far more.

CHAPTER SIXTEEN

IRIS KNEW THAT she had to leave the mountain. She'd been up there for more than twenty-four hours, and she could not spend another night. She didn't have cell service up here, and it was inevitable that her family would be concerned. Plus, she had everything with the bakery to get back to and a whole host of other things.

It was difficult to leave, though.

"I'll be back, with food."

"Yeah," Griffin said, running his hand over his hair. She had wanted to reach up and follow that same trail. Brush his hair off his forehead, let her fingertips drift down his face and linger at his beard. Instead, she just kissed him briefly, and told herself that her eyes were just stinging from allergies. Because there was a whole host of things in bloom, and that was the problem.

Why she felt strange, and her chest tightened. And her throat felt scratchy.

She started the drive down the mountain, and realized that she was shaking. She had just spent a day naked, mostly in the sun, making love with a man. And she tried to remember the woman she'd been when she drove up the mountain with that plate of cookies, unsure of what she was facing when it came to Griffin. A woman who had been so frustrated with the stagnant nature of her life, and who was looking to make some changes. And she just felt like…

That woman was silly.

Because she'd wanted changes, not knowing what it would mean. Not even having a clue that it wasn't as simple as before and after. That it wasn't as simple as not understanding sex and then understanding it.

She felt more mystified by the whole thing than she had when she'd started. She had known more as a virgin than she knew now. And that was a whole strange thing.

She wanted to believe that if her mother had been alive, she would have talked to her about this.

I'm sorry, Iris, Rose wanted to bake the cookies earlier, and you know how she gets. You and I will bake another time.

Sorry, Iris, I'm run off my feet. We'll talk tomorrow.

She rubbed her chest, and it felt sore. More allergies. Probably.

When she pulled up to Hope Springs Ranch, Rose was sitting on the porch, her boots up on the rail, her arms crossed.

"Hi," Iris said, getting out of the car, the dusky light providing a little bit of coverage for her expression.

"Well, *well*," Rose said. "The prodigal has returned."

"I'm hardly prodigal."

"You are a little."

"And where's my fatted calf?"

"Can I interest you in a rather skinny chicken?"

"If you're going to go throwing around biblical proclamations, then I expect a showing of biblical proportions."

"I was actually waiting for Logan. But where have you been? Ryder is… Well, he is not happy."

"I spent the night… With Griffin."

Of all the ways that Iris had imagined her sister—so brash and full of double entendres—might react to news like that, her face crumpling and effecting a shape that suggested deep concern was not on the list.

"Are you okay?"

Iris lifted a shoulder. "Yeah. I'm… I'm good."

Right then, Sammy came out the front door, a dish towel thrown over her shoulder. She was wearing a loose white dress, her blond hair free in the wind. Looking a bit like a guardian angel.

"There you are," Sammy said. "When you didn't answer your calls? Ryder got apoplectic."

"It wasn't my intention for him to be… Apoplectic. Or to be out of range for so long. I am sorry."

Rose looked at her, clearly asking the question of whether or not she could share what Iris had already told her. Iris didn't need Rose to do her dirty work.

"I spent the night with Griffin last night."

Sammy too reacted, not with hedonistic glee, which had been more her reaction to Pansy's proclamations, but with the same grave concern that Rose had shown.

"Are you okay?"

"Why are both of you acting like sex might have brought me irrevocable harm?"

"Because you're…"

"It's just that you…"

"What?" Iris asked, feeling frustrated.

"You're very…"

"Soft," Sammy finished.

Iris frowned. "I am not soft. You all do what I tell you to."

"Do we?"

"Who determines what we have for dinner?"

"Fair point," Sammy said.

"I'm fine. I'm fine, it's just… It's complicated. And…

I don't know. He's not boring, that's for sure." And then, something dug at her, beneath her ribs, and even though she felt like what had passed between herself and Griffin was too precious to make light of, she knew what Rose would do.

"I lost track of how many times," Iris said. "And outside too," she added. "No khakis in sight."

Rose looked abashed. "Really? You still have to go on about that?"

"I'm not boring. You're just not... None of you are right about me. I'm not weak. I'm not soft. I'm not boring. I can have affairs with brooding mysterious men. On mountaintops. And sometimes I'm not going to call home. Because I'm thirty-one. I am not fourteen. Or twenty-four. So there."

"Way to go," Sammy said, looking genuinely impressed. "I'm very glad to hear that your first experience has been... Satisfying."

"More than," Iris said emphatically. "He's a god."

"I really would like to see this man god who deflowered you in a meadow."

"I did not say he deflowered me in a meadow."

That was pastoral. They had come together during a storm. But that was something that no one needed to know. All the intensity between them. Or anything about Griffin's life. That was something he'd shared with her. It was private. Sacred.

It made her ache in a lot of weird ways just thinking about it.

"Where is Ryder? I need to talk to him."

"Wait a minute," Sammy said. "I have to... Did you use a condom?"

"Sammy," Iris said. "I do not need you to give me a safe sex lecture."

"Look, I know you're an adult and everything, but I just feel like... As the person with more experience..."

"You mean as the person who slept with my brother without protection and ended up accidentally pregnant with his baby?"

"Fine. Speaking to you as a supremely fallen woman."

"No," she admitted. "But I'm on the pill. For... You know. Stuff."

"Iris, you have to be careful about STDs and things."

"He is fine," she said.

"Sex gods on top of mountains can't be trusted."

"He hasn't been with anyone for a long time." She clenched the back of her teeth together. "He's been through a lot."

"How much?"

Pain stirred in her chest. "He lost his wife." That was as far as she would go.

"Oh," Sammy and Rose said at the same time.

Rose's expression turned cautious. "That sounds like kind of a project."

"You're with someone who experienced the exact same loss as you," Iris said. "Both of you are projects."

"That's different," Rose said. "Logan and I don't have to explain anything to each other. We just know. I mean it's a shared thing. Not an extra thing."

"Well, it doesn't matter. I'm not going to have a relationship with Griffin." It felt more like they were clinging to each other while they got through a particularly difficult time in their lives. He was... Maybe trying to come out of something. Finally taking steps to live in a way he hadn't in a long time. And really, she was doing the same. They had both been stuck. And sleeping together had given them a chance to be in a new space. To try something different. To try to be healed.

Not fully. The wounds that Griffin had would never fully heal, she was sure of that. Just as she would be forever marked by her parents' deaths. By the regrets that she had surrounding them. There was no getting past it. Rose and Sammy were looking at her with concern, because they assumed that she would be expecting something else.

"Don't go thinking that I believe this is my happy ending," Iris said. "I don't think that. He had his. And his wounds are pretty clear. More than that, he... Look, actually it's me. I'm beginning some things. I'm not looking for an ending. Not to anything. Because you're right, Rose, he's a lot. And I like the guy. I like him a lot. But that doesn't mean I want to take on his issues when I'm just kind of sorting out mine. I have a bakery to run."

That wasn't strictly...it. But her feelings on it were way too complicated to go into. It was too much ancient history and baggage and she just didn't want to go there.

"Buns not buns?" Sammy asked.

"You just used the same word twice," Iris said.

"Yeah. But I meant buns and buns."

"I know what you meant. It still doesn't work."

"Buns and *buns*," Rose said. "Why don't you have both? I mean, like you said, you know what you want. Why not enjoy him?"

"He's a man, not a carnival ride," Sammy said. "Unfortunately, I find men are more complicated."

Rose shrugged. "Doesn't mean they aren't fun."

"Sure."

"Okay. I am not conducting this affair by consensus. So that means you always have to deal with whatever I decide to do."

"Unfair," Rose said.

"You were very secretive about your own situation," Iris said.

"Because. Because Sammy is a turncoat. And therein lies a problem. She's going to tell Ryder that you had sex."

Iris looked over at Sammy. Sammy look chagrined. "I cannot lie to my husband."

"That complicates our friendship," Iris said.

"I know. I'm sorry. I mean, I'm not going to walk in there and say that you had sex. But that has more to do with my concern for his blood pressure than it does for you. The thing is, I don't think he actually wants to know your business. He doesn't care what you do. But he does care that you're safe. And he was worried. So if he asks..."

"I'm going to talk to him. I'm going to not say the word *sex* to him."

Iris walked up the stairs, and stomped into the house, where she was greeted by overly enthusiastic dogs. "You're menaces," she said, but she petted them on the heads before sending them outside. And there was Ryder. She could see him through the kitchen doorway, sitting at the table.

"Hi," she said.

He turned sharply, his expression fierce. "Where the hell have you been?"

"Out of cell range?"

"Right. Obviously. Except, you also could have been dead in a ditch."

"You're not my dad, quit doing an impersonation of him."

"Someone has to."

Suddenly, she just felt sad. Sad and overwhelmed, because there were all these tragedies, and she couldn't seem to escape them. Her own. Griffin's. Ryder couldn't either. It was why he was acting this way, because he hadn't known the whereabouts of his adult sister for a day.

Granted, some of that was that it was out of character. Out of routine. And of course that mattered. *Of course* that made a difference.

But still. She just felt sad. For all of them.

"Well, I'm here. I'm not dead in a ditch. Nothing's wrong. But I do need to talk to you."

"What do you need to talk to me about?"

"I'm moving out. Officially. I'm going to be living in the apartment above the bakery. I didn't know if Rose mentioned it to you, or Pansy. But I did already talk to them a little bit about it."

"You don't have to move out," he said.

"I know I don't have to. I love being here. In that I love being with you. And Sammy. And Astrid. But you all have lives, and I don't."

"This is a life, Iris. There's nothing to be ashamed of."

"I'm not ashamed. I'm not. But I am ready. To figure out what else there is for me. And I don't think that's unfair."

"Of course it's not."

"I'm just trying to figure things out. You know. My life."

"Of course."

"And that is going to include being out of cell phone range sometimes," she said slowly.

"You met someone, I take it."

She nodded. "I might have."

"Your boss? Landlord? Whatever he is."

"Griffin," she said. "And… I guess. But I wouldn't think of him primarily in that way."

"Just tell me you're being careful." Which could mean a host of things, but he was choosing his wording very carefully, and so was she.

"You're not going to have to give me away any time soon if that's what you're worried about."

"That doesn't worry me. If that's what you want, I would love to do that. If it's not what you want, then I won't do it. Whatever you want to do."

"I know that. I know that I always have your support."

She stood there and stared at him, the brother who'd also been a father figure. Who she'd partnered with to try and keep the whole family sane when they had endured such an unimaginable loss. Their relationship would always be so heavy. There was no way around it. They'd been through too much. They would always care an awful lot about what the other was going through. Again, inevitable. They had just been through so damn much.

She sat down at the table across from him, suddenly feeling very small. "How long did it take you to figure out what you wanted to do with your life?"

"Until about a year ago," he said.

She laughed. "Well, that's not very comforting."

"It's true, though. Things came together when I married Sammy. Started coaching the football team again. Just brought some things back in my life that I had decided I didn't get to have."

"Because you threw everything into taking care of us."

"Yes. But I know you did that too. And it's going to take you a while, to sort through everything. And if this isn't it, it's going to come along. You don't need to feel pressure to know exactly what you want."

"I don't, actually. I just kind of want to know that everything's going to be okay. Because this is all a lot of big changes for me, and I feel a little bit overwhelmed by it. Because I forgot what it was like to have dreams. And when I finally did again, I got a little bit more than I bargained for. I'm trying to plan ahead, but I don't know how to plan any of this."

"Focus on the bakery," he said. "I'm damn proud of you. It's going to be amazing."

"Thank you."

"You all did good," Ryder said. "And you have no idea how much that means. Because I was sad when Mom and Dad died. And I worried a hell of a lot for myself. But I just... Parents worry for their kids. Parents who are adults when they're raising them. And I was just so conscious that I was nothing more than a kid trying to make sure you all did okay. Trying to make sure you got to the other side safely. You're also much more amazing than I could've guessed you would be. And my life is a hell of a lot better that I thought it would be. And there's been stuff. You know, like dealing with my relationship with Sammy. Logan and Rose..."

"Were you really mad when they got together?"

He shook his head. "No. I was mad when Logan nearly ruined it. They love each other. That's so obvious."

"It is," she said. "You both make it look easy."

Ryder laughed. "Not easy. I don't know if you remember me growling around here like a bear when Sammy and I were trying to sort out what the hell our lives were going to look like. When we were trying to sort out how to be together. And Logan nearly ruined everything with Rose. It's not easy."

"Well, all the more reason for me to avoid it."

"Good luck to you."

She laughed, feeling hollow. "Thank you. I might need help moving."

"Oh. Is that really what this whole conversation is about? Let's have a heart-to-heart, can I borrow your truck?"

"Kind of." She smiled, unrepentant. And he smiled right back.

"I suppose I can help you with that."

"Very appreciated, big brother."

"No problem, little sister."

And she looked at him, and felt more like an equal than she ever had before. Like another person who had a life, and a future ahead of them, even if she didn't know what it was. But he didn't seem quite so much more older than her. She smiled. "The bakery is going to open next week."

"Really?"

"I mean, I'm being kind of optimistic. I have to make sure all of my permits come through, but I'm expecting the last one in a couple of days."

"That's fantastic. Are you going to have a grand opening event?"

"I thought that I might. The weekend after opening. I'll do a little soft open, see what people are liking best, and tailor it all to go with the big party."

"Well, you know we'll all be there. And we'll help in any way we can. Because that's what Danielses do."

"Damn straight," Iris said.

She stood and turned, preparing to leave the room. "Iris," Ryder said.

"Yes?"

"If you're going to go out of cell range for more than twenty-four hours, next time can you give me a heads-up?"

"Can't I just hang a tie on the door?"

"You're moving," he said. "So… I guess actually I probably won't know."

"Yeah. Things change."

"They surely do."

And after having been through many changes in her life

that were bad. That had signaled a change in things that she couldn't fix, or even comprehend. This kind of change seemed good. Life moving forward as it was supposed to.

"Better late than never," she whispered as she walked up the stairs to her bedroom for what she thought might be the last time.

CHAPTER SEVENTEEN

HE HAD ANOTHER voice mail from Mallory. And he was going to answer it sooner than he had been. He got up on the rock, and as soon as he had bars, dialed the number.

"Well, this is a surprise. Contact less than two weeks apart."

"Yeah. I've got… Well, I just wanted to make sure you were well."

"You wanted to make sure I was well?"

"Yes."

"I am. Thank you for asking."

"How's the practice, by the way?"

"Hmm. Complicated. You know, you wouldn't think that midwives would have a whole lot of inner office politics, but sadly, there are some."

"Is Rain taking the good birthing suite and all the good vibes too?"

"Can you not?"

"I mean, I can *try* not to. But it's fun."

"How come you still act like an immature brat when we get into having a normal conversation?"

"Because that's a normal conversation."

"You sound better."

He looked around through the trees. He put in a few hours on the house today, but the work hadn't felt quite so compulsive. It was strange, because he had imagined that telling Iris all about his past might make it all feel raw. Closer to the surface. But it hadn't been like that. Not really. Yes, it was there. But hadn't brought nightmares up any more ferociously than they'd been before. If anything, things had felt a little bit better. He breathed a bit easier.

"I like cookies," he said. Then he realized that sounded ridiculous.

"You...like cookies?"

"It's been a long time since I...liked anything."

The silence stretched out between them on the phone. "Griff," she said, and he could tell that her voice was thick with tears. "That is the best news."

"It's pretty good."

"Really. And thank you for calling me."

She told him a little bit more about the drama at the birthing center she worked at before they got off the phone, and there was something so aggressively normal about it all, that when he hung up he felt... Strangely light.

But then, he had. Ever since he had spent that day with Iris. He hadn't seen her since. He imagined that she'd been busy.

Which was fine by him. But he was starting to wonder... Starting to wonder what he should do. Because he wanted to see her again. And he didn't want to wait for her to come back up here.

It made him wonder if he needed to go to her.

He'd done it once before. Come down the mountain to repair that plumbing problem she had.

But she called him. It was different.

He meandered back down the path that led to the housing site and surveyed his progress. It was slow. But by design. There was no way to do a project like this by yourself and have it go quickly. Building this house had felt like action for a long time. He had never been one to sit around doing nothing, even when everything was terrible. There was always something to be done.

But he wanted to do something else. There was something else to do. And that, he supposed, was a gift.

One thing he'd always been was a man who knew what he wanted, and who took steps to get it.

But he'd been a whole lot of nothing for the last few years.

And at the point where he had no idea why he was still standing there with his hammer in his hand, rather than heading down the mountain to see the woman that he wanted to see, he figured he had better get going. Because he wanted to see Iris Daniels. And so he would.

Because life was short and uncertain, but he was breathing.

So he might as well do something with that breath.

HE DROVE DOWN the mountain, and things seemed a bit brighter. Once he was on the main street, he found that he felt hopeful. An experience he was no longer familiar with. When he pulled up to the bakery, he saw her through the window, standing on a chair and fiddling with what he thought might be a light fixture.

There was a sign hanging out front that read The Cookie Jar.

She'd mentioned that was the name. But he'd forgotten to ask her about it.

He got out of the truck, and walked up to the front door. She turned sharply, her eyes going wide, and then she scrambled down from the chair and went to the door.

"What are you doing here?"

"Came to see you."

"Really?"

"Yes."

"I thought…"

"I've been here before."

He stepped past her and made his way into the bakery. "I know," she said. "I just…"

"You just what?"

"I sort of thought that… I don't know. I didn't expect you to come down."

"There is a time for everything. And I've been avoiding the reality of that."

"Oh."

"I wanted to see you. And I couldn't think of any reason why I shouldn't."

"You wanted to see me?"

"I did. And I was standing up there, working on my house, thinking about you, and didn't see why you shouldn't be right in front of me."

Because she could be. That was the thing. She was here and so was he. So why waste any time?

"Well, I'm glad you did."

But she didn't make any move to kiss him, and he wondered if there was someone from her family around.

"Is anyone else here?"

"No. I'm all alone. Just getting some last-minute things done. My permits are all in, and I think I'm just going to open in a couple of days."

"Really? No grand opening?"

"My brother asked me the same thing. But I figured I would do a soft open and see how things go. And then…"

"Make sure that I know when your grand opening is." Except, as soon as he said that, he realized he wasn't going to give her an opportunity to make any other choice. He was going to be there. He was going to be around. And he was going to make sure that he knew what was happening with the business. First of all, her business was linked with him, and that meant he should be engaging in that. Second of all, he wanted to know what was going on with her life.

And much like the horse ride he'd invited her on, he wasn't going to do much worrying about why. He was just going to be in it.

"I like the sign," he said. "Like the name."

"Thank you. I... My mom always had cookies made." Her expression wrinkled, just for a moment. A small ripple of sadness that quickly vanished. "I like cookies."

"I noticed that."

She got a very sad, wistful look on her face, and he couldn't quite figure out why. "Does it make you sad? To think about her?"

"Not all the time. I mean, really not. She's been gone from my life for longer than I had her in it. That makes me sad. And sometimes thinking about the cookies makes me sad. It's just that you think you have all the time in the world to change things with people." She shook her head. "When she died, my younger sisters were really small. They were a handful, I mean they were little kids. And I was four-teen and things were changing in my life and I wanted... It doesn't really matter. It's just, I always wonder how it would have been if I'd known. It's just you always think you have forever, so much time. Until you realize you don't."

"That's the nature of loss," he said. "You have all kinds of perspective afterward. On what matters. On what you wish you would've done differently. Believe me. I have truckloads of perspective and nothing to do with it. And you know, you can share that with other people, try to pass it on, try to make sure that they maybe live their lives with a little bit more thought, but until they experience loss, they won't. Not permanently. And anyway, grief skews perspective. That's something I've learned. It makes the air seem thick and your head seem fuzzy. And how do you fight through it to figure out which part of the perspective you're supposed to keep? I've been in a grief monastery, but I don't know that it's benefited anyone. I know how important the people were that I lost. I know it down to my bones. I couldn't have any more perspective on that. But when it comes to perspective on living… Well, I've been pretty short on that."

"Me too," she said. "I wish that I wasn't. I wish that I hadn't spent so much time hiding myself away. I guess. I don't know, though. I talked to my brother a couple days ago. And he said it took him until last year to figure himself out, so… I'm four years younger. I guess I still have more perspective than he does. Or, at least, had."

"Well, there you go. You've got time."

"Opening this bakery is going to take a lot of time and energy. Plus, I'm still working up at your house…"

"Iris," he said. "Are you about to warn me off? Let me down gently?"

"I don't want to let you down," she said. "By which I mean I don't… I mean… Well, I would like to keep… Doing what we're doing. I just…"

"Honey, you don't need to give me the talk about what this is."

"I don't?"

"Being with you makes me feel good. And I didn't think that anything could. Not a damn thing, Iris. I haven't felt good in a long time. But that's all it is. It's just feeling good. It's not really…"

"It's not really your heart."

"There's nothing left of that."

"That's not true," she said. "There's a lot left of it. I know. I've seen it. But I get what you mean. And no worries. I'm in love with my bakery. That's the most important thing to me."

"Glad to hear it."

"But I would like to keep having sex." She looked around, like she was afraid she might get caught. "Because I do really like that."

"Well, very glad to hear that." He rubbed his chin and looked around the room. "All things considered, I don't need you to come up and bring me meals anymore."

She frowned. "Well, but then I won't see you as much."

"Iris, I don't even have indoor plumbing, and you shouldn't have to use an outhouse when we are together. I can rent a place in town if you don't want anyone seeing my truck here, or I can park around the block, whatever you want. I don't mind staying here with you, but it is up to you."

"You can stay here with me."

"Then I'll do that."

"I like your cabin," she said. "There's something magical about it. About... The way that it's like we're the only two people in the world up there."

She looked away, as if embarrassed. As if she had realized that that flew in the face of what they'd just been talking about. Not being romantic and having connections, just sleeping together.

He understood, though, because he'd felt the same thing. There was magic between them up there, and maybe that was all the more reason to bring it down into the real world.

He'd told himself that last time they were together up there that there wasn't a place for it here. But there could be. People did it all the time.

It was... A normal thing.

Two conflicting feelings hit him at the same time. Happiness, in a strange way. That he was considering something quite so normal. And a deeper emotion. Because nothing between him and Iris was half so basic as *normal*. There was something more to them. Something more to this. And up there on the mountain, he'd sensed it. Perfect moments. Perfect moments that stretched on and on, as long as he was holding her hand. As long as she was in his arms.

As long as he was in her body.

Looking into those beautiful eyes.

It was easy to get lost up there in his mind, on sun-drenched riverbanks, drunk on passion.

But they were standing down in town on Main. Talking about having an affair. And that was fine. That was fine.

"I just… I want to ask you something," she said. "But I don't want to overstep. I don't want to cross the line."

"I'm going to make a deal with you. This thing between us, whatever it is, no boundaries. If I ask you something, and it's a no go, you just tell me that. We move on. You can ask me things, if I don't feel like talking about it, I won't. And then we just get back down to what it is we're doing. You and me, we're a safe zone. You're learning how to be you, and I'm learning what it looks like to be human right about now. Not sure I know. So we're going to make some mistakes. But I think we might both need someone we can trust that way."

She nodded slowly. "Okay. So nothing is off-limits?"

"Nothing."

"Well, I'm going to have to think long and hard about some things then, because I have some questions."

"Other than the ones you were just going to ask me?"

"Yes. I have a serious thing to ask you. But when I'm done with that, I think I have some sex questions."

He laughed, in spite of himself. In spite of the fact that

this was a very strange experience, standing in a bakery, looking at the woman whose virginity he'd just taken a few nights ago, knowing that he was about to get asked something he probably wouldn't want to answer, and being amused by her all at the same time.

"Great. Though, I warn you, I may want to answer with an example."

"I'm fine with that," she said. "Absolutely fine with it. I…" She sobered, her face going neutral. "Is it weird for you? I mean, in the sense that… You haven't been with anyone since your wife."

He shook his head. "No. I haven't." He thought about that, long and hard. He had chosen to marry Mel. Because he loved her. And he had loved her till the day she died. In many ways, he always would, because nothing had ever come between them in life. But she was gone, physically. Sometimes he might talk to her spirit, her memory, because that was part of him. But it wasn't the same, and he knew it.

"I don't quite know how to explain it. I loved her very much. She was amazing. And being with her changed me. But it's not a problem to be with you, not in the way you mean. I wasn't keeping vows. I think I've been dealing with something a little more complicated. How could I even want to feel that good when they can't? When they're not here. Even down to eating food that I enjoy." He took a long, heavy breath. "But now I've done it. And I feel like… The world didn't end. It's not such a bad thing. But self-denial was easy when I didn't have the appetite for any of it. And then you brought it back. So here we are. I'm not confused about whether or not you're *you*, so we're clear."

He saw her shoulders sag slightly. "I thought you might have… I was a little bit afraid that you might be… Imagining someone else." Her cheeks went scarlet. "And I feel horrible saying that. It feels invasive and like I don't have a right... Like you would have every right..."

"Hell no," he said. "Iris, if I'm sleeping with you, you have every right to expect that it's you I'm thinking of. And I am. This is not... You don't have to be my medicine. I want you. Because you're you. Not to make myself feel better, not to make myself feel. You... You came first. I didn't want sex, and you were convenient. I wanted you, and that's why I was with you. Just so we're clear."

"Wow. I... I'm sorry. Here I am making speeches about things just being physical, and I'm being sensitive."

"I don't think there's any way we can pretend there aren't emotions in this. We have emotions. We're people."

She looked relieved by that. "Right. I... Maybe we are friends."

He stared down at that beautiful face, and wanted to laugh. And he didn't look at her and think *friend*. He didn't look at her and think a single word at all. It was something that bloomed inside of him that he couldn't quite articulate.

"Now, what are your sex questions?"

"I'm not sure I can ask them now."

"Why not?" he asked.

"It's inappropriate. We were being serious."

"Sex is pretty serious."

"I know. But asking about... Mechanics and things isn't," she said.

"I don't know. It depends on what you're confused about. There's a definite possibility that it could get serious."

"I'm not confused about anything, I just... I'm curious."

"Hit me with your curiosity."

"Is it always that good?"

His mind was blank. Of previous experience. And that did make him feel strange, because he'd spent a lot of years sleeping with the same person, and he knew that things between them had been good. But right now he couldn't... He couldn't compare the two things.

"What happened between us isn't typical. Or normal. And I can't say that I've ever felt anything like it."

Honesty. He promised her that. And he wanted it from her. Because they needed to be able to talk to each other, mostly because there wasn't anyone else he could talk to. And here she was, this woman he'd only known for a few weeks, who now had more of him than anyone else in his life. Who'd heard his whole story from beginning to end. Who he'd been inside. And he was the only man to ever be with her like that. They had fallen into an intimacy that was pretty deep and intense. And so... Honesty it was. Because what else was there?

"Oh."

"When I was holding you, down in the river. I thought that was the closest thing to perfect the world could offer."

"I thought that too," she whispered. "But I thought maybe that was just sex."

"No," he said, his voice rough. "It wasn't just sex."

And that threw a wrench in the whole just sex conversation they'd just had. But then, his whole life had been destroyed, and now he was standing there, on the verge of figuring out how to make something from it. Not just hide away. And maybe it was all right if he didn't have all the answers.

"Is there anything I can help you with here?"

"As a matter of fact," she said. "There are a great many high things that I'm having trouble reaching."

"Well, I'm happy to help with that."

CHAPTER EIGHTEEN

BY THE TIME they were finished, she was hungry. And more than ready for some kind of a break, and a snack. Baked goods weren't going to cut it.

"Do you want to get something to eat?" She immediately wished that she could take it back, because she did wonder if it wasn't good to ask him out. They could stay in. They could stay in and eat any one of her preprepared meals, but that's what they'd been doing.

"Sure," he said. "Want to go down to the saloon?"

She hadn't expected that. But it did sound like a pretty good idea. She was at war with herself, though. Because if she went to the saloon, the odds were high that she would run into someone she knew. She might even run into a member of her family. On the other hand, plain Iris Daniels, walking into the Gold Valley Saloon with a man as good-looking as Griffin on her arm... Well, she did kind of like that. Because not only was Griffin handsome, he looked kind of dangerous, and that was a compelling thought. Her, being with someone dangerous. Talk about challenging the status quo.

"Yes. I would like that."

"Great."

They walked out of the bakery, and down the street. She wondered if he would hold her hand. But of course that didn't mesh with what they were talking about doing with each other. That wasn't friendship in one room, and making love in another. And that was sort of what it seemed like they were trying to do. Because he was right. It was great to have somebody to walk into this new phase of her life with. Somebody she could ask questions of. Somebody she could gain experience with, and who she could trust. And she did trust Griffin. And he needed… Well, he needed somebody right now too. A woman who wasn't going to get needy on him. Because he had too much going on to have to put up with someone else's emotions too.

They could need each other in the right ways.

And that would work. It would.

But she was ashamed to admit that she did wish that he would hold her hand, and as they walked, their hands not touching, she felt somewhat bereft.

Don't be like that. You're older, you know better. You're not a sixteen-year-old girl. You don't believe automatically that having slept with him means that you're going to fall in love with him. And you don't even want that.

She didn't.

So she ignored the way that her knuckles burned as they hung so close to his during their walk. Ignored the fact that she did wish that he might take possessive hold of her as they did. That he might show the whole town that she was with him.

They walked into the Gold Valley Saloon, and he held the door open for her, and that did bring a flush of pleasure to her face.

She was disappointed to see that no one in her immediate circle was there. Laz was standing behind the bar, as always, his new wedding ring gleaming on his finger, and he smiled when she saw him.

Well, Laz would see her. So there was that. Griffin led

the way over to the bar. "I'd like a beer. Whatever you have on tap."

"Light or dark?" Laz asked.

"I don't know. What do you recommend?"

"That's a loaded question. We could stand here and talk about microbrews for quite some time."

"No thanks," Griffin said. "Just a beer. Hold the dissertation."

She saw a flash of who he'd been. Charming. Personable. Light.

Laz shook his head. "Beer is pretty serious business."

"I'll have a soda," Iris said.

"The lady will have a soda," Griffin added.

"Will she? Okay then." Laz looked between them with some interest, then went off to fulfill the requests.

The door opened, and Iris turned, and a sharp pang of glee hit her square in the stomach. Because there he was.

Elliott.

The khaki-wearing bane of the last few months of her existence.

The man that Rose had thought she should be with.

The man who had loved Rose instead of her, who had absolutely enraged her, because she hadn't even liked him, and then he had gone and hurt her feelings. That man.

"Stand closer to me," she hissed.

"What?" Griffin lifted a dark brow, his beautiful mouth turning down.

"Um, please stand next to me because the boring guy that my sister tried to set me up with just walked in, and the fact that I'm with you makes me giddy."

"Iris," he said. "Are you being petty?"

"I am. I'm being very petty. Down into my soul. But you are the most beautiful man that I have ever seen in my entire life, and knowing that Elliott will see me with you brings me great pleasure."

His lips quirked upward into a smile then. "I'm beautiful?"

"Yeah, kind of like a sheer rock face. Hard and dangerous."

"Craggy."

"In a good way."

He chuckled. And then, Laz returned with their drinks. Griffin lifted his glass, and clinked it against hers. "To your pettiness."

Elliott saw her then, and looked at her, frowned, then looked away. But he didn't come over.

Of course he didn't, he never liked you.

"He didn't like me," she said. "He liked my sister. It was the most embarrassing thing that has ever happened to me."

"Oh," he said.

"Like I told you when we first met. That day we went horse riding. My sisters are… They're really something else. I mean they're both adventurous and energetic and… and I'm just… Me."

"*Just you* has proven to be pretty miraculous for me."

Suddenly, she felt flushed with pride. And it didn't matter that Elliott had ignored her. She didn't like him, so what did he matter? Sure, there was the way that her feelings had been agitated during that whole experience, but he didn't matter.

Griffin did.

"I'm very glad to hear that." She stretched up on her toes, and kissed his cheek.

His hand went to her hip, and the casual contact that she'd made with him became decidedly un-casual. She was suddenly heavy with need. She could feel a pull starting low in her midsection and dragging down even lower.

"Griffin…"

The door opened again, and in walked a collection of her worst nightmares.

Her brother-in-law, West, her future brother-in-law Logan, Rose and Pansy.

The only silver lining was that Ryder and Sammy weren't with them. But honestly, of all the things, most of her family had to walk in. That was just annoying.

Is it? Or is it a little bit what you wanted…

She squirmed uncomfortably as that reality went home to roost.

All right. He was gorgeous, and showing him off was fun. And yeah, that was getting a little bit tangled. And she worried then, that she had thrown Griffin into something without giving him full warning about it. Because that wasn't fair.

Logan, West and her sisters saw her, and then redirected, heading straight for the bar.

"That's my family," she said, smiling and speaking quickly to Griffin. He still had his hand on her hip. "And they're coming this way."

"Okay, which one of the guys is most likely to punch me out?"

"Neither of them are Ryder, so you're good."

"All right." He pasted a smile on his face, and it was… A little bit rusty, but there was the ghost of something there she hadn't seen before. She'd seen him smile, but she hadn't seen him interact with other people. And the rustiness faded in a moment, and suddenly she could see…

Well, this was who he must have been.

The businessman who could work a room. He must have

been that man at some time. He had a family, a mother and father, a sister. He'd fallen in love and gotten married. He had probably charmed his wife's family, and he'd been a groom in a wedding.

He must have worn a tux, and said vows in front of a crowd. He would have smiled, and given a speech maybe.

For some reason all those images cut her deep, and filled her with hope all at the same time.

"Hi there, Iris," Logan said. "I don't believe we've met," he said, directing that to Griffin.

"We haven't," he said, extending his right hand in order to shake Logan's, but leaving his left on her hip. "I'm Griffin Chance."

"I see. Logan Heath. I'm Iris's brother-in-law."

"Not quite yet," Rose said, poking his ribs. "I'm Rose. I'm Iris's sister."

"Pansy," Pansy said. "Same." She was wearing her uniform, so she imagined that Griffin had probably guessed that.

"West Caldwell," West said. "Brother-in-law."

"Good to meet you."

"Well, we've all met," Iris said. "Griffin is my boss. My landlord." She could *not* introduce him as her lover.

Logan's gaze went straight to where Griffin's hand was resting on her. "Obviously."

"You all just out drinking tonight?"

"Indeed," Rose said. "Sammy and Ryder have a bad case of parenting exhaustion. So they aren't coming out."

"Well, that's too bad."

"How's the bakery going?" Pansy asked.

"Great."

"So," Logan said. "Griffin. Is it?"

"I think you know it is," Iris said, narrowing her eyes.

"What is it you do?" He continued speaking as if Iris had said nothing.

"Why don't you all order drinks," Pansy said. "We'll go get a table." She grabbed hold of Iris, and dragged her away from Griffin and the bar. Griffin, for his part, looked entirely relaxed, but she had a feeling that was because he didn't actually know what he was getting himself into. Her family was a whole thing. Then, so was Griffin.

"Damn," Rose said. "I mean, damn."

"What?" Iris asked.

"He is… He is so hot."

"So hot," Pansy agreed.

"He is, right?" Iris asked.

"I mean, you said that he was good-looking." Rose shook her head. "But you didn't say that he was that good-looking."

"Well, I thought he was. I mean, I really did. But you know, I didn't know if I was just biased."

"You knew. That's why you're sitting here looking smug."

"I do feel smug. Elliott is here."

"Really." Pansy looked around, until she saw him. "Oh, that is unfortunate. He suffers by comparison."

"He does," Rose agreed.

"And you," she continued, "look like a cat that got into the cream."

Iris squirmed. "Yeah, well, I kind of am."

"Respect."

The men came over to the table then, laden with drinks, and Griffin took a seat beside her. She turned to him. "You know, you don't have to stay."

"I'm not going to leave."

"I didn't mean it that way, it's just that… I know this is maybe more than you were expecting."

"I'm fine." He lifted his head and addressed the group. "West and Logan were just explaining to me which beer here is the best. I maintain that I don't have an opinion."

"That isn't going to fly here," Pansy said. "Everybody's very opinionated about their beer."

"Well, I confess I haven't had anything much better than a grocery store bottled beer in a long time. Until Iris started coming up and bringing me food. Because sometimes she's nice and throws a bottle or two in."

"You probably took that out of our fridge," Logan said.

"I probably grocery shop for it," she said.

She smiled, and Logan had the decency to look a little bit shamefaced. But only a little bit.

"But she won't be grocery shopping for us anymore," Rose said. "Because she moved out."

"That I did," Iris said. "So... I guess you're going to have to learn to be a little bit more self-sufficient."

"Or a little self-sufficient in general," Pansy said.

"I'm sure that Iris has explained to you our whole... Situation," Rose said.

"Yes," Griffin said. And he proceeded to make conversation and charm everyone, and in general be great. And by the end of it all, she had a feeling that if Ryder did ask about Griffin, he would get nothing more than a good report.

The evening wound to a close sooner than Iris expected, but she was glad, because she figured they would go back to her place and... She felt very ready for that.

But when they walked back to the bakery, they stopped in front of the door, and he kissed her.

Not a little kiss. A deep kiss.

"It was nice to meet your family."

"Oh yes?"

"Very much. But I should probably be headed home."

"Oh."

"I'm going to come down tomorrow. Is there anything I can get you from the store for the bakery?"

"What kind of thing?"

"Well, I noticed you had a loose floorboard up at the front of the store. I'd like to fix it for you. And, if you need anything else…"

"I was supposed to be cleaning your house," she said.

"I know. But I'd like to help you out."

"I… Yeah that would be good. And some putty or something to patch holes in the wall."

"I'm happy to do that," he said. "More than happy."

"Thank you."

He kissed her again, and then he left her standing there, unsure of what had happened, but absolutely certain that she had waded into deeper water than she had intended to. And she found herself wishing that they just had sex. Because somehow that felt like less uncharted territory than whatever had happened tonight.

HE WALKED IN to Big R, which was host to many different sorts of supplies, mostly focusing on ranching, but filled with basically anything you could want for most essential repairs, plus flowers and other garden supplies. There was a woman working the front, with a couple of dogs sitting behind the counter. The place was sparse, serviceable. No unnecessary decorations or anything like that. He'd been in a couple times since moving to Gold Valley. But it had been a while.

And this was the first time he wasn't shopping for himself.

He had a hammer and nails, and he brought that down with him from the homestead, but got some drywall patching kits and paint patching supplies, and then paused in front of a display with flats of flowers. Various blooms in many shades of pink that he thought might complement her cookie jar sign.

And he wanted to get them for her.

He wanted to make her smile.

He pulled a notepad out of his pocket and formulated a quick construction plan, picking up wood and soil, and every pink flower available.

There were great, tall windows at the front of Iris's store, and it would be the perfect place to build and install planter boxes. He could make a few matching planter boxes to go outside those upstairs windows of hers.

Just to add a little bit of cheer and color, and to differentiate her from the other redbrick buildings around her.

He loaded it all up in his truck and headed down toward The Cookie Jar, where he found Iris already hard at work scrubbing down counters.

"Good morning," he said.

She looked up at him, a strange expression on her face. "Good morning."

"I told you that I would come bearing supplies, and I have."

"Good."

He would surprise her with the flowers.

The first thing he did was set to work on that loose board, repairing it quickly, before moving on to any gouges or holes in any of the walls.

"I really appreciate you doing this."

"It's not a problem."

Really, it was a damn sight more than not a problem. A smile curved his lips. "You know, it's a weird thing, but I haven't done much to help other people in a long time. I mean, I give money. I told you, there is that equestrian center. I give money because she loved horses. And I love horses. I know I would've taught our daughter to love them too. So it feels like something. Something that I can keep that belongs to that other life. But I don't go there. I don't actually do anything. I realized that when I was picking up supplies for this place. That it's been a long damned time since I've actually thought of someone else. Even giving to the equestrian center is thinking about me."

"Well, I've done all kinds of giving over the last many years of my life. When people don't need you anymore it's..." She looked up at him, a stark horror filling her eyes. "It's hard when you have a lot in you, and people don't need you to give to them anymore."

He nodded slowly. "Yeah. It is. I had all that in me..."

He thought back to what he'd said to her that night. About how he wasn't a husband and a father anymore. About how the feelings didn't go away. And suddenly that felt all mixed-up inside of him. What he was, and what he wasn't. What he'd done was shut himself off. Was cut off an essential piece of him. He'd been a caregiver. That's what he'd been. He'd failed, and that had... Well, it had stopped him from doing any of it at all. And this simple act made him feel connected on a deeper level, to who he'd been, and who he was now.

It was bittersweet, in that way. But he'd been living in a world of bitter. So a little bit of sweet underneath seemed like... Well, a fresh-baked cookie after years of canned chili, quite frankly.

"Is there a... Back to this building?"

"Yeah," she said. "A little gravel lot behind."

"I'm going to pull my truck around. I have a feeling that the next project is going to have to be set about there."

"What did you do?"

"You'll see. Want to go for a very short ride in my truck?"

She went out, and started to scurry from the passenger door to the bed of the truck, but he jerked the door open. "Get in. Don't ruin the surprise."

He drove around the block, to the back of the building, to the barren lot behind.

"Am I allowed to get out of the truck?"

"Not quite yet." He looked at her for a long moment, at the expectant expression on her face. Those greenish eyes, full lips. And he leaned in and kissed her. She whimpered, and his body went instantly hard.

He regretted, in that moment, leaving her last night without taking her to bed.

He'd been about to. But he'd stopped. Because he'd gone out to the bar with her, and he'd met her family. Because he had wanted to do some things to fix her bakery as much as he'd wanted to strip her naked, and he'd... He just felt like he needed to build in more moments with her where they had clothes on. And maybe that was part of this real-life learning situation.

But whatever it was, he knew beyond a shadow of a doubt that Iris was special. She was special, and he wanted to be sure that he let her know it. She didn't feel it, he knew that. He remembered as much from that very first long conversation they'd had. That she felt for whatever reason her sisters were special, in a way that she wasn't. He liked her sisters. But they weren't her. Nobody was.

Iris was the woman who had come up the mountain and not flinched in the face of his anger, which he knew he wore like a shield over his grief. She was determined, and strong. She had taken her own trauma and turned outward, rather than inward like he had.

244 THE HEARTBREAKER OF ECHO PASS

She was innocent and sensual, honest. He had never in all his life met anyone quite like her. And he didn't think he would have appreciated her before.

Not before. But now, he was a man who had experienced a particular kind of hell. Who had been through something that few people would ever understand.

But Iris was a breed of flower grown in the rockiest of soil. Unique and blooming bright in spite of the adversity that she'd faced. And it was exactly what called to him now.

There was another person that could possibly walk out of the darkness with him.

He'd pushed his family away. Had felt like they didn't understand. They loved him, but they didn't know how to sit with his pain.

His friends hadn't been helpful at all. They had simply wanted him to go back.

He couldn't go back. Iris knew that without him having to tell her.

You could never be what you were before.

Grief like that marked you down deep in your soul.

But he was beginning to think that walking forward was possible in a way he hadn't believed before. Yeah, he was beginning to believe in that. And it was something of a miracle. One he wouldn't have found if it weren't for her. He didn't know all the ways he might honor that. But he wanted to.

Maybe she'd been right, after all. Maybe he still had some heart left, after all, because what was this if not...

Caring.

"Now you can get out."

She was slightly unsteady when she did, and he brought her to the bed of the truck and opened it. Her eyes widened, then brightened. "Flowers?"

"Yeah. I thought… I thought I might make a planter box. Actually, a few planter boxes."

"For my windows."

"Yeah. I thought it would look good with your sign. Pink."

"Griffin," she said softly. "That is the nicest thing."

"Weird, because I would've told you that I'm not nice. But you kind of make a man want to try."

She looked away, her cheeks turning pink.

"Why is it that me being nice to you seems to throw you off more than when I yell at you and tell you to leave my cabin?"

"A very good question," she said, looking up at him. "I just… I don't know. Thank you, Griffin. Nobody's ever done anything quite like this for me before. We all took care of each other, when my parents died. But you know, some of us were older, some of us were kids. It was up to the older ones to keep things going. That's just how it was. It's not a bad thing. It just is."

"But you were a kid."

"I was. And then I wasn't. It's all right. I mean, I was on the way to growing up. I wasn't the baby. Rose was… Rose was a firecracker. So much trouble. My mom had to watch her all the time. And then there was Pansy, who was also just kind of… A little bit wild. And I never was. So in the end, it was good. But they had me. Because if they didn't, then it might be a lot harder for them. And it certainly would've been harder for me. But I… You know. I liked being home. I liked baking."

"It doesn't mean you didn't want other things."

She tried to force a smile. "I forgot what they were. If I ever did."

"Is that true?"

She lifted a shoulder. "Maybe it's a choice. But it's true."

"Well, it's a different time now. You can have this. Want this. And I'm going to help."

"Why?"

"You're special, Iris. And you deserve everything."

The words came out of his mouth with so much conviction that they shocked him. Really, the only conviction he'd felt for the last few years was that life was hell, and he was stuck living it. But now he believed in something else. He believed in her. The realization was enough to knock him on his ass, but thankfully, he remained standing. Instead, he got the wood out of the back of the truck, and his notebook out of his pocket.

"I worked up a quick design for these while I was at the store."

"You can just… Do that?" She wasn't responding to what he'd said about her being special. Rather, gawking at the little drawing he'd done.

"Yeah. I've gotten pretty familiar with construction. With how things work. Since I've been…"

She looked at him.

"I'm building that house."

She nodded. But she didn't press.

Just like he didn't press her accepting what he'd said about her being special.

Apparently, no matter what they'd said, there were still some boundaries. Because if he pushed that, he had a feeling he was going to have to answer some questions inside of him that he didn't quite feel like answering.

And if she pushed about the house, it might lead to a deeper discussion than either of them wanted to have.

So they started to focus on the planter boxes. Iris hovered over him while he started.

"You know, you can go do other things if you have things you need to do."

"I know," she said. "I just… I like watching you work." She blushed. He loved when she did that.

"Well, appreciated. But I don't want to keep you from what you had in mind."

"Honestly, this is where I want to be."

She sat perched on the bed of his truck, he worked. She went and got some cookies and coffee from inside the bakery, and brought them out to him. And they both sat on the tailgate of the truck, eating pink frosted cookies with a sea of pink flowers behind them. And if he'd ever been told before that something like that might make him feel content, feel happy, he would've told them they were crazy.

The fact of the matter was, since leaving the business world behind, he hadn't been happy. Of course, there had been reasons for that. Circumstances. So he hadn't thought that he particularly liked country living. The slower life. This life where making things with his hands, and connecting to the world in a very real way was the way of it. A day spent building planter boxes, and just talking to someone. And not talking.

But feeling their presence, and sweet, quiet way. Yeah. He never thought that would be something he liked.

It hit him then that he hadn't fully taken on board the ways in which he'd changed.

Because that change had been enforced. Brought about by an initial trauma. It never occurred to him that there might be some good things in this life he'd chosen.

He didn't miss the city. And that had nothing to do with Mel. Or what he'd lost. That had everything to do with… Well, it was all linked. He couldn't really separate them out. But the problem was, he realized, that there were things in his life that were desperately shallow. Things he'd chosen when he'd wanted something different. And he'd been on a path that would lead him here, but mostly because it was what Mel had wanted. And he'd wanted to make her happy.

And in no scenario had he imagined himself living like this.

But right now, right now, things felt okay. Right now, they felt pretty good.

CHAPTER NINETEEN

THEY HAD SPENT the whole day together. He had kissed her twice. Iris felt… Strange. Everything that was happening between them seemed so… Well, not like what they had talked about yesterday. But then, he had met her family and they had gone their separate ways last night, and today he was… Well, he was being wonderful. She couldn't deny that. She never had anyone take the care that he was doing with her. But there was something about it that made her feel uncomfortable. Deeply so.

But then, the entirety of the last few months had been a study in discomfort. Maybe the last year. All the changes that were happening around her were intense, had jolted her out of her sense of purpose. And this bakery had brought it back. And to an extent, she had felt some of that with Griffin. Going to his house, cleaning. Bringing him food. It had been clear to her that he had been in some sort of depression for some time. But now he was here, and he was doing all of this for her, and… He was right. She was more uncomfortable with him being nice to her than she was with him trying to scare her down his mountain.

They were…friends. And that made things feel a little sharper. A little harder. But the friendship didn't change things. Not really.

"It's opening tomorrow," she said. "I'll put the sign out on the street, and then… It will be open. And then we'll

have a grand opening in a couple of days and… I can't believe it."

"You've done amazing work, Iris," he said. "Really
amazing. I think your parents would've been proud."

Something in her shifted. She pushed that compliment
away.

She found while she was in the kitchen that he had
placed a dinner order at Bellissima, the Italian restaurant
down the street, and then he went to pick it up, brought it
back and set it out on the table in the bakery.

And it was making her heart feel like it was too large for
her chest, all these small, sweet things that came together
to create something wholly new, something she was completely unprepared for. The pasta that he'd ordered was delicious, but she had such a hard time taking it. Such a hard
time feeling like he was just giving all of this to her. And
it was weird, because she never contended with this feeling before. She was used to being part of a family, where
she did a certain amount of caregiving. And it wasn't as if
nobody gave anything back to her.

But it was…communal.

They shared.

Today had been focused on her with an intense kind of
laser quality, and she didn't know what to do with it.

And she was afraid, so very afraid that he was just going
to leave her there again when the meal was over. So afraid
that, when she still had half a plate of food left, she reached
across the table and grabbed his hand. And it reminded her
of lying by the river with him. Because she realized it was
the only time they'd held hands. When they'd been naked
and basking in the aftermath of a climax.

But for some reason it felt different now.

Then, he'd been this man that she'd only known in the

context of his hermitage. And now, he… He'd come down and he'd done all these things for her. He'd shared with her. Opened himself up. Not just about his deep dark tragedy, but about things that he liked. About what he thought of her. She'd seen him talk to her sisters, and to her brothers-in-law. He'd eaten pink frosted sugar cookies next to her, and had built her flower boxes, and there was something about holding hands with him now that felt infinitely more complicated. Like they were holding something heavy and precious in their hands, and she wasn't sure she liked it at all.

His gaze was electric on hers. Far too sharp.

"I'm not leaving you tonight, if that's what you're worried about."

"Oh. I… I was."

He stood, and got down on his knees so that he was eye level with her, where she was sitting. "Iris," he said, his voice rough as he dragged his thumb over her cheekbone. "I just wanted to make sure you knew… You're more than me just enjoying pleasure after a long time of going without. I needed to make sure you knew that. This isn't just me needing sex. Granted, I like it, don't get me wrong. You're more than that. You matter. You could've sent a hundred different women up the hill before you, and they wouldn't have moved me at all. It was you. And you need to know that. Not my isolation. Not my sadness, my grief, my boredom. Not my ability to fashion you into someone else when I'm holding you in my arms, because I'm not doing that. It's you. I couldn't quite figure out why I didn't stay last night, not until I realized I wanted to build those flower boxes for you. But I realized it was about you."

Her chest felt full, like it might burst open, and she did the only thing she could think to do. She launched herself forward out of her chair, and into his arms, kissing him.

Deep and hard. Kissing him with every ounce of that unknowable emotion inside of her. Because it made her feel… Something. Made her feel better. Made her feel more like she could breathe. Because all of his words felt sharp and barbed, but his lips were firm and soft and magic all at once, and she was utterly and completely captivated by him.

By this.

So, she kissed him, because she didn't have words. And she didn't want his. Kissed him until she realized that even though they had blinds half drawn, they were visible to anyone who might be walking by, even though there wouldn't be anyone walking by at this hour.

"Upstairs?" she asked.

"Absolutely."

She didn't worry about the food, they would get that handled tomorrow morning. Right now, she just wanted him. Just needed him. Craved him.

Because this was clear. And this was sure. And she understood that he thought maybe he was… Devaluing her if he reduced it to sex, but this wasn't reduced to anything, not for her. It was big and magical and powerful, comforting. Because she didn't have to know answers. She didn't have to figure out what she could do to bring him pleasure, it just brought both of them pleasure. And that felt easy. And she desperately wanted easy. Because who would have ever thought that an entire day spent with someone doing nice things for you could feel so hard. Only that it did.

He picked her up. Like she weighed nothing. Like she wasn't any trouble or a burden at all, holding her against his broad chest as he walked her through the bakery, and up the stairs. When he got her inside, she abruptly flashed back to that night. To their first kiss. The night that he'd rejected her. She felt like they lived so many lifetimes since then. So many versions of themselves, stripped back and revealed. She hadn't known then what she knew now. Hadn't known about the pain that he carried around. And thinking about that spurred her on. She wanted to give to him. Wanted to thank him for everything that he'd done today. She pushed his shirt up, revealing his body. The hard ridge of his abdomen, his broad chest and shoulders. He was so beautiful. Impossibly so.

Like a gift she could never hope to earn.

He shifted, and those muscles flexed and bunched, and she felt an answering clinch echo inside of her body. Then his hands moved to the buckle on his jeans, and she helped him. As he undid his pants, she dropped down to her knees, started to pull at his boots and socks, and then tugging his jeans down all the way. He was so large and hard. So incredibly beautiful. His naked body was a work of art, and one that she would never tire of seeing. And she had never done this before, but she wanted to.

Yes, she wanted to an awful lot. She stretched up, curving her fingers around his hardness, testing the weight and strength of him.

Then she leaned in, flicking her tongue cautiously across that vulnerable skin. He tasted salty and musky, and there was something about it that made her whole body tighten with desire. It was so intimate. To taste him like this. And he was beautiful. A fantasy brought to life. She put her hand on his hip, traced the deep groove that ran from the bone there down to his thigh, bracketing the most masculine part of him. And then she took him in deep. His large hand came up and cupped the back of her head, forking through her hair. He tugged lightly, the pain sending sparks showering down through her body. It was amazing how she wanted him. Amazing the way that pleasing him ramped up her own pleasure. And she put everything into it.

For the flower boxes. For the day. For just being him. For the way that he was. He had said all those wonderful things to her. Amazing things about how she was special. And she didn't know how to respond in kind. Didn't know what to do or say. And didn't even know how to say thank-you for that. So she just put it all here. She showed him. Because it was all she knew how to do. It made her feel vulnerable. To want him to feel her gratitude so much. It made her feel vulnerable that he might know how much he mattered.

She didn't know why. Except it made her feel like she was bleeding inside. And all she could do to try to banish it was close her eyes and keep pleasuring him. His groans of desire created a deep satisfaction inside of her. Deep and wonderful.

He started to shiver. Started to shake. And then he pulled her away from him.

"Not like this," he said, his voice rough.

"Why not?"

"I want you. Too much. I want to be inside of you."

That harsh, guttural admission echoed inside of her, sent a thrill of pleasure through her body. He wanted her. He really wanted her. He was past the point of reason. Past the point of speaking words clearly, and it was because of her. It was because of what she had made him feel. And there was something so deeply wonderful and comforting about that something that made her feel… Fulfilled. It was beyond pleasure. It was somewhere at the center of what she was. Need. Deep and real, blooming inside of her. Inside of everything that she was. He carried her over to the sofa in the big, open space, and set her on the end of it. She was still dressed. Wearing the same floral dress that she'd had on the entire day. He reached beneath her skirt and yanked her panties down, finding her slick and ready for him. She would have been embarrassed, this display of how much she wanted him so obviously written in her body, except that he wanted her just as badly. That he was held just as captive to it as she was. Then he ducked his head beneath her skirt, tasting her.

She tried to push him away, because this wasn't what she wanted. She didn't want him to make it equal. But then, his mouth was back on her, and she couldn't do anything to deny him. Couldn't do anything to turn him away. Because she was lost in it. In him. And she forgot that she needed him to need her. And slipped into something more. Something deeper. This shared desire that wove a tapestry of sensation in her body. He pushed her higher, further, until she was gasping for pleasure. For release. He brought her to the edge. Over and over again, only to deny her.

This man.

This man who wanted her. Who craved her.

This man.

If she could just focus on what he gave her, on what they could give each other in moments like these. If she could just not want any more than this.

She hadn't known. She hadn't known that it could be like this. Not sex. She hadn't thought enough about it to make assumptions, not ones that went this deep. She hadn't known that connecting to another person could be like this. She hadn't known that there were things in life like this. That were intense because they were terrifying and yet, filled with joy for the same reason. That were bright and bold, frightening and inevitable. That were good and sharp and painful all at once.

She had known pain. Bright, white-hot grief that had

defined her. Who she was, and the way that people saw her. The way that she saw herself. But she hadn't known that good could come with quite so much danger. She hadn't known that the capacity for feeling existed inside a human body, not on this level. She just hadn't known. She felt a fool, really. Small and silly. For thinking that she might have been able to control something like this. For thinking she might have been able to know. She didn't know anything.

She didn't know anything at all.

He still wouldn't let her break. He wouldn't let her break, and she was suspended, in a world of fantasy and desire, of pain.

But he just kept bringing her higher, his hands, his lips, everything working together to create an intense, unending need inside of her. It was magic. But it was a black magic.

Finally, he positioned himself at the entrance of her body, and when he thrust inside of her, she broke. Stars burst behind her eyes, the night sky shattering and falling around her, pieces of endless glass pleasure embedding themselves inside of her.

Sharp and sweet.

Nothing half so simple as pure sweetness.

But nothing was good when it was too sweet. That was the problem. There had to be something else with it. It had to have another side.

It was just the way of it. It was just the way. His claiming of his own desire was fierce, his fingers digging into her body as he chased his own release. The raw, guttural growl that he let out as he slammed into her one last time, as he spilled himself in her, created another ripple inside of her. A second release on the heels of one she would have said would have been it. All she could handle. All she could take.

And when it was over, he picked her up off the couch, carried her across the room, and to her bed. This was a new room, so she didn't have a host of memories stored up in it, but she had brought her bed and bedding over, even though there had been one there already, which she had used a couple of times. Ultimately, she had preferred her own. And being with a man, on that familiar quilt... It was a whole strange thing.

He pushed the blankets back, guided her beneath them and lay down beside her. Then he wrapped her up in his arms.

They were going to sleep together.

They had done that at his place. But that had been... It had been so different. Spontaneous. And everything between them had been a storm. There had been a lot of anger. A lot of sadness. This had been different. She hadn't felt those same barriers. That same sense of trauma. Where they had both been bleeding out some kind of darkness, trying to soothe the other.

She ignored the hitch in her chest that reminded her it wasn't like she'd been without her own darkness tonight.

It wasn't. It was true. But they were here now. And he wanted her.

She could... She could help him. He'd said so.

As he walked on this path trying to figure out being human again. And she would. She would be there for him. She would be exactly what he needed.

She let her mind go blank at that thought. Let herself take in nothing more than the scent of his skin, the sound of his slow, steady breathing.

Tomorrow, her new life started.

CHAPTER TWENTY

IT WAS HER very first day open, and she was... Not nervous. She had everything ready to go. Most of her stock she'd been able to make ahead, and some of it she had prepared from dough that morning. Everything was set out, and looking beautiful. The display cases were full of cookies, all colors. Pinks, lavender, yellow, green, regular chocolate chip, chunky varieties that were filled with nuts and fruit. There was cake, pie. A rack filled with bread. It was a superhuman effort, and she was incredibly proud of it.

What had really surprised her was when Griffin had come downstairs, freshly showered, come into the kitchen, put on an apron and asked what he could do to help.

It was almost comical. He was a superior specimen of masculinity, an absolute god of testosterone, and the apron was... Well, that black apron over his broad chest, tied over his slim waist, was legitimately one of the sexiest things she'd ever seen. He hefted trays in and out of the oven, brought in new stock. She wasn't incredibly hard-hit, it was a weekday, after all, and Gold Valley only had the usual foot traffic, as tourism wouldn't really pick up for another couple of weeks. But there were people, and they were very excited to have a bakery back in town. Living above it would mean that Iris could devote time to simply being there. In her opinion, the previous bakery hadn't lasted because their hours had been very uncertain and strange.

She intended to provide stability, and to fling herself into it, and given the deal Griffin was giving her, her overhead was so low it was nearly unrealistic.

The enthusiasm of the place… That was what truly fueled her.

The looks on people's faces when they saw the brightly colored goodies. She tied up several pink boxes and put little Cookie Jar stickers over the top of them, filling them to the brim with cookies, cupcakes and muffins. She had a lot of discussions with people about her refrigerator meals, and quite a few people ended up taking some home for that night.

The door opened, and Sammy entered first, Ryder holding it open for her. She had baby Astrid on her hip, and was grinning.

"Iris," she said. "This is absolutely stunning."

"Thank you," Iris said.

"This is really something else," Ryder said.

"I want one of everything," Sammy said, waving her free hand.

"You literally get free treats from me all the time. And anyway, whatever people don't buy, I'll be boxing up and sending to you."

"Not if I buy it first," Sammy said.

Griffin chose that moment to come in from the back. Looking delicious and bearded, and very obviously who he was.

"Hi," Ryder said, eyeing the other man. "You must be Griffin."

"And you must be Ryder." Griffin didn't miss a beat. He reached out and shook Ryder's hand, leaning over the counter to do so.

"Guilty as charged. So you're…" Ryder lifted a brow. "Protecting your investments?"

"Assisting. With whatever she needs. Though, it's not much. She's pretty much got this locked down."

"She's brilliant," Ryder said.

"I agree."

Ryder sized Griffin up. Iris half expected the words *what are your intentions toward my sister* to come out of her brother's mouth. But thankfully, they didn't.

"How's business been?"

"Great," Iris said. "Honestly, considering it's not the grand opening, and we just turned the sign, much better than I expected. I'm hoping that this Saturday is really amazing. I'm going to set up a table outside and give away free sugar cookies."

"Well, we'll all be there with bells on. Whatever you need."

She wrinkled her nose. "For you not to wear bells?"

"No. Definitely coming in bells. Maybe only bells."

"Please no."

"All right. I'll behave. Can't promise anything for Sammy, though."

"I never behave," Sammy said. "Not if I can help it."

"Hey," Ryder said. "What time you closing up shop here?"

"Oh, probably about five."

"Well, it just so happens that we were going to barbecue a rack of ribs over at the house. You should come."

"Oh, well…"

"You should both come," Ryder said, looking directly at Griffin.

"Both of us," Iris said.

"Yeah. I think it would be nice if I got to know your boyfriend."

"He's..."

"Always up for ribs," Griffin said. "Then we'll see you tonight around six. Don't bother to bring dessert. Sammy's buying one of everything."

She wrapped up the desserts for her brother and Sammy, and tried not to react to what had just happened. It was horribly uncomfortable, the idea of Griffin spending an inordinate amount of time with her family. After all, they were... They had just spent all last night...

Well, when she thought about where he had his mouth...

And then thinking about him being anywhere near her family... She didn't know how people did that.

Rose and Logan had sneaked around. How had they managed? She really didn't quite know.

"I can hear you thinking," Griffin said.

"You don't have to come to my family's house tonight. I mean... Ryder was being nosy. Intrusive."

"Polite. And I would like to go to your family's house."

"Why?"

He paused for a moment. "They're important to you. They are an important part of who you are. Anyway, I haven't been to anything like that in a long time."

"And you're... Okay with that?"

He nodded. "I'm starting to realize something, Iris. The real tragedy of going through something like I did is that you don't want to heal. Because it doesn't feel right. I've been avoiding getting better, because I thought it would be a disservice to them. I'm still struggling with that, I'm not going to lie to you. Because I keep telling myself maybe this is just easier than staying secluded. Maybe I'm taking some kind of easy route. But then... This isn't easy. It's not.

But I need to do it, and I want to. Because it's not living that does them a disservice, it's refusing to live well when they're not here to do it themselves. What kind of attribute is it to shut yourself away?"

"Griffin... Well, I'm glad for you then."

"I think I can handle your family. Don't you worry about me."

"I don't know. They're a bit much."

"Who haven't I met?"

"Colt and Jake. My cousins. Officially, two of the biggest, brashest idiots in the world. At least, that's my opinion."

"What makes them idiots?"

"Bull riders."

"As in, rodeo bull riders?"

"Yes. They're definitely... Well, they're definitely them." She shook her head. "But anyone who thinks to themselves that throwing themselves on the back of an eight hundred pound animal and getting flung around is a good idea is pretty much half-cocked."

"I think I'll like them."

"You probably will."

"You don't have to worry about me," he said. "I could have said no if I didn't want to go."

"Right. About what he said. The boyfriend thing, I..."

He turned to face her, gripped her chin, his eyes blazing into hers. "Iris," he said. "I'm not running scared. Don't worry."

"I'm not worried." It was a lie, though.

This had been so clear in her head. Friends. Two people helping each other. Not one person with heavy feelings wishing, working, for the other person to feel the same.

No.

The problem with things like this, the problem with *help-*

ing was that it was so easy to confuse it with love. That the way you were appreciated, and someone else appreciating you was…enough.

But it was a one-way street. And it was never enough.

And when you weren't needed, people moved on. "I just didn't want you to think I was trying to trap you," she said. "We both know this is…friendship. I know you love your wife."

"Of course I do," he said, his voice fracturing. He looked like he didn't know quite what to say. "You matter to me, though."

She'd mattered to a lot of people. She'd helped a lot of people. It was a good thing, a good feeling.

As long as she didn't want more.

"I just wanted to make sure you knew that I…that I know what this is."

He huffed a laugh. "Do you? Because I'm not sure I do."

Her heart twisted and she reached out and touched his face. "We're helping each other."

And she smiled even though she sort of wanted to cry.

HOPE SPRINGS RANCH was beautiful. There was a wooden sign above the entry of the driveway, with horses and words proclaiming the name. It sat off the main highway, backed by forests and mountains, wild and beautiful, with a farmhouse that avoided being too pristine, a whole passel of dogs and horses out in every pasture.

This was where she had grown up. With siblings, and no parents for a time, a group of kids all depending on the land then each other.

It fascinated him that she had come out of it as she was. As determined and pure as she was. She wasn't cynical.

She wasn't angry. She wasn't filled with hatred or bitterness. At every turn, Iris was incredible to him.

Though, she was clearly finding his invitation to her family's house problematic. So that could just be because she didn't really love the idea of her being around his family. Which he could understand.

He thought about his parents, back in the Bay Area. And he wondered what they would think of Iris. What Mallory would think of her.

His dad had a way of cutting down to the heart of things, and he would like how Iris was no-nonsense in her way. His mom would like how she cooked and cared for things.

Mallory would like her.

Mallory was a practical girl, even if her taste in men had always been kind of suspect. Well, her taste in one man. Granted, she never talked to him about Jared, so he didn't really know where the two of them stood these days. But that was just because Mallory knew better than to bring him up.

Griffin was not a fan. Not in the least.

It was clear Mallory didn't care all that much about Griffin's opinion. If she did, she wouldn't have been trapped in a fifteen year, off-and-on relationship with a man she had once insisted to him she was fated to be with.

For all that Griffin wasn't best friends with fate, or the concept of it, he didn't think—if the concept was real—it was actually his brilliant, driven sister's fate to end up cohabitating with a guy who rarely had a job and who seemed to consider commitment flexible.

He wondered what Iris would say about that. And then he felt guilty. That he was going to spend time with her family when he had spent so long ignoring his own. But he didn't have a place to invite them to in town. He supposed, though, they could stay at the bed-and-breakfast at the end of Main Street. An old Victorian, that was run by an elderly woman whose biscuits were famous about town.

If Mallory could get a break from the clinic. His parents had retired long ago and he knew they could come whenever.

Was he really planning ways for Iris to meet his family?

He stopped his truck in front of the house, staring at it.

"You can still turn back," Iris said.

"No," he said. "Not remotely tempted to. I was promised barbecue. So I'll have it."

They were greeted enthusiastically by the dogs when they got out of the truck, and Iris patted them while professing annoyance.

"What's the matter?"

"They know they're annoying," she said as they made their way up to the front porch.

"So this is your house."

"It's where I grew up, yes."

"And lived until just recently."

"Well, yes. I guess so."

She opened the door, and they both walked in. The entry way was cluttered, and cheerful, the floors of the home scarred and well used. There was a leather couch that looked like it had been around since Iris's childhood.

It was warm and cheerful, very different to the modern house his parents had. He and Mallory had been born so far apart that while they'd been close, the house hadn't been filled with a lot of kid noise the way this one must have been.

"Everyone must already be outside." They filtered through the house, and went out the back door and indeed, everyone was already in the backyard.

West, Logan, Pansy and Rose were sitting in lawn chairs. There were two men he hadn't met before, and a teenage boy. Then, there was Sammy and Ryder, and the little baby they'd been holding yesterday.

"Hi," Iris said.

Everybody turned to look at them, as if they were surprised to see them.

"I told you I invited them," Ryder said.

"Hi," Griffin said. "I'm Griffin Chance."

The first man, tall and broad, stood up from the lawn chair and stuck his hand out. "Colt Daniels."

The next one, just as tall and broad, and with similar features, stood also. "Jake Daniels."

The kid, tall, but not at all broad, stood up. "Emmett Caldwell. West's brother."

"And the rest of us you met," Ryder said.

Colt and Jake then moved and enveloped Iris in a group bear hug.

"Haven't seen you yet," Jake said, tugging at her ponytail.

"No," Iris said, smoothing herself like an angry cat. "I've been busy."

"Too busy to come see us?"

"Not on purpose," she said.

"You're going to be seeing a lot more of me," Jake said. "I just bought a ranch up the way."

"Did you?"

"Yep. Getting tired of living on the road. I figure it's time to think about retiring. You get to your thirties in bull riding and start considering that stuff."

"Not me," Colt said.

"Yeah, just wait. You're going to fall the wrong way

one day and end up where I am. Realizing that your back has a shelf life."

"I'm a full thirteen months younger than you. So, I'm good for a while."

"The confidence of youth," Jake said. "The grand opening of your bakery's in a couple days, right? I want to make sure that I get there for that."

"Yes," Iris said. "It is."

"Looking forward to it. You know, you're the best cook I've ever known."

"You've had very few people cook for you," Iris said.

"Not true," he said. "I've had any number of women cook me breakfast."

"Liar," Colt said. "You're always out the door before breakfast."

The corners of Jake's mouth pulled down. "True."

"See," Iris said to Griffin. "Bull riders."

"There's some time before the meat gets done. And that means, we can play football." That proclamation came from Ryder. And was met with both groans and enthusiastic sounds. Emmett was the most enthusiastic.

And was the most likely to get absolutely clobbered.

"Wait a minute, tell me about the football," Griffin said to Iris.

"It's Ryder's first love, and he coaches the local high school team."

"So, should I play?"

He couldn't remember the last time he'd thrown a football around in a backyard. Maybe never? He wasn't actually sure he knew how to play. He knew the rules from watching it, but...

"Yeah," Ryder said. "Get in there. I'm obviously going

to be judging what manner of man you are based on how well you do."

He didn't doubt that. Not for one second.

"All right," Ryder said. "Men, in positions."

Griffin got an assignment given to him from Ryder, and took it, the teams were divided up haphazardly and the game commenced. The full-scale violence surprised Griffin, but he found that he enjoyed it. Who would've thought. Pink iced sugar cookies in a violent backyard game of football.

It was entirely possible that Ryder was trying to kill him for sleeping with his sister. Griffin couldn't discount that.

But, mostly, it was good-natured, and he didn't end up too close to death by the end of the game, even if he was limping.

Ryder's team beat his soundly.

"You did a decent enough job," Ryder said, clapping him on the back. "I don't judge you too much."

By then, the meat was ready, along with baked beans, macaroni salad and any number of other delicious foods. Colt brought out his guitar at one point, and did some passable country songs, pretty impressive for a casual backyard performance, really. And Griffin just kind of listened. To everyone talking. To them interacting. To family.

Family.

That word settled in his stomach like a rock.

He'd avoided family for so long. The sense of it. The need for it.

He'd avoided his own, because they were so linked to that piece of family he'd lost.

But right here, he saw a family bonded together by loss. It was…he didn't have words for it.

He went over to the cooler, and opened it and saw that it was out of beer.

"More in the house," Ryder said. "Come on, we'll get some."

Iris gave him a look, but he shrugged and followed Ryder indoors.

"Is this the part where you ask me what my intentions are toward your sister?"

"Yeah," Ryder said. "I'm pretty proud of myself for not saying it in front of her."

"Your whole posture kind of shouts it, though."

"Only because you feel guilty."

"I don't feel guilty about anything," Griffin said. "I think your sister is amazing. I'm not using her. If that's what you're worried about."

"Good. I wanted to be sure of that. My gut is that you're a pretty good guy. And I have an all right gut. But you're some rich guy who came down here from California, and I have to admit, that makes me a little bit nervous. Ingrained prejudice."

"That's not exactly the whole story," Griffin said. "I don't know what she told you. My wife died a few years ago. I came here to lick my wounds."

Ryder jerked back. "Right. Shit. I'm sorry."

"It's a… I'm learning to accept it? I don't know. Figure out how to exist?" He thought back to that little baby. That little girl of Ryder's. It made him ache. It made him ache, but it was a fact of life. And he was glad there were babies in the world. That other people had their little girls. But he always thought of his own, and that was difficult. It always would be, he realized. It always would be, and there was some kind of grace and acceptance in that. Grace he hadn't realized he needed.

"I... I lost my wife and my daughter," he said to Ryder.

Ryder's face turned to stone, and he knew it was the last thing a new father wanted to hear. Hell, if he'd been a new father, hearing his story would have destroyed him. But living it was worse. He knew that for certain.

"So I'll tell you something. Something real and I'm not... I'm not great with feelings so bear with me. Your sister feels like a miracle to me. Because I didn't know if I would ever enjoy the taste of food again, much less find somebody who made me feel like this. So I don't know what my intentions are toward her. I just know that I think she's amazing. Pretty damn near perfect. And I know that I would never do anything to hurt her."

"I don't know what to say," Ryder said. "She didn't tell me about your daughter."

"I had a hard time telling her about it myself. I have a hard time talking about it. But now I told her. I told you. You say it enough times and it becomes real, you know? I've been doing a lot to try and make it not real. And now I'm kind of finding my way back into the world I'm trying to figure out what living looks like now. Right now, it's looked the best with her."

"I don't know how you're... How you're still standing," Ryder said. "I don't know..."

"I wasn't. Not for a long time. You lose something like that, and the only thing that keeps you going is knowing that living is something they can't do. But I've just been surviving. Not really living. She's showing me something different. So believe me when I tell you, she matters to me."

Ryder nodded. "But you can't make any guarantees."

"No," Griffin said. "I've... When I do, she'll be the first to know."

"I respect that."

"Thank you for inviting me over. The other thing I haven't done in a long time too is sit with a family. And it's been good to see yours. I kind of abandoned mine. My parents, my sister. I couldn't really cope. Not after losing Mel and Emma."

"I can understand that."

"I figured you probably could." He shook his head. "Iris, and everything that's coming to my life by extension of her, is helping me realize there are some things that I need to start piecing back together."

"Well, we're glad you're here."

"Thank you."

Ryder took two beers out of the fridge, held his out and clinked it against the edge of Griffin's. "You're always welcome here."

"Thank you."

And he hadn't realized what it might mean to have a place like that. One where he was welcome. Another place to go.

His isolated personal map had grown just now. He'd made connections. And it was the kind of thing he could just sit and marvel at. The kind of thing he didn't take for granted. Because of course he didn't. Of course he didn't take any of this for granted. How could he?

He'd spent the last five years in a fog, and coming out of it was like breathing. For the first time. Like seeing for the first time.

"Now, let's go rejoin the party. Iris is probably dying of distress, wondering if I took you in here to kill you for living in sin with her."

"Were you going to?"

Ryder shook his head. "No. I have no room to judge."

"Doesn't mean you wouldn't."

"That's right, you did mention you had a sister. So you know how it is."

"I do know how it is."

And he realized that Ryder, unlike any of the friends he had back home, actually did understand him. A little better than most. Husband and father, a man who'd experienced loss. A man with quite a few younger sisters that he'd had to protect.

He'd expected to come meet Iris's family, what he hadn't expected to do was find a friend.

He would've said that he didn't need friends.

He was remembering. All the things that made life worth living. All the things that made life matter. Because of Iris.

Because of the feelings that he had for her.

Ryder had probably wanted some guarantees, and Griffin had said he couldn't give them to him.

But he was starting to think that might not be the case.

He was starting to think that this was more than he had imagined it could be. That there was more left for him on earth than he had ever thought possible.

THERE WAS AFTER dinner football, because of course there was, because Ryder had a completely captive guest in Griffin, who was obviously doing his best to be part of things, which was leaving Iris absolutely agog.

"He is really something," Sammy said from beside her.

"He... Yes."

"I mean, he is smoking hot."

"Dial it down about twenty percent," Iris said, shooting Sammy a warning glare.

"I would," Sammy said, "but I can't."

"Well," Iris said.

"Here," she said, "hold Astrid."

Sammy dumped the little bundle of softness gently into Iris's arms, and her heart contracted.

She looked over at Griffin, who managed to choose that exact minute to look over at her. While she was standing there holding a baby.

A strange expression filtered across his face, his features going tight. And Iris suddenly felt panicky.

"Take her," she said to Rose.

"All right," Rose said, taking Astrid in her arms.

"When are you going to have one of those?" Pansy asked.

"Maybe never," Rose said, but Iris could see by the expression on her face when she looked at their niece that that was absolutely not true. She smiled softly. "I don't know, maybe in a couple of years. She's so beautiful."

Iris had to agree, but she felt enervated over the fact that Griffin had just seen her holding a baby, and what if he thought she wanted a baby? Or what if it hurt him to see a baby? She hadn't even thought of that. She wondered if he was okay, or if he was upset. He had looked a little bit upset.

Because of course he wouldn't be wanting... And the picture that she would've made holding her was so domestic. That concerned her. Honestly concerned her.

The whole thing made her feel jumbled up. More than she should feel.

"What about you?" Pansy asked. "Are you going to marry him?"

"No," Iris said. "I already told you that. No."

"You brought him home to all of us. You brought him home to meet the family."

"I didn't... I didn't do it on purpose. Ryder invited him."

"So, what's the problem? He's gorgeous, and here and charming. And plays football. Ryder seems to like him."

"The problem," Iris said, "is that... It's hard to explain."

She looked at Rose and Pansy, two of the people she loved most in the whole world, and she didn't know how to explain that so much of the heaviness she carried inside her was because of the way she'd cared for them.

"Try," Pansy said.

"He was married," she said.

"So?" Rose asked.

"He's widowed. His wife died. He…he loves her and he's…he's my friend. I needed someone to help me start a real life and he needed someone he could be with to help him heal and I'm good at helping people."

The words were ash in her mouth.

"You're more than that," Rose said.

"I need to make sure I am," Iris said.

Her brain felt like a minefield of memories. And she chose not to have any of them. Standing there with her sisters.

I need your help, Iris.

You know how Rose gets.

Rose just needs me.

I don't have time to bake with you.

Your dad is so mad at Pansy, I just have to go and manage that.

They need more care than you. They need more attention.

She shoved all that aside.

But then, more memories flooded in.

Thank you so much for taking care of them.

I love it when you help around the house.

I appreciate it so much.

She felt tired just then.

Finally, when the game was finished, and she and Griffin made their way back to the bakery, she leaned back in her seat. "I'm tired tonight," she said. "I might need to be alone."

He frowned. "All right." He paused for just a moment. "Did I do something wrong?"

"No," she said. "You didn't do anything wrong. It's just me. I'm tired. I'm tired and I need a little bit of time to think."

"Whatever you need, Iris. You know I'll give it to you."

"I appreciate it."

But when he finally dropped her at the bakery, she couldn't sleep. And she ended up just being angry with herself that she hadn't asked him to stay.

Because no matter how much she told herself this was temporary, her bed already felt too empty without Griffin in it.

And that was a problem.

CHAPTER TWENTY-ONE

IT HAD BEEN a few days since Griffin had been up to the build site, and he'd decided to go and take stock. Had felt compelled to do so today.

For so long Griffin hadn't thought of the house as anyone's house in particular. At first, it had been Mel's house.

Because it had been the place that she wanted, on the site that she wanted. But she had no part in the design of it. He had no real idea if it would've been something she liked. He'd known her, well enough to be able to guess, but it wasn't like it had come directly from her. He was building it. And the fact was, she couldn't live in it. He didn't think of it as his house, because he couldn't imagine getting to a space where he actually wanted to live in it. It was just something he was doing.

He stepped out of the truck, and surveyed the site. The skeletal walls, so far from completion, and as long as he did it by himself, he had a feeling it would remain pretty far from completion.

He needed a team. He needed a crew.

He couldn't finish this by himself.

And before that hadn't mattered, because not only had it been nobody's house, there had been no rush because he had no idea who might live in it. In fact, in his head he had imagined it as a mausoleum. Nothing more than an empty tomb. Containing nothing, least of all life. A monument to death. Was that what he'd been building?

Well, the fact was, it was what his life had been.

A monument to death.

Certainly not a monument to love, or to the life that he'd once had.

A piss-poor tribute to the people who had once loved him more than anything on earth. The people he loved so very much still.

It was complicated. They didn't need him to love them in the way he once had. They weren't here for him to care for.

They were... They were safe.

And all of this that he'd done, this isolation, living up here... He'd been protecting them. Because he was still a husband. He was still a father. That love had not been removed from his body. He hadn't lost who he was. He carried it with him.

But they were safe.

He believed that in his soul. They were cared for. They didn't have the same needs as those who were still left on earth, living life.

He didn't need to protect them.

But he could do a better job of sharing who they'd been. Of sharing the good that they'd done for him as a man. Because it had been a lot. Their legacy didn't just begin at the hurt that he felt over losing them. And it shouldn't. Their legacy was bigger than that. His wife's existence had enriched the lives of so many, not just him. She was more than just his wife. And she was more than just his pain. And his little girl... She was more than that too. She was more than her death. She was smiles and giggles and a deep, real joy that he'd felt. That he knew existed. They had taught him that deep and beautiful things existed in the world.

Their legacy should be hope.

Their legacy should be love.

Wasn't that a better legacy than death?

And wasn't it up to him to carry that forward?

This house.

He had built it with his grief. He had fueled it with the sweat and tears that poured from him as he had hammered each and every nail. But somewhere along the lines, sometime in the last month or so, the tenor of the hammer hitting the nails had taken on a new sound. A new purpose.

Because he could see a life lived in that house. He could see it filled with people. Filled with love. Filled with children. He could see a future where he lived there. Not by himself in a cabin with no electricity, no water, no. He could see a future where he didn't just survive. He could see a future where he lived.

And he wanted that future.

For the first time in so long he wanted.

And that had to matter. It did matter.

But it could only matter as much as he let it. And he had to be brave. He had to be brave, and step out and demand that life give him something more. There was fate, and he was beginning to believe in it. In the form of one petite woman who had come up the hill carrying a plate of cookies not knowing who she would meet at the top of it. A woman who had seen a sign on a bakery for rent, who had come into his life when he had needed her most.

But fate couldn't do everything. Not for him and not for anyone. It didn't just dish out the bad, it brought the good, but you had to be able to reach out and take it. You had to do that last bit of hiking yourself. She could have stopped when she saw the tree in the middle of the road but she didn't. She kept on going.

And now it was up to him. It was up to him to keep on going.

It was up to him to let her know how much she mattered to him.

He still couldn't see the future. He still didn't have a name for all of this, but he was willing to find it.

He was willing to walk ahead until he did.

Because for the first time in a long time, the living mattered to him. And he was willing to do more work for them than he was going to do for the dead.

Because the dead didn't need him.

Mel and Emma did not need him the way they once had.

Neither were they gone.

They were with him. In his heart. Had become a part of who he was, the air he breathed. In his actions, in his choices. In the changes that had occurred in him in the last five years.

There was something profound in that shift in thought, in feeling.

One made him the guardian of a tomb. The other made him a man.

Iris Daniels had reminded him he was a man.

A man who had some living to do.

IRIS WAS DETERMINED that her grand opening would be absolutely the best ever. Griffin had offered to come down and help, but her sisters and Sammy were with her, and she had pushed him off, feeling the need for a little bit of time with her family. At least, that's what she told herself.

And so now, they were icing a mass number of pink sugar cookies, preparing them for a giveaway.

"These are adorable," Sammy said. "And delicious."

"Very delicious," Rose agreed.

Pansy made for a comical picture, sitting there in her uniform, but she had to go to work as soon as they were finished and it hadn't made any sense for her to be in her plainclothes.

"This really compromises your image," Sammy said. "Police Chief Pansy Caldwell covered in pink frosting."

Pansy rolled her eyes. "Everything about me already compromises my image. Police Chief Pansy basically covers it."

"Yes, but you're fearsome."

"Formidable," Rose agreed.

"I wouldn't want to get in a fight with you," Iris said.

"No indeed," Pansy said. "Honestly, I don't mind. It allows me to surprise people."

"I like to surprise people," Rose said cheerfully.

"With the fact that you're a giant marshmallow, and not half as tough as you would like people to believe?" Sammy asked.

"I'm tough," Rose said, frowning. "I could take you."

"I never said you couldn't," Sammy said. She smiled brilliantly. "I'm a lover, not a fighter."

"How nice for my brother," Iris said.

"He would tell you different. I'm sure."

"So where is The Handsome Man?" Rose asked. "I expected him to be here."

"I told him that I wanted some time with you." Everyone was staring at her. "What? I told you, it's not like we're living together or anything. It's casual."

"I have to tell you, after the whole thing with the barbecue, it does not seem casual." Sammy spoke sagely.

"It is casual," Iris insisted.

"Again," Sammy said. "Doesn't seem it." She paused

for a moment. "Ryder really liked him. He told me a little bit about... You know."

Iris looked away. "I thought he might."

"What?" Pansy asked.

"I told you Griffin lost his wife. But, until he decided to tell anyone the rest of it, I didn't feel it was my place. He lost his daughter."

"Oh," her sisters chorused together.

"That's exactly it. I don't think he likes everyone to know just for that reason."

"Well, how is anyone supposed to react? That's terrible," Rose said.

She felt suddenly an immense burden resting on her soul, and she didn't want to think about why the idea of *love* felt quite so heavy to her. Why it felt like quite so much work.

Because it is. It's baking and cleaning and proving. Over and over again.

And other people just get to be. And it seems like enough.

She felt guilty. Over the resentment those thoughts built up about her sisters. About the resentment it made her feel toward her mom, who wasn't even here anymore.

Not now, Iris, I'm tired. I had to keep Rose busy all day while you were at school.

Oh, thank you so much for helping with dinner. What would I do without your help?

"Yes," she agreed. "It's terrible. And he needs a friend, not someone asking for a commitment and...it would be a disaster to fall in love with him. He's not ready for it. I'm not ready... I... Look, sometimes you talk yourself into taking something because it's better than the nothing you had. Elliott is a great example."

Rose scoffed.

"I'm serious," Iris said. "I was interested in Elliott because I thought it was better than nothing. I was a virgin and Griffin is great, but is it just because there's never been anyone else? And you know he…he was alone and he was so…so sad. And right now I think I look good to him because he's been broken for years. He needs someone to take care of him, and I've been doing that. But that will pass. And he won't need my help anymore. And then I think he'd see our… You can't build a life on that stuff."

"You don't know that," Pansy said, gently.

"No, I do. I don't want to fight," Iris said. "And I don't know how to say this without it coming out wrong. But I've done a lot of helping. And in the end you all grew up and moved on and what did I have? It's one thing to do that with younger siblings, but I'm not doing that with a man."

"I… I'm sorry," Pansy said. "Do you really feel like we… we really took a lot from you didn't we?"

"I don't like to talk about it," Iris said. "It's not fair. You were kids and I wanted to take care of you, I did."

"But you weren't our mother," Rose said. "You didn't choose it."

"No, but you're my sisters, and I'd do it all over again. But you can see why I don't want to get into anything like that in a relationship."

"You don't know that it would be like that," Rose badgered.

"I won't be taking the risk," Iris said. "I have the bakery. And I have…his friendship." She forced a smile. "And his body. Which is hot. And that's all I want."

Rose and Pansy exchanged a glance that said they clearly didn't believe her.

Fine.

They didn't have to.

"Well, let's set up for cookies," Rose said brightly,

changing the subject, as she seemed to sense Iris's extreme discomfort.

They set out a little sandwich board, pink balloons and the table filled with cookies. It was the weekend, and the first seasonal summer concert of the year was being held in the outdoor amphitheater in Gold Valley. People often came from hundreds of miles away to go to the shows, and it brought a massive influx of tourism into the community. That meant that today the streets were alive with people, and they gave away so many cookies, along with cards, information on how to place birthday cake orders and myriad other things.

She had set Rose at the register inside, and they sold a fair number of goodie baskets that she put together especially for the concerts. Many cakes, and little bottles of iced coffee. And she was feeling almost giddy with the relief of it. Until Griffin showed up, and the feeling of intensity overtook her.

She thought about everything she just said to her sisters. About feeling like it was too much. Like he was too much. And she realized she was caught in the middle of a somewhat unsolvable problem. Because her new life was inextricably linked to him whether she wanted it to be or not. Because no matter that she had made bold proclamations about the fact that this wasn't permanent by design, she found that she...

She wanted him around. She wanted him to be there.

It was difficult to imagine this without him, and that was sobering.

"This is amazing," he said. And then he wrapped his arms around her and kissed her, in full view of everybody.

"Thank you," she said, her cheeks heating. Rose was inside, but Sammy and Pansy were there, looking on.

"Is there anything I can help with?"

She was about to say no, but then another wave of people came and Griffin immediately set to work charming them and handing cookies out. And she couldn't deny that he was a pretty great asset when it came to female customers particularly. Today, he had on a tight black T-shirt and his cowboy hat, and he was looking...

Well, he was looking pretty perfect.

When all was said and done, her sisters offered to help with cleanup, and she was about to decline, when they started furiously working anyway.

And that left the five of them all doing things together, with Griffin talking to them effortlessly, as if he'd known them for years.

"We'll get out of your hair," Sammy said.

"You really don't have to."

"I think we do," Rose said. "Anyway. Logan was cooking dinner tonight, and I really hate to squander a good opportunity to be waited on hand and foot."

"Ryder might heat up a frozen pizza. But honestly, I wouldn't eat his cooking if he offered."

"Yeah, that sounds like Ryder."

"He means well," Sammy said. "And is very accomplished in other rooms."

"Gross," Rose and Iris said together.

"Goodbye, Griffin," Sammy said. "It was nice to get to see you again."

"You too."

And that left just the two of them, standing there in the empty bakery, again.

"You know, the concert just started," he said. "You want to walk up to the top of the hill over there and see if we can hear some of it?"

"I… Sure."

They had a couple of concert baskets left over, and she grabbed them and the two of them walked out of the shop. She locked the door behind them, and Griffin took the boxes from her, and then grabbed hold of her hand.

Her heart squeezed tight as he walked her down the sidewalk, their fingers laced together in the way that she had sort of hoped he might do just a week ago when they'd gone to the Gold Valley Saloon.

Had that only been a week ago? It was so difficult to imagine her life before this. Before him.

And that made her heart stutter just a little bit.

They walked away from the main street, up the hill that went toward the amphitheater and then off a little path that led to a grassy hill. The sky was purple, the air hanging warm and low around them. She could smell the grass, the crickets, the smell coming up from the food trucks at the venue. And the music from an old country duo filtered through that summer air, adding to the magic.

"I don't know why I never do this," she said. "It's really nice."

"It's easy to take for granted the things you have around you. The things in your hometown."

"I suppose so."

He opened up the first box, and took out a cake and offered it to her. She took it gladly.

"There have been all kinds of things I took for granted in my life," he said. "It occurred to me that you may not know this. I feel like you lost the assurance that things would be all right very young."

She nodded slowly, chewing the cake thoughtfully. "Yes. I did. I never assume anything. I never just assumed…"

"I did. My whole life. My parents had money, and I assumed that I would go to school. My father was successful in business, so I assumed that I would be. I was surrounded by people who made successes of themselves, and as a result it seemed pretty damn easy. I always assumed that a wife and kids would be out there somewhere. And when I met the woman that I wanted to marry, all those choices seemed easy. Love felt like something pretty easily won. We planned on having a daughter, and we did. And that all just seemed like how it was supposed to be. Until everything wasn't. Until I found myself in a position that's not natural any way you look at it. Until I was forced to bury my wife. Until I had to bury my child. And that was when I realized... Every good thing in life is a minor miracle. If not a major one. You can't just assume that you'll have anything. Or keep it. Not really."

"I guess that's true."

"And I also thought... I was *sure*... I was sure that losing that meant I was never going to have anything like it ever again. That was just done for me. Just like I assumed that I'd have it, I assumed that having it once meant... That was it."

"Of course." His words made her chest get tight.

"I was wrong, though," he said, his words steady and sure. "And it's sort of a miracle, the biggest one I can think of, to realize that I can have these feelings. And it doesn't feel like having them again, it feels like something completely different."

"Griffin..."

"No, listen to me. It feels like something entirely different to be able to care again when you didn't assume that you could. To be able to care about the world again when you were absolutely certain that you couldn't. To be able to think ahead to a time where I want to share my life with other people. That I might be able to have a new future. Not just have my wife back. Not just have my daughter back."

He took a sharp breath. "This whole idea of moving forward... It's painful as hell. And I don't know what it means. I feel disloyal. To be honest with you, I don't feel perfectly healed, perfectly put together. I feel a little more broken, in fact, than I did the day before. Like making a change rebroke a bone that had healed...badly and now I have to heal a different way. But I care for you. A whole lot. You are something all your own, Iris Daniels, and I'm captivated by you."

She didn't know what to say to that. She felt overwhelmed, tears filling her eyes, she didn't know what to say. She didn't know what she wanted to say.

She didn't know what she wanted to feel.

"Griffin..."

"You don't need to say anything. I'm not asking for anything. I'm not sure what I'm offering either. I'm a little bit messed up, and just trying to deal with all this in the most honest way possible. I don't want to go back to the mountain. I want to stay with you. For now, I want to stay with you."

"I see."

"Do you?"

She blinked, her chest feeling sore. "I don't know, I... What about Mel?"

"Mel is gone," he said.

She nodded. "Yes. You love her, though. She was your wife. I'm...not."

He nodded slowly. "I'll always love her."

"You should."

"She was my first love. But she isn't here now." His

voice was rough and heavy with regret and it hurt. And it was foolish to feel hurt by it.

But she envied that woman, which was the least fair thing. Mel wasn't here anymore. But she knew the man he'd been. The one she'd seen bits and pieces of when he smiled with her family.

He'd put a suit on for her and married her.

You weren't supposed to do this...

She wasn't doing this. She wasn't.

It was just she cared so much, but she knew this wasn't forever. She was okay with that.

"I need you."

That word fed something inside of her. That word suddenly grounded her to the spot. She looked at him, at his beautiful, lined face. At the brokenness she saw there.

He'd said he didn't have it all figured out, but that he wanted her. And she could help. She could do something for him. Fix him. Be what he needed. For the time he needed it.

But she realized when she'd seen him today that she couldn't quite imagine a situation where she'd be happy without Griffin in her life. Couldn't pretend that she was going to walk away from it unscathed. Why shouldn't she take what he was offering? A chance to be together. A chance for her to help him heal, just like they'd been talking about before. But maybe this would be a little bit longer. With him around a little more.

As long as she knew what it was, it would be okay, wouldn't it?

She'd given her sisters such a convincing story earlier but when she looked at him it burned, and...and she wouldn't get confused. If she was happy helping, it was okay that it wasn't love.

He loved his wife. He'd loved her first.

Iris would love her bakery and care for him.

It was okay.

"I want to be with you," she said.

"Good," he responded.

"What does that look like?"

"I suspect we'll figure it out as we go. Though, still, your place is a bit more practical than mine."

"Yes."

"You won't send me away at night again?"

"No," she said. That scared her. Because it was compromising any distance she might have from him. And some distance had been comforting. A facade that maybe this wasn't half so serious as it was becoming.

"I don't really have much to bring down. Except some food from the ice chest."

"You might as well leave it. If you're going to be working on the house."

"Yeah. True enough." He shook his head. "I didn't want to ask you to work through this with me."

"I don't mind. Griffin, whatever you need, I can be there for you. I can… I can take care of you. I can." And if it all felt really similar to another time, to another moment, and it made her feel a little bit afraid, she didn't let it sink in. Didn't let it show.

She got out the little bottle of iced coffee and took a sip. And then she just sat with him, in silence, everything he'd said echoing in her.

That he had feelings for her. That he wanted to continue.

One thing she knew for sure, she wanted him in her life. And she was willing to do whatever work she needed to keep him there.

CHAPTER TWENTY-TWO

AFTER THAT, HE essentially moved in with Iris. It was weird to be down in town, where he could actually have an internet connection, and where his phone worked all the time. He decided to go ahead and get his old computer out, and engage a little bit more with the business, which his business manager was thrilled with.

The other person surprised by his sudden availability was Mallory.

"Hey," he said, answering on the second ring one day.

"You... You have service."

"I do."

"What's going on?"

"Well, I'm still about the homestead sometimes, but I... I moved."

"You moved."

"I'm with someone, Mal. Her name is Iris."

"Iris. Really?"

"Yeah."

He proceeded to tell her the whole story of Iris, how they'd met and how he was trying this, in spite of the fact that it was pretty intense.

"I can't believe it. I mean, honestly, Griffin, I can't. I was so sure..." Her voice caught. "I was really sure that we were going to lose you. I was afraid."

"Yeah, well, you might have. If it wasn't for her."

"Well, I want to meet her."

"You should come up here. You and Mom and Dad."

"And Jared?"

"Are you back with him?" The disgust infusing his voice hadn't even taken thought or effort. No prep required. Just knee-jerk dislike taking the wheel.

"I'm never not with him," she said, suddenly defensive.

Amazing how his name came up the minute things were a little bit defused.

"Well, he seems to think that sometimes you're not with him, which means he gets to behave as if he's single."

There was a biting pause. "It's complicated."

"I take it to mean he's back crashing on your couch, though."

"Not on my couch. But yes. He's back at my place. At our place, Griffin. You haven't been home in five years, you don't really…you don't know how it is."

"Fantastic." He chose to ignore that. "But I want you to know, I have a pretty big property, and hiding a body on it would be easy."

"You know, a couple of months ago I would've been seriously concerned you might have meant that. But it sounds to me like you have something to lose now."

What a strange turn of phrase. *Something to lose.*

It was true. He did.

And he could see that just a little while ago that might have stricken fear into his heart, that he loved something enough now he stood to lose more.

But it was weird to him that he wasn't afraid.

He was… He was happy. Because life was better when you had something to lose.

He'd been a man with nothing. A man who wanted nothing, who loved nothing, and it was hell. It was hell. He would much rather be vulnerable.

"Come up and see us, though," he said.

"Us," Mallory said. "Seriously, Griffin. I'm so happy for you. You're my hero. I hope you know that. I hope you know how much I miss you."

And suddenly right then a lot of things seemed possible. Even going back to California. For a visit. Gold Valley was his home now, and he was resolved in that. But he could see taking Iris back there, introducing her to his parents. Bringing her over for dinner. And the idea didn't draw comparisons between the time he'd done it before, and wanting to do it now. His and Iris's relationship was its own. That much was clear.

He went downstairs, prepared to go up and put a couple hours working on the house, and when he walked into the dining room, Iris jumped up. "Do you need anything?"

"No," he said, frowning.

She'd cooked him breakfast this morning, a huge spread, way more than what he was used to, she certainly didn't need to be offering him anything else.

"I'm headed up to the house. If you need anything from the store before I get back…"

"I shouldn't. Anyway, even if I did I have plenty of time to grab something for dinner. Will you be back for dinner?"

"Yeah. I aim to. Six o'clock?"

"Yes," she said.

"Good. Hey, I invited my sister and my parents to come up and visit. I'd really like for them to meet you."

Iris shifted uncomfortably, her face turning pink. "Really?"

"Yes. Really. You're important to me."

She blinked, and he could sense her discomfort. He

didn't know why that bothered her, any more than he understood why she'd gone into a kind of manic service mode since he'd moved in. But then, he realized this was new for her. Sharing space with another person in the way that they were. It had been a long time for him too. And he couldn't say it was anything like he'd experienced before, because Iris wasn't anything like he'd experienced before.

He got in his truck and headed up the mountain, headed to the building site. To the house.

The *house*.

He stood there for a long while, surveying the place and thinking, the revelation he'd had up there the last time he'd come turning over in his head.

And then...

Then he started thinking about the talk he'd had with Ryder. About what he'd said to him.

I can't give you any guarantees...

Why not? That was the thing.

Why not?

The realization hit him in the chest like a brick, and it hurt. It hurt like hell.

Because the last thing he'd ever wanted in all the world was to find another woman that he wanted to marry. Was to navigate falling in love and...

He thought back to when he'd seen Iris holding her niece.

It was so painful. That image. Because it should make him turn away. It should make them feel some kind of deep, unending trauma. And instead, it filled him with longing. And for so many years the image of a woman holding a little girl had been a futile kind of longing. A longing for a child he no longer had. For a wife he no longer had.

But now when he saw that, he thought of possibility. He thought of a potential future. A wife he could have. A child they could make together, not just an avatar for the one that he'd lost.

And it wasn't about simply replacing them. No. Not ever. Because they...

Mel and Emma were part of him.

That was the simple truth.

He had thought of them as gone, and had thought of himself as no longer a husband and father. But he had known that love, and he carried it in him. He knew a father's love. It was still part of who he was, of everything he was, everything he did. And he was... He wasn't honoring their life by choosing not to carry that love forward.

If he kept it to himself, hid it all away, then their memory went along with it.

It was a waste. That's what it was. And it always would be in its way. There was no way around it. You couldn't resurrect the dead.

But there were better ways to honor their memory than what he'd been doing.

Building the shrine to a life he could no longer have. To people who would never live in it.

He was...

What if he could *marry* Iris?

What if he could *love* her?

Oh that hurt, it hurt like a bullet, at the center of his heart.

The risk in that. To *love* again...

Loving somebody again.

He'd been ready to accept that he cared. Love was a whole other thing.

But it wasn't a decision. That was the thing. It just wasn't. It was a reality. She'd come storming into his life, and with it, she brought his heart back into the world. He told her he couldn't feel those things anymore, and when he'd said it, it had been true.

But she created in him something new, something miraculous, something he hadn't thought possible. An alchemy of hope that joined together with desire and created love on a level he never thought he could experience.

This was new. It wasn't recapturing something old. No.

It wasn't an easy realization. It wasn't an easy thing to want. There had been a time, when he'd been a young man with his entire life set out before him. Every dream he could've possibly conceived of like brilliant, pristine diamonds lying on the surface of the ground. There to be picked up, to be marveled at.

But now he'd had them, and he'd lost them. And finding dreams now, was getting down on his hands and knees and digging through the rocky soil with his bare hands. Coming up with bloody knuckles and bruised and battered fingers.

Now, mining for dreams was to know the cost of them.

He had wanted a wife, and he had wanted children because it was a natural thing. The order of the world.

And then, he thought he had that, and never again. But he'd thought of it back then in terms of replacing.

Now he saw it for what it was. To take a heart that had been so scarred, so bruised and cut, flayed open, and ask it to love again, was not the same. To ask it to dream again.

And the fact was, it had gotten there all on its own. Or rather, Iris had served up hope on a plate of cookies, and had made him realize all the more that there could be.

Had started his heart longing again far before his brain had caught up. Far before he'd started to realize.

He'd let everything good burn away in that fire. And that wasn't tribute to anyone.

He'd had diamonds, and he hadn't taken the remaining diamond dust forward.

He wouldn't *move on*. He realized that now. Because he was forever changed. Forever altered. But love, he thought then, was a lot like fire. It could destroy. It could hurt so very badly. It could be a nightmare of endless proportions. But you needed it to survive. Needed it to breathe. To make a life.

Not just survival.

And he couldn't say that he felt unburdened by the realization of all of this. No, he was bloody knuckled, bruised and battered.

But the man he'd become loved Iris Daniels. He wanted to do the work that needed to be done to be what she needed.

Because he didn't have a monopoly on hurt. On loss. On need too.

Because being a partner didn't mean taking all the comfort on offer for yourself. No, it surely didn't. It meant being a partner. It meant figuring out how to be whole enough to offer as much as he took.

What an interesting thing, to fall in love as this man. Who wasn't young or idealistic, or simply assuming everything would work out.

He'd had everything. And he'd lost it.

He'd come out the other side as someone entirely different. Someone who wanted peace and quiet. Who never wanted to have another shallow business conversation again for as long as he lived. Who didn't particularly want to put on a suit and go to a party. Who enjoyed a slower pace. Who wanted to build flower boxes, and houses with his bare hands.

He looked around this place, that house, that shrine he'd been building to grief, and his stomach hollowed out.

Mel didn't need this house. But he did. And somewhere along the lines in the last couple of weeks, his intent in building it had shifted.

Maybe part of him had been working toward this the entire time.

He was building a life.

A life that he could share with Iris. And suddenly, the stars above him seemed like diamond dust. Bright and hopeful and beautiful. He was overwhelmed then, by a deep sense of peace. They were with him. Part of him.

Shining above him.

Losing them had left a hole in his heart. But loving them... Loving them gave him some of the best parts of who he was now. A gift, one that he could scarce say he deserved. No, he didn't deserve it at all. But his nonetheless. To squander, or use.

And he was determined now that he would use it.

He was determined now to love.

THE THING THAT surprised Iris the most in the first few days since the grand opening was that Elliott appeared. She hadn't expected that. She really and truly hadn't expected to see the man who had acted like she was basically invisible the last time she'd seen him at the Gold Valley Saloon, come to patronize her bakery.

But then, she was the only bakery in town, so it might have more to do with her cakes than with her specifically.

"Iris," he said.

"Hi," she said. "Can I... Help you?"

"I haven't had the opportunity to try any of your baked goods. And I remember a few months ago we talked about them. Remember, we shared some recipes."

Yes, she remembered. She remembered that Rose had introduced them, and they had ended up talking about bread, and they had exchanged recipes and Iris had believed, really and truly believed, that he was interested in her. And it was the first time any man had actually seemed like he might be, so she had felt immensely flattered.

"Yeah, I vaguely remember something to that effect. I saw you the other night, I wasn't sure if you saw me."

"I did," he said, the words coming out slightly rusty.

"Oh. Well. You didn't really… Greet me."

"Sorry. I was surprised. Is he… That man… Are you… With him?"

Was she with him? Well, he had made some pretty bold declarations about wanting to pursue a future, and wanting to be with her. And he had moved in. He made love with her ferociously every night. She was always exhausted when she fell into bed after a long day at the bakery, but then… Griffin was in her bed, and there was something magical about it. And she didn't want to turn away from him. Couldn't even if she had wanted to. Because he was magical, and amazing, and he created feelings in her body that only he could.

Because there was something as wonderful as there was unsettling about him. And being with him.

"Yes," she said.

"I see. It seems like I kind of missed the boat with the Daniels women."

Even now, he was lumping her in with her sister? She couldn't even parse what he said enough to realize that he was expressing regret over not being with her. It didn't matter. She was second pick. Second pick to Rose. It was worse than not being picked at all. To know that he was working his way down the list, and she was beneath… Just like she had always been. Why was that how it was for her?

She was so happy to have Griffin in her house. And she had committed to keeping him in her life, but the fact of the matter was, he hadn't said that he loved her. He cared. He wanted to see where it went. But he was in love with his wife.

He had loved her first and best, and he always would.

And you help him. And you know how happy that makes people...

Her entire life she had felt like she was playing second fiddle to someone else. To sisters who were brighter and more intense. Sisters who had required more attention. A special kind of love, while she had been trustworthy, so she had had to be a caregiver. Even when she was a little girl. So she hadn't gotten all the attention. And then it was too late. It was too late, and her parents had been gone and she had to fill the void. She had to fill the void, because they weren't there and there was no other choice.

And if she didn't take care of them, who would?

But who was going to take care of her?

Griffin takes care of you.

That felt uncomfortable. It felt sharp and painful, and she didn't want to think about it. It was better to focus on what he needed from her.

Because if he didn't love her she was going to have to do a whole lot to keep him there.

She knew how that went.

To matter, you needed to be doing something that mattered.

She hadn't mattered to Elliott. She didn't want to matter to Elliott. It was clarifying, standing there, wrestling with these hurts, these doubts, these thoughts. It was clarifying, because through this whole thing she had convinced herself she had feelings for Elliott when she really didn't, and she had found that somewhat... Disturbing. That she had been so willing to settle. For somebody who didn't light her on fire, or even start a smoldering in her soul, just because he had given her some measure of attention. Or, she had believed that he did.

Knowing that she had been somewhere on his list validated that he had, in fact, been flirting with her. Maybe even hedging his bets.

But that wasn't it. That wasn't the thing that got her. The thing that got her was the realization that the real pain that had come from this was being chosen second. Was that he had loved Rose, and hadn't seen her.

Because that played a much bigger role in her life than she had realized before. It had brushed up against the edges of her consciousness, yes, and she could remember having that discussion with Griffin. About how her sisters were beautiful and special in a way that she wasn't.

But she hadn't realized...

She hadn't realized that it stung in quite this way.

And until she married it to the situation with Griffin and his wife, she really hadn't quite understood how deep of a wound it was.

Maybe there's something wrong with you. Maybe that's just it. Maybe you are just a backup. Second-rate. Second pick.

Some people are.

You're strong.

Griffin's words echoed inside of her.

You're strong.

He had said that early on, he had seen something in her that she hadn't before seen in herself.

But strong might just mean strong enough to endure this particular kind of life as a Clydesdale. Steady, working.

Taking care. Not a Thoroughbred, who existed to simply be out there in the field, tossing its mane and being beautiful.

Something useful.

Utilitarian.

And what woman didn't dream of being utilitarian?

"I don't think that's the only reason you missed out," she said. "A word of advice, talk to women about something other than water filtration. And maybe don't use one to get to her sister."

"I…" he sputtered. "I'm very secure and stable."

"So is a table. You have to be more than that. Be a little better than that. And don't tell me how nice you are. Because you know what, you're not that nice. You made me feel like garbage. And you made my sister feel bad. And the whole time, she blamed herself, and I kind of blamed her too. But the fact of the matter is, you led us both to believe something else was happening. And I think you did it because you knew that that's what Rose wanted. I don't think you were at all surprised that Rose didn't like you. I just think you thought you could put on a good show with me and make her see you differently. But Rose likes cowboys. And you know what? So do I."

Then she grinned broadly, and produced a pink frosted sugar cookie. "Have a cookie. And a very nice day."

He actually did take the cookie, which surprised her, and lowered him even more in her estimation, because if he was really angry, he'd have thrown it back at her. And just then, she realized, that for all her bad feelings, she did basically have two men who wanted her. And whatever Elliott's motives were, there was that.

It was intriguing, and different for Iris.

Griffin was an adventure.

And she didn't know where he was leading. She needed

to get back to that place. Where she saw him as an experience. It was just hard. Now that he'd met her family. Now
that he'd moved in. Now that he'd expressed a commitment
to her, that went somewhere beyond just sleeping together,
but stopped short of everything.

You said you didn't want everything.

Sex was complicated.

What she wanted to do was call Pansy and yell at her.
Because Pansy had been all for a fling, as if it was possible. And honestly, her younger sister had no evidence that
it was. Because the idiot girl had married the only man
she'd ever slept with. In fact, both of her sisters had done
that, and their encouragement toward an affair with Griffin rang hollow for that reason.

And you knew it at the time.

And you did it anyway.

She reached into the bakery case and took out a Mountain Climber. Griffin's cookie. Because God knew she
needed some sugar. And some caffeine. She wasn't in a
bad space. She was in a good space. And she was having a
little bit of relationship drama. But internally. Externally
there was no drama at all. Externally, Griffin was incredible. She wanted to do things for him. She wanted to make
him happy. She wanted to make sure that he was happy in
this place with her. It was important.

But inside… Yeah, things felt a little bit less stable.

But that wasn't his fault. It wasn't…

She blinked rapidly, suddenly feeling teary, and on the
heels of her surge of positive feelings, it was weird and
unexpected.

Was this just how it felt to be… Involved with someone
quite this intensely? Maybe.

She was starting to think that it was overrated.

She thought back to when her deepest hope had been to have a feeling so intense it surpassed the sadness that she felt the day she lost her parents. And she felt that with Griffin. Many times over. She'd realized during sex there was an intensity, that was like a handful of broken glass and a handful of glitter and grind them together until she was cut up and sparkling, that it wasn't necessarily going to be all good.

She had accepted it there. In bed.

It was harder to accept outside of it. Harder to accept that sometimes she was just going to be sitting in her bakery, which was a personal triumph, and feel… A driving sense of urgency to be with him. To be away from him. To hold on to him forever. To push him away, before he hurt her.

All those things competing at once.

But she was in a room filled with cookies. So she would have one.

And she would focus only on the taste of that cookie.

Because right about now, it was the only thing she could handle.

And so she thanked God for baked goods. Without which, she would have lost her sanity a long time ago.

CHAPTER TWENTY-THREE

Ever since his realization that he loved Iris, ever since his realization that he wanted her to be his wife, Griffin had been trying to figure out the perfect time to bring it all up. He had been trying to figure out the perfect time to take her to the house. And then he realized there wasn't going to be a perfect time. And you couldn't wait for things.

It was crazy, because they'd known each other just over two months. And he was pretty certain that a lot of people would think this was too quick.

But he'd lived several lifetimes in his thirty-eight years. And in the last five years he'd lived none.

Until her.

And in these two months he had fit years worth of healing and joy, pain, regret and finally hope. Why would he wait another minute to tell her everything he felt? It didn't make any sense.

So he told her they needed to head up to the cabin to do a few things, and had managed to tear her away from cleanup at the bakery just a little bit early. He was grateful that things were structured so they could still see each other, even while she was working seven days a week, all day every day. But that had been her goal, given that she felt she needed to keep the business open as often as possible, and there was no way she could afford an employee.

He could pay for one. That was the thing. He had a lot

of money. And honestly, all the better reason to get them married and joined together. So that they could join their finances. So that the bakery really was hers too.

He was thinking he was going to sign it over to her. So that it could be hers. But he would be there, to back her every step of the way. He wanted to join everything he was, everything he had with her. He had never been so confident in anything in all his life.

When they got out of the truck, he took her hand.

"What?"

"I just want to… I've never shown you. Not really. I got mad at you, and I chased you away, and I didn't really show you." They went up the path, and she was silent, as he led her to the building site of the house.

"This is going to be the front door." He led her through a big wide open space. "We'll have a big wide one. One that makes you feel welcome." He showed her the big, expansive rectangular cuts in the wall across from them. "The living room. There will be a fireplace there. All made of rock. And you'll just see mountains. Just mountains. And not another living soul." He turned her around so they were facing the other wall. "And the kitchen. While you're standing at the sink you'll be able to see all these trees. Just nothing but pine. All that wilderness." They walked across the open plywood floor, to a hallway that led down to another mass of space. "Master bedroom, bathroom. Two walk-in closets. And this is my favorite view. Because here you can see just through the trees and off the mountain, down to the valley below. To Gold Valley. And you know why they call it that, don't you? Because when the sun spills over the mountain and down to the fields and houses and Main Street below, it's like it's covered in gold. It's magic."

"This is beautiful," she said, muted. "But I'm not sure why... I mean, I love it. You've done an amazing job."

"I've been working on it alone. So it's taken all these five years to get this far. Though, to be honest, I didn't work on it solid the whole time. But I didn't care when it was finished. Because truth be told, I couldn't imagine a life here." He met her gaze, conviction blazing in his chest. "But I can now. That's the thing, Iris. I can now. I can see exactly what kind of life I could have here." He swallowed hard. "But it won't be by myself."

"Griffin..."

"I know it's convenient to live above the bakery, but I don't want you there forever either. I want you here. I want you here with me. I thought that I was here building a monument to the past. I was devoted to my grief like a monk devotes himself to the church. But I... It's not what I want anymore. I couldn't see a future, because it didn't matter. I could barely see the hand in front of my face. Every nail and board in this place was done in a kind of blind faith I didn't realize I was living. That someday I would want to live here. That someday I would have a reason to really be... Living. I didn't know that. I didn't think of it that way. And some time in the last two months it shifted. And I wasn't building it just for me anymore. I thought of you while I hammered these nails. And I thought of being here with you, living here with you. Building a life with you. And right now, standing here, my only regret is that when I took you up to the top of that hill and shared that picnic with you, I didn't tell you I loved you then. But I wasn't ready."

He took in a breath. "Realizing that I was in love again... That's been a special kind of grief, Iris, because I've had to let go in some new and different ways. But it's not moving on or forgetting the past. It's moving forward. Because time does move forward, no matter how you sequester yourself up in the top of the mountains, it's true. The people that you care about all live life without you. You can freeze yourself, but you can't freeze the world. And truly, there's no point to it. I was lying to myself. Thinking that if I stayed up here I wouldn't have to accept it. That I wouldn't have to accept anything. But I do. And I have."

"Griffin," she said. "I understand that you're… That you're hurting. And of course you are. And I want to be there for you. I do. I can… I can help heal you. I understand what it's like. To lose like we did, and I know it isn't the same, but…look, helping isn't the same as…loving. It's not."

"No, don't you understand? I don't need you to help me heal. It's not that. I don't want for us to just hold hands while we walk into a different life. I don't want to do that and then say our goodbyes. We're not each other's medicine. I think we could be more than that."

"I don't know what to say. I don't know… I don't know."

"Just say that you love me."

"I don't understand why you think you love me. I mean… I don't understand."

"I just do. It's that simple."

IRIS LOOKED AT GRIFFIN, and terror streaked through her. She could not for the life of her figure out why this was happening. Figure out why this beautiful, wonderful man was telling her that he loved her. And why it made her want to run away. Why she had to run away.

"I need you," he said.

And that rooted her feet to the spot. And she had to wonder, if that could be enough.

He doesn't really love you. Not like that.

He can say whatever he wants, but he loves you because you cook for him.

He loves you because you're steady.

Because you're everything you've always been.

He loves you the same way Mom loved you.

When you can do what you're told. When you can help.

She felt like her heart had been torn open, every disloyal thought she'd ever kept buried, deep in the sea of her uncertainty, coming flooding out. She couldn't do anything about it. Couldn't do anything to change it. It was... It was terrible. More than terrible. And now that it was careening around out in the open like that, in endless torment, there was nothing she could do to stop it. Nothing at all.

And it hurt.

It hurt worse than anything ever had.

Second.

Less.

He was beautiful. And he was first. And he was perfect.

Maybe being needed was enough. Maybe it could be enough.

Because that was the kind of love he meant, and he might not think so, but she knew.

Because other love just wasn't for a girl like her.

She'd wanted to be the one for someone. Someday. Deep in her heart she'd always wanted that. She'd been a romantic, and she'd been starving to feel...to feel like she was the one who mattered. Not just useful. Not just the one who could take care of people.

This wasn't what she'd dreamed of.

But now he was all she could see and looking at him hurt.

With tears pooling in her eyes, spillover from that flood happening in her soul, she stood up on her tiptoes and kissed him. She kissed him like she was drowning in every-thing. Like she was drowning in all these feelings that were rolling through her. Because she was. And he was like a lifeline.

And he was the tide.

Her temptation, her salvation. Her danger and her res-cue all at once. This man.

He was everything.

What would it be like to be everything?

She felt so small and dirty even considering that. So sad and silly. But it didn't change those thoughts echoing inside of her. So she kissed him. To silence them. To si-lence herself.

He wrenched her T-shirt up over her head, out there in the open, in this half built house that had been started for someone else. But he had her in here instead. And he'd said so many things. So many beautiful, flowery things, and she was certain that he believed them. Certain beyond a shadow of a doubt that Griffin thought everything he said was true. Because he was a good man.

That was the problem.

If he'd been a liar, if he'd been manipulative, it would be easy to walk away. If he'd been any of those things, she wouldn't be clinging to him. She wouldn't be kissing him. She wouldn't be trying to lose herself in the pleasure that only he could offer her. Only him.

So when he unsnapped her bra, she didn't stop him. No, she clung to him, to his shirt, to his broad shoulders, as they kissed each other deeper, longer. Rough, calloused hands roamed over her body, his large palms cupping her breasts, his thumbs teasing her nipples. It was everything. And so was he.

This brilliant, singular moment in time a gift and the glory that she would never take for granted.

Because Iris Daniels had waited her entire life for magic like this.

But she should have known that it would cost more than she had to give. Eventually it would, that was the problem. Eventually she'd fail him and she'd see how thin it all was.

She'd felt this already, with her mother. And she just couldn't stand it, not anymore.

She should have known.

She pushed her hands beneath his shirt, her fingertips skimming the hair roughened ridges of muscles on his abdomen, all the way up to his broad, perfect chest. She made quick work of his T-shirt so that she could look at him, so that she could drink him in hungrily. So that she could marvel at him. He wanted her, that much was true. Needed her in many ways, she knew that too. She could glory in that. Because the fact remained that while she might have reservations about the way that he cared for her, he did want her, not anyone else.

You were the only one that came up the mountain.

She squeezed her eyes shut, and then opened them again, because she would keep her eyes open while she did this. Because it didn't matter what he felt deep down, not right now. It was about what she felt. And she did love him.

Oh, she loved him with everything she was.

She had never been in love with another person. And she didn't know if she ever would. She had never even wanted another man before she'd met him. He held a claim on her. Body and soul. Like a shackle that she had no hope of escaping. And she hadn't wanted this. No. Finding her way to him... No.

It was supposed to be about the bakery. It was supposed

to be about sex. It was supposed to be about growth. And it wasn't about any of that. The most important part of this entire road seemed to be Griffin, and there wasn't anything that she could do about that. There wasn't a damn sorry thing that she could do to make anything else loom larger than the mountain that loomed before her now. All muscle and heat and desire. Everything.

To her.

And so she clung to him, her hands resting on that chest, feeling his heartbeat rage against her palms.

She clung to him.

And she kissed him. With everything that she had. Everything that she had ever been before, everything she ever would be. She kissed him.

Then she moved her hands down to the buckle on his jeans, undid it slowly. She teased herself, tormented herself with the revelation of his body. He was so beautiful. There had never been a man this beautiful. She was sure of that.

This man. Her man. Her mountain.

Like a rock, so hard and brilliant. So good. Created by God's own hand, and there was no denying it, because nothing but a divine creator could have ever produced something so perfect. He was like that.

His hands made her feel small and strong all at once. Made her feel cared for, and made her feel like she was in the gravest of danger. She was so very aware of his strength. And so very aware of how gentle he could be. He was like that.

He made her feel like an endless world of possibility existed beyond them, between them. He made her feel like she was the only one in the world, for just a moment. Until she remembered that she shared him with the life he should have had by rights. He was like that.

And she hated that she wanted there to be something more. She really did. She hated that she needed there to be something more. Because a better woman wouldn't. A better woman would know that it was good and right that he continued to love the wife that he lost in the way that he did. That it was a sign of his strength that he had gone to a mountain for five years and buried himself in his grief. But he had continued to build this house for her, in the place that he had promised her.

Yes, a better woman would be okay with all of that.

She would know that it meant he was good. She would know that it meant he was strong. She would know that he deserved his grief. That he deserved to carry that love, and that she deserved to have it.

Iris knew all those things. She knew them all and still felt them chafe against her, and that was what made her bad. But then...

Everyone had always had such confidence in her supreme goodness. In her ability to give and give and give. Her mother, her father, everyone had acted like it was God-given. Like she was just a caretaker. No. That wasn't it. It never had been. She was just afraid. Afraid that if she didn't do that, if she didn't break herself open and pour out, over and over again, that she wouldn't be anything. That she wouldn't be enough.

And she was afraid of it now. With him.

She wasn't good. She was a coward. She was selfish. She had just never been given the chance to be. And oh, now she had it. Now she felt that, coursing through her veins. So this was maybe what it meant to be thirty-one years old and faced with a declaration of love that she knew had an asterisk behind it. Because she was on her own now. And she was free.

And maybe this was the journey that she had to go on. This journey to realizing that she had never been a beacon of anything.

But she had been protecting herself, but not from the world. From the rejection of the people that she loved the most.

And now, kissing him, touching him, feeling small and mean and petty, she wanted to protect herself again.

But she shut her brain off. She shut her brain off and she gave herself this moment, because she needed it. She needed him more than she needed anything in the entire world. More than she needed to breathe.

He got on his knees and tugged her jeans down, kissing her thigh, her stomach, teasing her. He sat down on the pile of clothes that they had left there on the ground, and he brought her down over him. His jeans, spread out beneath him, offered a cushion for her knees as she straddled him, the slick heat of her coming into contact with his arousal.

And he brought her down slowly over him, and she arched her back, bringing her breasts right into contact with his mouth. His beautiful, perfect mouth. He played a symphony of pleasure there, looking at her, sucking her, making her his.

She was his. And it wasn't fair.

He owned her. It was so deep. So real.

She was his. And he would never be hers. Not really. She would always share pieces of him with the universe. Pieces of him with people who weren't here.

Pieces of him with a woman that he would never hold again. And he'd said that he never thought of her. He did.

But she couldn't blame him if that was a lie.

She couldn't blame him.

Was it a lie?

He has never lied.

No. He hadn't. And she didn't believe that he would. Again. Not on purpose.

But if she had asked her mother directly, to her face, do you have a favorite daughter, her mother would've said no. But it was written in her actions. Her every single one.

And that broke her.

But then, his wicked hand came up to tease her, torment her, and he filled her, absolutely and completely, his each thrust up inside of her easing the pain in her mind, if only for a moment. They were connected now. They were here. And it was real and physical and guttural. And whatever they felt, whatever emotions were out there, unable to be grabbed, unable to be contained, they didn't matter, not right now. Because what they had right now was real. It was raw, and it was something.

She had been Iris Daniels, locked up in a box for longer than she cared to admit.

Afraid.

Whatever thing she had been afraid of, afraid she'd been. And she had never imagined that she would make love to a man on the floor of a half built house, with the sky brilliant and blue and the trees swaying overhead, with uncertainty clamoring in her heart.

But she was this woman.

And if she was this woman now, maybe she could be this woman forever. Maybe. Just maybe.

Maybe it was possible.

His thrusts became erratic, the cords in his neck standing out as he pushed them both further, faster, higher.

Pleasure gathered low in her belly, and when he thrust deep inside of her on a growl, pulsing, crying out his pleasure, she did the same. They went over together, sweat slicked and delirious with pleasure.

He brought her backward, laying himself down on the bare wood, letting her rest over his chest.

"Iris," he said. "You have to know how much I need you."

She did.

She did.

She extricated herself from his hold, her stomach pitching, because she felt ill. She brought herself to her feet with shaking knees. "I know you do. And I know you think it's love. But I can't do this, Griffin. I can't."

"Iris…"

"No. You don't understand. I was supposed to change my life. I was supposed to get independence. And instead I'm… I'm obsessed with you. I'm obsessed with this and obsessed with when I can see you again, when I can touch you again. It's nothing like it was supposed to be. I feel… So small and so stupid. I did exactly what I said I wasn't going to do. I fell for the first man I slept with. At the worst time. And you're my landlord and…"

"Is it so bad to fall for me?"

"Yes," she said, every small, petty thing that she just thought rising to the surface, but she tamped them all down, because she was too ashamed to say them. She was awash in shame.

All the shame she had felt for years. Years and years, as emotions had bubbled up inside of her she could never give voice to. Because how could she?

"Why," he said, his voice fierce. "Why is it so bad?"

"Because. Because we were helping each other out of a tough place and that's all it was and help isn't love. But that's the thing. You just…you needed help. And when you don't need it anymore you're going to see that this wasn't what you wanted. When you don't need me you'll move on."

"I don't believe that's the problem," he said, his face like stone. "You tell me what's really going on."

"That is what's going on," she said. "I feel for you. I do. And I care. I'm not saying that I don't. But, Griffin, we are two very broken people, and I can see the merit in us walking each other out into the light, but dammit, at a certain point we have to be honest with ourselves."

"What about, Iris?"

"We're playing house," she said, her voice breaking.

"Who's playing?" he asked, his voice rough. "This is real, Iris." He hit his fist on the wall. "This house is real and what I feel for you is real."

Iris wanted to hide from the intensity in his eyes, from the demand there she was so sure she couldn't meet.

"I think you believe that. Because I don't think you would lie to me. But you…" She couldn't bring herself to say it. She just couldn't. She would rather hurt him in a thousand different ways. Tell a thousand different lies than say what was really in her heart. Because she was embarrassed by it. Sick with it.

She didn't want to beg.

Didn't want to beg for him to love her most and best because…oh she'd begged her own mother for it and she couldn't ever forget that.

Why can't you just love me as much as you do Rose and Pansy?

I do. You're such a big help.

And she'd heard the truth in those words.

I do *when* you're such a big help.

He said nothing. He only stared at her.

"No, Griffin, it was fine when we were supposed to be

friends. Friends helping each other. Because what is our time around the dinner table going to look like? The anniversaries that we have to mark. The things that we remember. And we'll just pass it all forward. If we have children… Griffin, neither of us are going to be able to handle that. Because you're going to be afraid you're going to lose me, that you're going to lose the child. I'm going to be afraid that somehow we'll leave them behind. There's reasonable, and then there's baggage no one can carry."

And she'd love him. And try and try and he'd realize when she couldn't be as useful as he needed her to be that it wasn't love like he'd felt for Mel. That maybe it wasn't love at all. And she couldn't bear it.

"Stop carrying it," he said, his voice hard. "That's a choice you can make. It's a choice that I'm making. Because you know what? They didn't give it to us. We gave it to ourselves."

"That doesn't make any sense. That's not what it means when you say you have baggage. Nobody chooses to pick it up."

"Yes, you fucking do. You choose it every day. And I have. Believe me, Iris. I have gotten up in the morning and I have picked the heaviest ones and I have put them on my shoulders and I have carried them around. I know what it means to choose sorrow. I know what it means to choose grief. To choose to live my loss rather than living the love that I had. I know what that looks like. And I know what it looks like when you choose to remember the good instead of only marinating in the bad. I know what it feels like. Yes, you have a choice. To be what happened to you, or to find a way to be you. You don't have to carry the darkness."

"Fine then," she said. "It's me. And if it's me, then you should feel free to be rid of me."

"I don't want to be."

"You don't have a choice." She scrambled, putting her clothes on, a sick weight settling in her stomach. "I can't. None of what you're saying rings true for me and I don't even think it's going to be true for you tomorrow. I think you want it to be true. I think you want to be healed. But I don't think you are."

"I'm not broken," he said. "I'm not because I refuse to be."

"We don't get to make a choice."

"We do. And I think that's what scares you. You could live whole, right now, with me if you wanted to and you're running out of excuses. You've got nothing but fear."

"I'm being smart. And I was the virgin, Griffin, you're the one who should have known better."

"You know what I know? I know how dangerous it is to have a life you love. I know what happens when you lose it. So when I stand here and I show you the life that I want, the life that I want to have, you better damn well listen to me. And you better understand what it costs. Don't you tell me what I feel, what I don't feel. Don't tell me I'm not smart. I know I'm not smart. I am wildly, incredibly hopeful. I have faith. And you know how much it cost me to find it? I had to piece together bits of a tattered soul that I wasn't even sure had enough left to it to make a damn thing. And now I want a life. And I want it with you. That is brave. It isn't easy. There is nothing easy about it."

"No. And I want easy. I don't want this." She stumbled back, out of the house. There was only one car. Dammit. Dammit all. She hated everything. She really did. Everything was a mess. It was a disaster. She started walking down the driveway.

"Don't you dare."

"I'll call my sister."

"The hell you will, Iris Daniels. Get your ass back here. You are not walking down the road by yourself with no cell service for God knows how long."

"You don't get to tell me what to do."

"Somebody has to. In all your ranting, did you ever stop to think of all the ways I took care of you? I have earned the right to tell you what to do. Because I actually know you. Because I actually did take care of you. Because I actually care. I didn't just let you take care of me with a serene smile on your face. Keep on scrubbing my floors. Keep on giving to me. Did I let you get on your knees and pleasure me with your mouth and give you nothing back? No, I didn't."

Heat assaulted her, shame. More shame.

"I gave to you. And I would keep on giving to you. These are just more lies you're telling yourself because it makes you feel safe. That's all it is. You're afraid. What happened to the woman who brought me a plate of cookies? You can't even look me in the eye now."

"She was just a dumb virgin," Iris said. "She didn't know anything. She thought that she could just go out in the world and make it all happen. But I know better now. And I suppose I have you to thank for that."

"Why are you standing there acting like I just smashed your heart with a hammer when all I did was offer you a home, love, my heart?"

"Because you don't mean it. You don't mean it. You're in love with your wife. And you should be, Griffin. It's fair. But this house is hers. And your heart is hers. And whatever you say to me, I know that's true. I know that you think you want something new. I know that you think you want me. But how can I ever know that when you look at me, you won't wish it was another woman walking down the aisle toward you? Is it going to be the wrong wedding photo? Is it going to be the wrong baby in my arms? It's not fair. None of it is. I know that." Shame lashed at her and pain that was unimaginable. "I just think you want to replace them."

"I don't," he said. "Believe me that has been the hardest thing that I've had to contend with in this whole thing. To be certain that's not what I'm doing. To be certain that I'm not putting a Band-Aid on anything. But I'm not playing games with myself."

"I just can't... I just can't."

"I can't do anything to convince you. I can't do anything but tell you the truth the way that I always have. And you know what, it's not fucking fair. It's not fair that I had to lose them. And that losing them is going to make me lose you. But until you grow up a little bit, I don't think we can make it work. But I will drive you down to town."

"I don't want you to."

"Get your ass in the car. Consider this your plate of cookies. You rescued me when I needed it, now let me do the same to you. And before you say anything, no, you don't deserve it. It doesn't matter, though. Because that's how love works."

She got in the truck mutely, and the entire way down the mountain tears fell silently down her face. She had never felt so small. She had never felt so low.

And it was all done at his expense.

He dropped her in front of the bakery and she stared at it. She would lose it now. Of course she would.

Why would he continue to rent to her after all of this?

But when she stumbled inside and dropped to her knees and gave in to the anguish in her heart, it wasn't the bakery that she cried over losing.

It was Griffin.

And no matter what she told herself, she couldn't make it otherwise.

IRIS FELT SMALL and sad. She didn't know what to do about her current situation. She was having trouble getting out of bed. But she still had a bakery to run. And she didn't know quite how she was supposed to do it. What she hadn't expected was this to feel like she was dying. But it did. She knew grief. She knew it well. She hadn't thought that simply choosing to walk away from a person would make you feel like that. Like it was final and terrible, like you had lost in such a deep and momentous way. But she did.

Ever since he'd gone it was like she'd been watching their breakup on an endless loop in her mind.

And when it wasn't that, it was her relationship with her mother. Uninterrupted and raw. And she was angry. Really, really angry.

She'd been a kid, and she'd needed her mom to let her know she loved her unconditionally.

And she was also sure her mom hadn't realized how Iris felt.

She was angry that time hadn't been sufficient for them. That they'd never been able to sort it out. That it…simply was.

She managed to get the bakery open, but she was an hour late. She kept expecting Griffin to come in like an avenging angel and hand her an eviction notice. She almost hoped that he would, because then she could see him. But he didn't. The days bled together into a kind of gray haze, making a mockery of the sun that was outside. The sun wasn't real. She didn't feel it. She didn't feel it in her bones, on her skin or in her heart. The sky looked clear, but everything in her felt foggy, so she couldn't make it seem to matter.

She was mad at him. For not coming.

And on the fifth day, she got a letter in the mail with Griffin's company name on the top, and a visit from her brother.

The bakery was empty, the early afternoon lull, after lunchtime and before people were done with work, leaving this couple of hours slow. She stared at the letter, not wanting to open it. And then she looked up at Ryder.

"What exactly is going on?"

"What?"

"Don't give me that. Not while I'm looking at you. You look like a tragic panda that got punched in both eyes. You haven't been sleeping. We haven't heard from you. You want to tell me what's going on with you and Griffin?"

"I don't. I never did. That's the thing. You inserted yourself into my life, you brought him over to the house, you did all kinds of things without asking me. I didn't want you involved. Any more than I wanted him to be overly involved with us. I just didn't want it. But you didn't ask. You just stuck yourself right in the middle of it. And I resent it, Ryder. I do. I didn't say that you could. But you did anyway. And now you're here, demanding to know what's going on. I don't want to share. I never did."

"You never do," he pointed out.

"Pot, kettle," she said,

"Maybe. You've always been a tough nut, Iris. You've always been self-contained. And I haven't done the best job of communicating with you, because I'm bad at communicating. If I was better at it, I probably would have ended up with Sammy a lot sooner than I did."

"It's not your fault. None of this is your fault. It's my

fault. It's…" Tears filled her eyes and she looked at the letter. "It's my fault. But I don't know what to do about it. I panicked. He said that he loved me."

Ryder paused. "And that panicked you why?"

"I… I'm embarrassed."

"Iris, there's nothing to be embarrassed about."

"Yes there is. Our mother and father died in a way that must've been terrifying. Really terrifying. And I'm here with my two feet planted firmly on the ground. I'm acting like love is the scariest thing that I could ever come into contact with."

"Because love is scary. It is. Tell me what's higher stakes than your own heart in this world? I mean sure, we can worry about our physical health. We can worry about our bodies. But when it comes to… Everything, tell me what's more important than the people you care about, and the people who care about you? Nothing. Of course it's scary."

"Well, I made it worse. I made it terrible. It's my fault and I don't know what to do about it. I'm miserable. And I'm… I'm not brave. And I'm not good. I feel like you all think I am. Like I'm this bastion of light and hope, and I'm just not. I took care of everyone because I was afraid. I took care of everyone because I was scared that if I didn't, I wouldn't matter. Because I didn't…" She closed her eyes. "I told him that I was angry that he loved his wife. That he didn't love me first."

Ryder looked at her, long and hard, and she felt herself shriveling up. Felt herself shrinking. "I know," she said. "What kind of person does that? What kind of person is jealous of a dead woman? It isn't fair."

"It isn't fair, but it's how you feel."

She wanted to curl up into a ball and cry. She wanted to shrink up small and be like the little girl she hadn't been allowed to be. She wanted to howl and pound her fists against the floor. She was already broken by the submission. Already broken by what she was. She wanted to make it bigger, brighter, bolder.

She wanted him to understand. Just how messed up she was. Just how messed up this was.

"I've always come second. And I chose to. I let myself. But I felt like I had to. I felt like if I didn't, none of you would love me. I felt like..." A tear fell down her cheek. "I felt like if I didn't, Mom wouldn't love me."

"What?"

"I don't like to talk about it. I don't like to think about it. We all lost her. We all lost her and Dad. And I think they were good parents. I do. But the other girls... The other girls were work, and Mom needed help. And if I didn't help her she would get mad at me. Then I... I wanted to be cared for the way that she cared for them. But as soon as I was the oldest, as soon as I wasn't the baby anymore, I just had responsibilities. And I didn't get to be cared for. Rose was so much work. Pansy too. And I was good. But there's no reward for that, Ryder. There is no reward at all, except that nobody notices you. Except your sister thinks you should be with a boring man in khakis, and your mom doesn't have time to bake with you and everybody depends on you because they know they can, but you can never fall apart. You can never freak out. And then everyone moves on without you. When they can't use you anymore. When there's no point to you. And I'm just... I'm starting from second place with him, and I hate it. I hate all of this." She took a deep, ragged breath. "She was never happy with me when I wasn't helping. And Rose and Pansy didn't have to help, they just got to be. I couldn't bear living a whole life with him trying to work my way up to that first, best love that he had, not when I already know I can't measure up."

Ryder looked at her like he didn't know what to say. And why would he? Everything that she just said was so vile and poisonous she could barely stand to listen to it, much less have the sentiment live inside of her.

"Iris," he said, his voice rough. "I had no idea you felt that way."

"Because I didn't tell anyone. Because I don't know how to talk about it. Because I don't want to say anything about… About Mom. Because I don't want to admit that I'm angry with her. I'm angry with her for dying before we could work that out. Before we could get to where maybe we'd have a better relationship. When the girls had grown up and she didn't feel quite so stressed. I… I wish that we would've had time, and we didn't. And now I'll just never know."

"I'm not an expert. And I'm not going to claim to be. But I think you might be mad at the wrong dead woman."

"What?"

"Griffin's wife. I think she's the wrong dead woman to have bad feelings about. I think it's easier, maybe, to feel bad about her. Because you didn't love her."

"No, I know that I'm angry at Mom…"

"You're putting it on him, though. You know it's not fair, but you're trying to split that pain up anyway. Did you ever think that second love isn't second best? Because when you've been hurt, when you've been really hurt, loving isn't the easy way out. Believe me. Sammy and I had to go through this. She'd been hurt so badly by her parents that choosing to be with me was hard. It was more than hard. And making the choice was brave. Really and truly brave. And as far as he goes… I can't imagine the pain he's been through. He told me his story, and I… It kills me. As a husband, as a father, to know he went through that. What it must take to decide to go on. That's not second-rate love, Iris. That is brave, first-rate love. That is deep. He must love you an awful lot."

Tears spilled down her cheeks, and she couldn't stop them. She felt so afraid. Like she was trembling inside. "Maybe I'm not worth it, though. I mean, maybe that's it, Ryder? Maybe I'm not worth that. He should find somebody else. He should find somebody that's better. He should find somebody that's not so…"

"Not so what?"

"Me," she exploded. "Someone who's not me." She took in a shaky breath. "There is nothing about me that is special. There is nothing about me that's up to… Up to this. And I won't be able to be enough. And then he's going to realize that…"

"Iris, let me tell you something. Whatever you felt before. Whatever Mom made you feel. You don't earn love. Not real love. It can't be bought. It can't be borrowed. You can't work for it like you're hoeing the yard. It can only be given. And all you can do is accept it. That's it."

"No," she said. "That doesn't seem right."

"It just is. It's the way of it. The way of things. Maybe it doesn't make sense. Maybe it seems too good to be true. But that's just the thing. When you find someone that seems too good to be true, and they stand in front of you and they say they love you, you take it."

"But what if…"

"There's no what-if. You're already living the what-if, kiddo. You don't have them. You're broken. You're not safe."

Tears filled her eyes. "I bet this is my eviction notice." She tore the top off the envelope, and with shaking hands pulled the papers out that were inside.

But it wasn't an eviction notice. Instead, it was the title to the building. With a place for her to sign.

"Griffin…"

"What?"

"He… He's signing the building over to me."

"I knew I liked that guy."

"But I don't deserve it. Not after everything I said to him. Not after how… How many ridiculous things I've thrown in front of him just admitting that I don't think I'm good enough. All the things I said to him…"

"That's love. You can't earn it or buy it, and you can't chase it away all that easy either. Remember how I was when Sammy left? I was a mess. I went to find her, didn't I? And all was forgiven. On both our ends. Because we chose love over fear. Or anger. Or anything else. A man who sends that out… Well, I bet you he's willing to do the same."

Iris sat with that for a long time. And then at four o'clock, two hours early, she turned her sign, got into her car and began to drive toward Griffin's place. She didn't know what she was going to say. She didn't know what she was going to do. But she just needed him. She needed him.

And when she got up to the top of the mountain, she saw that his truck wasn't there.

Looked around. She couldn't hear the sound of his hammer.

She ran up to the front porch, walked into the cabin, which of course wasn't locked. The icebox stood open and empty, the bedding on the mattress gone.

There were no boots by the door. Panicked, she ran down the steps, down the trail toward the horses.

And saw that they were gone too.

Griffin was gone.

And he might have left her a bakery, but he had taken her heart.

And she didn't think that she would ever get it back.

CHAPTER TWENTY-FOUR

IT HAD BEEN a long damned time since he had peach cobbler. He wished he could enjoy it more. He sat at the kitchen table of his childhood home, and looked up at his mother, who was staring him down. His father was beside her, leaning against the countertop, holding a mug of coffee. Mallory sat next to him at the kitchen table, with her own bowl of cobbler, a scoop of vanilla ice cream melting over the top.

Jared was lying on the couch in his parents' living room, and he could hear the sound of whatever stupid game he was playing on his phone filtering through.

"I'm going to go in there and crush that thing," he muttered.

"His phone?"

"His head."

"You're mean," Mallory said, looking at him with eyes that were an identical color to his own. "You've only been here for a day, and you're already being mean."

"Not to say we aren't glad you're back," his father said. "But you know, some explanation might be nice."

Griffin looked up. "I didn't think much was required."

"Well, you don't look much happier than the day you left," his mom said. "I was hoping that..."

He sighed and pushed the bowl back. "It's complicated."

"How is it complicated?" Mallory asked. "I thought you were going to bring Iris to see us."

"Iris doesn't want to come back with me. Because Iris doesn't want to be with me."

"She said that?"

"Yep," he responded.

He got up and went over to the counter, and took another scoop of the hot cobbler and put it in the bowl. "I told her I loved her, and she rejected me."

"So you came home then?" his dad asked.

"Yes. I came home then. What's the problem with that?"

"Seems to me you haven't learned anything," his dad said.

"How is that?"

"You ran instead of talking things through last time. Now you just ran back home. But it's the same thing. You're running from state to state, from your biggest problems."

"Dad…"

"It's true. There is no negotiating to be done for Mel and Emma, I get that," his dad said, his voice breaking on their names. "No bargaining. But you got this girl, and sounds like you had a problem. But she's not gone."

"She was pretty definitive."

"But she's alive. And so are you. There are going to be hiccups. Going to be problems. But you got to stay and face them."

"I thought you wanted me home," he said.

"I do," his dad said. "But you know, I'd like it if you were home happy."

"I was happy," he said. "It was the damnedest thing. She made me happy."

"Then you need to try again," his mom said.

"Right," he said, turning to look at Mallory. "So, you're from a different generation. Practically a different generation than me. If a woman says she doesn't want you, what do you do?"

Mallory looked up, a strange, hollow look in her eye. "You know, if you love her, maybe it wouldn't hurt to say it more than once."

"I did say it more than once."

"I just... If you love her, maybe you should make her reject you a couple of times."

"Really?"

"Well, running feels better than having to do all the chasing. I bet."

He gritted his teeth. Her loser boyfriend had nothing to do with any of this. But then... He did wonder. He got up and walked out of the kitchen, out to the front porch. His dad followed. "What happened? I mean, tell me the story."

So he did. Because he hadn't talked to his old man like this in years. Maybe not since he was a teenager and they had gone out and ridden horses together. Maybe not in all that time. He told him about Iris and how she had come up with cookies. How she had given him back something he hadn't thought he would ever have again.

"She's hurting," his dad said. "Sounds to me. Scared. Because all that stuff she said to you, that's what scared people do. You want to know. You said some pretty awful things to us when we offered you love. When we tried to pull you back. It's what happens when someone isn't ready to accept the love that's on offer."

"That doesn't make any sense."

"No," his dad said. "It doesn't. But you think about it, Griffin. Think back really to what happened when you left. The ways we tried to help you, and all the ways that you rejected it. Pain doesn't make sense. Fear doesn't make sense. It just is. It's only when it quiets down that you can

MAISEY YATES

331

start to listen to other voices. Don't you think you'll want to be there so that once hers quiets down... Yours is the voice she hears?"

"So why didn't you come after me then?"

"Because I had a sense that you needed to listen to your own voice. And it sounds to me like to an extent you did. Now I'm just here to guide you a little bit the rest of the way. You've been through things that I haven't been. You're a strong man, Griffin. Hold out here. Be as strong as she needs you to be."

"I'll go back," he said. "And when I come back here to visit you, I'm going to hope that she's with me." Purpose filled his chest. His heart, his soul.

He would be there. When she was ready. And somehow it all became clear. He didn't actually need to go after her. Because one thing he knew, when Iris wasn't listening to fear, she would hear her own voice loud and clear. And she would know what it was she wanted.

"Thank you," Griffin said.

"You're my son," he said. "And I would've given anything to take this from you. To take all the pain on myself."

Griffin understood that. And he believed it.

"I know." He shook his head. "I'll be back again. Sooner than I was last time."

"I'll hold you to it."

He frowned. "Why do you let that asshole into your house?" He knew his dad knew exactly who he was talking about.

His dad sighed. "Because if I don't, then I won't see your sister. I wish I would have put a stop to that back when they were sixteen."

"He's useless."

"She doesn't see it yet. And like I said, fear can't be the loudest voice."

"You think she's afraid?"

"What things look like without the things she's used to. Yeah."

"You're pretty smart, did anyone ever tell you that?"

"No. I've been waiting thirty-eight years for you to tell me. I'll take it now."

He stepped forward, and embraced his father. Then he went inside and gave his mother a hug. And gave one to his sister too. He knew what he had to do.

He had to go home. Not here.

Home to Gold Valley.

Home to Iris.

SHE HAD MADE the trip every day. Every single day. And this time, when she arrived at the top of the hill, when she arrived at the top of the cabin, his truck was there. She held the plate of chocolate chip cookies close to her chest, and tears streamed down her face.

He had come back.

She had known that he would.

She started to take a step forward, but then the cabin door opened and she saw him. And her knees went weak. She dropped down onto them, the dirt and rocks biting into her knees. "Griffin," she said. She held the cookies down in her lap, shaking as she cried.

"Iris," he said, coming down the stairs, sinking down to the ground with her and wrapping her in his arms. "Iris. Don't cry."

"I am crying," she said. "I can't help it. Because I can't believe that you came. I can't believe that you're here."

"I just got back."

"I've come every day. With different cookies. They're all over the counter inside. A plate for every day that I've been up here looking for you. To tell you that I'm sorry. To tell you I didn't mean what I said. I was afraid. I was so afraid. I have spent all my life feeling like I wasn't enough. Like I wasn't the one. The special one. The pretty one. I've been good and serviceable and I was afraid that I was just that to you. And it hurt me. But mostly, most of all, I was afraid that I wouldn't be able to keep you. That I wouldn't be able to keep you with me once you realized that I wasn't everything you thought I was. Because you're right, it's got nothing to do with coming after your wife. I know you loved her. And you've never lied to me, not once. And I know you wouldn't. My brother says that loving after tragedy is brave. The second love isn't second-best for that reason and as soon as he said that I knew. And I knew it was true. It's just that I… It's me. It's not you, it's not her. It's me. You know, the day before my mother died, I asked her to bake cookies with me. But she was too busy. Too busy with Rose, and she needed me to read Pansy a bedtime story. And she was just too…"

Iris took a shuddering breath, her whole body aching. "Griffin, I asked her once why she didn't love me as much. She said she loved how I helped."

"Oh, Iris. Sweetheart."

"I just was so afraid our relationship was too…buried in that. And at the same time I wanted you to need me and I hated it because it…it made me feel like it wasn't love. But then if you didn't need me you wouldn't want me and…"

"Iris, if you never did another thing for me but breathe beside me, I'd love you forever. It's just you. Being with you."

Iris heaved a sob. "I needed to hear that. I really did. I… It's so silly and I can never fix it. She needed me to take care of myself. And I didn't feel like I was one of her girls. Not in the same way that they were."

His hold on her tightened. "Iris. You're my girl. And you are more than enough. Don't ever doubt that I was just waiting for any old person to come up that hill. It had to be you. With your cookies and your determination. With your innocence and your fire. With everything you are. I have been in love before, Iris. But it wasn't the same journey. It wasn't the same at all. It was easy. Everything fell into place. This has been hard. Brutal. And it means more to me than anything ever has. Because I know the cost of losing something. And now I know what it feels like to lose you, and I just... But my dad reminded me that it wasn't final. That you were still here. Do you believe in fate?"

"I try not to," she said. "Because it seems kind of impossibly cruel when you've lost things the way that we have."

"I have to believe there's something bigger. I just do. Otherwise I don't think there's any way to go on. So fate, the hand of God, whatever you want to call it, it led you to me. I know it did. But fate can't do everything on its own. We have to do the rest. We have to be brave. Our hope has to be stronger than fear. Our light has to be brighter than the darkness."

"I love you," Iris said, her voice small. "I love you with everything that I am. Do you think that will be enough? Because I'm really scared. I'm going to have to learn a different way to think about myself. I need you to be patient with me. You have given me nothing but goodness and honesty. You have given to me. In ways no one else ever has. It's not more work you have to do. It's just... Work I have to do."

"No," he said. And her heart stuttered. "It's not work you have to do. It's work we'll do. Together. Because neither of us are alone, not anymore. You are singular, and you are special. And my love for you is second to nothing.

And I will tell you that and show you that every day for the rest of my life."

"Thank you," she said. "For not giving up on me."

"You're the one who had to march up the mountain every day and deal with me. You're the one who didn't give up on me. Iris, you're the one."

Her heart expanded, so full she thought it would burst. She believed him.

"You're the one, sweetheart," he repeated. "The only one who could have ever pulled me out of my exile. The only one I want. The only one I love. Everything I am, everything I've become, wants this life. This life with you." He slid his thumb across her cheek. "Iris, my love for you is like nothing else I've ever experienced. It is singular, and you are special. It's true, I was married before. But when I make you my wife, you will be my only wife. I'm not holding on to anything but you."

"I want that life you told me about. When you walked me around the house. I want that. With you."

"And we'll have it. I'm ready. I'm not holding anything back."

"Me either."

"Just let me know what you need from me."

She looked at his face, his stunning, handsome face. "I'm just going to love you. And you just have to accept it. So long as I can do the same."

That simple. That hard.

Iris Daniels had wondered if there was a formula just changing her life. Maybe not a formula. Maybe a recipe.

For chocolate chip cookies. And love.

"It's a deal."

And then he kissed her, and she forgot about everything else but how much she loved him.

EPILOGUE

SHE DID WORRY when she found out she was pregnant. She worried that it would be hard for him. But when their son was born, and Griffin held him, tears pouring down his face, Iris knew that she didn't have to worry at all.

Griffin was a wonderful father. Protective, but in a reasonable way. And seeing him with their son only made her love him more.

She pulled out the little photo album that they'd put together of Emma. Because they had vowed that they would tell Jack about his sister in heaven someday. Because they were going to share all the love between them. And that included the love and loss that had built Griffin into the man that he was.

The husband he was. The father he was.

She wasn't afraid of it anymore. She saw it as a testament to his strength.

The man that loved her. Loved their son. And didn't hold anything back.

He put their little boy down in his crib, and then looked up at her and she felt...

Beautiful.

Loved.

Whole.

She felt more than good enough. She no longer felt like she didn't fit her name. And it wasn't because she suddenly thought she was more like a flower than she'd ever been before.

It was all in the way he said it. Like an Iris was the most beautiful, cherished thing in all of creation.

And he said it, just then, and took her in his arms, kissing her deep and long.

Iris was Griffin's.

And that was more than enough.

* * * * *

SOLID GOLD COWBOY

To my Gold Valley readers,
thank you for loving these books

CHAPTER ONE

LAZ JENKINS WAS in the business of giving out advice. Okay, technically he owned a bar, and was in the business of selling booze. But that job came with a certain responsibility. He took the position of armchair psychologist very seriously. He had been part and parcel of more happy endings in Gold Valley, Oregon than he could even count at this point. He had wondered—often—if he should start some sort of matchmaking service. Though in fairness, he wasn't the person who matched people up, he just told them when to quit being dumbasses and work it out with each other. His *choose love* speech was so well-worn, so tried-and-true, that he could freely mix it up whenever he wanted to.

But when the door to the bar opened after last call and he looked up to see the silhouette of a woman wearing a voluminous dress standing in the doorway, he had a feeling that there wasn't going to be a *choose love* speech that would fit this moment.

"You're closed, aren't you?"

He would recognize the voice of his best friend anywhere. But his best friend was not supposed to be here today. She was supposed to be getting married. Technically, she was supposed to already be married, and off on her honeymoon with the pointless asshole that she called a fiancé, having that fabled, sparkling wedding night in a fancy hotel in San Francisco, like she had been so look-ing forward to.

Of course, she appeared to *not* be there. Something he might have picked up on sooner had he actually gone to the wedding earlier.

He hadn't.

But he had hoped he wouldn't have to have that conver-sation with Jordan so soon after. And he had sort of been hoping that after she'd gone on her honeymoon she might not really care. They'd been planning on going to Hawaii.

"Since when has it mattered to you if I'm closed?"

He pressed both hands on the bar and waited. And he thought back to that first time she'd walked in his bar.

"You're closed? Aren't you?"

"Yeah, last call was a full half hour ago, princess." But he looked at what she was wearing—a light sweater and what looked like pajama pants and he was…well, concerned and curious. "Why don't you come in and sit for a minute. I'll make you a cup of hot tea."

She stood there, just staring for a moment, as if she were stunned by the offer. Then she mobilized. Crossing the wide, empty room and making her way to the bar. "Oh you don't have to do that." Even as she sat down.

"I insist."

He wasn't about to send her off at two thirty in the morn-ing looking that vulnerable. He'd never forgive himself if something happened to her.

She walked closer and he could see she looked familiar.

"I should have gotten dressed," she said. "I have to be at work in like…an hour and a half. But I just live down the street."

"Sugar Cup," he said, suddenly putting her face into context. "You work at the coffeehouse."

He didn't recognize her without her guard up, that was the only way he could describe it. He'd gotten coffee from her a couple of times and she was…sullen. But not now. Now she just looked soft, vulnerable and a little sad.

"Yeah, so this bout of insomnia is getting intense."

"Insomnia, huh?" He poured some hot water into a mug and added a tea bag—he only had one kind, this was a bar, after all—and slid it toward her.

"Yeah, I've always had trouble sleeping but it's gotten worse lately. Just…having trouble sleeping."

"Sorry to hear it. I'm Laz, by the way."

She blinked wide blue eyes at him. "I know. I'm Jordan."

And that was the first of many, many times over the past decade that he and Jordan had shared a cup of tea in his bar at an ungodly hour. From that they'd built a friendship that he wouldn't have known how to explain if asked. But fortunately, he wasn't in the business of being asked about his life, nor was he in the business of explaining himself.

It was hard not to go around the bar. Hard not to put himself on the side of the bar she was on. But he didn't. Because he wanted to know what the hell was happening.

"Haha…hahaha." He looked at his friend whose shoulders were shaking with the force of her very fake laughter. "Funny story. I didn't get married. Which, you would know, had you been at the wedding."

"Looks like you might not have been at the wedding, Jordan. So why do you think I wasn't?"

"You would have called me. And you didn't. You haven't talked to me for three days, actually, Laz."

"Well. Was there anything to say?"

"Well, I don't know. We are pretty close, aren't we? I thought we were."

Their friendship was a strange one. He could honestly

say that he had never been friends with women. Not really. Women liked him. He had absolutely no trouble getting play when he wanted it. He owned a bar, after all. He saw the women who ended up not leaving with the person they wanted to. The women who came to hook up, but didn't find any they were interested in, except him.

As a blanket policy, he never went home with a woman who had had more than two drinks. Because he was a gentleman like that. And hell, he wanted a woman to know who she was with. And he wanted her to enjoy it. And the fact that he wanted desperately for Jordan to want to be that woman... Well, that was something that stuck in his craw more than he would like to admit. He didn't do unrequited longing. And hadn't before he met her.

She'd come in about once a week at first. And in that time he'd managed to collect more and more information on her.

He could still remember the first time she'd mentioned Dylan. Dylan, the eternal boyfriend, who had then become an eternal fiancé. Who had then been intended to be a husband. But was not, it turned out.

"I've been with him forever."

"Is that why you're still with him?"

She wrinkled her nose. "Weird question."

"No it isn't. We get in habits."

"He's a person, not a habit."

He shrugged. "Just checking."

"Well, no he's not. He's amazing. And he liked me when I was the sad girl in high school with no coat and shoes that were too small. And do you know how many people liked me or tried to know me back then? Approximately no one, that's how many."

"All right. Fair. But I bet a whole lot more people like you now."

"I got busy."

"You got busy. Great."

"Are you going to castigate me for declining to come to the wedding that you clearly didn't have, or are you going to actually tell me what the hell happened?"

"There's no point talking about it," she said, wading deeper into the bar, kicking the tulle and lace of her dress out of the way. It did something weird to his heart. Made it get tight. Also made it feel too big for his chest all at once.

It was hell. He didn't like it.

He hadn't imagined her in such a fussy wedding dress. Jordan was… The thing about Jordan was she wasn't actually sullen. She was reserved. She took a while to get to know, but he knew her. And he had a feeling it was her almost-mother-in-law's fault she was in such a fluffy dress.

"I'm not the person that my mother-in-law… My future mother-in-law would've chosen for her son. She told me that. I had a lot of changing to do to be…remotely acceptable. Trailer trash and all that."

"She called you that?"

"Oh, not in so many words. She's a good churchgoing woman, she would never say it. But she thinks it. I know she does. She was so generous to me, and she gave me a place to stay when I needed one, but it has always come with strings."

He could remember every conversation they'd had at this bar. For someone who talked to hundreds of people every week, it was telling when he could have a conversation with one person and know it was important.

He'd made good friends with West Caldwell. The guy was an ex-convict from Texas, wrongfully accused of a crime he didn't commit, who had married the town police chief. There was just something about the guy, easy to get to know, easy to talk to, as well as not talk to. But, he had never once been tempted to kiss West. There were several reasons for that. But it was just one of the many ways that Jordan herself was unique.

Their connection had stuck. That conversation had stuck. And it had bloomed into a friendship. One that took place between the end of his shift and the beginning of hers. That was another thing about Jordan. She often wandered the streets of Gold Valley from 2:00 a.m. to 4:00 a.m., captive to her insomnia, which had become the foundation for their relationship. And he had just… Well, he'd forgone a lot of sleep and a lot of sex for the privilege of talking with her.

"There's no point talking about it, and yet you're here. In the place where we talk about it. All of it. So you might as well go."

"I just couldn't do it. I just couldn't do it. I got to the day, and I couldn't do it. And I owe them everything."

He knew what she meant. She didn't just mean Dylan. She meant his whole family. Jordan had been kicked out by her parents when she was sixteen, and it was her boyfriend's family who had taken her in. He knew that her connection with them was complicated, and went far beyond a simple romantic entanglement with one person. She was enmeshed in the entire family. And she spoke about it in terms of affection and irritation in pretty equal turns. But one thing was certain—always certain—she loved his family. She loved him too, though less often doubted that she loved him the way that a woman should love a man. She carried a lot of affection and obligation for him.

He wasn't actually an asshole. It was just that Laz didn't think he was right for Jordan.

And you think you are?

For all his speeches on love, he'd never been in love himself.

He'd been married to this bar for more years than he could count. After moving to Gold Valley to care for his grandmother and work on her ranch, he'd set new goals for himself. And those goals had included buying a piece of the main street of the town that he had come to love so much.

So he'd done that. But along the way… Along the way he hadn't done the whole marriage and family thing. It had never seemed all that attractive to him. His parents had been steeped in icy silence, the success of their professional lives not compensating for the solid wall of ice that existed in their personal lives. There had just been so much resentment. And if they'd hated being obligated to each other, they hadn't been a whole lot more excited about Laz and his extracurricular activities either.

It was why Gold Valley had been an easy choice. It was why he left home at seventeen. Chosen to graduate from Gold Valley High rather than the high school in Portland he'd been going to. Because while his grandmother had been stern and firm, running the place with an iron fist, there had also been peace in her house. Long talks late into the night, her particular brand of soul food, and sweet tea, owed to her upbringing in Louisiana. She had been a hard-working woman, and she had run the men who worked the ranch, and her house with unfailing energy.

"I can't believe that she's gone." He poured a shot of *whiskey for himself, and then one for Jordan. He set both on the bar.*

"I'm so sorry," Jordan said, her hands on his. And he wished it could be more. *"I wish I could have met her."*

"She has been pretty poorly ever since we met. Didn't

come down to town really anymore." He knocked the shot back. But he wished that his grandmother had met Jordan too. He'd have liked to get her take on them.

"To your grandma." She took the shot, then gasped. "Oh Lord. I've never done that before."

"Well shit. Didn't tell me that. I wouldn't have thrown you in the deep end."

"It's okay," she said, wheezing. "I'm fine."

He laughed. Absurdly, even while sorrow rolled through him. "She would have really liked you."

"I can't think of a better compliment."

And he couldn't either. Except... Except that Jordan was Jordan. And that in and of itself was a compliment he knew she would never be able to take.

"She would have liked you. So fuck Dylan's mom."

She laughed. "Don't say that. She took me in. She's been really good to me."

"She makes you feel bad about yourself. That's not good."

"Yeah. I guess not."

"You're special. Don't ever forget that."

"Laz..."

But he was done talking about himself. Just profoundly done.

"Do me a favor. Help me get up to that apartment up-stairs tonight. Because I'm not going to be able to drive."

"Whatever you need."

He didn't need to think about that. The one night he'd needed someone to be there for him. Gladys would have scolded him. She wouldn't have wanted her grandson getting sloppy drunk over her, that was for sure.

She'd been a staunchly independent woman. The only one in her family to move from Louisiana to the West

Coast. She'd forged her own path, and she'd done it with a firm, uncompromising spirit. She wasn't a woman to raise her voice, but she wasn't holding in anger. She just spoke her piece when it needed speaking. She did what needed doing. She didn't have entanglements she couldn't handle. And she seemed happier for it. Her husband had died before Laz was born, early in his father's childhood.

And while she had mourned her husband, she had been content with the life she had built for herself on her own terms.

He'd always admired that. It also internalized that you just couldn't have the life that you wanted, not down to the final detail, if you shared it with someone else. His parents were unhappy because they had each other, and him, and it was one too many obligations.

Gladys had been good to him. She'd come to his football games at the high school. She'd come to his bar until it had been a bit much for her to make it into town. Her freedom left her free to love him a bit better, and to shine all the brighter.

And he'd wanted to be like her. Not his parents.

His brand of solitude had worked for him.

He saw enough people in the bar.

But then along had come Jordan, and a slow shift of things had begun to make him question whether or not it was what he wanted for always. But then, Dylan had always been a factor. Always Dylan.

"Do you ever wonder if you've made a mistake?"

"What kind of mistake?"

"I don't know. I can't tell if it's a big one or small one. But I just feel like. I don't know how to explain it. My life was never easy. I mean, I'm not trying to be a victim or anything like that, it's just that it was always tough. Grow-

ing up in my house. And I took the first available hand that got offered to me. And sometimes I just wonder. I wonder if I'm in the wrong place. Or maybe I'm the wrong person for the place. I don't know. I really don't know."

"I understand in some ways. I think my parents always felt like they made the wrong choice. Live the wrong lives. And what the hell can you do with that?"

"I don't know. I guess it depends on how determined you are to keep living in that life."

Until now, maybe.

"So, what changed?"

"You know, the needing to stand there and say vows. I kept going through them in my head. Over and over again. We didn't do anything sappy like writing our own vows. You know I hate that shit."

Jordan liked to play she wasn't sentimental at all. A holdover from being that girl with no winter coat. But he knew she was. He knew she loved Christmas lights. Just a few months ago the town had been all lit up for Christmas, and it had snowed. And there was Jordan, two in the morning even though it was freezing.

"We should go for a walk."

"It is fucking freezing."

"But it's beautiful outside. The Christmas lights are up."

"And we're going to be the two crazy people wandering down the street at three in the morning."

"Come on."

She took his arm, and it was something like torture, and they walked down the street together, a strange pressing sense of panic making him want to choke. Because it was domestic. Because it was close to what he wanted, and what he could never have. Not with her, with anyone.

But then the clear Christmas lights illuminated her face and he couldn't worry about it. Not anymore.

"Dylan will never do this with me."

Dylan. How he hated the mention of that guy. That guy got to spend his days with her while Laz just got her nights, not in the way that he might like.

The streets were completely empty, the evergreen garlands illuminated by the thousands and thousands of lights wrapped around every support beam and every porch rail on Main Street. And then they stopped in front of the town Christmas tree, Jordan still clinging to his arm. She looked up at him, and he couldn't breathe for a space of time. If she had been any other woman he would have kissed her. But if she had been any other woman he wouldn't have gone on a romantic Christmas light walk two days before Christmas either.

"You need to figure out your sleep," he said.

She laughed softly. "I don't really want to. Because then we wouldn't have this."

"Yes," he said, remembering the way the Christmas lights lit up her eyes. "I do know you hate that shit."

"So it was perfect. Just the words. The regular words. The ones that you're supposed to say. So I'd already heard them, and it was easy to practice. When I imagined saying them to him, when I imagined them being… Permanent and binding, I thought I was going to be sick. When I was supposed to go to the church I thought I was going to be sick, so instead of going to the church I went to the bathroom and got on my knees and got ready to throw up." She looked over at him. "Not in the dress." She put her hand on her forehead. "So then I started driving to the church. After I put my dress on. And then I just kept driving. I kept driving and driving and I didn't stop driving. I went to Medford. I went to In-N-Out Burger and ran in and got a milkshake. They still put the Bible verse on the bottom of the cup, did you know that?"

"I didn't know there was a... I didn't know that was the thing."

"It is. I dipped French fries in the milkshake and sat on the bumper of my car and stared at nothing. There's a mall there. That's all there is to look at. I couldn't go in to any stores, because I was in a wedding dress. So I just sat there. I considered driving to California. At that point, you're only forty-five minutes away. I checked on the map."

The image of her eating French fries triggered another memory. This one a lot more recent.

"The wedding is in two weeks." She dipped a French fry into some ketchup and shoved it into her mouth. "And I... I'm not excited. Which scares me a little bit. Maybe it's just because I don't think it's going to change anything. I'll be legally bound to his family, which used to be the only thing I ever wanted. But... You know, you can't choose your family. Like I can't choose mine. Which is why I never speak to my parents, but they are still my parents. But I'm not sure... His family modeled a functional family for me but I'm not sure that I fit in with them any better. And I actually am choosing them, aren't I? Except I always feel like they chose me and I have to be grateful for it."

"Do they actually say that?"

She looked away. "I mean, a little."

"That's bullshit, Jordan."

"Well. I'm the child of a couple of addicts that they would never even speak to, much less choose their daughter to marry their son. I just..."

"You're going to let people make you feel like the daugh-

*ter of addicts for the rest of your life? Make you feel like
that's all you are?"*

"*That's not... It's not them. It's not... It's just that I'm
very conscious of the fact that I have to be careful. That
I have to be mindful of what I could turn into if I'm not
careful.*"

"*That's not fair.*"

"*Maybe it isn't. But I don't have anyone else either. I'm
so afraid of what's going to happen to me if I end up alone.*"

"*You'll never be alone. Not as long as you have me.*"

"All right. So then you..."

"I kind of blanked out. I mean, I'm not really sure what
all I did. I drove around. I just drove around. And then I
turned back around and came here. And then... I came
right here. Because it was the only place I knew... There's
nowhere else I can go. I don't have anyone else. I just alien-
ated everyone who has ever loved me."

He chuckled. "Okay."

"Except you. I... I'm not going to be able to sleep. This
is when I can't sleep anyway."

She picked at a scarred part of the bar top.

"Let's get out of here," he said.

Her head shot up. "And go to where?"

"My house."

"Your house." She frowned.

In fairness, he had never had her out to his house before. She was his best friend, and he would claim that in
pretty much any circle, but they had only ever really seen
each other here. But then, that was pretty normal for him.

"What am I going to do at your house?"

"You're going to sleep, Jordan. You are not staying up
for more than twenty-four hours. You are not marinating in

your own misery to the point that you can no longer stand on your own two feet."

"Am I not?"

"No," he said.

A new purpose turned over inside of him. And he realized... Well, he realized that he should have done a little telling her what to do a while ago. Because she wasn't taking care of herself. And she hadn't been.

"Let's go."

"Right now? I didn't even get a drink."

"You shouldn't have a drink. Not in your current state. Don't go using it like medicine."

She frowned. "Oh please don't be my Jiminy Cricket. I'm in my own head enough about all this stuff."

"I am not a damned bug. But I am going to tell you what's good for you. You're already milkshakefaced. Let's leave it at that." He rounded the bar, and walked over to where she was sitting. She just looked up at him, with big blue doe eyes. Jordan was never doe-eyed. He put his hand low on her back, which made his stomach feel hollow.

He walked her out the front of the bar and closed the door behind them, locking it. "You have any clothes other than the wedding dress?"

"No," she said. "And all of my clothes are at Dylan's."

"Right. Let's just go to my place." He sighed. "I'll get you one of my T-shirts."

That didn't do anything to improve his disposition.

They walked down the sidewalk, a healthy distance between them. He shoved his hands in his jacket pockets. And then when they got to the truck he went to the passenger side and opened the door for her. "Get in."

She obeyed. And he helped her tuck the wedding dress up into the car.

And as he lifted the mountain of tulle up into the truck, their eyes met. And his stomach hollowed out.

"You're coming to my wedding, aren't you?"

"I thought we were situational friends."

She looked hurt by that. Angry. Well, he was hurt and angry about the whole thing.

"We're friends," she said. *"The best friend I have and I thought that you would come to my..."*

"Yeah," he said. *And even then he knew he was lying. "I'll come to your wedding. I'll sit there and stare at you as you walk down the aisle. And I'll behave myself."*

"Good. Not the behaving yourself. That you'll be there. You know you're important to me."

"Yeah."

But he couldn't say what he wanted to. And there was no point to it anyway. So he said nothing. Because he'd been over this with her repeatedly. And there was no point arguing. She had doubts, but she was going to do it.

It was best if she did.

He released his hold on her. Closed the truck door decisively. Then he got in and started the engine. Neither of them spoke.

They drove up the winding road that led to the little ranch that had been in his family since the 1960s. The house itself was still much as it had been back in those early years. He'd updated it, fixed it up with his own hands mostly.

The barn had been expanded. Because his true passion was horses, and while he didn't much care about having every modern convenience in his house, in his barn was another matter.

"This is it," he said.

"It's nice," she responded.

He pulled up to the front and she sat rooted to the seat.

"You can get out, Jordan."

She started to unbuckle her seat belt, and before she could make a move to get out, he was exiting the truck, rounding to the other side and opening the door for her.

"You don't have to do that," she said, swinging her legs around and pushing herself out of the truck, ball of white tulle first.

"Maybe not," he said. "But it seems like the thing to do when somebody has just run out on their wedding."

"What am I going to do, Laz? I can't go back to Sugar Cup. Everybody in town is going to know. Everybody in town must already know."

"I managed to make it through a Friday night without hearing about it."

"Great. They are protecting me. Because they hoped I was going to come back. That's what it has to be. But I wasn't going to come back. I was never going to come back."

"Why didn't you just break up with him before the wedding, Jordan. If that's what you were feeling?"

"Because I was afraid. And I thought that wanting to be part of his family... I thought that wanting to do it was the same as being in love. But it's not. And beneath all my wanting to do it, I desperately didn't want to do it. I don't know if that makes sense."

"Makes sense to me. I understand."

"It's such a mess, Laz. I really made a mess of it."

She was looking up at him, pleading, and he really couldn't take it.

"Sleep," he bit out. "Don't talk about messes. And don't think about whether or not you should be cleaning them up. You can't do anything when you haven't slept."

"I should know," she said. "I've spent years not sleeping."

"Me too. Occupational hazard."

He led her inside, and ushered her through the house, into his bedroom. He gritted his teeth. Jordan was in his bedroom. And who the hell was he that it made him feel this way? He had spent years having casual sex. The desire was easy. The getting there was easy. The saying goodbye was easy. But the scary thing was that Jordan had said hello one day, in the wee hours of the morning, and he had never even considered saying goodbye. That was the problem. She mattered. And he didn't really know what to do with someone who mattered quite this much.

Except give her a place to stay.

"I'll get you a T-shirt."

He reached into the top drawer and pulled out a gray T-shirt. He almost grabbed a white one, but thought that was a shade too masochistic. Imagining her in nothing but a white T-shirt was enough to destroy him completely. Imagining her in a gray one was only going to render him partially reduced.

"Thanks," she said.

"I've got sweatpants too but they're not going to fit you." Laz was over six feet, Jordan was maybe five-two. She was a tiny little thing. Tiny, feral and angry, and that was all the things he liked about her. All the things she was always trying to cover up. To be acceptable to that boyfriend and his damn family.

"I'll sort it out," she said.

"I can go down to town and get some of your things to-morrow if you want."

"Would you do that?"

"Yeah. Help me figure it out."

"Well, maybe he went on our honeymoon. If he did…"

"You think he'd go on your honeymoon by himself?"

"Oh, not down to San Francisco. But to Hawaii, yes.

We were flying out of San Francisco because we got a deal. Those tickets aren't refundable. I bet he's getting on a plane."

"Too bad plane tickets aren't transferable anymore. That's one of those made-for-TV romance movies waiting to happen. He could grab one of your bridesmaids."

Jordan laughed. "I don't have bridesmaids."

And he should have known that. Because the fact of the matter was that he would call Jordan his best friend and she would call him hers.

"It hurt my feelings that you weren't there," she said. She smiled. "You know, somewhere between here and Medford."

"When you realized?"

"Yes." The corners of her mouth turned down. "You didn't come to find me. So I knew you didn't know. I knew... Laz, I knew you would have come for me."

His breath stopped. Right there in his lungs.

"We'll talk about that later."

She nodded. "Did you just think I wouldn't do it? Is that what you thought? Did you know that I was going to walk into the bar?"

He wished he could say yes. But the fact was, for him, that would've been optimism. And he didn't traffic in that level of optimism. He was a realist. But then, maybe he was going to have to forget about that. Because it was not realistic that Jordan had come to the bar in her wedding dress at 2:00 a.m. when she was supposed to be Mrs. Dylan Walker.

And was instead Jordan.

His Jordan. At his house.

"Get some sleep. We'll talk in the morning. Eggs and bacon?"

"Please don't tell me that you cook."

"I live by myself, Jordan. Of course I know how to cook."

And with that, he left her. By herself, to change into his gray T-shirt.

Laz had never considered himself a saint. But at this point he was considering applying.

CHAPTER TWO

JORDAN WOKE UP completely disoriented. She was not in San Francisco. That much she knew. She was on a bed buried beneath a flannel comforter, breathing slowly. She moved the blankets down and looked around the room.

Laz's *room*. She was at Laz's *house*.

Well, this was a predicament.

She sat up, and realized she was still only wearing a T-shirt. But she could also smell bacon, and she was pretty sure her desire for the bacon was going to outdo her need for modesty.

It was Laz, after all.

She tried not to think about the first time she'd met him. She had stumbled into his bar thinking that it was open, when in fact it had been past last call. And she'd seen him. Standing behind the bar. He was tall, broad shoul- dered, with black hair and dark skin, a chiseled jaw. His mouth was… Well, it was just immediately sensual, and she couldn't quite figure out why. Because she saw men every day and managed to not think about their mouths.

And all of that stuff entered into her system as an instan- taneous thunderclap. Not a series of individual thoughts, but a hot jolt of realization. And along with it the sense that he was somehow meant to be standing there, and so was she. She didn't typically go into the bar because she had a job at the coffee shop, and it required she get up early. But her insomnia—which she'd been struggling with for six months or so—was starting to bore her to tears, and so she had taken to walking around. She had looked in the bar on a few different occasions, and tonight had decided to go in.

And something had whispered through her soul that sounded a lot like fate and it had terrified her. But instead of running, she had gone to sit at that bar.

She had told herself multiple times over the past ten years that the kind of fate Laz was had been to be her very best friend. And he had been. He had been a pillar to her these last few years. Helping her sort through all manner of different traumas from her past, and God knew she had many.

She had done her very best to shove her attraction down very deep. Because Dylan's family had always been there for her. Because Dylan was supposed to be the one. He always had been. But when she met him she hadn't felt a thunderclap. And to be quite honest she never felt one in all the years since.

But she now had a solid seventeen years of being Dylan's girlfriend, and she wasn't really sure what came after that. So she had simply stayed. And Laz's words about habits had echoed in her head, growing increasingly louder. And she just ignored them. Until yesterday.

She groaned, she climbed out of the bed, and was greeted by air that was far too cold for her liking. Plus the shirt rode all the way up her thighs, and she was pretty sure that given the cold, her nipples were absolutely visible, like little Tic Tacs through the top. She grimaced and grabbed the flannel blanket from his bed, wrapped it around her body. And she decided that she was going to take her chances on humiliation and brave her friend this morning.

She walked down the hall, taking in the details of the

place. There were framed photos in that hallway, but they were so old she couldn't imagine that he'd put them up. A little boy that must've been him, posed in a portrait studio holding a red ball, wearing overalls to match. And a series of such pictures, all of them likely taken at a school. There was a photograph of a wedding, one that looked to be the early eighties, with a couple that was a perfect blend of Laz's features. And then one framed picture of an older woman in a floral dress holding a chubby baby with wild curly hair. Laz and his grandmother. Her heart clenched. That was the one time Laz had let her be there for him in any kind of emotional sense. When his grandma had died seven years ago. He'd gotten drunk. And he never did that. He was so smooth and easy and always in control. Always the one who knew what to do. But he hadn't known what to do then. And she'd wanted to comfort him in a deep way. In a physical way that had scared her. She had reached across the bar that night and put her hands on his. And she had felt… She wanted to press herself against him. To give him all of her as a means of comfort, and it had scared her enough that she had backed way off.

Because she was with someone else and she had to be. She had to be.

It was that *had to be* that had echoed inside of her yesterday. Because why? Why had she built for herself a series of *had tos*? Why was she so hamstrung by rules that she had created for herself?

She touched that photo, briefly, Laz and Gladys, and then went down the hall.

"Good morning," she mumbled.

She hated this feeling. When she did sleep, this was how it was. A brief few hours and in the wrong space of time.

"Oh good," he said. "You're up."

"Is it early?"

"No," he said. "Very late. But, this is about when I get up anyway, and this is when you should be getting up."

"You have another bedroom?"

"No. The spare room is an office now."

"Where did you sleep?"

"The couch. It's a nice couch."

"That's not fair. You didn't have to sleep on the couch."

"Where was I going to sleep, Jordan?"

Those dark brown eyes met hers and she faltered. Because there was no real answer for that that didn't make her skin feel like it was too tight.

"Well. I will take that bacon."

"I have bacon. Because I always deliver on my promises."

"I know you do," she said.

It was one of the things about him. He was just always there for people. For everyone. She'd heard stories over the years… He had single-handedly solved more romance crises in the town of Gold Valley than she could have ever imagined one small community could have had. He was good. At listening, and consequently, sometimes good at hearing things that other people didn't even realize they were saying. And yet… Well, and yet. Here she was. He hadn't fixed her issues.

She felt a little bit salty about that.

"Have a seat."

She did, careful to tuck the blanket underneath her legs so that not too much of her thigh made contact with the cold wood on the chair. The dining table was nice. Solid wood.

"This is…" She looked around. In fact, for all the place was small everything in it was solid. Well made. She could feel the history of the house, and the quality of everything inside. There was a heaviness to it. Not like the new, neighborhood tract house that she and Dylan shared.

"I made it," he said.

"Get out. You made this?"

"Yeah. I have a wood shop. In my spare time I…"

"Your spare time?"

"I don't have a family, Jordan. I don't have anyone to answer to. My time is my own. I come home from the bar, I make sure that things on the ranch are running smoothly when I get up in the morning, handle the payroll for all the staff. For the bar and the ranch. I go to the shop and I wood work. Sometimes I go for a ride. One or the other."

"How did I not know that about you?"

He shrugged. "I don't know. Don't talk about it much."

"Right. I guess people tend to not ask about you."

He shrugged. "That's not really my job."

"Well, you know about everybody else. You know all about me and all about my issues."

"You've seen some of my issues, Jordan," he said, his eyes suddenly getting serious. And it made her feel warm.

"Yeah. I guess. But it's still not the same. People drink, and they tell you everything."

"You don't drink. Not really."

"Fine. I just tell you things because I like you."

"Great," he said.

There was a tension in his shoulders as he moved around the kitchen. He went over to the coffeepot and poured a generous mug. "Coffee?"

She laughed. "Well, technically I have a hard time drinking coffee that I don't make. Because I make it so well."

"You know, making drinks is kind of my thing too," he said.

"But not coffee."

He held the mug out toward her, and she took it, their fingertips brushing. It made her stomach go tight. "I drink coffee. And I don't like drinking anything that doesn't taste good."

"All right, so you're trying to make sure I know you're not a disgusting bachelor?"

"Oh, I'm a disgusting bachelor. But also discerning. That's just how I am. So."

"Right. So discerning."

Silence stretched between them. "Why didn't you tell me not to marry him, Laz?"

She hadn't meant to say that out loud. Not at all. She hadn't meant to... She felt stupid. Her face got hot.

His eyes went sharp. "You would have welcomed that?"

"I don't know. It's just that you... You give advice to everybody. I know you do. You tell them what they really want. You tell them what's good for them. But you didn't tell me not to marry Dylan."

"Look, Jordan, did I know that you weren't in love with him? Yes. But was there any way to say that? Come on. Be honest with me. If I had said that to you..."

"Fine. But I just wish "

"Sorry, little girl. You gotta take responsibility for that all on your own. And I know that's not fun. But the fact of the matter is, it's nobody's fault but yours that you let it get up to the wedding day and then let it dissolve."

"Teller of hard truths," she muttered.

"Right. So, how do you want to get your clothes?"

"I think Dylan is gone," she said. "So it should be pretty easy for you to go back and get them. If you don't mind. There's a spare key to the house under the flowerpot by the front door."

"Wow. Very secure. Why don't you just not lock your doors?"

"That wouldn't be safe," she said, deadpan.

"At least give the burglars a scavenger hunt."

"Well, I didn't. But it should be pretty easy for you to get in. My… I have a packed suitcase."

"Great. I'll grab it."

"I don't know where I'm going to go. I'm going to have to get a place. But I don't make enough money at Sugar Cup to just magically have a deposit for an apartment."

She wasn't just an employee at Sugar Cup, she was a part owner. She had bought a stake in it a few years ago, and she had never been more proud of herself. In hindsight, it was a telling thing, really, that Dylan had been worried about how much time it would take away from their relationship, and Laz had been extremely proud of her.

That should have been clarifying all on its own. Why should her friend be happier for her than her fiancé?

"I'll tell you what. You were supposed to be on vacation the next couple weeks anyway. Why don't you work for me instead. Hide up here and earn some money."

"Laz… There's no…"

"I can pay you whatever the hell I want."

"I'm *not* taking charity from you." She couldn't do charity. Because she'd done it. Too many times. There were always fake grins and an expectation of gratitude. She'd often thought people were waiting for her to put on a Cockney accent and do a dance number with a chimney sweep when they'd given her canned food as a child. And then of course there was Dylan's family.

"You're my best friend," he said. "If you don't take charity from me, who are you going to take it from? Anyway. I will give you jobs to do. Don't you worry about that."

She wouldn't point out that she had in fact taken charity many times. When she was a kid and it was that or go hungry.

"Why are you doing all this for me?" she asked.

"Jordan, I think that you have been under the delusion that the only people that were going to ever do anything for you were Dylan and his family. I get that your parents did a hell of a number on you. And I don't blame you for being skeptical about the fact that there are more than just four good people in this world. I get that his mother and father and brother have been there for you. And I get that in some capacity he has been. But that's not a good enough reason to marry somebody. And it doesn't mean that nobody else wants to be there for you. I want to be there for you. So let me."

There was really no other option. What he was giving her was the best chance at getting her life together that she could have ever thought of. He was giving her an opportunity to hide. To earn money.

"Well, where are you going to sleep?"

"You're very concerned about me, as if I'm not a grown man who hasn't spent a hell of a long time taking care of himself."

"Well, then what do you want me to do?"

"I miss my grandmother's cooking. I miss having the house a little bit tidier. If you could be my housekeeper for the next couple of weeks…"

"I'm not going to be able to cook like your grandma."

She recalled Laz bringing in some of the things his grandmother had made to the bar. Gladys Jenkins's cooking had Southern roots, and while Jordan was handy—especially when it came to baking—she didn't know anything about food from Louisiana.

"That's fine. I eat all kinds of food. Just know that I'll appreciate it."

"All right," she said. "I'll do it. Thank you. Because I just don't know what else I would've done."

"That's what I do. I take care of people."

And she couldn't deny that, but there was something about that assurance that rang hollow to her, and she didn't know quite what to do with it.

CHAPTER THREE

WELL, HELL. LAZ hadn't meant to go and get himself a room-mate. But, here he was. Engaging in a high level of torture that he hadn't intended to fling himself down at the mercy of.

And as he drove down through the main street of Gold Valley, looking at the familiar redbrick buildings and pondering his life choices, he realized that there had never been a choice. Not really. He could be as irritated with himself as he wanted, but that didn't make it... Well, any less than it was. He was going to be there for Jordan. Whatever she needed.

He just would. Because there were certain things that he... There were certain things he could give her. And certain things he couldn't. And all of that was a tangle around what he wished.

Why hadn't he asked her *not* to marry Dylan?

Because it would have been a self-interested demand. He wanted her. It was plain as that. He wanted her in his bed, but he didn't know how to have someone else in his life.

And he wondered if he was like Gladys. Too stubborn and too solitary to ever really settle down. He had often wondered that about his own dad.

His dad was a faithful husband. He would never leave his mother. He had been dedicated to them, always. But he'd also flung himself into his work as a doctor. His practice had taken precedence over everything else. And it had caused endless issues between his parents, because his mother's work as a lawyer had been extremely demanding and she had felt like his dad didn't give enough at home. They had never fought. No. At least, not shouting and screaming.

It had been death by a thousand cuts.

Pinpricks of passive aggressiveness that marred every single day. And Laz himself felt like he was walking on eggshells constantly. Just trying to avoid all of that. But he knew firsthand how parents could be there for you physically, and yet hold everything back emotionally. How people could be in a marriage, and simultaneously not be in it. Technically doing all the right things, but emotionally not managing it. And he just... He had no interest in failing somebody that profoundly. And at the end of the day, that was his concern. That he would profoundly fail the person that he tried to enmesh in his life.

When he pulled up to the little house that Jordan shared with Dylan, he felt a strange turn of envy.

Well, she didn't share it with him anymore. Now she shared his house with him. So what about that?

He walked up to the front door, and lifted the little pot with the geranium in it, grabbing hold of the key that was indeed there, and then he fit it into the lock. But just as he did, the door jerked open. And there was Dylan, looking enraged. Laz was no stranger to a bar fight—at least breaking one up. But it wouldn't even be fair to engage in a scuffle with Dylan, who was about half his muscle mass and at least three inches shorter. Basically, Laz could kick his ass by breathing on him too hard.

"She didn't think you'd be here."

"Oh," Dylan said. "She's with *you*. I should have known."

Laz had briefly met Dylan a couple of times over the years. On the odd occasion that they'd come into the bar to eat a meal. He'd never been hostile toward Laz, but Laz had always gotten the feeling that he didn't particularly like him.

It was fine. He was used to that. Often men found him intimidating. Because Laz was the kind of guy who could absolutely steal your girl if he felt like it. It was just that he didn't want drama, so he didn't often feel like it. And when it came to Jordan… He cared too much. He had always cared too much. To just seduce her. To ask her for a fling to scratch the itch that echoed through his whole soul.

"Yes," Laz said. "She's with me. Because she came to me, and she needed a place to go. And I'm her friend."

"Yeah," he said. "You're her friend. Your reputation precedes you," Dylan said, stepping forward, and to his credit, Laz had a feeling he pretty much would challenge Laz to a fight at this point. So he had to give the guy at least a little bit of props for that. Apparently he'd go all in in a fight for Jordan. It was just too bad he would lose.

"Look, her coming to me has nothing to do with that. Her not marrying you has nothing to do with me." He wished it did. Even if it wasn't fair.

"I don't believe that."

"Feel free to go on not believing it. But it's true. I'm here to get her things."

"Where is she staying?"

"None of your damn business. She'll talk to you when she's ready. But she needs to sort herself out."

"I'm her fiancé. You're nothing to her. You're some guy she moons over in the bar. Don't think I haven't noticed. She practically drools when you walk by."

"Then I guess that's your fault for not giving her something to moon over. If I'm irresistible to her, that's your damn fault. You should have been more irresistible, I guess. And before you say anything, that's got nothing to do with looks. I listened to her. How long's it been since you've done that."

He pushed past Dylan. "I just want her suitcase."

"This is my house."

"I have a key. Because Jordan told me where it was. It's her house too. You all are going to have to sort that out, but I am here to sort this out. Because she asked me to. Because I'm her friend. I don't care if you don't understand that."

He saw the suitcase, sitting there by the sofa. And he grabbed it. He didn't have to ask if it was Jordan's, because it had flowers on it. Which was funny, he hadn't taken her for the kind who would have a flowered suitcase. And somehow he knew it had been a gift. A gift she'd been given that just didn't fit her at all. He would buy Jordan a black suitcase, and sure, it would be harder to find on the luggage carousel, but it would at least suit her demeanor.

Jordan didn't like to draw attention to herself. You had to dig deep to get to her humor. You had to dig deep to get her loyalty. But it was worth it. And he had to wonder if any of these people who had cared for her had ever dug for the parts of Jordan that made her... Her.

He took the suitcase and hefted it into his truck. He had just enough time to get back to his place, deposit all this and get back to the bar. He didn't have to be there every day. He had a good staff that handled things for him, but mostly he was just used to it. It was his life. Just the way he was fundamentally put together, he imagined. His grandmother had made the ranch her life. His father had made his medical practice his life. And Laz might not be a doctor, but he loved what he did. And he cared about it. It earned him a living, and gave him a sense of accomplishment.

He drove back up to the house, and was greeted by the smell of baking bread.

Yeah. This was a good idea. "Here are your things," he said.

"Thank you," she said.

"I'm hungry."

"Well. Good. The bread is almost done. And there's soup. Do you eat when you get home from the bar usually?"

"Usually. You don't have to…"

"I don't sleep, remember?"

"Right. Well. If you don't mind…"

"I don't. I'm going to earn my keep. I'm not just going to let you give money to me because you feel sorry for me."

"I don't just feel sorry for you." He sighed. "Dylan is not gone."

"Dylan's not gone?"

"No. He was at the house when I went there."

"Oh… Shit."

"Yeah. So, he knows that I know where you are. But he doesn't know where you are."

"I'm just not ready. But that's the problem. I wasn't ready when I needed to be. Because you are right. I shouldn't have let it get to the day."

"I understand what you did. It's complicated."

"Yeah," she sighed. "Extremely complicated."

They had lunch after that, and it felt disturbingly domestic from Laz's point of view. But then he had to get down to the bar to open, and he welcomed the distraction. There had been some pretty heavy drama down at the bar recently anyway. The Daniels family had provided him with enough entertainment to last him a good while. And he told himself that he didn't want to miss anything.

Not that he was afraid of what might happen if he was alone with Jordan for too long.

CHAPTER FOUR

THE PROBLEM WITH cooking and cleaning was that it made her mind wander. Not just wander, but go down paths that she preferred not to walk on. Turning over possibilities and ideas, and different things that she had spent a long time rejecting.

But it was what Laz had said about people helping her. About how she had other people in her life who cared.

And when she thought about it, she knew that it was true. She and Lars—who she knew most of the customers referred to as Grumpy Chef—had a decent relationship at Sugar Cup. He was another of the part owners, and she knew that he would do anything for her if she told him that she needed it. Because the reality was, even though his demeanor was gruff, he was a very nice man. And then there were Katrina and Susie, who also worked there. And while Jordan might never have made best friends with them—they were young, in their early twenties—they were sweet. And they didn't hate her or anything. But she'd somehow decided that it was…safe to lean on Dylan's family. And not safe to really lean on anyone else. And that line of thinking led her back to her parents. Straight to trailer parks and addiction and the kind of sadness she just didn't like to… Didn't like to excavate. She had always wondered why they were like that. And why she hadn't been enough to fix it. She hadn't gotten kicked out because she was rebellious. She had gotten kicked out because she'd gotten rid of their heroin. She did think sometimes that she was lucky they hadn't killed her. At least her dad. He'd lost it.

She'd been thrown out, but she also had to run away. And she could still remember her dad's last screaming rant at her. That she thought she was better than she was. That this was in her blood and she would never escape it. That she couldn't just run away to the suburbs and be different.

And maybe that was the problem. Dylan's family had represented something so much more than just Dylan alone. They were normal. A deeply normal suburban family, and when she'd first started dating him she'd been terrified that he was going to…reject her when he knew just how messed up her family was. He hadn't, though. And his parents had been kind enough to let her live with them. She had her own bedroom—because they were not about to have the two of them sleeping in the same room.

She and Dylan had moved out when they were twenty, and gotten their little house off the main part of Gold Valley. And then for the past twelve years they'd…coasted. That was all. Neither of them had really made a solid move toward commitment. They'd taken forever at it. And then in the end she'd been the one to balk. But she'd waited too long. And she had to wonder if they were actually just both victims of their own apathy more than anything else.

She hadn't known what other life to live, so she hadn't pursued it. And it had been largely motivated by fear. Yeah. She was just so afraid of what was on the other side of that life that she had actually found was so comfortable. Because secretly… Secretly she was sort of convinced that it was Dylan that kept her away from that future that her father had promised she would find.

She didn't really believe that. Her parents had made their

choices. They couldn't simply blame genetics. No matter how convenient that might be for them. They had to take responsibility for their actions. The same as she had to own the fact that her life had turned out good in part because of herself. It wasn't just because of Dylan. But there was a part of her that…

She sighed. It was one thirty in the morning. That was normal for her. She had decided to go ahead and make Laz a hamburger when he came home. So she had everything prepared, but she didn't want to start it too early.

Not that he couldn't have had a hamburger at the bar. Maybe you wouldn't want the same kind of thing he could have had there at home.

She stood there questioning herself until she saw headlights.

They always met in this space. In these strange hours. When her mind started to fray and she was desperate to avoid sleep.

She blinked.

Was she desperate to avoid sleep? Had she just been avoiding it in Dylan's bed?

And dreams.

The dreams that she found so disturbing.

Of a different life. Completely different. She swallowed hard.

She heard heavy footsteps outside, and then the front door opened. "You want a hamburger?" she asked.

"Hello to you too," he said.

"Sorry. It's just… It occurred to me that you could have had one at the bar."

"Sure. I eat at the bar sometimes, but generally don't. But it's not because I don't like hamburgers."

"Why?"

"I mean I did at first. But I get sick of… Even the way the oil tastes. Just a little bit too much work."

"I guess that makes sense. I'll make the hamburgers then."

"Did you wait to eat?"

"Yeah. I mean… My body clock is basically screwed for life. So there's no point me being precious about meal-times."

She walked over to the stove and put the premade patties on the cast-iron griddle that attached to the propane burners.

"How was work?"

"Good," he said, having a seat at the table. "How was here?"

"Great."

"The place looks amazing."

"You're pretty neat. I just did some deep cleaning."

"I can tell. It feels lighter."

"Good."

She didn't know why this should be awkward. Well, except that they had never done this. With her making things for him.

But she had to wonder if anybody ever made things for Laz. His grandmother had. She knew that. She knew that she had been a firm woman, but that Laz had loved her more than anything.

He didn't really talk about his parents. Something they had in common.

"Do you ever speak to your parents?"

He looked up at her, his brow crinkled. "I talk to them once a week."

"Oh. I just… You never talk about them."

"Well. I… I don't really like Portland. So I don't ever

have the desire to go back and visit. I do, a couple times a year. But it has to fit around their schedules. They're busy. They've always been busy."

"Oh. I guess I didn't... I didn't realize that."

"My dad is a doctor. My mom is a lawyer. They're very business-oriented. They're very...invested in their careers. That's fine. But there's a reason that I came out here when I was seventeen. When Grandma Gladys said that she needed help... I jumped at the chance. To get out of the city, to get out of my house."

"I didn't know that you left home at seventeen."

He nodded slowly. "I mean, I had my grandmother. So it's not quite the same."

"Yeah. I was sixteen when my parents kicked me out."

"You never did tell me why."

"Throwing out their heroin."

Surprise flashed through his eyes and she couldn't decide if she was sad that he now knew just how bad everything had been when she was growing up, or gratified that she had managed to shock him.

It was all just so sordid and sad. And it had been one thing to tell him her parents had addiction issues, and another to connect it to what had happened. Because even now she wanted to...protect them in some ways.

It was so toxic and messed up, and she knew it. But it was one thing to know you had some issues, another to just not have them.

And on some level she just hadn't wanted Laz to have too clear a picture of her life back then. She wanted him to see who she was now. To not have all that in his head.

"Well, I didn't figure that."

She laughed, trying to shift the sadness in her chest.

"Did you think that I was rebellious? Especially with a guy like Dylan."

"I don't know. I figured they found condoms in your backpack or something."

"Ha. No. Actually, they would have probably found that to be very responsible of me."

"I see."

"We were just white trash. But with a lot of drugs. I don't have any happy memories of my childhood. Well now, that's not true. There was this one Christmas when my mom was trying not to use. And my dad had his use kind of under control. I mean, he was able to shoot up and then kind of be around. And I don't know. We got these little TV dinners with slices of turkey and gravy and we had a tree made of tinsel. And it was nice." She could still see the living room. Fake wood panels and that shiny little tree. They'd eaten their meal on TV trays on an old green couch that had a hole in the arm, with foam protruding through the end.

She had presents under the tree that year. It had made her very happy. Her parents had been pretty happy.

They had been sometimes. That was the thing. Because for years it was a back and forth between them and the drugs. Child services and all of that. They had tried. Intermittently they had tried. But once she had been a teenager they just stopped. Like they'd thrown up the white flag of surrender and just jumped right in headfirst to addiction rather than making it a dance where they put their feet in and then ran back to the shore.

"My dad told me I was going to end up just like them."

"Jordan…"

"Always kind of thought maybe I would. It terrifies me. That thought. And I thought… I don't know. Dylan's family was so normal. It was so wonderful to be a part of that. I remember the first Thanksgiving that I spent with them, right after my parents kicked me out. And they had…this huge turkey. And mashed potatoes and gravy, and nobody got in a fight. And nobody fell and cut themselves on a glass or screamed at me or locked themselves in the bathroom. And I didn't know that people like that really existed. I mean, logically I knew they had to. But I'd only ever seen them on TV."

"You feel like they saved you."

She nodded. "They did. I mean, that's the thing. Because what would've become of me?"

"I wish I would've known you then," he said.

"Yeah. Well. You would have been too old for me then," she said.

And then she felt immediately silly, because he wasn't offering her anything but friendship. And she hadn't really meant it the way that it had come out. It was just…

"You know what I mean. Because sixteen-year-old girl, twenty-six-year-old man, that doesn't really work. But this works."

"Right," he said.

But he was appraising her a little bit too closely. She scampered back to flip the patties, and then just went ahead and hugged the stove top so that she could keep her distance between herself and him. And the crackle of heat in her stomach.

Because she wasn't in a relationship. Not anymore. And that… That felt just a little bit too revolutionary in the moment.

But Laz was still her friend, and he was her only lifeline. She'd gone from having Dylan's family to having Laz, and she needed to be careful.

"You wanted to know," he said. "Why I didn't ask you to not marry Dylan."

"Oh," she said, feeling jarred by the subject change. "Yes."

"Well, it took me a little bit to realize the answer," he said.

"Let me guess, it's not because you thought we made such a great couple?"

"No," he said. "It's because it would have been selfish."

"What?" Her heart slammed into her chest.

"I thought that it would have been selfish of me to ask you to not marry him. Because I'm not disinterested, Jordan. No matter how much I might want to be. And then I went over there and I saw that flowered suitcase that you had…"

"His mother got that for me for Christmas."

"You said that you were afraid that if you weren't with him you might become like your family. I get that, but you spent the past… It's been a hell of a long time in a family that never even really knew you. I knew you didn't pick that suitcase. I knew it. And you know, I didn't see any point in saying anything, all things considered. I didn't see the point in disrupting anything further than it already has been, but you wanted to know. And it's not because I didn't care. And it's not because I'm afraid to say the honest thing. But I was afraid of leading you somewhere that I wanted you to go. But that was when I at least thought… I thought they knew you. At least. But they never did, did they?"

"I don't understand what you're saying."

"I want you," he said. "That simple. I have. Since the first time I met you."

She could not believe that those words had just come out of his mouth. With the hamburger on a plate in front of him. Not that the hamburger was incredibly relevant to the situation, it just kind of added to the absurdity of it. They'd been friends for years. And he never said anything. He never even indicated...

And all those feelings that she had the first moment she met him came flooding back.

But she... She suddenly felt so small and unworthy. She had never given a lot of thought to how she looked. Because she had a boyfriend for half of her life. She had never wanted to attract another man. She had always been so grateful for Dylan. She did what she could with what she had, but that was basically it. Laz was beautiful. There was no doubt about that. No argument to be made. Classically masculine and handsome in a way that took her breath away. But even in that moment when she'd first seen him she hadn't given any thought to whether or not she could attract him, because why would she?

He had experience. Lots of different women, that much she knew. They didn't talk about it, but it was implied in a lot of different conversations. She had Dylan. That was it. And an increasingly dull sex life that had waned entirely in the face of her increasingly bad insomnia.

And he hadn't been too upset about it. And she hadn't really known what to make of that. The fact that he had let her reduce their sex life to zero had begun to bother her. And it had turned into a sort of game where she tried to see if anything else would happen.

If she waited him out, if he would finally get fed up with it.

It had actually made her start to question her desirability. Something that she really hadn't thought much about before.

But now she wondered. If she could actually be enough

for a man like Laz. A man who had felt like fate from the moment she had first seen him. An impulse that she had denied because...

Well, she was used to denying her impulses. Used to questioning her instincts.

Because hadn't she been told—by everything her parents had done, by everything they'd said—that she could not trust anything that she was inclined toward? Yes. She had been told that. And so when she had walked into the bar and seen Laz, known that he was the most beautiful man she had ever laid eyes on, felt like she was peering into a future that she wanted more than anything... She had questioned it. Absolutely and completely.

Maybe she shouldn't have. Maybe that was the lesson. Above all else, maybe the lesson here was that she wasn't always wrong. And there was a concern, of course, that if she closed the distance between them, their friendship might be ruined. But that moment when she had first laid eyes on him existed in a place inside of her that couldn't be denied. It didn't question anything. Because it knew exactly what it wanted. And had from the first moment she had ever seen him.

He had been there for her... He had been there for her. And so many ways over all that time. And she knew that closing the space between them could never break what they were.

She had built her foundation with Dylan on need. Not physical need, but an emotional need that had been very deep and very real. But her relationship with Laz wasn't built on that. She had met him, and she had wanted to know him. She had found him easy to talk to. And she found him beautiful.

It was such a different thing. Such a different thing to

want without feeling a sharp, fearful side to it. Without being worried that she might lose everything if she couldn't give him what he wanted.

"You really want me?"

"Yes," he said, his voice rough. "But he's always been there. He's always been in the picture, and…"

"You should have told me to get rid of him."

You didn't tell me not to marry Dylan.

Her earlier words echoed between them.

"I wanted what was best for you. Whether you believe that or not. I did. And if it wasn't… This, then…"

"Why?"

"You know how it is for me. I don't share. My life is mine. In… Look, I give to people all day every day. It's part of my job. And when I come home, I do what I want. I don't rely on anybody, I don't ask for anything… And that's the way I like it. Somebody in my position can't ask someone else to give up the future, to give up a marriage for…"

"For what?"

"There's not a name for it, is there?"

"Friends with benefits?"

The words made her stomach feel hollow. Because they couldn't just be that.

"Yeah. Friends with benefits."

"You know, you actually could have asked me to do that," she said, her throat getting tight. "The first time I saw you… I felt like my world turned over on its head. But I was a coward, and I couldn't understand what my life might look like if I stepped off the path that I'd carved out for myself. And more than that, I was afraid of it. So I… I ignored it. I ignored that I felt that way. I ignored that I wanted something else. But I knew that something changed. Forever when I first met you. And it did. Because you gave me the confidence to do what I did the other day. You gave me the confidence to walk away from Dylan, not because I could have you instead, but because… I have our friendship. And you made me feel something about myself that he didn't. You made me trust myself in a way that I never did before. But it's taken me all this time to realize…that I could remove those supports and I would still stand." She cleared her throat. This next bit felt important. "I've only been with one person."

"I figured as much," he said.

"I might be bad at sex."

He chuckled, and the warmth that spread through her body sent tingles all the way from her scalp down to her toes. "You will not be bad at it."

"How do you know? Maybe I am inept when it comes to handling penises."

"There's no way that you could be inept when it comes to handling me."

And he was the one that closed the space between them, and she was grateful. He came right where she stood and wrapped his arm around her waist, and the air rushed from her lungs.

And there were words that hovered on her lips that terrified her, so she swallowed them. Didn't say them. She looked up into his brown eyes.

She suddenly wanted to cry. Because it felt like fate. Because it felt like the answer to a thousand prayers that she had never been brave enough to say. Because she felt like a new woman in a way that she hadn't, when she had decided to leave Dylan at the altar.

That woman had been afraid. She'd been numb. And she hadn't known what the next step was. Hadn't known what she wanted or what she was going to do.

And all right, she still didn't know the answers to all that, not in a broader sense. But she wanted him. She really, really wanted him.

And she felt like if she could be this brave, brave enough to reveal the secret part of herself. Brave enough to expose just how deep her desire for him ran...

Then maybe she could be brave enough for anything.

She put her hands on his face, finally touching him the way that she wanted. She smoothed her fingertips over his stubble-roughened jaw, and ran her thumbs beneath his bottom lip. "I can't believe this is happening," she whispered.

The fire in his eyes burned brighter, and he didn't let her speak again. Instead, he lowered his head, kissing her, hard and deep. Stealing her breath. Stealing her reservations.

It was a revelation, this kiss. And any concerns she had about being bad at sex or undesirable were burned away by the heat in it.

Because she realized then that it actually didn't matter what kind of experience she had. Because there were kisses, and then there was kissing Laz.

Because there was sex, and then there was just the act of wanting him, which touched somewhere deeper than any other sort of desire ever had.

He was big and muscular, and when he held her in his arms she felt small. Delicate, fragile but sheltered.

She had been given shelter before. By a wonderful family who had taken her in and showed her how to change the shape of herself so that she could fit. But that wasn't what Laz was doing. Not now. She was in a shelter made from his strength, and it fit around her. In a profound and deep way, and whether or not it was supposed to mean something like that. Whether or not she was supposed to feel it so deep... She did. He kissed her all the way down the hall, taking her into the bedroom she'd been sleeping in, and removing her clothes from her body. And she wasn't nervous. She wasn't self-conscious. It wasn't time or inevitability that made her feel attractive, it was the way that he looked at her. Like she was the most precious thing he had ever seen.

"Now you," she said.

He took his shirt off slowly, revealing acres of dark, smooth skin. Well muscled and strong.

She put her hand on his chest, thrilling at the feel of him. Because she had certainly never seen such a gloriously masculine man in the flesh before.

Not so close that she could touch.

And maybe it was a little bit petty and a little bit mean to compare pale, thin Dylan to Laz, but she did. In the moment, she did.

Maybe he's fate, or maybe he's just hotter, a voice whispered.

Maybe he's both. Because she wasn't going to enter into the business of doubting herself. Not now. Because it wasn't just about him being hotter. It was about the way he'd been there for her. All this time.

Then his hands went to his belt buckle and her throat went tight. Her entire body seizing up in anticipation. He pushed his jeans and underwear slowly down his lean hips, and kicked his boots off along with them.

His thighs were muscular, sexy. Indicative of all the hard work that he did on his ranch.

That was what the man did. He worked. Whether it was at the bar or on his land, and he wore the evidence of that in every hard, chiseled line on his body. And then there was... Well, him. That most masculine part of him, thick and proud and so much more than she had ever dared imagine.

If she were going to engage in comparisons again—and she was—Laz came out ahead there too. By a lot.

She swallowed hard.

And then she decided there was no point being a coward. Not about anything. Because this was what she wanted. Plain and simple. And she was going to take it.

She reached her hand down, wrapped it around his hard length, soft and hot and hard all at once. She squeezed him, watched as his face went pained. A tortured look there.

She moved her hand up and down his length, until he caught at her wrist with his hand. "Careful," he bit out.

"Why? I'm tired of being careful. I'm tired of being what I'm supposed to be. I'm tired of being whatever he thinks I should be. All I have done for all these years is tried to... Tried to stop myself from turning into a monster. I almost committed myself to a life that was going to make me nothing but miserable. Because I was such a coward. Because I wasn't brave. So now I want to be brave. I want to be brave as I can be. I want to do whatever I want."

"Well, I am here for being your playground, Jordan, but I don't want this to end too quickly."

And that was how she found herself being picked up off the floor and deposited on the bed.

Flat on her back on the soft mattress. And he lifted her thighs, draping them over his shoulders and lowered his head to the heart of her. That part that was slick and wet with desire for him. And she gasped.

She grabbed the back of his head as he tormented her. Pleasuring her with his tongue and his hands.

She writhed against him, arching up off the bed as she found her release, shuddering out his name.

"That's right," he said, moving up her body, gazing down into her eyes. "Don't forget who's with you."

"No chance," she said, her voice weak and shaky.

He took a condom from his nightstand, and sheathed himself quickly as he positioned himself at the entrance of her body.

"Laz," she whispered, bracketing his face with her hands. And then he thrust inside of her, and she lost her breath.

Because it was him. Finally.

He was something she hadn't let herself want. This was something she hadn't let herself want. And it wasn't until she had stripped away all those other people in her life that had had so many expectations of her that she was free. Free to feel what she did. Free to want what she did.

And she wanted him.

And as he established a steady rhythm that drove them both to the heights, as he thrust into her body, over and over again, he forged in them a bond that she didn't think could ever be broken.

She felt utterly devastated by it. By him.

And she was glad of it.

Him. And only him.

She broke open, right there with him, pleasure a torrent that poured over, and he growled out his own release too, trembling, this big, sexy man. Trembling because of her.

And the words that she had held back on her lips echoed inside of her, reverberated inside her soul, joining up with that mystical sense of fate, and it all made sense.

It was more than fate. It had felt like it in that first moment. But over a decade of friendship and conversations, of building something genuine and real, had transformed this.

She loved him.

She was certain.

It felt nothing like loving Dylan. Nothing at all. It was its own thing, unique and wild.

And she was terrified with it. But maybe… Maybe the thing about loving Laz was that she had to accept that her future would look different than the one she had imagined with Dylan. Because she had been married to an idea of domesticity. Of having what his parents had. Of having that magical, normal sort of thing that she had never gotten to see in her childhood.

But maybe loving Laz meant being his friend. Sharing his bed. And letting him have his own life. Would that be so bad? She could be herself with him. More herself than she had been all this time. And maybe that was good enough?

Maybe it would be good enough.

Maybe she could accept that. Because she couldn't imagine going back to not having this. To not having him.

So maybe accepting what was on the table wasn't a bad thing.

Maybe the problem was that what she wanted was never going to fit her.

And she could take more in terms of what she felt, but less…

Checks and balances. It was reasonable. And as she lay there in his arms, safe and sheltered, buzzing with pleasure after what had just occurred, she decided that it was okay.

More than okay.

Friends with benefits with Laz was better than the promise of marriage and forever had ever been with Dylan.

And for the first time she could remember, without pacing herself to exhaustion, driving across half a state or tossing and turning for hours, Jordan fell effortlessly, deeply asleep.

CHAPTER FIVE

WHEN LAZ WOKE UP the next morning, he could smell bacon. And he still felt sated and satisfied after a night spent in Jordan's arms. That sex... The woman had blown his head off.

And now she was cooking for him.

He shook his head.

Yeah, it was what she had been hired to do, but this felt different.

It just did.

He had to wonder why.

Guilt crept over him. Guilt at the speech he'd given her. At what he told her about how he intended to keep his life separate.

It was true, though.

It was all he had to give. All he had.

But he got up, and had breakfast with her, and instead of going out to his wood shop, he ended up taking her back to bed.

And when she got down on her knees and took him into her mouth, her blue eyes a wild spark as she looked up at him while she pleasured him, he figured it was all right that for now, this was all he wanted to do.

He called his bar manager and told her that he wouldn't be in tonight.

Instead, he made dinner for himself and Jordan, and she baked a cake. Then they made love on the floor of his house in such a way that he almost felt like he needed to apologize to the portrait of his grandmother that hung at the end of the hallway.

And it went on like that. For days.

Because he felt like he'd found something in her that he never anticipated. She made him want to disrupt his schedule. She made him not care so much about being at the bar every night.

He didn't feel quite so compelled to go out and check on the ranch personally every afternoon. He just let his foreman handle it.

What he wanted had been reduced to his little house. What he wanted had been reduced to Jordan's arms.

And what surprised him was how okay that seemed.

He had consciously gone out of his way to never wind his life around another person's.

To never need them. And he was skating perilously close to something he had always vowed he never would. He felt guilty about the things he'd said to Jordan when they'd first gone to bed together, but he stood by them too.

There were just some people that were better off solitary.

Some people who didn't bend that well because they would just break.

And he was one of them.

He finally gave in and went to work after about a week of being at his place with Jordan, and it was a good thing. Because she was going to have to leave soon. She was going to have to go back to her job. Or maybe not. Maybe not. They hadn't really talked about it.

But that will amount to her basically living with you.

He gritted his teeth. Sure. That wasn't going to work. He did know that.

But one afternoon when he ventured down into town, he

walked into the Western wear store and perused the stock. And inside he found a black suitcase.

Inside, the suitcase was lined with loud, retro cowboy art. Horses and men with six-shooters held high in the air. And it was funny. A little bit of hidden strangeness inside a sedate-looking bag. And it reminded him so much of Jordan he had to get it.

Which was how he found himself hauling a suitcase up to the house that night while he blew off his regular shift.

When he walked into the house, Jordan was standing at the stove, stirring a pot.

"Oh," she said when he walked in. "I didn't expect you for dinner. I have a cake in the oven but…"

A cake. She baked him a cake.

All over his house little touches of care were evident. All these things that she'd done for him.

You paid her to do them. Don't go making it sentimental.

"I brought you this," he said, shoving the bag toward her.

She blinked. "You… You brought me a suitcase."

"Because the flowered one is all wrong. This is what you like. You don't want anything as loud as that flowered thing."

"You're right," she said, staring at him, wide-eyed. "I don't."

"It's got… I mean it's got cowboys inside of it."

She blinked. "You shoved a couple cowboys in there for me? That was thoughtful of you, Laz, but you're about the only cowboy I can handle."

He unzipped it, and showed her the lining. "It's just… It's interesting inside. But you have to work hard to find that out. Like you."

It was very strange, and he was pretty sure he was hovering around the edge of a romantic gesture, but having never actually done one before, he didn't really know.

"Laz," she said. "That is… The nicest thing. And… And you're right. It is exactly what I want. It's exactly what I would choose." She let out a hard breath. "I love you. I just… I'm not expecting anything back. But I love you. And I needed to say it."

Something went tight inside of him and twisted.

It was like the world had gone still and his heart along with it. Jordan. Beautiful Jordan who had turned his world upside down the first day she'd walked into his bar, loved him.

Not another man, but him.

And he had no response to it. There wasn't one.

Not in the whole, dark well of pain inside of him.

"Right. Well. When do you start work back up again?"

She blinked, looking as if she'd been slapped. "I… Next week."

"Are you any closer to finding yourself a place to stay?"

"No," she said.

"How about above the bar. There's a place up there you… you helped me use it one night. I can have it cleaned and it would be ready for you quickly."

"You don't… You don't have to do that."

"I want to."

And he realized that he was basically offering her a position as his kept woman. And he could have offered her that apartment from the beginning and he hadn't. He had kept her close to him. Kept her with him, and now she was saying that she loved him.

And it didn't escape him that he was keeping her close so that he could still access her. Because he was an absolute dick, and even while he realized that, he couldn't stop himself from making the offer.

And he knew that she wouldn't be able to refuse.

"I… All right," she said. And she blinked furiously, trying to hide her hurt.

He would never reject Jordan's love. He couldn't do that. But he couldn't have her living in his house and he couldn't make her promises that he didn't want to keep.

That he *couldn't* keep.

Except he kept feeling like *didn't want to* was closer to the truth, no matter how hard he tried to convince himself otherwise.

He didn't want to hurt her. Not for anything.

But he wanted things to keep working the way that he wanted them to. "I'll help you move in as soon as it's clean."

"Well, thanks. You gave me a suitcase."

And he remembered the words from an old movie, twisted to suit the moment. She'd given him her heart and he'd given her a suitcase.

And he didn't do anything to fix it.

"What kind of cake is it?"

"Chocolate," she answered.

"Great. You need help with anything?"

"No. I'm fine." She swallowed hard and nodded, and he felt a cloud of guilt. And he didn't do anything about it.

And that was how things changed between them again. Not with shouting or screaming or anything like that. Just with a suitcase and the throat full of unspoken words.

And that was when Laz realized that he really was his parents.

And he knew there was no way that he could explain that to her. Because that wasn't something he did. He wasn't the one who shared.

He gave advice. And that was it. And he didn't quite know what to do with being at a loss.

Except keep on down that road.

So that was what he did.

CHAPTER SIX

JORDAN HAD BEEN wrestling with feeling like she'd been gutted alive for the last few days. All the while that Laz had that apartment fixed up for her. And all the way up to moving day.

But she didn't say anything. Even though she should have. Even though she wanted to. She didn't say anything when she packed up that suitcase that he brought her, that brief, shining evidence of the fact that he knew her, followed by a devastating strange sort of half rejection.

It's actually not unreasonable for him to not want to move in with you.

She knew that. But she had said that she loved him and he hadn't said anything back. And she hadn't said it again since.

And you were willing to accept something different, remember?

Except, it turned out that actually what she really wanted was for him to be in love with her.

But she would continue to see him. Of course she would.

Because their relationship was good in so many other ways, and it was grounding and...

She stood in the center of that apartment, frozen.

And what would happen if she was really alone? If she had to face the town, completely unprotected by her relationship with Dylan's family, and even with their censure rolling through the community. If she had to go on without her friendship with Laz, without him sharing her bed.

If she was just a woman who lived alone, and had to cope with herself and any potential demons…

What was she?

And when Laz came up with the last box, she turned to face him. "We can't keep sleeping together," she said.

He stopped. "We can't?"

"No. So if you moved me here to have easy access to me, bad news."

"Why can't we?"

"Because I love you. But I don't need to be in a relationship with you to keep myself safe from heroin, or whatever it is I've been thinking all of my life about all of these relationships that I have. I denied my first instinct with you, because I didn't trust my instincts at all. I was so sure that they were going to land me in a bad spot that I… That I denied them. And I denied myself. But Laz, I'm not doing that anymore. I love you. Like as more than a friend. But I don't want to accept a half-life where we don't have a future. I thought that I could. I thought that I could sleep with you and do the friends with benefits thing and that that would be enough.

"But it isn't. And hanging on to that is just something I'm doing out of fear. Because I don't know what my life looks like if you're not in it. Because I'm afraid of who I'll become, but I can't stay with people for that reason. Not anymore. I've done too much of that. I'm not going to do it anymore. Not for you. And not for anyone."

"Jordan…"

"No. I made a lot of mistakes with Dylan, not least of which was letting it get to our wedding day, and then running away rather than having a conversation with him. But

I'm not doing that anymore. The one brave thing buried in all those cowardly decisions that I made was I was willing to change my life. Willing to dramatically change it. And I still am. But I need you to be willing to meet me halfway. I can't do this. Because I've already done the relationship where I make all the compromises because I might be broken."

"It's not you who's broken."

"You're not broken either. But you're going to have to decide to be whole, I can't decide that for you. Any more than Dylan could decide it for me, and you can't make a relationship work with someone that dedicated to living in their pain. Believe me. I know." She looked around the room. "So thank you for the apartment. I will pay rent on it. And I'll still… Speak to you. And be your friend. But I can't be in between. I just can't. I love you too much to let either of us accept that."

She blinked. "You didn't want to ask me not to marry him because you were afraid you were being selfish. Well, I'm asking you to change. For me. And maybe I am being selfish, but maybe it needs to be said."

"I can't," he said.

He looked tortured. He looked like he wanted to say yes, but couldn't. And for the life of her, Jordan couldn't understand that.

"I'm sorry," he said.

"Me too," she whispered.

Laz set the box down, turned and walked out of the apartment. And she somehow knew when he closed the door, he wouldn't be opening it again.

Jordan stared blankly ahead. But she didn't want French fries. And she didn't want a milkshake. And she didn't want to drive aimlessly for hours while she decided what to do.

She'd made her decision. And she knew she made the

right one. Because while she had kept herself on a short leash, doubted her instincts and always secretly believed that she was a bad person inside, waiting to come out and ruin everything she'd built, she just…didn't think that anymore. She was a woman. One who deserved everything. One who deserved love, one who deserved to feel confident in her decisions.

She was a woman taking a risk.

A woman who was trying to put herself on the road to having everything.

And if she had to take this risk to get there, then so be it.

And even though she was left bereft and sad, and so lonely feeling, she also felt more resolute than she ever had before.

Because she was no longer a prisoner of those words her father had spoken to her all those years ago.

She was free. And with freedom came some pain that she wished would go away. But she hoped she'd be able to overcome.

But in that pain, in that moment came clarity.

She was Jordan Whitfield. And she was not going to be defined by the words of other people. She was going to define herself. Going to define her own life.

And she was going to stand on her own two feet. Because that was the strength that Laz had given her.

Because he had shown her that shelters existed that could expand to accommodate her. And even though that was the gift that had broken them apart, it was also the gift that had made her strong enough to ask for what they both needed.

Now all she had to do was have faith.

And since Laz had always felt like fate, she had to trust that in the end it would work out okay.

A lot of trust for a woman who had never really seen it work out before. She knew how hard life could be.

But she wanted to know just how beautiful it would be.

And this was the only way.

CHAPTER SEVEN

Laz was in a foul temper, and he wasn't in the mood to talk to any of his bar patrons, which he knew was a big no-no, but he didn't much care. He shouldn't be at the bar. Not if he couldn't get it together.

"Another drink."

He turned around and tried to force a smile, only to see West Caldwell standing there, along with Ryder Daniels and Logan Heath. He had advised all three men on their romantic issues in the last year. And he was not happy to see them. Grinning, with wedding rings firmly on their fingers. "Comin' up."

"You don't look so good," West said.

"Agreed," Logan said.

Ryder didn't say anything, he only nodded. But then, Ryder was bound by strict codes of honor, and most certainly to not meddling in other people's business, so it stood to reason that he hadn't verbally chimed in.

"Everything's fine," Laz said, lying through his teeth.

"Is it? It's just that I heard that Jordan from Sugar Cup ran off and didn't get married, and that she was shacked up with you."

"This town is a scourge."

"Yeah, but generally reliable when it comes to gossip. So is that true?" West pressed.

"True enough," he said. "She's my friend, and she was on some hard times. I offered to help out."

"Right. That's how I always offer to help my friends. Little friendly bunking together," West said.

"If I recall right," Ryder said. "That is how you helped my sister."

"And look how that turned out," West said, grinning.

That wasn't exactly true. West had become his now wife's landlord by default. And that had forced them into a proximity where things had gotten friendly real quick.

"She was staying with me, now she's not. She's renting a room above the bar, in fact. No gossip to be had there."

"Is that why you're in a bad mood? Because you're definitely not in the mood of a kinda man who's getting regularly laid," Logan pointed out.

Well, he *had* been getting regularly laid. Actually until yesterday.

But it wasn't about that. Of course it wasn't. But Jordan didn't understand. She didn't understand that…

That what? You're not willing to change? Is that really what it comes down to?

No. There was some clawing, burning fear that kept snarling in his chest, and he couldn't define it any more than he could fight it.

"Should tell us what's going on," Logan said. "It's only fair. After all… You helped enough people over the last few years that you deserve a little help with your own."

"And we wouldn't be any kind of friends if we didn't stick our oar in."

Laz could only stare. Because this was the last thing he'd ever expected. That all those conversations he had over the years in the bar might actually come back and benefit him. That they wouldn't forget his happiness.

He'd seen it as a no-cost business transaction, but that wasn't how they were treating it.

And maybe… Maybe that was it. Maybe he'd been lying to himself all this time. Maybe he wasn't half so solitary as he believed. Maybe never had been.

"She's in love with me," he said. "But I… I'm set in my ways. I live alone. I like things done my way."

"That's dumb," West said. "I would do things any kind of way if I could keep Pansy in my life. We could do them her way, hell, we could do them the Bhagwan Shree Rajneesh's way, I don't care. Whatever she wants, I'm all in. Because I'm not happy if she's not happy. I'm not happy if she's not with me."

"Same," Logan said.

"Same," Ryder said.

"My parents have a terrible marriage," Laz said. "That house growing up was miserable. They never had time for anybody but themselves, and they resented their relationship as much as they resented me. I just don't have any desire to live that kind of life."

It was West who looked at him just a little too acutely. "Do you not want to live like them? Or do you just want to go back to living like you already do? Is it just not wanting to need someone a little more than they need you?"

That landed. Right square in his chest. And he felt… Well, he felt damned foolish.

Because it was true. He had moved out of the home where nobody seemed to want or need him, and into his grandmother's house where he'd been able to help. And she had to accept, whether she liked to be solitary or not. And then he'd started work at this bar, where he gave advice, and everybody valued him. Either for his ability to dole out whiskey or sympathy. But taking back… That was what got him. That was what was so difficult.

"I…"

"I didn't take you for a coward, Laz," Logan said quietly.

"You were all cowards first."

"Not me," Ryder said.

"Really?"

His brothers-in-law were staring at him. "You were coward enough while you loved Sammy for seventeen years and didn't say anything. Just because she's the one who left you right before you worked everything out…"

"Fine," Ryder said. "But the point is. Fearing change doesn't much get you anywhere. You gotta be willing to change with life, or it's just going to run you over. So you can keep yourself safe in one way, but it's not going to protect you from the heartbreak of not having her."

"So… What? You just…say yes, knowing that in the end it could destroy you?"

But he already knew the answer to that. Because it was the answer that every single person in his bar had found over the years.

The conclusion they'd all come to.

It was just that simple. And that hard.

To say yes instead of say no. To protect yourself instead of running scared.

"Sure. But you hope. And you love. In between those two things… It can turn out pretty great," West said.

And he knew it was true. Because he was looking at the evidence right in front of him. Because the evidence had been in and out of his bar for years. Carved into the wall of his bar bathroom. Even though he'd asked them to cut that shit out. But that was just it. It worked all around him all the time. And sometimes it didn't. It hadn't in his home, no matter that his parents had stayed together. And they'd made him feel... Well, they'd made him feel like he didn't matter, and he had never wanted to go back to that.

But Jordan made him feel like he mattered. And she had from the beginning. And what the hell did it matter what had come before if they could decide what came after? Because that bullshit was just like what her father had put on her. Telling her that she was doomed because of who her parents were? He knew enough to know that wasn't true of her. So why couldn't it be just as untrue of him?

"Keep an eye on the bar," Laz said.

He took the inside staircase and went right up to the apartment, pounding on the door. Jordan opened it, looking wary. "What do you want?"

And he didn't say anything. He just pulled her into his arms, because it was what he wanted to do. Because he hadn't held her for days, and he was sick of it.

"I'm sorry," he said. "I'm sorry that you had to be the brave one."

"You are?" The question was muffled against his chest.

"Yes. You deserve better than that from me." He held his arms out straight, looked into her eyes. "I love you."

It wasn't a revelation. It didn't shock him. But it did make him feel... Like a piece of himself that had been missing for a long damned time was finally in place.

"And I will turn my whole life upside down. I will paint the inside of my house pink, I will get a cat, I will do whatever the hell you want if you will be with me. I don't need my time, I don't need my space. What I need is you, Jordan. And I had to be brave enough to say that. Say that I needed someone. Because I'm a hell of a lot more comfortable with other people needing me."

"Laz," she said, wrapping her arms around his neck and

kissing him. "You know what, I'm glad I had to be brave. Because it made me realize something. I've had myself on probation for years. I'm tired of it. And that's what gave me the strength to tell you to go away until you sorted yourself out."

"Was actually West and Ryder and Logan that sorted me out."

"When?"

"Just now."

"In the bar?"

"In the bar," he confirmed.

"That's... Well, I think that's no less than you deserved."

"Thank you. You know, my parents might not have been as terrible as yours. But they made me feel like I didn't matter. I never wanted to feel that again."

She put her hand on his face. "You won't. Because you matter to me. And even more importantly you taught me that I need to matter to me. That my own feelings matter."

"I love you, Jordan. I have from the first moment you walked into my bar. And the real reason I didn't tell you not to go through with the wedding is that I knew that you deserved to have something more offered to you. And I was too cowardly to do it, not too good."

"Well, are you too coward to do it now?"

"Not at all. Will you marry me? Invade my space and change my life?"

It wasn't sudden at all. It was ten years of late-night conversations, walking together in the streets of the town, sharing themselves. They might have only kissed for the first time a week ago, but they'd fallen in love, deeply, truly, a lot longer ago than that.

"Yes," she said. "I will."

"Good. Hey, do you know about the tradition of carving your name in the bathroom of my bar?"

She narrowed her eyes. "Yes. I have heard about that."

"I think it's high time my own name was put in there, don't you think?"

"Laz!"

"What? People are already going to talk. So let's really give them something to talk about, Jordan."

And then she smiled. Really smiled. That smile that only he ever saw. That spark in Jordan that she kept buried deep, and didn't show the world, but only a very few people who were lucky enough.

And he was lucky enough.

"You have yourself a deal."

EPILOGUE

IT WAS THE funniest thing, when Jordan moved in with Laz— for real—she started sleeping.

She worked out a schedule where her mornings weren't as early, he adjusted his so it wasn't as late.

Laz liked sharing his life. That was the biggest surprise of all. He liked sharing his meals, his space, his wood shop. Jordan decided to learn to knit, and she got a chair that she put out there, and she sat while he worked. They often didn't talk at all, they were just together.

Most of all, they learned to talk, and trust. Each other, and themselves.

He was the Laz Jordan loved, not the boy who had felt unloved by his parents. And she was the Jordan he loved. Not a daughter of addicts. Not a woman who had to keep herself on a tight leash for fear she might do something wrong.

Just Jordan. Just the love of his life.

Just everything.

He used to be in the business of giving out advice. But now, his biggest business was just to love her. Every day, with all of his heart.

Forever.

* * * * *

SPECIAL EXCERPT FROM

⊕HARLEQUIN

DESIRE

*Tired of being Nashville's most eligible bachelor, Luke Sutherland
needs a fake date to the wedding of the year, and his ex-lover
Cassandra Taylor needs a favor. But as they masquerade as a
couple, one hot kiss makes things all too real...*

Read on for a sneak peek at
Fake Engagement, Nashville Style
by USA TODAY *bestselling author Jules Bennett.*

Cassandra couldn't believe how perfect this day had gone. Hannah
Banks was just as sweet in private as she'd seemed in public. This
wedding would be such a fun and rewarding event to work on.
And hopefully Cassandra would be so busy with this project, she
wouldn't have too much time to devote to her "fiancé."

Once they were back in Luke's truck, he pulled out of Hannah's
drive. Cassandra smoothed her hair over one shoulder and adjusted
her sunglasses against the bright sky.

"You're really good at your job," he said.

Cassandra glanced over to Luke, who was keeping his eyes on
the road. "You sound surprised."

"Not surprised at all, actually," he admitted. "I knew you'd be
amazing at this. I've just never seen you in your element before."

A little taken aback by his admission, Cassandra smiled. "Well,
thanks. I love my job and I always think that if you're doing what
you love, then it never feels like work."

"I agree. Owning bars was always my goal. I love the atmosphere,
the people... Well, I did love the people until I was bombarded
with women ready for me to make them Mrs. Sutherland."

A burst of jealousy surged through her, but that was ridiculous. She had no claim to Luke, and it wasn't like the man hadn't dated over the years. Maybe he'd even had a serious relationship. None of that was her business or concern, which was why she shouldn't be thinking of it.

When Luke pulled in front of The Beaumont, where she had rented the penthouse for the next few months, he killed the engine and stepped out. Before she could get her own door, Luke had opened it and reached his hand inside.

Cassandra shifted her gaze to his and found that intense stare looking back at her. She slid her hand into his, and there was no ignoring the familiar jolt that had always aroused her. Apparently, now was no different than eight years ago.

When she stepped out of the truck, he didn't move back, and instead he caged her against the opening and smiled.

"What are you doing?" she murmured as their bodies pressed together. Instant bursts of arousal coursed through her, and she cursed herself for allowing herself to feel such worthless emotions.

"Practicing."

And that was all the warning she got before his mouth descended on hers.

Don't miss what happens next in...
Fake Engagement, Nashville Style
by USA TODAY *bestselling author Jules Bennett,*
the next book in the Dynasties: Beaumont Bay series!

Available July 2021 wherever
Harlequin Desire books and ebooks are sold.

Harlequin.com

HDEXP23296MAX

Welcome to Gold Valley, Oregon, where the cowboys are tough to tame, until they meet the women who can lasso their hearts, from *New York Times* bestselling author

MAISEY YATES

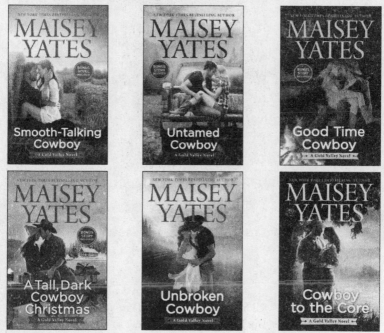

"Fans of Robyn Carr and RaeAnne Thayne will enjoy [Yates's] small-town romance." —*Booklist*

Order your copies today!

HQNBooks.com